After All Is Said And Done

Belinda G. Buchanan

The characters and events in this book are fictitious. Any similarity to real persons, living or dead, is purely coincidental and not intended by the author.

For Bruce, the love of my life

After All Is Said And Done

Sarah Williams leaned against the wall, letting Gavin's lips roam along her neck and throat. The excitement in her started to build as he moved against her in long, even strides. His hands, strong, sure, and familiar, slid down her backside, touching her in all the places she liked. She suddenly stiffened and let out a low moan as her body began to throb. This launched Gavin into action, and the harder he thrust, the more intense it became, making her breaths come out in gasps.

She laid her head upon his shoulder and shuddered until the last bit of pleasure inside of her was gone.

Gavin tenderly brushed his cheek against hers before turning away to get dressed.

Wishing to hold on to him just a little longer, she slipped her arms around his chest and hugged him tightly.

"You know," he said, looking over his shoulder at her, "I've got surgery in twenty minutes."

"I know," she answered with a sigh. "Will you be very late?"

"Shouldn't be. I'll probably be home sometime around eight."

After giving him a lingering kiss, Sarah left his office and blissfully made her way down the corridor towards the elevator. With a hiss, its doors opened, inviting her in.

Taking the rare opportunity to be alone in a hospital elevator, she smiled and closed her eyes, wanting to remember every single second of what had just happened. She breathed in deeply, catching the last lingering remnants of Gavin's aftershave. Things had not been this exciting for a long time between them, and she felt encouraged that this was a new beginning.

The elevator stopped and chimed, making Sarah reluctantly open her eyes. Her mood, and her smile, quickly dissolved when she saw Jessica Harrington step on.

Neither acknowledged the other as the doors roughly slid closed and began its downward descent.

Sarah folded her arms, intent on ignoring her as she watched the light jump from floor to floor, but a sudden jolt caught her off-guard. She gripped the rails behind her as the elevator jerked, and then screeched to a halt.

Jessica straightened up and pushed the button for seven. Nothing happened. "Great," she muttered, reaching for the red phone next to the panel. "Yes, this is Dr. Harrington. We're stuck in elevator B on the south side." She looked up at the number that remained lit above the door. "We're somewhere between ten and twelve." Her eyes flicked towards Sarah as she listened. "They'll get somebody on it right away."

She groaned inwardly. That meant they could be stuck in here for a few minutes, or a few hours.

Twenty minutes later, they were still waiting.

Sarah sullenly leaned against the back wall, disliking the thought of having to make polite conversation with her for the next hour or so. She looked up at the light, trying to move the elevator with sheer will until she gave herself a headache.

"How's Ashley?"

She turned slightly, surprised that Jessica had spoken first. "Fine." Tension began to swirl inside the tiny box, making her realize that she was going to have to say something in return. "So are you hoping for a boy or girl?" she asked, trying to sound genuine.

Jessica tenderly caressed the bump protruding from her stomach and shook her head. "It really doesn't matter to me, as long as it's healthy." She paused a moment to smile. "But I think Ethan's secretly hoping for a boy."

"I think all men wish that," Sarah mused. "Do you have any names picked out?"

"Olivia Grace if it's a girl, and Ryan Michael if it's a boy."

The elevator shuddered and made a loud whining noise, but remained motionless.

Jessica suddenly doubled over and took in her breath.

"What's wrong?"

Her lips pursed together as she held her side. "That was a really strong kick."

Sarah nodded, remembering how excruciating little feet could be.

Jessica's breath seemed to catch in her throat as she turned towards her. "I think my water just broke."

Sarah felt her chest begin to tighten. "It's not water," she whispered.

Jessica glanced down and saw the bright red blood seeping through her scrubs. A guttural cry fell from her as she held her stomach and sank to her knees.

Sarah grabbed her cell phone from her pocket and knelt beside her.

"Fourth floor Labor and Delivery."

"Listen carefully," she spoke into the phone. "This is Dr. Williams. I am stuck in the south elevator somewhere between ten and twelve with Dr. Harrington. She is hemorrhaging. I want you to tell that maintenance crew to get us out of here right now!" She stopped and took a deep breath, trying to regain control of her voice. "Then I need for you to page Dr. Ethan Harrington and tell him what's happened. I'll stay on the line." She pushed the speaker button and laid the phone on the floor next to her.

Jessica was sitting rigidly on her knees, clutching her abdomen.

Sarah helped her sit back. "I need to see what's going on, all right?"

She nodded, her face turning paler by the second.

A pool of blood spilled out as Sarah slipped Jessica's pants down. Thinking quickly, she took off her lab coat and pushed it between her legs, trying to stop as much of the bleeding as she could.

"Sarah?"

"I'm here, Ethan," she said, loud enough for him to hear her.

"What's happening?"

She hesitated, hating to tell him this over the phone.

"Hello?"

"She's hemorrhaging, and I believe she's having contractions."

There was a long pause.

"Can I talk to her?" he asked in an unsteady voice.

She held the phone to Jessica's ear. "It's Ethan," she said, urging her to speak.

Jessica blinked, unleashing a swath of tears. "Ethan? I'm so scared."

Sarah had never felt more helpless in her life. The only thing she had with her was her stethoscope; a useless instrument in this situation. The lab coat, along with her hand, were both drenched in blood.

Jessica tilted her head back, exposing the veins in her neck as she cried out.

Realizing that she had to do something, Sarah removed the coat, only to have her fear confirmed; the baby's head was beginning to crown. Panic quickly spread through her, knowing that the baby would die within minutes if it weren't delivered soon.

"Jessica!"

Upon hearing Ethan shouting, she saw that Jessica's eyes had closed. She dropped the phone and tapped the side of her cheek. "Jessica? Jessica, stay with me. I need you to try and push. Do you hear me?"

The elevator suddenly dropped, knocking her off balance. It then caught itself and slowly began moving downwards, eventually groaning to a halt.

Before the doors had fully opened, Ethan Harrington was stepping through them. Without speaking, he scooped up his wife's lifeless body and put her on a waiting gurney.

The nurses draped a blanket over her and whisked her down the corridor towards labor.

Gavin stood at the other end of the hall, his eyes fixated upon Jessica as they wheeled her past him.

Sarah picked up her phone and stumbled into the nearest bathroom. She leaned heavily against the sink, watching the blood from her hands swirl down the drain. She pressed the soap dispenser several times until she had a large glop of the white liquid in her palm. As a doctor, she was used to seeing blood, but she had never gotten over its smell.

By the time she walked out, the crowd of onlookers had vanished. The aroma of bleach hung thick in the doorway of the elevator she had just been in; an orderly stood inside, silently mopping up the blood.

"Sarah?"

She spun around to find Gavin.

"I was looking for you."

"I needed to wash up."

"What happened?" His tone was accusing.

"I don't know," she replied, trying to stop the shaking in her voice. "She just started hemorrhaging and then went into labor."

A strange look crossed his face as he pressed the button for the other elevator. "Why don't we go grab some coffee?"

~

Sarah poured the small container of cream into her coffee and stirred until it turned a milky brown. She could feel the heat from the liquid as she brought it near her lips.

Gavin sat across from her scrolling through the numbers on his cell phone.

"What happened to your surgery?"

"Postponed until tomorrow," he answered, pressing the phone to his ear. "This is Dr. Williams. Is Jessica Harrington still in surgery? ... What's her condition?"

Sarah took another sip of her coffee trying to ignore the concern she heard in his voice.

He hung up and lay the phone on the table.

"What'd they say?"

"They don't know anything." His eyes suddenly flooded with emotion, causing him to look away.

Sarah took a final sip from her cup and pushed her chair back. "I'm going to make my rounds and then head on home."

He nodded. "I'll be there in a little while."

She stood by the table for a moment, hoping he might react to the curtness in her voice, but the only thing he did was look back down at his cell.

~

Sarah tilted her head back, letting the hot water spray down upon her face and mouth. She breathed in deeply trying to put the day's events behind her, but the lingering scent of Jessica's blood made it impossible for her to do so. She began to scrub vigorously as her mind replayed what had happened. Several minutes and three raw fingers later, she realized that the incident itself wasn't bothering her nearly as much as the way Gavin had behaved afterwards.

The feeling of warmth left behind by their rendezvous in his office this afternoon was quickly trampled by the memory of his affair with Jessica last year. It was an affair that had left nothing but carnage in its wake, causing separations in both their marriages.

Forgiveness had not come easy for her, but she had swallowed her hurt and let him come home, making a promise to herself that she was going to be everything to him that she hadn't been before.

The steam that was now circling the ceiling told her that she'd been in the shower long enough, yet it was with great reluctance that she shut off the water.

Gavin was sitting on the bed with his back to her when she came out of the bathroom. "Please let me know if there are any changes," he said, hanging up the phone.

"Any news?"

"The baby was delivered by cesarean. He's in NICU."

"And Jessica?"

He didn't say anything for a long time. When he finally spoke, his voice was uneven. "She's in ICU...still unconscious."

"What's bothering you, Gavin?"

He bowed his head and ran his fingers through his hair.

His silence only confirmed her suspicions that he still had feelings for this woman. "What is it?" she pushed, feeling compelled to hear him say it.

He stood up and turned around, his face wracked with guilt. "If she dies...it's all my fault."

Sarah blinked, and then began to shake as the reality of what he had just said sank in.

"I'm sorry," he murmured. "I'm so sorr—"

She slapped him across the face. "You *son-of-a-bitch!*" Her anger immediately turned to tears, making her chin tremble as she fought to speak. "*Goddamn* you," she whispered.

"I never meant for this to happen," he said miserably.

"Get out!" She put her hands over her ears not wanting to hear anymore.

"Sarah, please."

He reached out to hold her, but she shoved him away. "Get out!" she screamed.

Chapter Two

Ethan Harrington sat quietly in the ICU trying to hold his emotions inside. His wife's small, still body lay in the bed. The baby wasn't due for five more weeks, and although her last checkup had showed her placenta was low, there was nothing to indicate that it was going to rupture.

Jessica's blood pressure had been dropping steadily throughout the night, and he knew the consequences could lead to her suffering a stroke or seizure. Her kidneys were already showing signs of stress.

He gently touched the side of her face, wishing that she would open her eyes. He knew everything that could be done for her had already been done. All there was left to do now—was wait. Wait for the hours to pass by and hope for some improvement.

"Dr. Harrington?"

He turned to look at the nurse.

"I'm sorry to bother you, but Dr. Nichols needs to see you in NICU."

Ethan stood up abruptly and brushed past her. Deciding that it would be quicker to take the stairwell, he bypassed the elevator and hurriedly made his way up the steps to the fourth floor.

When he arrived, he went past the nursery and through a set of double doors. This was where the babies requiring intensive care were treated. There was no plate glass window for proud parents to gaze through here—just rows of incubators.

Dr. Nichols met him at the door.

"What's going on?"

The woman put her hands in the pockets of her lab coat, her expression grim. "Ethan, I want to arrange to have him taken to St. Joseph's Children's Hospital in Bar Harbor. They are better equipped to take care of him. They've handled this type of trauma dozens of times."

He cleared his throat. "What's his blood count?"

"It's still extremely low." Nichols voice was matter-of-fact. "I understand this is hard for you, but I wouldn't be asking if I didn't feel it was absolutely necessary."

He folded his arms and looked at the floor for a moment. "When do you want to do it?"

"First thing in the morning."

He glanced at his watch. That was about four hours from now. The last thing he wanted was to be separated from the baby, but he knew he couldn't leave Jessica. "All right," he heard himself say.

Dr. Nichols left to make the arrangements.

Ethan stepped through the doorway and walked over to the incubator. The baby was tiny, frail, and very gray; a breathing tube covered most of his face.

He reached behind him for a latex glove and slipped it on before laying his hand on his son's chest. He wanted him to know that he was here. He took a deep breath and held it, waiting for the ache in his throat to go away. In a single moment, his whole world had been turned upside down.

Chapter Three

Sarah splashed some cold water on her face and took her time patting it dry before scrutinizing herself in the mirror. The skin around her eyes and nose was red and blotchy from having cried for most of last night.

After applying her makeup, along with a liberal amount of concealer, she sat back to see. A bit of the redness was still there, but she figured it would be gone by the time she got to the hospital. Feeling somewhat satisfied, she let her eyes wander from her face to her fiery red hair; thick and wavy as it fell down her shoulders, it was easily the most striking thing about her.

Her reflection offered her the smallest of smiles amidst trembling lips. Sarah tossed the tube of makeup into the sink as tears welled up inside her once more. Despite all her assets, she knew she was no comparison to blonde-haired, blue-eyed Jessica.

Refusing to let them fall this time, she grabbed her purse from the vanity and made her way downstairs. Her feet moved her along at a snail's pace as she headed towards the garage. The hospital was absolutely the last place she wanted to be, and if it weren't for the fact that Ethan wouldn't be there today, she would have called in sick.

~

Ethan checked his watch as he waited impatiently for the elevator. It was nearly seven and he knew they would be transferring the baby soon. He pushed the button again and felt a strong, familiar hand on his shoulder. He turned and found his father standing behind him.

"Someone from my office told me this morning what had happened. I wish you would had called me."

Ethan found himself searching for the right words to say, but nothing came to mind. "I didn't want to worry you," he finally said.

"How's Jessica?"

"She hasn't regained consciousness."

"I'm sorry," his father said softly. "Is there anything I can do?"

He shook his head and checked his watch again. "I've got to get to NICU."

"Would you mind if I went with you?"

The two of them rode together in silence to the fourth floor.

Everett followed him down the corridor and through a set of double doors. Inside the room, there was a glass incubator with an index card taped to its side. The words, 'Baby Harrington', were printed neatly on it.

He stepped closer to get a look. The baby lay unmoving on its back with tubes and wires covering most of its tiny body. He shifted his eyes to Ethan; the pain was evident upon his face as he stood gazing at his son. He began to hurt inside for him. "He's a good-looking boy," he said, trying to ease the moment.

Ethan gave him a smile, but it was half-hearted, at best.

"Dr. Harrington? The chopper's about ten minutes away."

He nodded at the nurse. "Is Dr. Nichols here?"

"She's on her way up."

"What's the chopper for?" Everett asked.

"He's being moved to St. Joseph's in Bar Harbor."

The nurse had a stack of papers for Ethan to sign and initial for the transfer.

Everett stepped back as a flurry of activity started around the incubator. He listened as Dr. Nichols and Ethan discussed the baby's condition, using medical terms that he did not understand. Feeling that he was being more of a hindrance than help, he silently slipped out the doors.

~

Sarah sat in one of the padded chairs outside ICU waiting for Ethan to return. She had called Gavin's scrub nurse a little while ago and learned that he would be tied up in surgery for most of the morning.

She leaned against the back of the chair, but quickly sat forward, unable to squash the anxiousness that was swarming inside her. Not having to worry about bumping into Gavin right now was a welcome relief, but it was only part of her apprehension.

"Sarah?"

She jerked her head to see Ethan coming towards her. "Hi," she said, feeling her heart start to pound. "The nurse told me about the baby. Is he on his way to St. Joseph's now?"

He sat down wearily beside her and nodded. "I was hoping that he would improve and it wouldn't come to that," he said softly.

"How's Jessica?"

"There's been no change. We just have to wait—" He stopped and looked away.

"Ethan, I know things look pretty bleak right now," she said, fighting to hold back her own tears as she watched him struggling to regain his composure, "but you just have to have faith."

He nodded, but found no comfort in her words.

She suddenly leaned over and hugged him. "Everything's going to be all right," she whispered. "It's going to be okay."

Surprised by her unexpected display of emotion, he quickly pulled back as everything inside of him came dangerously close to rushing out.

She let go and wiped at the corner of her eye, the way women do when they're trying not to smear their mascara. He reached behind him and grabbed a tissue for her.

"Thank you."

His eyes darted nervously back and forth, refusing to focus on her distraught face. "Thank you for helping her yesterday. I'm glad you were there."

She shook her head. "I wish I could have done more."

Silence settled around them as he glanced towards the doors of ICU.

Realizing that he was anxious to go back inside, she stood to go. "I'll stop back by a little later."

"Thank you," he said, rising from the chair.

Her heart sank for him as she watched him walk across the floor and disappear into ICU. Things were far worse than he could ever possibly imagine.

Chapter Four

Gavin closed the door to his office and collapsed onto the sofa, uncaring that his scrubs were drenched in sweat. He closed his eyes and took several deep breaths, trying to ease the ache in his shoulders and neck.

What should have been a simple bypass, had turned into a six-hour ordeal due to unforeseen complications. He lay there recounting every detail of the surgery, mentally making notes of the things that he needed to follow up on.

In the middle of his note taking, his thoughts turned to Sarah and he was immediately overcome with shame. He had felt more with her yesterday afternoon than he had in months - and now she wouldn't even speak to him.

He sat up angrily and swung his legs onto the floor. He had not intended to sleep with Jessica again, but what had started out innocently enough, had quickly heated up.

He rubbed his eyes, trying to form a thought of clarity. He hadn't wanted to tell Sarah the truth the way he had last night, but everything had happened so fast. Now, Jessica was in critical condition and might not recover. And the baby, *his baby,* might die.

"Dr. Gavin Williams report to CCU."

With a heavy sigh, he stood up. Besides his own patients, he now had to take care of Jessica's.

As he left his office, he found himself wishing that he could go and see her, but figured it would be best if he stayed away. He knew that Ethan would not appreciate him being there.

~

Ethan sat in the waiting room outside ICU talking on the phone with Dr. Michaels from St. Joseph's. The news he was giving him wasn't great. The baby had shown no visible signs of improvement since his arrival, and his vitals had dropped.

He was listening closely when he saw a nurse hurry into Jessica's room. A moment later, her obstetrician, Dr. Cali, went in. Panic struck him and he stood up, telling Dr. Michaels that he had to go.

Dr. Cali met him at the door.

"What's wrong?"

She held up her hand to calm him. "Nothing's happened. She's beginning to come around."

He brushed past her to go inside but she grabbed his arm.

"Ethan, wait. I know this is going to be hard on you, but you have to be positive about the baby. She has to believe that he's okay."

"I understand," he said, swallowing hard. He went through the door and to his wife's side. "Jess?"

Her eyes slowly fluttered open. They were confused at first, but immediately changed to fear when she felt of her stomach. "The baby! Is the baby okay?"

"Shh..." He reached out and touched her cheek to calm her. "The baby's fine."

She looked at him, searching his face. "Really?"

"Really."

Hearing the confidence in his voice, she let herself relax.

He smiled down at her. "You gave me a beautiful baby boy."

"We had a boy?" Her eyes began brimming with tears. "And he's okay? I mean, really, there's nothing wrong?"

"He's got all his fingers and all his toes. *I counted*. Everything's where it should be."

"Can I see him?"

He was quick not to hesitate. "When you're stronger, I'll have him brought to you. I promise."

Chapter Five

Sarah arrived home that night to find Gavin waiting for her. She noticed the table was set as the smell of chow mein permeated her kitchen.

"I brought home Chinese," he said, sounding about as contrite as he could be. "I thought we could have some dinner and then talk."

"There's nothing to talk about."

He reached out and grabbed her by the arm as she brushed past him. "Sarah, please…"

She took off her coat and begrudgingly sat down, refusing to look at him. For the next ten minutes, the only sound heard was that of the ice clinking in their glasses. Having no desire to eat, she stirred her food around, occasionally glimpsing at Gavin out of the corner of her eye. The outline of his jaw was rigid as he picked at the contents in front of him.

He suddenly pushed his plate aside, making her cringe. She had managed to avoid him at the hospital for the entire day, but now that they were both here, she knew with absolute certainty what was about to come.

"Sarah, I know I hurt you," he began. "But I need you to understand something. I never meant to do so."

She gave him a cold look. "Then why did you sleep with her again?"

"Truthfully…I don't know."

"You don't *know*?" She got to her feet, feeling her face flush with anger. "Do you have any idea what you've done, Gavin? What you've *both* done?"

He stood up, letting the napkin fall from his lap. "Please don't get upset," he said, holding his hands up as if doing so would calm her.

"How could you do this to me, Gavin? *How?*"

"I didn't do it on purpose, Sarah," he said, in what sounded like a very condescending tone. "It just happened."

Knowing the tears that were streaming down her cheeks were misleading, she tapped a finger angrily against his chest. "It was your *fucking* choice to *sleep* with her, Gavin! It didn't just *happen!* You knew exactly what you were doing!" No longer able to stand the sight of him, she hurried out of the kitchen and started up the stairs.

"Sarah, we're not going to get anywhere if we can't talk through this."

She stopped and turned around. "There's nothing left to say." She gripped the edge of the banister in order to hold back her sobs. "We can't just pick up the pieces like last time and go on."

~

Ethan came home and poured himself a tall drink before heading upstairs to take a much-needed shower. On the way to his bedroom, he couldn't help but stop and look in the nursery. A sad smile formed upon his lips as he viewed the empty room. They hadn't wanted to know the sex of the baby, so he had painted the walls a soft green. Stuffed animals and a slew of baby toys adorned the rest of the space, along with a dresser and changer table. The crib, however, still lay in pieces on the floor.

He reached into his pocket for his cell phone and checked his voice mail. There was still no word from Dr. Michaels. He leaned against the doorjamb, feeling a slight stinging in his eyes. All these months of planning and waiting could all be for nothing. He wouldn't even allow himself to call the baby by the name they had chosen for him, as he was afraid of getting too attached.

Taking a sip of his scotch, he turned away and went across the hall. Jessica's blood pressure had steadily climbed throughout the afternoon, and Dr. Cali had upgraded her condition to stable. He rubbed the grit from his eyes as he lay back against the bed. In the morning, he knew he would have to tell her about the baby.

It was still surreal to him that he and Jessica were parents. Ethan had never wanted anything more in his life than to be a doctor, and after achieving that goal, he threw himself into it body and soul, never giving much thought to having a wife or family. But all that changed when he'd moved here, to Serenity Harbor.

The corners of his mouth turned upwards, remembering the first time he'd met Jessica. It was his second day, and he'd stood nervously next to Sarah as she introduced him to the other doctors and members of the hospital board. He shook all of their hands and exchanged pleasantries before they took their seats at the table.

He silently looked around the room trying to remember everyone's name. The man talking was Phillip Martin; he was the chief of staff here. Sitting beside him was Grace somebody or other. He couldn't remember her last name, but knew was a psychiatrist. Next to her, sat her husband, Paul; he was an attorney for the hospital.

Then there was Meredith Van Owen, a rich widow in her mid-fifties, who had drooled all over him before the meeting. Ethan studied her for a moment, wondering how many face peels she had endured. Her skin was so tight it looked as if it were going to crack.

Meredith saw him looking her way and gave him a wink.

He quickly flicked his eyes in the opposite direction pretending not to have noticed. Seated to his immediate right was Sarah, and her husband, Gavin. He was the head of cardiology. There were still a couple of others on the other side of the table whose names he had already forgotten.

The meeting seemed to drone on forever, and he was becoming quite bored with statistics and logistics when the door suddenly opened. A woman in blue scrubs hurried in and sat down in the empty chair on Ethan's left, apologizing to everyone for being late.

Throughout the rest of the meeting, he couldn't stop himself from looking at her. She was the most beautiful thing he had ever laid his eyes on. He wanted to reach out and touch her silky, blonde hair as it fell down her back.

She turned slightly, catching his eyes with hers.

Ethan felt his face turning red.

Seeming amused by his embarrassment, she gave him a broad smile.

After the meeting was over, Dr. Martin introduced them. "Jessica, there's someone here I'd like you to meet. This is Dr. Ethan Harrington. He'll be working in the clinic with Dr. Williams."

Her blue eyes sparkled as she took his hand. "It's nice to meet you."

"Jessica is a cardiothoracic surgeon," Phillip continued.

That was fitting for Ethan because he felt that he was going to need one. He thought for sure she could see his heart beating through his shirt.

It took him nearly two weeks to gather up enough courage to ask her out on a date. She accepted and they eventually wound up at her apartment talking until the wee hours of the morning.

After that, except for when they were working at the hospital, they were rarely apart. Four months later, they had flown to Cancun and eloped.

Ethan sighed and took another sip of his drink. That all seemed like a lifetime ago.

Chapter Six

Ethan could hear his wife yelling all the way down the corridor when he stepped off the elevator the next morning.

"Why won't they let me see him?"

Grace, Jessica's best friend and cousin, stood beside the bed trying to calm her down. "I don't know, sweetheart, but I'm sure everything's fine."

"There's something wrong! If there wasn't they would let me see—" Her voice fell silent when she saw Ethan's face.

Grace dropped her arms helplessly against her side and took a step back, allowing him to come closer.

Jessica's eyes began to well up with tears as he took her hands in his. "There were complications when he was delivered," he said delicately. "He was airlifted yesterday morning to St. Joseph's in Bar Harbor."

"No." She leaned forward and buried her face in his chest. "No, Ethan," she said, sobbing. "No... no...no."

~

Sarah stared at the incoming call on her cell phone. It was Gavin. Realizing that any conversation at this point would be nothing more than a repeat of what had been said last night, she declined the call. She sat down uneasily in her chair, accepting the fact that there was nothing else that could be said or done to fix their marriage.

Feeling more miserable than ever, she glanced around at the cramped office she shared with Ethan. It was only an area about twelve feet wide and fifteen feet long. To the left of the door, two desks were pushed together, facing each other, in order to save valuable floor space. A yellow sofa, that had seen better days, sat on the opposite side with a picture of the ocean hanging above it. The painting wasn't very colorful, or even pretty for that matter, but it did a good job of hiding a large crack in the drywall. Next to the sofa, a door led to a narrow hallway that held two examination rooms.

She and Ethan were partners together in the clinic, which was open to low income families, and those without insurance. The hours were long and sometimes unrewarding, but she and Ethan both agreed that there was a need for this type of service.

The problem was that the hospital board *didn't* agree, and although both of them were *on* the board, they usually had a hard time getting the funding they needed. The money was more likely to go to pediatrics or research before they saw a dime.

She stared at the stack of paperwork and medical charts that lay scattered about both desks. She half-heartedly flipped through some of the papers. The thought of working today didn't excite her in the least, but there was no way of knowing when Ethan would be back.

Hoping that going on rounds would put her in a better frame of mind, she walked over to the coat rack and picked her stethoscope off one of its wooden pegs. One of Ethan's ties slid to the floor. With a heavy sigh, she bent down to retrieve it.

She suddenly found herself wishing that she could go back to two days ago and recapture what she'd felt for Gavin the moment after they had made love. Her desire to do so, however, was immediately replaced by a surge of bitterness. She shook her head, feeling the anger return. How could she have been so stupid?

~

Ethan sat in the chair next to Jessica's bedside, scrolling through his emails. She had calmed down somewhat, and for the past few hours, hadn't said much of anything.

"Ethan?"

"Hmm?"

"Did you take a picture of him?"

He looked up and shook his head slightly. "No, I'm sorry. I never thought to do it."

"It's all right," she said, seeing the sudden agony in his eyes.

More silence passed by.

"I think you should go to Bar Harbor to be with him."

He slipped his phone back into his pocket and leaned forward. "I don't want to leave you," he said quietly.

She lay her palm on the side of his face and gave him a faint smile. "I'll be all right, but I would feel better if you were there with him."

"Am I interrupting?"

Looking over his shoulder, he saw Grace standing in the doorway.

Jessica motioned for her to come in. "Of course not."

Ethan offered her his chair, and walked over to the corner of the room to check his voice mail. Dr. Michaels was supposed to have called him over an hour ago, and despite his normal ability to remain calm, he felt himself growing more and more anxious with each passing moment.

"How are you feeling?" asked Grace, kissing her on the cheek.

"Better. Dr. Cali is going to move me to a private room in the morning."

"That's good news…"

Ethan's cell phone rang as the two of them talked. Recognizing the number, he excused himself from the room.

Jessica picked up on his apprehension as he walked outside.

Grace saw it too and tried to distract her. "Is there anything I can bring you from your house?"

She shook her head, her eyes fixed intently upon Ethan as he stood just outside the doorway. She watched, refusing to blink, as she searched his mannerisms for any signs of distress.

"Thank you," he said, before slipping the phone into his pocket.

Jessica's breath grew ragged as he returned to her bedside.

His eyes were moist as he took Jessica's hand in his. "He's breathing on his own."

Chapter Seven

Jessica lay in her bed on the maternity ward. The room had been brightly decorated with flowers, cards, and blue helium balloons. Several of the staff, along with her colleagues, had stopped by during the day to wish her and the baby well. This had left her feeling weak and tired, and she sank farther into the pillow as she talked quietly with her father-in-law.

"Have you spoken with Ethan today?"

"Not yet," she said, shaking her head. "But he promised he'd call as soon as he talked to the doctor."

Everett smiled down at her. "You know I saw him after he was born."

"You did?"

"I did. He's a handsome little chap."

She grinned, finding his accent, and the use of that word, charming. "I can't wait to see him. Ethan's going to email me some pictures later today."

"You know," he said, taking her by the hand, "you had that son of mine scared to death." His voice was gruff in a teasing way.

"I know," she whispered. As the light filtered through the blinds, she couldn't help noticing that Ethan bore no resemblance to Everett whatsoever, and gathered that he must take after his mother. Her father-in-law was fairly tall, but a little overweight. A thin mustache and goatee, with muted shades of gray, helped to soften the hard edges of his jaw.

"Thank you for giving me such a beautiful grandson."

She nodded, finding herself unable to answer as the shame of what she'd done returned.

He leaned over and gave her a peck on the cheek. "I'm going to let you get some rest. You're going to need all of your strength when that little rug rat comes home."

~

Ethan solemnly followed Dr. Michaels down a long hallway at St. Joseph's. They had been walking for close to a minute now, and there seemed to be no end of it in sight. Finally, they veered to the right and went down another hall, then turned left and went through a set of sliding glass doors. Ten incubators, each one about two feet from the other, lined the middle of the room.

Dr. Michaels stopped abruptly at the fourth one and reached for a chart that hung off the end of it.

Ethan looked down and saw his last name taped to the glass. The baby was asleep with his hands curled into tiny little fists beside his face. His color had vastly improved since he had last seen him.

Dr. Michaels studied his chart for a moment. "When he was born, his Apgar score was only three. Is that correct?"

"Yes."

"I scored him an eight this morning," he said, signing off on the chart. "He seems to be responding well."

"What's his blood count?"

"Much better than before. It's still low, but within normal range. In the morning we're going to try feeding him with a bottle."

"Dr. Michaels report to the third-floor lab," an indifferent voice called over the P.A.

"Excuse me for a moment."

As Dr. Michaels disappeared through the door, the baby suddenly stirred and began to cry.

Instinctively, Ethan reached in to pick him up but stopped, knowing he couldn't. He looked around until he got the attention of a nurse.

She came over to check on him. "What's the matter, sweetie?" She undid his diaper and took a peek. "Oh, he's got a wet diaper. Yes, he does," she cooed.

Ethan watched as she reached under the incubator for a fresh diaper and some wipes.

"Would you like to change him, Dad?"

"Um, sure." He slipped on the pair of latex gloves she was holding out for him, and nervously undid the diaper before setting it aside.

"Here, you have to keep the old diaper over him until you're ready to switch them. Little boys have a fire hose," the nurse explained sweetly.

The baby's cries got a little louder, making him want to hurry. His tiny legs seemed to be made out of rubber bands, for every time Ethan pulled them down to fasten the diaper, they would draw back up again. Finally, the task was complete, and he stepped back to admire his handiwork.

"You know we've been calling him Baby Harrington all this time. Have you got a name picked out for him?"

He smiled. "It's Ryan."

The baby looked around the room as Ethan spoke.

The nurse gave him a nod. "He knows your voice, Dad."

Ethan felt himself well up with pride.

~

That evening, Gavin cautiously peered inside Jessica's room, making sure she was alone before entering.

Upon seeing him, she smiled and held out her hand.

"How are you?"

"I'm fine."

He squeezed her hand and swallowed hard, forcing the lump back down his throat. "You had me so worried," he whispered. "I'm so sorry for all of this. I never meant for this to happen the way it did." He was unable to stop the words as they came tumbling out.

"It's not your fault, Gavin."

Her answer was met with silence as he sat down in the chair beside the bed and sighed miserably. "How's the baby?" he asked quietly.

"He's getting better. Would you like to see?" She reached for her cell phone on the tray.

His eyes grew moist as he stared at the screen. "He's beautiful," he murmured.

As he continued looking at the pictures, she couldn't help noticing that he was starting to get just a touch of gray on his sides, even though he was only thirty-six; two years older than Ethan.

After a moment, he laid the phone back down on the tray. "I need to tell you something, and I don't want you getting upset."

She sat forward, feeling a slight sense of alarm.

He glanced at the door to make sure they were still alone. "I told Sarah the truth."

"*Why?*"

"I had to, Jessica. I couldn't live with the guilt a second longer. I was scared that you were going to *die*."

She felt her stomach beginning to churn. It was as if Pandora's Box had been opened—it stood poised and ready to ravage all of them. "I'm guessing by the look on your face, she didn't take it very well."

He leaned back in the chair and cast his eyes upon the floor. "She's asked me to move out."

~

Sarah flipped her pillow over to the dry side, and wiped her eyes with the sleeve of her nightgown. Earlier this evening, Gavin had taken a few items of clothing and told her that he would sleep in his office until he could find an apartment.

The moon shone through the slits of the blinds, illuminating the emptiness she felt inside. She knew that it was pointless to lie here wallowing in self-pity, but it was the only thing she had left.

Her eyes wandered over to the picture frame sitting by itself on the nightstand. It was a photo that Gavin had taken of her nearly two years ago. Grinning and dressed in a billowy pink shirt, she stood sideways for the camera, proudly showing off the bump in her stomach.

Sarah picked up the frame and traced the outline of it with her finger. Three weeks after this picture had been taken, she had miscarried; it was a loss that had sent her and Gavin reeling. Things went quickly from bad to worse when complications from it forced her to have a hysterectomy.

Further adding to her misery, was the fact that her daughter had just left home. Ashley had barely turned eighteen when she met and subsequently fell in love with Ted, unleashing a whole new set of problems. The first one being that Ted had been accepted into a university, which happened to be on the other side of the world, in Sydney, Australia. And the second problem—was that he had asked her to marry him.

She and Gavin were against it from the start, telling her that she was too young. Ashley met their answer with hostility.

Tension in the household grew thick, and after weeks of arguing, Sarah began to realize that her daughter was going to do this even without their blessing. Against Gavin's wishes, she gave in. Ashley and Ted were married the day before they left.

It wasn't long before Sarah found herself miserable without her. Having given birth to Ashley at the age of twenty, it had always been just the two of them until she'd married Gavin five years ago. He quickly took to the role of stepfather, treating her as if she were his own.

But now, for the first time in their marriage, they were alone with only one another. There was no teen angst to deal with, no curfews, and no school functions to attend. She'd never realized up until that moment just how much of her life had revolved around her daughter.

Gavin started spending more and more time at the hospital, as did she. Sometimes, days would go by before they saw each other at home. When they *were* together, they usually fought, and their lovemaking became less and less frequent, until it stopped altogether.

It was about that same time that rumors began to circulate about him and Jessica. Sarah tried ignoring them, but soon began to have her doubts that he was being faithful. When she had expressed her concerns, he had angrily brushed her aside telling her that she was being paranoid. Feeling that he was probably right, she let it go and tried to focus on healing the rift in their marriage.

Then one night she came home to find him talking on his cell phone. He was laughing and speaking to the person on the other end in a very casual tone. When he noticed her standing there, he changed his demeanor and hung up.

Having aroused her suspicions once again, she waited until he'd gone upstairs to take a shower before looking at his call log. She pressed the last number dialed and waited.

"You hung up so fast I didn't get a chance to tell you how much I enjoyed this afternoon." The voice was unmistakably that of Jessica's.

Sarah turned over on her side and swallowed the new batch of tears that was forming. Looking back, she really didn't know why she had forgiven him. At the time, she thought it was because she still loved him, but now she wondered if it was her fear of being alone that had driven the reconciliation.

Burying her face in the pillow, she began to sob.

Chapter Eight

Jessica sat in her kitchen blissfully eating the comfort food that Grace had prepared for her.

"Was the food that bad at the hospital?"

She swallowed and shook her head. "No. You just don't know how good of a cook you are."

Grace smiled, seeming delighted by the compliment.

"I wish I could cook like this."

The older woman raised her eyebrow. "You could have learned if you'd just stayed in and helped out once in a while."

"True," she said, laughing. "But I was having too much fun."

The two women were cousins, and had grown up in the same house together. When Jessica was just six, her mother had decided to marry some rich Texan and move to Houston, leaving her behind in her aunt's care.

It was a bad time as Grace's brother, William, a private in the army, had been killed just weeks before, but Jessica's mother couldn't see past her own selfishness to wait.

Bound by tragedy, she and Grace quickly became best friends. Jessica idolized her older cousin, eventually choosing to follow in her footsteps to becoming a doctor.

The two of them had been through their share of good times and bad times, but Grace had always been there to pick up the pieces, including being there for her when her mother had died. Sometimes, Jessica felt as if she clung to her like a child, but the older woman didn't seem to mind.

She wiped her mouth with a napkin and sighed. Where had the years gone? Grace now had a grown son, and was a grandmother to twin girls.

"Are you excited about tomorrow?"

Jessica laughed again. "As if you didn't know." Ethan was coming home tomorrow with the baby. "You know, Grace, I don't even have diapers for him."

"Well," she said with a chuckle, "you make a list, and I'll run to the store for you before I go home."

"Thank you."

Grace put the leftovers in the fridge and began cleaning up the dishes. She knew how happy Jessica was right now, but couldn't help wondering if she had forgotten about the elephant in the room. She didn't want to ruin this moment for her, but felt she had to say something. "Jessica, I know you're very happy right now, but I think you're forgetting about the most important thing, aren't you?"

Her smile immediately faded. "I haven't forgotten about it," she answered in a clipped tone.

"Well then, I think you're choosing to ignore it."

Jessica looked away. Grace could be extremely blunt sometimes. "No, I'm choosing to not think about it right now. I just want to hold my son and be with my husband. I'm not thinking beyond that."

"He needs to know the truth, Jessica—"

"I know," she said cutting her off. She sat there for a moment trying to hold back the tears. "I know, but I'm scared to tell him. I don't want him to leave."

Grace sat down in the chair across from her. "You can't let Ethan go on thinking this is his baby."

"Why not? What he doesn't know won't hurt him."

She gave her an exasperated look. "That's not the point, is it?"

Her cell phone rang. "It's Ethan!" she said excitedly as she hurried into the other room to talk.

Grace felt an uneasiness settle in about her. She knew Jessica's reasons for not wanting to tell him were valid, but she also knew if Ethan ever found out the truth on his own, he would be devastated.

Chapter Nine

Jessica sat in the nursery, silently rocking her son. It was hard to believe that he was almost six weeks old. The last few days had been spent interviewing nannies, which had not been an easy task. It seemed that whomever she wanted to hire, Ethan did not, and vice versa. Going back to work was going to be hard enough, let alone leaving him with a total stranger.

They had finally agreed upon a woman by the name of Ellen Chambers. She seemed nice enough and came with glowing recommendations. She also didn't seem to mind the fact that she would need to be available twenty-four hours a day. With her and Ethan's schedules, it was extremely difficult to guess when they would be home.

From where she was sitting, she could see out into the backyard. A small guesthouse, covered in white siding, sat on the edge of the property. She thought it would be best if Mrs. Chambers lived there, as this would allow her to be available at a moment's notice, yet still give the three of them their privacy.

She put Ryan in his crib and tiptoed down the stairs, being careful to avoid the squeaky one near the top. The home she shared with Ethan was a big, rambling Victorian situated on a quiet street in the older part of town. It had been in a sad state of disrepair when they had bought it eighteen months ago, but looking around now, you would never know it.

Her sandals clopped quietly on the concrete that lined the inground pool, which at the moment, was still covered with a blue tarp. She began making her way along the narrow stepping-stones that led up to the front door of the guesthouse. As she drew near, she guessed that the use of that word was deceiving. A guesthouse implied a house, whereas this was really no bigger than a studio apartment. It consisted only of a bedroom, bathroom, living room, and galley kitchen. Jessica turned the knob and went inside, hoping that Mrs. Chambers liked small spaces.

Ethan was standing on a ladder, painting the far wall in the living room. He had been working down here for the last couple of days, trying to get it in shape.

"Oh, that color's going to look great."

"I didn't hear you come in," he said, looking over his shoulder. "Is the baby asleep?"

"Mmm-hmm."

"You know, I thought I remembered saying that I was never going to pick up a paint brush again after we finished the house."

She began to giggle. "But you're so good at it."

He gave her a smile before turning his attention back to the task at hand.

Jessica watched him for a moment, noting that if anyone ever fit the bill of being tall, dark, and handsome—it was Ethan. Lean, slightly muscular, and standing at six foot one, he had a pair of smoldering brown eyes, and thick black hair that he kept parted on the left. His locks would often fall forward and hang loosely above his brow, making him look boyish at times.

Besides being chivalrous to a fault; a trait that she found charming, even if it did get on her nerves at times, he was also kind, considerate…and always just a little unsure of himself.

Jessica folded her arms against her and sighed, knowing that her affair with Gavin had only added to his low self-esteem. She was deeply ashamed for what she'd done, but also couldn't explain it.

A few months after they'd bought this house, Gavin had started flirting with her. She'd found it amusing and flirted back. At the time, she felt there was no real harm in it, and quite honestly, she liked the attention. Ethan was usually attentive to her, but there were times he could be a little withdrawn.

Then one evening, Gavin said something to her in jest like he always did, and she said something back and laughed. Then he kissed her. But it wasn't a peck on the lips. It was long, and hard, and passionate. Before she knew it, they were half-naked on the floor in her office.

This went on for months, even as the rumors about them escalated. They snuck around, seizing any opportunity they could. It was sexually driven.

It abruptly came to a halt when his wife found out about the two of them by accident. Gavin and Sarah's sudden separation only fueled Ethan's suspicions, and he confronted her one night, demanding to know the truth.

A small shudder went through her as she remembered her admission of guilt. The look in his eyes that night was something she would never forget. Three days later, he moved out.

They remained separated for three months, and it was on very shaky ground that they'd reconciled. But the damage had been done. It seemed that Ethan had become a different person. He became increasingly obsessive about her whereabouts, and was constantly berating Gavin. It would take nothing to set his temper off, which seemed to increase greatly when he had been drinking.

They still had their moments of laughter, but their constant bickering overshadowed it. When they made love, she could tell he was holding back. The passion was gone, and any intimacy they had with each other grew smaller, until it stopped altogether.

On a particularly warm summer night last July, Ethan had flown to New York for a medical convention. Jessica was in her office getting ready to leave for the evening when Gavin stopped by and asked her out for a drink. She politely declined, not wanting to put herself in that position again, but he was persistent—and she was vulnerable. She felt herself coming to life as he undressed her, his lips touching hers.

A few weeks later, she learned she was pregnant.

She became terrified of losing Ethan after that. He had to think that the baby was his. So one night soon after, she met him at the door with a bottle of wine, wearing nothing but a black negligee. It didn't take long for her to arouse his interests.

Chapter Ten

Sarah gazed out her office window wishing that she were home. She longed to be in the solitude of her own company right now.

The door behind her opened and closed.

"Are there any more patients to see?" she asked wearily.

"No, the waiting room's empty."

She glanced over her shoulder at Ethan. "Would you mind if I took off the rest of the day?"

"No, of course not. Is there anything the matter?"

"No."

Ethan watched as she began gathering up her things. For weeks now, she had been distant with him. She was his best friend, and he knew that he was hers; but lately, her actions didn't reflect it. "Sarah, have I done something to make you mad at me?"

She looked up. "Why would you ask such a thing?"

"Well, for a while now, you just seem like you don't want to be near me. You've been very quiet."

"I don't mean to be. I guess I've just got a lot on my mind."

"Like what?"

"Nothing." She felt her voice beginning to falter.

He took her by the arm and led her over to the couch. "What's wrong?"

She pursed her lips together, trying to stop the lump in her throat from coming up.

"What is it?" he asked tenderly.

Her chin began to quiver as she drew a deep breath. "I've asked Gavin for a divorce."

He physically drew back, startled by her reply.

She turned away, embarrassed to be crying in front of him.

Sometimes there are no words in the human language that can take someone's pain away. Ethan could think of nothing to say to comfort his friend, so instead, he leaned over and hugged her.

She buried her face in his shoulder as the tears came rushing out.

~

That evening, Ethan was upstairs in the nursery giving Ryan his bottle. He smiled as he rocked him back and forth, finding that holding him in his arms always took away his frustrations of the day.

"Hi," Jessica said, walking into the room.

"How was your first day back at work?"

"Terrible! I missed my baby." She bent down and kissed Ryan on the forehead. "So, how are my two favorite men getting along?"

Before he could answer, the phone rang. It was the hospital calling for him.

Jessica took Ryan from him as he went into the hallway to talk. "Did you miss Mommy?" she asked, nuzzling the side of his face. As she held him, she caught a glimpse of herself in the mirror; her figure had almost come back.

"I have to go check on a patient," Ethan said, returning to the nursery. "I'm sorry I can't spend any time with you." He gave her a quick kiss on the cheek and whispered goodbye to Ryan.

Jessica placed the baby in his crib and followed him into their bedroom where she promptly sat down beside him. "How long will you be?" she asked, running the tip of her fingernail over the back of his neck.

"Don't know," he answered, leaning over to tie his shoes.

She placed her other hand on the inside of his thigh. "I'll wait up for you."

He stood up quickly, slightly irritated with himself that her touch had such an effect on him. "Don't bother. It will probably be very late when I get back."

She felt the sting of tears as he left the room.

Ethan got halfway down the stairs and stopped. Sarah's news today had left him shaken, but he knew he was going to have to overcome this anger if he and Jessica were going to make their marriage work. He returned to the bedroom and found her still sitting on the bed.

"Did you forget something?"

"Yes." He bent down and cradled her head in his hands. His lips pressed tenderly against hers for a moment. "I'll be home as soon as I can."

~

A week later, Sarah was in her office, going through some of the paperwork on her desk when she came across a bill that was due the fifth. She looked at the calendar and frowned. Today was the twenty-fifth. She scrawled her signature on it and started to send it to accounting when she realized that she needed Ethan's signature as well. He had gone down to radiology over twenty minutes ago.

She left the office and headed for the third-floor X-ray, knowing that accounting would cut the check today if she got it in by three o'clock.

While waiting for the elevator, she could sense people staring at her. News of her pending divorce had spread like wildfire throughout the hospital. She grimaced as she stepped through the doors; it was hard enough getting through the day without having to deal with the whispering and pointing going on behind her back.

The elevator deposited her on the third floor, yet she saw no sign of Ethan by the time she got to radiology. Pivoting around on her heel to go, she nearly bumped into Jessica. Sarah immediately grew rigid. She had not seen her since that fateful day on the elevator.

Jessica glanced around nervously. "Can we talk for a minute?"

She took a step closer to her, and in a voice barely audible said, "I don't have *anything* to discuss with you."

Jessica reached out and grabbed her sleeve as she brushed past her. "I'm sorry, Sarah. I never meant to hurt you this way."

"I find that hard to believe," she said, pulling her arm back.

"It's true. I can't even begin to tell you how sorry I am. And I know that Gavin is, too."

She shook her head and began walking away, not wanting to hear anymore.

"He still loves you, you know."

She spun around. "Don't you *dare* stand there and tell me that!" she said, prepared to have it out with her. It was then that she noticed the number of nurses and technicians that were now watching them. Rumors, like diseases, thrived in this hospital. Realizing that this was neither the time, nor place to do battle, she turned and walked away.

Deciding it would be best to take the stairs, her sensible shoes carried her up two flights of steps, but she was still seething when she returned to her office.

Ethan looked up as she slammed the door shut, but didn't say anything.

She felt herself becoming mad at him. Why couldn't he have been here ten minutes ago? "I need you to sign this," she said, handing him the bill.

"Why am I signing a paper wad?" he asked, arching his brow.

She sighed. "It's an invoice. I accidentally threw it away."

He scribbled his name on it and handed it back.

She glanced at the clock on the wall. It was after three now, and too late to give it to accounting. Wondering how much more miserable this day could get, she plopped herself down in the chair and grabbed the next invoice on top of the pile.

She glumly began going over it as she hunted for her pen. After several seconds of searching, she looked across the desk at Ethan. "Did you take my pen?"

"No, this is mine," he said innocently.

She narrowed her eyes at him.

He broke into a lopsided grin.

"You're hopeless," she said, feeling the corners of her mouth turn up. "You know that, don't you?"

"Yes, but you're stuck with me."

Sarah opened her middle drawer to retrieve another one, but found her smile fading when she saw the small package hidden near the back. She hesitated a moment, then took it out. "I almost forgot," she said softly. "This is for you."

"What's this?"

"It's a present for Ryan. I'm sorry it's so late. I've had it for weeks, I just forgot about it."

"You didn't have to do this."

She waved her hand in the air. "Oh, just open it."

Ethan tore at the wrapping and opened the box.

She swallowed hard as he parted the tissue paper and held up the tiny bib. The words, 'I Love My Daddy!' were embroidered on it in red stitching.

He seemed delighted. "Thank you, Sarah."

She smiled inwardly. Ethan had been born and raised in England, but had lived in the U.S. for a number of years. Most of the time, his accent was barely detectable, yet she found it amusing that it became more pronounced whenever he got excited.

~

That evening, Sarah was making her way out the south entrance, happy to be going home when she though she heard someone calling her name.

Looking over her shoulder, she saw Everett Harrington coming towards her. "Hello, Everett."

"Hello, my dear. Are you heading home?"

"Yes, but Ethan's still upstairs if you're looking for him."

He shook his head. "No, actually I'm headed home as well. I just stopped by to see Phillip. Do you mind if I walk with you?"

"Of course not."

Everett was the owner and president of Harrington Enterprises, a multi-million dollar business, whose sole purpose was buying and selling other companies.

As they walked, they made conversation about various things. They talked about his grandson, the weather, and of course, business.

Everett was on the board of directors at the hospital, which usually placed her on opposite sides with him when it came to getting funding for the clinic. When he had first joined the board, Sarah thought he would be a great help in getting money their way since Ethan was his son, but Everett Harrington was not interested in anything that didn't turn a profit. He made it known how much he disliked the clinic, and what a waste of time he thought it was.

"How does it feel to be a grandfather?" she asked, realizing the conversation between them had lulled.

"Oh, don't get me started, my dear."

Sarah smiled at him, finding it hard to hold a grudge. Outside the boardroom, Everett was very likeable.

They said goodnight and parted ways.

As she unlocked her car, a sigh fell from her lips. Another mundane evening to look forward to.

Chapter Eleven

Jessica sat rigidly in Gavin's office, knowing that she had made a terrible mistake. For the past half hour, they had been discussing the consequences of telling Ethan the truth.

He had been pushing her for months now, and she suddenly found herself wishing that she'd never told him the baby was his in the first place.

The blood drained from Gavin's face, leaving him pale. "Are you sure?"

Jessica nodded.

"And it's –"

"It's yours."

He leaned back in his chair and put his hand over his mouth. The look on his face was a semblance of anger and devastation.

Her body trembled as she waited for his response. She knew that telling him was not going to solve the problem. If anything, it was probably going to make matters worse; however, this was a hard burden to bear alone, and she desperately needed to find comfort somewhere. Her best friend, Grace, had offered her none.

"How many weeks?"

"Four and a half."

He subtly glanced at the calendar on his desk.

"It's yours," she repeated, feeling the anger rising in her.

"How can you be positive it's mine?"

She clasped her hands together. "Ethan and I haven't been together in two months."

This revelation was followed by several minutes of silence.

"What are you going to do?"

"I don't know."

He clenched his jaw and looked away.

She knew that wasn't the answer he was hoping for.

"Are you going to tell him?"

A surge of fear swept through her, more powerful than the one from last night.

"Jessica?"

She fought to find her voice. "I don't know."

He began to shake his head as if in disbelief.

"Are you going to tell Sarah?"

"Tell her what?" he said angrily. "Tell her that you and I slept together again? My marriage to her is just barely hanging on as it is." He pushed his chair back and stood up. "You have put me in an impossible situation, Jessica."

She felt her mouth drop open. "I've put you in an impossible situation?" She forgot just how goddamned arrogant he could be sometimes. "It took two, Gavin! Don't you lay this at my feet!"

He held his hands out to his sides. "What did you expect me to say?"

She stood up. "I don't know, Gavin," she said, feeling the sting of tears. "I guess I thought you might be a little more sympathetic, that's all."

"Jessica, did you hear what I said?"

She returned her attention to him. "What?"

He placed his hands on his hips. "Do you want me to be there tomorrow night?"

She pushed the memory aside and shook her head, trying to gather her thoughts. "I don't know. I don't know if your being there will help, or just make matters worse," she replied, wishing he would just drop the subject.

"You're not going to back out on me are you?" he asked warily.

"I don't think you understand just how hard this is going to be on him…and me."

He crossed his arms. "I know *exactly* how hard it's going to be. I've already been through it, remember?"

She tried taking a more direct approach. "I just don't think I'm ready."

"Maybe I should tell him."

"Yeah, that would go over well," she said sarcastically.

Her words were followed by silence.

Looking up, she saw the muscle in his jaw twitch, and realized that he was serious. An uneasiness began to gather around her, making her rise to her feet. "Gavin—"

Ring! Ring!

He scowled as he turned to answer the phone. "This is Dr. Williams."

Realizing that this would be a good opportunity to slip away, she opened the door while his back was still turned and headed down the corridor. As she walked towards her own office, she found herself wishing that she had kept the secret about Ryan's paternity to herself. Living with the consequences of what she'd done would be a lot easier if no one else knew about it.

"Dr. Jessica Harrington to ER stat. Dr. Jessica Harrington, report to the ER stat."

She pushed open the door to the stairwell and hurried down the steps. Paramedics were wheeling a patient into trauma when she arrived.

Gavin was already there, doing an assessment.

"What do we have?" she asked, reaching for a pair of gloves.

He had a worried look about him. "You'd better call Ethan."

~

Trish Holloway's thick, curly brown hair bounced up and down against her shoulders as she accompanied her favorite doctor on his morning rounds. Every now and then, Dr. Harrington's arm would brush against hers as they walked. His touch made her feel giddy inside, like an adolescent schoolgirl.

As she listened to the instructions he was giving her regarding one of his patients, she pressed the clipboard tightly against her chest in hopes of drawing his attention to her cleavage.

A voice sounded over the P.A. "Dr. Ethan Harrington, report to CCU stat."

He handed her back the chart. "I'll finish up with you later, all right?"

She sighed to herself as she watched him heading down the corridor in that long, deliberate stride of his. Like most of the nurses here, she had a huge crush on him, but sadly…he only had eyes for his wife.

~

Ethan walked up to the nurses' station outside CCU. "Did you page me?"

"Your wife did. Just a moment and I'll get her for you," the nurse said, picking up the phone.

A moment later, Jessica appeared around the corner.

"What's wrong?" he asked, noting the grim look she was wearing. "Is it one of my patients?"

She took him aside. "Ethan, there's something I need to tell you," she spoke slowly. "Your father's had a heart attack."

He shook his head, as if he didn't understand. "What?"

"He came in by ambulance a little while ago."

Ethan looked at her for a moment, his face unreadable, and then turned to go into CCU.

Through the glass window, he could see Gavin talking with one of the nurses. When he saw him standing there, he came out to meet him.

"How bad is it?" The words jerked from his throat.

Gavin exchanged glances with Jessica before answering. "It's bad..."

Ethan put his hands on his hips as he listened to him explain that his father had suffered a massive heart attack.

"...was cyanotic when he was brought in. He's sustained severe damage to his left ventricle."

"Is he conscious?"

Gavin shook his head. "Does your father have a history of heart disease, or any medical conditions?"

Guilt suddenly washed over him. "I don't know."

~

It was late in the night as Jessica stood over her father-in-law, listening to his heart. Looking at Everett now, she noticed for the first time just how old he really was.

Age had never been a factor for him before, as he was always shuttling back and forth from this meeting to that one. His energy had seemed endless. He had once told her that running his business kept him young. She let the stethoscope rest around her neck and stifled a sigh. The man who'd said those words was now just a shadow of the one lying in the bed.

She shifted her eyes from him to Ethan. For the past three hours, he'd been sitting in a chair by the corner, staring at the floor. Up until a year ago, she didn't even know that his father was still alive. He'd been vague when she questioned him about it, saying only that he and his father led very different lives. His sister had been a little more forthcoming, however, telling her that the two of them had a falling out about sixteen years ago over the fact that Ethan wanted to be a doctor instead of following in his footsteps.

"It's late."

The room had been so quiet, that she jumped at the sound of Ethan's voice.

He slowly got to his feet and stretched. "Why don't you go on home? There's no point in your staying."

She slipped her hands in the pockets of her lab coat, wishing that she could argue the point. "Are you sure?"

He nodded. "I'll see you out."

They walked in silence as he escorted her out of CCU and over to the elevator.

She stepped on and turned around, placing her hand upon his chest. "Try and get some sleep, all right?"

He leaned in and put his arms out to keep the doors from closing. "I'll see you in the morning," he said, kissing her softly on the lips. "Give Ryan a kiss for me."

"I will," she said, giving him a meager smile.

As the doors slid shut, he began making his way down the dimly-lit corridor towards Intensive Care. The halls of the hospital were strangely quiet; free from all the noise and bustle of the day. It was a welcome change.

He stopped to speak with the nurse at the station about Mr. Samuels' condition. He had been injured by a hit and run driver, and had sustained internal injuries; the most serious of which, was a ruptured spleen. His advanced age was complicating matters, and there had been no improvement since he was brought in.

"Dr. Harrington?"

He looked over his shoulder to find Mrs. Samuels.

"Has something happened?"

Ethan motioned for her to sit down. "There's nothing wrong," he said, kneeling in front of her.

She smiled and put her hand over her heart. "When I saw you, I thought..." She closed her eyes, unable to finish.

Over the last few days, Ethan had learned that the two of them had been married for nearly fifty-seven years.

"Dr. Harrington, is he going to be all right?"

As a physician, he couldn't count the number of times he had been asked that question, and yet he always found it difficult to answer. Seeing the desperation in her face, he feigned a small smile. "We're doing everything we possibly can to see that he will be."

A tear followed the lines in her face as it cut down her cheek.

He patted her hand reassuringly. "Now listen. He's going to need all your strength and support when he goes home, and you can't very well give him that if you're sick yourself. Now, I want you to promise me you'll try and get some rest."

She wiped her eyes and nodded.

He gave her a quick wink as he stood up to go.

The deserted elevator took him to the fifth floor in record time. He unlocked his office and flipped on the lights before making his way over to his cluttered desk. He rummaged around in the top drawer for a moment, before finding the piece of paper he was looking for.

He sat down wearily in his chair, and pulled out his cell phone.

After five rings, a sleepy voice with a Spanish accent answered. "Westcott residence."

"May I speak to Renee, please?"

"She's out of town. Not come back 'til tomorrow."

He hesitated a moment.

"Que?" the voice said, sounding impatient.

"This is very important. Please tell her that her father has had a heart attack and she needs to come right away."

There was a slight pause. "I tell her when she get back. Who is 'dis, por favor?"

He sighed. "This is her brother calling."

As he hung up, he rifled through the junk in the drawer until his hands closed around a small bottle. He emptied two of the ulcer pills into his palm and absently glanced over at the coffee machine. It sat quietly on the other side of the room, having been turned off and cleaned by Sarah hours ago.

Spying his mug by the phone, he picked it up and peered inside. A thin brown liquid stared back at him. He popped the pills into his mouth and reluctantly took a long swallow of it, shivering at its bitterness.

The nurse on duty was in the process of changing his father's I.V. bag when he returned to CCU.

He waited for her to leave before easing himself down into the chair. He let his head fall back against the cushion and closed his eyes, trying to rid himself of the throbbing pain coursing through his stomach.

He must have fallen into a deep sleep, because the next time he opened his eyes it was after seven.

Jessica bent down and touched him softly upon his cheek. "I didn't mean to wake you."

"That's all right," he said, looking over at his father. "How is he?"

She knelt in front of him and placed her hands on his knees. "I'd like to run a catheter into his pulmonary artery to determine why his blood pressure isn't coming up."

Trepidation began circling him. "What do you think it is?" he asked, knowing that she most likely had a suspicion.

"It could be a lot of things."

"That's not what I asked."

She patted his knee like she would a child. "Let's wait and see what the test shows, all right?"

Ethan sat forward in the chair and rubbed the back of his neck in an effort to hide his emotions. Anytime his wife refused to answer him was because she wanted to spare his feelings.

Jessica tenderly brushed his hair from his forehead, wishing that she could take his pain away.

"Ethan?"

Upon hearing Sarah's voice, he raised his head.

Jessica got to her feet, angry that she had interrupted such a private, and intimate moment, between them. Daggers flew from her eyes as Sarah walked across the floor.

"I just took a call from your sister. She said to tell you that she's coming in on the six o'clock flight from D.C."

"Thank you." He cleared his throat before speaking again. "How are things upstairs?"

"Don't worry about the clinic," she said reassuringly. "Just concentrate on your father."

Jessica felt her anger beginning to smolder. How Ethan could allow himself to be friends with this woman was beyond her. "Excuse me," she said in a clipped tone. She had more important things to do than stand around and listen to Sarah's drivel.

Ethan rose from the chair, taking note of the awkward silence that had been left behind in her wake.

"Is there anything you need?"

"No, I'm fine," he answered, returning his attention to Sarah, "but would you mind looking in on my patient in ICU?"

"I'd be happy to."

As the conversation died out, there was nothing left to do, but stare at his father.

"Has he regained consciousness at all?"

"No," he answered, shifting his feet.

Sarah looked past him, visibly struggling to find something else to say.

"So, how are things with you?" he asked, hoping to change the subject.

She suddenly cracked a smile and began shaking her head.

"What?"

"Do you realize that you have asked me that same question every day for the past few weeks?"

He scratched his head and gave a short laugh, feeling some of his tension leaving him. "No, I guess I hadn't. But I only ask because I care about you."

"I know you do," she said softly. "And thank you. But I really am okay. I'm getting on with my life."

He smiled down at her. "Okay. I promise I'll stop asking you that question."

~

The morning slowly waned into the afternoon for Ethan as he sat in the chair, listening to his father's monitor. Over the past few hours, he had grown accustomed to the abnormal rhythm it was giving off.

His blood pressure had been dropping steadily, and a little while ago, Jessica had tearfully informed him that the catheter had showed that the blood was backing up into his lungs. His father had developed Cardiogenic Shock, and given the damage his left ventricle had sustained, Ethan knew that it would only be a matter of time.

He leaned forward and held his head in his hands. He had always thought that he would be more than ready for his father's death, but things were stirring inside of him that he hadn't been prepared for at all.

A sudden movement caught the corner of his eye. Jerking his head up, he saw that his father's hand was hanging off the side of the bed.

He went over and picked it up, figuring it was just his muscle contracting, but it immediately closed around his fingers. Startled, he moved his gaze upwards; his father's eyes were now wide open. Unable to speak because of the intubation tube, he made a small sound in the back of his throat that sounded like a cry.

All those memories and feelings that Ethan had locked inside of him suddenly came rushing out—and they hurt.

His father looked at him for the longest time, eyes pleading, and then went limp.

"Dr. Harrington?"

Ethan squeezed his father's hand and waited. There was no reaction.

"Dr. Harrington?"

He set his jaw to mask his emotions before looking over his shoulder.

"I'm sorry to interrupt," the nurse said quietly. "But you're needed in ICU. It's Mr. Samuels."

"Tell them I'm on my way."

By the time he arrived, Mr. Samuels was in full cardiac arrest. He, along with an intern and two other nurses worked to get his heart started again.

"Charging..." said the intern, handing the paddles to Ethan.

Just then, the switchboard operator came over the P.A. "Code blue in CCU! Code blue in CCU!"

Ethan showed the slightest hesitation before taking the paddles.

A second later, another page came over the speaker. "Dr. Ethan Harrington report to CCU."

Gavin and Jessica worked frantically trying to save Everett.

"Charging...charging...clear!"

Gavin placed the paddles on Everett. His body rose and fell.

"Still no heartbeat," the nurse said to Ethan.

"Again."

"Clear!" Ethan laid the paddles on Mr. Samuels.

"Nothing."

Gavin nodded at Jessica. "Set it to 400. All right. Let's try again."

She set the machine.

"Clear!"

Everett's body convulsed and jerked as the electricity ran through it.

All eyes were on the monitor.

"We've got a heartbeat!" the nurse said excitedly.

Ethan looked at the monitor and saw the pulse moving across the screen. He gave a barrage of orders before heading out the door.

Taking the stairs two at a time, his legs felt as if they were going to collapse beneath him before he made it to CCU. He burst through the door and skidded to a halt.

Jessica hurried over. "Ethan, I'm sorry," she said, throwing her arms around him. "I'm so sorry."

He felt his breath catch in his throat. Through the glass, he could see that the color of his father's skin had already turned gray.

Jessica led him over to a chair against the wall and sat down beside him.

The nurse on shift came up to him. "Dr. Harrington, I'm very sorry for your loss."

"Thank you," he said numbly.

"If you can tell me which funeral home you want, I'll go on and call them for you."

He ran his fingers through his hair, unable to form a coherent thought. "I don't know," he said in a broken voice. "Jess?"

"How about Chandler's?"

He nodded in agreement.

The smallest of sobs fell from Jessica's lips as the nurse stepped outside to make the call.

Ethan put his arm around her, drawing her to his side.

"I'm sorry," she whispered, sounding angry with herself.

"It's all right," he replied, although he couldn't help wondering who her tears were for.

"They're on their way," the nurse said, returning to the room.

Jessica gave her a weak smile as she wiped at her eyes. "Thank you, Denise."

"Dr. Harrington, I'm sorry, but I need you to sign this release form," she said, kneeling in front of his chair.

Ethan took the pen from her, only to have it fall from his fingers.

"That's all right, I've got it," she said, picking it up from off the floor and handing it to him once more.

His hand was trembling so badly, he couldn't even press the tip of the pen onto the paper. It was at that point that Jessica casually laid her hand upon his forearm to steady him.

Denise took the clipboard and went inside the room where his father still lay. She methodically began unhooking all the I.V.'s and monitors.

"Are you ready to go home?" Jessica asked, squeezing his wrist.

"I need to clear my schedule first," he replied, getting unsteadily to his feet, "and then I'll have to swing by the airport and get Renee."

"Why don't you let me do that for you?"

"*What?* Are you a glutton for punishment?" he said, smiling down at her. "*I* don't even want to pick her up."

She tilted her head and looked into his eyes. "Are you sure you're okay to drive?"

His smile faded as quickly as it had come. "I'm fine. I'll see you at the house in a couple of hours." He walked out of CCU without giving her the chance to reply.

Chapter Twelve

Renee Westcott checked her makeup as the seatbelt sign flashed inside the cabin. The sleepy lights of Serenity Harbor twinkled down below. The last time she had been here was about a year ago. It was also the last time that she had spoken to her brother.

She sighed and put her compact away, thinking back to when they were younger. Ethan had always been a solemn, quiet boy who spent his days in his room reading, or down at the stable tending to his horse. She was the typical, annoying little sister, but he always tolerated her.

Then one morning in June, she woke up to find him gone. She shuddered, remembering how angry her father had been that day—yelling and slamming things around. Their nanny, Greta, had sat at the kitchen table with her head cradled in her hands as she'd cried.

Renee did not know the whereabouts of her brother for almost ten years. She was in between marriages at the time, and working in New York for one of her father's subsidiary companies, when out of the blue she received a Christmas card from him. In the card, Ethan wrote her that he was working at a hospital in Detroit.

They slowly began to rebuild their relationship, keeping in touch with phone calls and emails. He even visited her on occasion, but had always made her promise not to tell their father where he was. She agreed, understanding his reasons.

Renee kept the secret for nearly five years, eventually using it to try and repair her own relationship with their father, which had been hanging by a thread. She had angered him over the years with her many marriages, and had hoped giving him Ethan's address would put her back into his good graces. It worked, but her actions had not come without consequences.

She absently began twisting her wedding ring around her finger. Looking down at the exquisite diamond that sat nestled atop a band of gold, she couldn't help sighing at its insignificance.

Currently, she was the wife of James Westcott, a high-powered attorney in Washington, but it was nothing more than a marriage of convenience. She gave James money and power, and he gave her a high place in society, along with prestige. It was easier for her to *use* the men in her life rather than love them, having given up on that concept years ago.

Her brother, however, was a different story. He was absolutely head over heels in love with his wife, Jessica—a woman whom Renee had disliked from the moment she'd met her. She had always doubted her sincerity about loving him, and unfortunately, her suspicions were confirmed last year when they had separated because of her infidelity.

She felt the plane's wheels touch down on the runway, and instinctively turned her mind back to her father as she gathered her things. A sense of urgency surrounded her as she made her way through the gate and into the building.

"Renee?"

Spinning around, she saw Ethan walking towards her, his face ashen.

~

Jessica finished tucking the sheet between the mattresses and reached down for the comforter. She had worked up a sweat trying to get the guest bedroom ready for Renee.

A pair of headlights flashed in the window, causing the anxiousness inside her to grow. She absolutely dreaded the thought of having to see her sister-in-law again. Renee was constantly undercutting her in front of Ethan, as well as in private, with words that were meant to be as malicious as they were cruel—and she shuddered to think that she was going to have to live under the same roof with her for the next few days.

She heard them come through the garage door off of the kitchen and reluctantly headed downstairs to meet them.

Seeing Renee's makeup streaked with black, she temporarily put her animosity towards her aside as she forced herself to embrace her. "Renee, I'm very sorry."

"Thank you," she said tearfully.

Ethan took her bags upstairs, leaving Jessica alone with her.

"Why don't you come sit down?" she said, motioning for her to follow her into the living room. "I'm sure you're tired." She listened to the points of Renee's heels clicking across the hardwood as they walked.

"It must be hard trying to lose all that baby weight."

Jessica bit her tongue as she sat down. Her sister-in-law had a way of making simple statements that left no room for rebuttal. "Can I get you anything?" she asked, sincerely hoping that she wasn't hungry, because there wasn't much in the house to eat.

She plopped herself down in the chair and shook her head. "No, thank you," she replied in an accent that was more pronounced than Ethan's.

Jessica could almost feel her dressing her down as they sat looking at each other, and immediately began to regret the casual slacks she had chosen to change into. She was more than a little relieved when Ethan came into the room carrying Ryan.

He knelt down beside Renee's chair. "Ryan, this is your Aunt Renee."

She watched with disdain as her sister-in-law cooed over the baby. Ethan seemed delighted that she'd taken such an interest, but Jessica knew that she was only doing it in order to pacify him. "I'm going to go make him a bottle," she said, having seen enough.

Ethan motioned for her to sit back down. "I'll get it." He left for the kitchen, leaving the two of them alone once more.

Renee looked at the baby for a long time and then smiled. "He's just as handsome as my brother."

Jessica smiled back in spite of herself. That was one of the nicest things she had ever said.

A few minutes later, Ethan returned with the bottle for Ryan, and a glass of scotch for himself. "Would you like to feed him?" he asked, holding the bottle out to Renee.

"Uh, no. I'll just be a spectator," she replied, handing the baby back to him.

"Here, Ethan. I'll feed him." Jessica held her arms out to take him.

Ethan sat down wearily on the sofa and took a long swallow from his glass as Renee watched.

"Have you made any arrangements yet?"

He breathed in as the liquid traveled downward. "Not yet. We're supposed to call the funeral home in the morning."

"We're not going to have it here, are we?"

"Where were you thinking we'd have it? Manchester?"

She nodded. "He should be buried next to our mother, don't you agree?"

Jessica saw him clench his jaw.

"No."

"Why not?"

He took another sip of his drink and rubbed his eyes.

"Why not?" she repeated.

"Look, I don't want to fly his body all the way over there just to put him in the ground next to her. It's pointless."

Renee leaned forward in her chair. "It's not pointless, Ethan. She was our mother for *Christ's sake!*"

"He remarried. If anything, he should be buried next to Greta. They were together longer."

"No. I want him next to our mother," she said flatly. "He was married to her first, and he loved her."

Ethan slammed his drink down on the table and stood up. "Well, tell me something, Renee. When you die, which husband do you want me to put you beside? Stephen? Or will it be—what's his name—your second husband..."

"Charles," she said, giving him a steely look.

"Charles," he repeated. "Oh, and let's not forget about number three—or is it number four? I honestly can't keep track anymore!"

By this time, Renee's cheeks had turned a dark crimson, and Jessica couldn't help feeling sorry for her.

"So which one will it be, Renee?" He stood in front of her, waiting for an answer.

"You've made your point," she said quietly.

Seeming satisfied that he had, he grabbed his drink and stalked out of the room.

Renee uncrossed her legs and stood up, taking a moment to smooth the edges of her hair. "I *am* rather tired all of a sudden. I think I'll head on up to bed."

Jessica opened her mouth, wanting to apologize for her husband's behavior, but she realized that doing so would probably only make matters worse.

Instead, she told her goodnight and carried Ryan into the kitchen where she found Ethan standing by the counter. "Renee's gone to bed," she said, hoping he heard the curtness in her voice.

He filled his glass to the top with scotch and lifted it to his lips.

She watched as he made the liquid disappear in one swallow. "Would you like something to eat?"

"I'm not hungry," he answered, reaching for the bottle.

The familiarity of this conversation played out in her mind. She knew it by heart, but wasn't going to finish it this time. "Well, I think I'm going to put Ryan down and take a shower."

He nodded. "I'll be up in a little while."

She turned and slowly made her way out of the kitchen. She could hear the bottle clinking against the glass as she climbed the stairs.

~

Jessica was turning down the covers when he finally stumbled in. The fatigue on his face was apparent as the events from the past twenty-four hours had caught up to him. She sat down on the bed and patted the mattress. "Why don't you try and get some sleep?" she said, pushing her anger aside.

He kicked off his shoes and fell backwards onto the bed, using her lap as a pillow.

With the tip of her fingernail, she lightly began stroking the side of his face.

After a moment, the tightness in his jaw went away and he closed his eyes.

"Who's Greta?" she asked softly.

A sigh fell from him. "She was our nanny and housekeeper before my father married her."

"So she was your stepmother?"

He opened his eyes to look at her. "I had already left home."

"What happened to her?"

When he spoke, his voice was distant. "She died of cancer about five years ago."

Jessica continued stroking him until his breaths became long and deep. Reaching over, she turned out the light and leaned against the headboard, embracing the darkness.

She awoke at two in the morning to the sound of the phone ringing. In one fluid motion, she was out of bed with the receiver in hand. It was a quick reflex she had mastered since becoming a mother. "Hello?" she whispered, hurrying out of the room so as not to wake Ethan.

It was the hospital calling for him. The nurse on the phone needed to inform him of a patient's condition.

"Can't this wait? I really don't want to wake him."

The nurse hesitated a moment. "I'm sorry, but Dr. Harrington left strict instructions before he left to call him if there were any changes to Mr. Samuel's condition."

Jessica knew the nurse was just doing her job, and she also knew Ethan would probably be very angry with her if she didn't tell him. "Just a moment."

She went back into their bedroom and sat down on the edge of the bed. "Ethan?"

He didn't move.

It was then that she realized he was sleeping on his good side. He was partially deaf in his right ear. "Ethan?" She gently shook him.

He jerked his head up. "What is it?"

She held the phone out to him. "It's the hospital."

He seemed disoriented as he looked around.

"It's the hospital calling for you," she repeated.

He swung his legs over the side and took the phone from her.

Jessica got back under the covers as she listened to him talking quietly to the nurse. "Everything okay?" she asked, after he had hung up.

"His vitals are improving," he replied, placing the phone back on its cradle.

She watched as he stood up and began to undress. The moonlight outlined the edges of his slender frame as he pulled his shirt over his head.

"I must have really been out of it. I didn't even hear the phone ring."

Out of it was certainly one way of putting it, but Jessica remained quiet, deciding that this was not the time to start a fight.

Ryan's cry came through the monitor on the nightstand.

With a sigh, she pushed the covers back to get up, but Ethan motioned for her to stop.

"It's okay," he said. "I'll get him."

~

Renee wandered down the stairs and into the kitchen where she found Ethan standing in front of the stove. A smile formed on her lips as she watched him cradling his son in his arms. This was a side of her brother that she had never seen.

"There we go. It's all warm," he whispered. A startled look came over him when he turned and saw her standing there. "Couldn't sleep?"

She shook her head and pulled out a chair.

They sat in silence for a long time, listening to the rain as it fell softly upon the roof.

"I talked to him a few days ago," Renee said softly. "He seemed fine."

Ethan watched Ryan sucking contentedly on his bottle. "Sometimes, a heart attack can come on without any warning."

She cleared her throat as the sting of tears began to form. "Did he say anything to you?"

"No. He never regained consciousness."

Drawing in a jagged breath, she began wiping her eyes.

"I'm sorry for what I said earlier," he said, keeping his eyes on Ryan. "It's just that neither one of us has lived in Manchester for years. It makes more sense to have him here. He was doing all of his business out of Serenity Harbor anyway."

Renee tilted her head, finding his apology, or rather, his *lack* of one, somewhat off-putting. "I suppose you're right," she finally said, deciding it would be best to just let it go.

He switched Ryan to his other arm and leaned against the back of the chair.

"I like what you've done with the house," she said, looking around the kitchen. "It's lovely."

"Thanks. I guess it *does* look a little different than the last time you saw it."

"*A lot* of things have changed since the last time I was here." She watched him as he held the baby. "How does it feel to be a father?"

"It feels great," he said with a grin that nearly covered his face.

"I'm glad you and Jessica worked things out."

His smile immediately turned into a scowl. "No thanks to *you*."

She crossed her arms. "I know you're still angry at me over what I said to her."

"It was none of your business."

"You're my brother, and I care about you. That makes it my business."

His eyes flickered. "No, Renee. It doesn't. What happens between Jessica and me is nobody's business but our own. Understand?"

She sat there stone-faced.

"How's James?" he asked, changing the subject.

"He's fine. I talked to him a little while ago. He said that he'd try to be here for the funeral."

"He'll *try*?"

"He's got a lot on his plate," she said definitively.

Ethan raised his eyebrow. "I'm sure he does."

She looked away for a moment trying to curb her anger. "How are things at the hospital?"

"Very busy right now."

"Why don't you forget about that bloody clinic and go into private practice?"

"I like what I do," he said, half-smiling. "I've never had any desire for my own practice."

A long sigh fell from her lips as she shook her head. "You're a true bleeding heart, Ethan."

Chapter Thirteen

The next morning Jessica found Ethan in the kitchen impatiently drumming his fingers on the counter as he waited for the coffee to finish brewing.

"I didn't know you were up."

"Who was at the door earlier?" he asked, keeping his back to her.

"Grace. She brought over a breakfast casserole. Would you like some?"

He picked up the coffee pot and began filling the mug in front of him. The liquid was still pouring from the machine, and hit the burner with a distinct hiss. "No thanks."

"Are you sure?"

He took a big swallow from his cup and turned around. "Is Renee up, yet?"

"I haven't seen her," she said absently. If possible, he looked worse this morning than he had last night. She reached into the cabinet beside him for a plate, and began spooning some of the casserole onto it. "Are you certain I can't get you some?"

"I'm sure," he replied, sounding irritated. "Do you remember which funeral home we were supposed to call?"

"Chandler's. I spoke to them already. We have an appointment later this morning."

His voice, and his eyes, softened. "Thanks."

She gave him a small smile. "You're welcome." She picked up the plate and took him by his arm. "Why don't you sit down with me and have something to—"

"*Goddamn it,* Jessica," he said, jerking away. "Would you please stop falling all over yourself pretending to care about me?" Clenching his jaw, he turned and hurled his coffee mug across the room.

She drew back, startled by his outburst.

His shoulders slumped forward as he suddenly dropped his head. "I'm sorry."

"It's all right," she said, blinking back a tear.

"No, it's not." He took a step towards her and held out his arms. "I didn't mean what I said just now."

Jessica could feel him shaking as he embraced her. "I know," she said, pretending to be unscathed by his words.

He kissed her on top of her head. "I didn't mean it," he repeated.

Out of the corner of her eye, she noticed Renee standing in the doorway. Her eyes went from the two of them, to the coffee dripping down the wall. Something between a smile and a smirk began to form on her thin lips.

~

Later that morning, Ethan stood in the living room watching the rain as it spattered against the French doors. He turned when he heard Jessica's footsteps. "What time are we supposed to be there?"

"Eleven-thirty," she answered, noticing that he looked a lot better since he had showered and shaved.

He rubbed his eyes and sighed.

"Are you all right?" she asked cautiously, hoping not to get a repeat performance of this morning.

"I'm fine," he said, looking at his watch. "Where the *hell* is Renee?"

"I'm right here," she answered, walking into the living room.

Jessica spun on her heel and suppressed a groan. There stood Renee, dressed to the nines. Even in circumstances of death, she had to make a fashion statement.

~

Resisting the urge to tap her foot in the elevator, Jessica clamped down on her tongue, and watched the light jump slowly from floor to floor.

A pleasant sounding bell chimed and the doors finally slid open, depositing her and Ethan, along with Renee, on the fifteenth floor.

Jessica drew a deep breath, trying to quell the anxiousness inside of her as they walked to the end of the hallway. Her emotions rose to the top when she saw the door with the numbers 1505 embossed on it.

Ethan inserted the key that he had gotten from the manager of the building, and turned the knob.

The first thing Jessica saw when she walked inside was Everett's briefcase lying open on the coffee table. There were a few papers stacked neatly beside it, and she guessed that he must have been preparing to go to work when it happened. Her eyes stung when she noticed the phone on the floor. She remembered one of the paramedics had told her that Everett had been able to call 911.

Ethan picked it up without speaking and placed it back in its cradle before heading upstairs.

Jessica turned to follow him, but stopped. "Are you coming up, Renee?" she asked, thinking that she would want to help pick out the suit.

Her sister-in-law sniffed and shook her head. "No. I don't think I can go up there."

Hearing the fake quiver in her voice, Jessica continued up the steps, doing everything she could to avoid rolling her eyes.

The quietness took hold of her as she stepped through the doorway. Her father-in-law's wallet and watch rested on the top of his valet; his shoes sat neatly underneath it. Ethan stood in front of the closet door, seeming as cold and distant as the room felt. She watched as he solemnly chose a dark suit for his father along with a black and white striped tie.

Remembering that he had a handkerchief that matched, she opened the dresser's drawers one by one until she found it. "What do you suppose Renee's doing?" she asked, sitting down to fold it.

He zipped up the garment bag and slung it over his shoulder. "She's probably downstairs looting the place."

As they were getting in the car to go to the funeral home, Jessica saw that Renee's coat pockets were bulging ever so slightly. She began to chuckle inwardly. Ethan knew his sister very well.

Chapter Fourteen

Jessica hurried up the stairs to her bedroom, where she quickly pulled on her pantyhose, and then began applying her lipstick. They were running late as usual. Ethan was across the hall in the nursery tending to Ryan. Renee was in there with him, and she could hear the two of them talking through the monitor as she put on her earrings.

"You got in late last night," he said.

"I had to go over the financials with Clint Owens at Dad's office. It ran long and then I joined him and his wife for dinner."

"Did you sleep okay?"

"Ugh, who could sleep with all that crying?"

Ethan laughed softly. "Well, he's a baby. They do things like that."

"You know something, Ethan? He really doesn't look like you."

Jessica dropped her earring. Her heart pounded in her throat as she went across the hall and peered around the doorway.

Ethan seemed to be studying Ryan. "You don't think so?" he asked, leaning over the crib.

"No—"

"Mrs. Chambers is here," Jessica blurted as she stepped through the door. "Are you ready to go?"

Renee swiveled around and narrowed her eyes. She acted as if she knew Jessica had been listening outside just now. For her benefit, she gave Ryan a long look and then glanced at Ethan, before arching a thin eyebrow at her.

"I'll meet you downstairs," Ethan said, not having noticed the exchange.

Renee sauntered towards her and stopped.

Jessica folded her arms across her chest, bracing herself for what she might say, but she just smiled with that cocky, little smirk of hers before walking out.

~

Sarah rummaged around in her purse for her lipstick, feeling rushed. She had closed the clinic at noon so she could attend Everett's funeral, but it was already half past.

She was on her way out when she looked down and noticed a run in her stockings. She threw her purse down on the desk and began searching through her top drawer.

Knock-knock.

"It's open," she called out, finding the fingernail polish.

"Hi." Gavin meandered inside.

Sarah looked up at him. "Hi," she said curtly, unscrewing the cap.

"Are you getting ready to go to the funeral?"

She put her leg on the chair and began painting the run. "I was just on my way out."

Gavin couldn't help staring at her legs. They were beautiful from stem to stern.

Sarah looked up at him again.

He quickly dropped his gaze to the floor.

"Gavin?"

"Hmm?"

"Is there something you wanted?"

He slid his hands in his pockets. "Um...I thought that maybe we could ride together."

She began shaking her head.

"Please? I really hate going to these things by myself."

"All right," she said, grabbing her purse. There was no time to argue with him.

He smiled, revealing his trademark dimples. "Thank you."

As she brushed past him, she almost returned the smile, but caught herself.

~

Jessica walked slowly around the room, stopping to read the cards on all the baskets of flowers that had arrived. Low murmurs and whispers surrounded her, and she surmised that there were at least thirty or forty people here already. She felt a warm hand on her shoulder and turned around.

"How are you holding up?" Grace asked.

She shrugged. "I'm good."

"How's Ethan doing?"

"I don't really know," she said, glancing in his direction. He was standing across the room with his head slightly tilted towards Paul who was introducing a gray-haired man to him. Ethan nodded politely and shook his hand. Jessica stifled a sigh. She had lost count of how many hands she had shaken this morning and knew that he had to be tired of it as well.

Renee, however, seemed to be thriving on all the sympathy being poured her way. She mingled throughout the parlor, turning on the tears whenever necessary. It suddenly occurred to her though, that she hadn't seen or heard her in the past five minutes. After scanning the area, she finally found her in a darkened corner with her husband, James, who had arrived this morning. They seemed to be embroiled in a serious conversation.

"Jessica?"

"Hmm?" she said, returning her attention to Grace.

The older woman gave her a curious stare. "Did you hear what I said?"

"Sorry."

"Sometimes, it takes a while for someone to accept death. He may still be in shock. It could be weeks or even months before he can come to terms with it."

Jessica nodded at her cousin's advice, but there were times she wished she could just talk without using her psychiatric degree.

"Is there something wrong?" she prodded.

"No," she answered quickly. She wasn't about to inform her of what went on in her kitchen yesterday.

Grace gave her a knowing look, inviting her to tell her.

She clamped down on her tongue, finding her inquisitiveness today infuriating. "Ethan's been distant and angry with me…and I don't even have a clue right now as to how he's feeling, Grace." The words came rolling out too fast to stop.

Her eyes softened. "Give him time on that too, Jessica. He needs to learn to trust you again," she said quietly.

Grace's words stung, making her drop her gaze to the floor.

~

Sarah signed her name in the registry book and started to hand the pen to Gavin when she realized that she'd already written both their names together on the same line. Shoving the pen back into its holder, she stepped inside the room. Traffic had been bad, making for a painfully long and awkward drive.

The dimly-lit parlor was filled with a sea of people all talking in hushed tones. She felt Gavin's breath on the back of her neck and walked farther into the room. "I'm going to talk to Ethan," she said, turning to him.

He shifted his feet. "I'll talk to him later."

"Fine," she said, wondering why he'd insisted upon coming with her in the first place. Fortunately, trying to figure out what went on inside that man's head was no longer a concern of hers.

As she approached the front of the room, she saw that two elderly men were talking with Ethan. Not wishing to interrupt, she went over to the casket to pay her respects while she waited. Looking down at Everett, she saw that he still had that grumpy expression he always wore.

"It's nice to see a familiar face," Ethan said, offering her a weary smile after the two men had walked away.

"Are most of these people from Harrington Enterprises?" she asked, turning from the casket.

"Some of them are," he replied, glancing around the room. "Others apparently did business with him."

Sarah took his hands in hers. "How are you doing?"

He suppressed a sigh having heard that question for the hundredth time today, but he knew Sarah was genuinely concerned, and not just making idle conversation. "I'm fine."

"Your father was a good man. I'm so sorry."

"Thanks."

"Hello, Dr. Williams." Renee sidled up next to Ethan.

Sarah had met Ethan's sister once before and had not been impressed. "Renee," she began, "I'm so sorry for your loss. Please accept my condolences."

"Thank you," she answered, dabbing at her eyes.

"It's been a while since I last saw you," Sarah said, trying to be polite.

Renee looked at her brother and latched onto his arm. "Yes, Ethan and I were just talking last night about how everything had changed so much in a year's time. I mean, he's a father now, and he's back together with Jessica." She stopped and pursed her lips. "Oh, I'm sorry. You must think I'm being terribly insensitive."

"Excuse me?" Sarah said, giving her a puzzled look.

"I heard that you and your husband are getting a divorce."

Ethan gave his sister a sharp look. "Renee, I think James is looking for you."

"It's such a shame. I thought since my brother and Jessica reconciled that the two of you would be able to work things out as well."

Sarah felt her face turning red.

"Renee," Ethan repeated.

She continued on, ignoring him. "You two have weathered so much together. It's just such a–"

"*Renee!*" Ethan's expression told her to shut up. "James is looking for you," he said, accenting each word.

Renee smiled sweetly at Sarah, having accomplished what she'd set out to do. As soon as she'd heard about their impending divorce, *specifically*, the timing of it, she became suspicious that Gavin might be the father of Jessica's baby. "Excuse me," she said before sauntering off.

Ethan started to make an excuse for his sister's behavior, but couldn't think of any plausible thing to say. He shook his head and sighed. "I'm sorry, Sarah."

She forced a smile. "It's okay," she said, pretending that she was unharmed by Renee's remarks.

~

Jessica stood near the back wall, trying to have a quiet discussion with Gavin. "You may think I'm being paranoid, but I believe Renee knows about the baby."

He stepped closer. "Why do you think that?" he asked in a low voice.

"Because—" She suddenly stopped when she noticed Renee staring at her from across the room. She was wearing the same smirk that she had on in the nursery. Jessica crossed her arms and looked at the floor for a moment. When she raised her eyes, she did her best to pretend that she was having a casual conversation with him. "Because," she whispered, "this morning she made a remark about him not looking like Ethan."

"How could she possibly know? She just got into town the other day."

"Yes, but I overheard her telling Ethan this morning that she'd had dinner with Clint Owens and his wife last night. Clint's wife, Debby, works for Holt and McNamara."

Gavin frowned as he rubbed the back of his neck. "They're handling my divorce."

"Exactly."

"Do you think Ethan suspects anything?"

"I don't think so."

Gavin glanced over at him to make sure he wasn't watching them. "Jessica, I think we need to tell him as soon as possible, before he finds out on his own."

"I know that Gavin, but I can't tell him right now. Not after he's just lost his father. Don't you agree?"

He sighed and ran his fingers through his hair.

"Gavin!"

He shook his head and slid his hands in his pockets. "I *agree* with you Jessica," he said sharply. "But I don't necessarily like it. It's time we ended this charade."

~

Ethan stood next to Paul as he listened to an older gentleman telling them about a business deal involving his father. He smiled and nodded, trying to be polite as the man droned on, but his patience was wearing thin.

Out of the corner of his eye, he noticed that Paul's smile seemed to be wavering as well. He was extremely grateful to Grace's husband for being here today. Since he was the attorney for Harrington Enterprises, he knew practically everyone here.

The man's story had no sooner ended, than he launched into another one. Paul and Ethan both shifted their feet, looking for a way out.

Without warning, it suddenly sounded to Ethan as if everyone in the room was shouting instead of whispering, making his ear throb. His heart pounded against his chest as the floor beneath him started to move.

He quickly excused himself, leaving the man to talk to Paul as he shuffled out of the room.

A faint breeze provided him with some relief as he stepped outside and leaned against the white brick building. His legs shook as he sat down on the steps and unbuttoned his collar. After taking a few deep breaths, the noise inside his head slowly began to diminish.

He clasped his head in his hands and looked at his feet. He didn't want to hear another story about his father's business ventures, and he didn't want to shake another hand. He just wanted to go home and be alone with Jessica and the baby—and knowing that he couldn't right now, only made his desire to do so worse.

Thinking that it would be nice to at least have a cup of coffee with her, he forced himself back inside and began searching the room for her.

"Are you all right?"

He turned to find Sarah standing behind him. "I just needed some fresh air."

She eyed him curiously for a moment, and then reached up to touch his cheek.

He drew his head back, and away from her hand. "So, how are things at the clinic?" he asked, trying to hide his irritation.

"It's been pretty slow," she lied, not wanting him to feel guilty about being off.

He nodded. "And how are things with *you?*"

Sarah opened her mouth to protest, but he held his hands up in the air. "Oh, I'm sorry. I forgot that I'm not supposed to ask you that anymore," he said smiling.

She laughed. "Thank you for remembering."

The smile suddenly disappeared from his face as he looked past her.

She glanced over her shoulder and saw Gavin approaching.

"I just wanted you to know how sorry I am about Everett," he said, extending his hand as he came near.

Ethan sighed. The last thing he wanted to do right now was shake hands with the man that had screwed his wife. It was with a clenched jaw that he finally took it. "I know you did all you could for him. Thank you."

~

Later that evening, Ethan was lying on the sofa with his drink balanced on his stomach.

"Still have your headache?" Jessica asked, walking into the living room.

"Mmm-hmm."

"Raise up for a second."

He sat up, allowing her to sit down, and then laid his head in her lap. She began stroking his hair, letting her fingers caress his forehead. He closed his eyes as a contented sigh fell from his lips. "That feels nice."

The sound of high heels clicking on the hardwood made him open one eye. When he saw it was Renee, he closed it again.

She plopped herself down in the chair and cleared her throat.

"Where's James?" Jessica asked.

"He had to fly back to D.C." she replied, watching as she played with her brother's hair. "Ethan? I talked to Paul Cummings earlier."

"About what?" he asked, sounding disinterested.

"He said if it's all right with you, he would read the will tomorrow."

He opened his eyes and sat up. "What?"

"*You* heard me."

Ethan set his drink down and shook his head. "We just buried him two hours ago, Renee."

"I'm well aware of that, but I have to head back to D.C. tomorrow evening."

He stood up and walked around the sofa with his hands on his hips.

"So, do you mind?"

"*Yes,* I mind!"

Jessica sighed inwardly. For the past couple of days it hadn't taken much to set Ethan's temper off, and Renee's presence only seemed to serve as a catalyst for it. She listened to the two of them arguing back and forth until he finally gave in. The reading of the will would take place tomorrow afternoon.

~

Later that night, Ethan stood over the crib watching Ryan sleep. His little chest moved up and down as he sucked contentedly on his pacifier. A sudden sense of loss came over him as he thought about his father and how his son would never know him. He had always hoped that giving him a grandchild would somehow strengthen the ties between them.

Refusing to allow the misery to settle into his heart, he shoved the thought from his mind and crossed the hallway.

Jessica was sitting on their bed with her back to him. He watched as her long, slender fingers reached under her dress and began sliding her nylons down. He closed the door, remembering that Renee was in the house.

Kneeling on the bed, Ethan brushed the hair away from her shoulders as he softly kissed the side of her neck. She leaned against him, letting his lips caress her. He slipped the straps of her dress off her shoulders, and turned her around to face him.

His eyes were filled with desire as he bent down to kiss her again. She fell back against the pillow, pulling him with her. Within moments, they were slowly writhing together.

~

Ethan sat down in one of the leather-gloved chairs in Paul's office, wondering why he had even bothered coming. He seriously doubted that his father was going to leave him anything—and he honestly couldn't blame him. This was going to be nothing but an embarrassment for him and he began to grow angry all over again for having allowed Renee to talk him into doing it today.

He looked over at his sister as she sat perched on the edge of her seat. He could almost see her eyes calculating the money.

Paul slipped on his reading glasses and cleared his throat. He quickly read through a few paragraphs of legal jargon before getting to the main point. "To the Serenity Harbor City Hospital, I leave the sum of one million dollars."

Jessica and Ethan exchanged glances. The hospital must have meant more to Everett than they realized.

"Well, there's a true waste of money," Renee muttered under her breath.

Paul continued reading. "To my daughter, Renee..."

She instantly perked up at the sound of her name.

"I leave the sum of my estate."

"How much is it worth?"

Paul rifled through the stack of papers before finding the one he was looking for.

"At this time the total sum of his estate is valued at just over eleven million dollars."

"And what about his company?" she asked, disinterested in the small change.

"I'm getting to that," Paul replied, peering at her over his glasses. "If my son, Ethan, has children of his own, I leave my shares of Harrington Enterprises, which total eighty percent, to him. All the earnings made shall be placed in a trust for his child, or children, until they reach the age of twenty-five."

Renee leaned forward. "You can't be serious! My father would never have left his company to *him*," she said, pointing at Ethan.

Ethan sat motionless, too dumbfounded to speak.

"There *is* one contingency," Paul said. "But it really is pointless, now."

"What is it?" Renee asked, coming out of her seat.

"If at the time of my death, Ethan is childless, I give him two years. If, at the end of those two years, he still remains childless, my shares of Harrington Enterprises will go to my daughter, Renee." Paul looked directly at Jessica as he finished reading.

She felt her face burning as she shifted in the chair uncomfortably.

"I want a copy to give to my attorney," Renee demanded.

"Paul, this is ridiculous," Ethan said when he had found his voice. "I don't know the first thing about running a company. There must be something you can do."

He came around the desk and put his hand on Ethan's shoulder. "Listen, why don't you go on home, and after things settle down a bit," he said, glancing at Renee, "we can discuss your options."

It was a miserable drive back to the house.

Once they were home, Ethan headed straight into the kitchen where he pulled a bottle and a glass from the cabinet.

Renee followed on his heels. "How could he leave you the company? You don't even care about it! You never have! I was always there for him, even when you weren't! How could he do such a thing?"

Ethan unscrewed the cap from the bottle and slowly filled his glass, ignoring her.

"You know, he flat out told me once, that he was *ashamed* of you!"

He took a long swallow of his drink and flicked his eyes in her direction. "Are your bags packed?"

Her face darkened. "Don't bother driving me to the airport," she said, turning on her heel. "I'll take a cab!"

Ethan felt his own anger rising. "You know," he called after her as she headed upstairs, "we wouldn't even be in this situation at all, if you hadn't told him where I *lived!*"

~

When Renee returned with her suitcase, she seemed to have calmed down somewhat, but the expression she wore upon her face remained indignant.

Jessica came out of the living room holding Ryan. "Goodbye, Renee. Have a safe trip."

Renee ignored her well wishes and stepped forward to give the baby a kiss. "I still don't think he looks like you, Ethan."

Ethan said nothing as he carried her bags outside to the waiting cab.

"I'm going to fight to have this will overturned," she said, following him.

"You can do whatever you want. I really don't care," he answered with a sigh.

"The writing isn't as black and white as it seems," she continued. "You need to read between the lines."

"Meaning?"

She opened the cab door and slid into the seat. "I'm sure you'll find out soon enough."

Jessica was still in the foyer when Ethan returned. His face was expressionless as he closed the front door. She swallowed nervously wondering what Renee said to him.

He turned around and saw her staring. "Anything wrong?" he asked, smiling.

She relaxed and smiled back. "I'm sorry, but I'm really glad that she's gone."

He nodded in agreement. "She's not really my sister, you know. She was left on our doorstep by trolls."

Jessica laughed, feeling some of the tension drain from her body.

Chapter Fifteen

Sarah arrived home from work the next evening to find Gavin waiting for her in the driveway. Swerving around him, she hit the opener with her thumb and pulled inside the garage.

He got out of his car and followed her in.

"What are you doing here, Gavin?"

"I'd like to get the rest of my things. There's still a lot of stuff here in the garage."

She turned and surveyed the cluttered shelves behind her. Practically everything in here was his. "Fine," she said, slamming her car door. Leaving him to it, she hurried up the steps and went on inside the house.

She sat down at the kitchen table and began going through her mail, but couldn't relax. It made her uncomfortable to know he was here.

Hoping that a cup of tea would help, she got up and began filling the kettle with water. The sound of boxes being dragged across the concrete floor could be heard, along with lots of clanking. She shook her head, wondering how the hell he was going to fit all of that into his car.

"Sarah?"

She turned from the sink to find him standing in her kitchen. "Are you done?"

"Almost," he said, wiping his hands on his pants. "I just need my golf clubs, and I'll be on my way."

"They're still in the closet by the front door," she replied.

He walked past her and into the living room. "I've got a brand new box of balls somewhere," he called to her as he opened the closet. "Have you seen them?"

Sarah set the kettle on the stove and sighed. The longer he stayed, the angrier she felt herself becoming.

"I think they're in the bedroom closet," he said.

She moved to the doorway where she could see him. "*Where* in the closet?"

"Up top."

"I'll go look for you," she said, knowing he would never find them on his own. She hurried upstairs to her bedroom and jerked open the closet door. She really wished that he had arranged to do all of this while she was at work. It would have made things much easier on her. Just as her eyes spied the box, she heard movement behind her.

"Did you find them?"

"Up there," she said, pointing.

He reached over her head and got them down.

"Is that it?" She hoped he heard the impatience in her voice.

He set the box down on the shelf beside him and shook his head. "There's something I need to say to you first."

She folded her arms against her, certain that this was going to be another poor attempt by him to apologize. "What?"

He stared into her eyes, and then brought both hands to her face. Without hesitation, he bent down and kissed her on the mouth. It was soft at first, and then grew more intense.

Sarah felt her body tingling as he pressed against her, walking her backwards towards the wall. She closed her eyes, seeing right through his ruse, but found herself wanting him more than anything in the world right now.

Unfortunately, she had always been able to exude logic over emotion, and right on cue - her logic turned on. She drew back, remembering what he had done. "I think you better go."

He responded by kissing her harder.

Hot tears began to form as she berated herself for feeling this way. She put her hands against him and pushed. "I want you to go."

"Please, Sarah."

She picked up the box of balls and shoved them into his hands. "I mean it. Go."

~

Sarah stood in her office the following afternoon, staring through the window at the park across the street. The first warm day of spring always brought people out there in droves.

A chirping noise sounded behind her, and she knew what it was without looking.

"Do you know if we have any batteries left?"

"No," she said absently.

"No, we don't have any? Or, no you don't know?"

She pursed her lips for a moment. "I don't know."

A heavy sigh fell from Ethan, followed by the sound of him opening and closing the drawers of his desk.

Turning from the window, she reluctantly sat down in her chair and began searching through her own drawers. The effort seemed futile until she spied one hiding in the very back. "Here you go."

"There's not another one is there?"

"That's all I see," she said, snapping the drawer shut.

He blinked, seeming surprised by her tone.

Sarah returned her attention to the pile of paperwork in front of her, finding herself wishing that Ethan had not come back to work today. Guilt immediately followed her silent admission, making her banish the thought.

The incident from last night had left her with a great deal of anger; something that she had never been good at hiding—and it was for this reason that she desired to be alone.

The chirping noise sounded again, drawing Ethan to his feet.

Sarah watched as he lifted the clock off the wall and extracted its battery.

"I'll replace it tomorrow," he said, catching her gaze.

She offered him a small smile, hoping it would make up for her snippiness.

The door to their office swung open.

"Can I talk to you for a moment?"

Her smile fell from her face. "I'm busy."

Gavin walked farther into the room. "It won't take long, I promise." As he waited for her to answer, he casually flicked his eyes in Ethan's direction, but didn't acknowledge him.

Ethan finished putting the batteries in his beeper and clipped it to his waist. "I'm going to make my rounds."

Sarah watched as he brushed past him and went out the door. It used to be that the two of them couldn't pass each other by in the hall without making a spiteful comment, but lately, they seemed to have found a happy medium, which was to completely ignore one another.

A moment of silence passed before Gavin spoke. "I think we need to discuss what happened last night."

"There's nothing to discuss," she said, steeling herself for what was to come.

"You call what happened, nothing?"

"It was just a kiss, Gavin. It still doesn't change anything."

"It changes everything. I still have feelings for you."

She pushed her chair back and stood up. "Feelings of what?"

"I don't know...just feelings. And I think you do too, you're just too stubborn to admit it."

She rolled her eyes. "The only *feelings* you have for me, Gavin, are primal ones. When are you going to learn that you can't fix everything with sex? My sleeping with you isn't going to change how I feel!" She held her hands out in frustration. "Gavin, don't you see? This *isn't* going to work out."

"No, it's not going to work out if you won't give me a chance."

Sarah stared at him with her mouth open. "Are you serious? How many chances have I given you, Gavin? *How many?*"

He clenched his jaw. "Don't you stand there and pretend to be so *damn* self-righteous. I'm not proud of what I've done, but you're no *saint*."

"I never claimed to be one."

Something that sounded like a disgruntled laugh came from his throat.

She folded her arms, refusing to go down this road with him. "I'm sorry if you're confused by what happened last night, but don't think that a kiss means I forgive you."

His face grew dark as a swath of red converged on his cheeks. Spinning around, he reached for the door and jerked it open. "You are unbelievable!"

~

Jessica sat in the cafeteria, having a much-needed cup of coffee with Grace. It was near the end of the day and she was trying to unwind, a difficult task considering the subject of their conversation for the most part had been about Renee.

"Do you think she's going to try anything?"

"I really don't know."

"Well, if it's any comfort, Paul said that she can't legally do anything for two years. There were no loopholes in Everett's will."

"That's the first good news I've heard in a while," she said smiling.

Grace sprinkled the packet of sugar in her cup. "How is Ethan handling all of this?"

"I think he's a bit overwhelmed by it. He told me that he wasn't cut out to be a businessman."

"Well, I know all of this must be hard for him."

She nodded in agreement. "I think it's put an undue amount of stress on him," she replied, hoping that would curtail any possibility of her continuing to push her to tell him the truth about Ryan.

Grace tore open another sugar packet.

Jessica took a sip of her own coffee, trying to hide her smile. Her cousin was hopelessly addicted to sweets; however, one would never know it by looking at her rail-thin frame.

"Why don't the four of us go out to dinner tonight?" Grace said, swirling the stick around in her cup. "I think we could all use a break."

"That would be wonderful," she replied, wishing she could. "But Ethan's gone over to clean out his father's condo."

Grace's eyebrows furrowed together. "I don't think it's such a good idea for him to go there by himself."

Jessica shook her head. "I told him that I'd go with him tomorrow, but he insisted on doing it alone."

~

Ethan stood solemnly in his father's bathroom, clutching a prescription bottle for high blood pressure. The pharmacy that had filled it was across town, as was the doctor that had prescribed it. After a moment, he slipped the medication into his pocket, deciding that he would give it to a patient at the clinic who couldn't afford it.

He finished the task of cleaning everything out of the cabinet and returned to the bedroom.

Several cartons containing his father's clothes sat by the door. The manager of the building had promised him that he would take the items to the homeless shelter in the morning.

Grabbing an empty carton, he knelt in front of the nightstand and slid open the top drawer. There was nothing inside but some old business papers. Ethan ran the tip of his finger over his father's handwriting that was scrawled over the margins. The sentimental part of him wanted to keep them, but his rational side asked him what the hell he was going to do with a bunch of papers. With a sigh, he tossed them in a garbage bag and moved on.

He opened up the next drawer, expecting to find more of the same, but found a small cardboard box instead. Several items lay inside it, but a black and white photo of himself and Renee was what caught his attention.

He sat down on the bed and studied it. In the picture, he appeared to be only five or six which would have made Renee about two. She was in pigtails and wearing a cowgirl skirt with fringe on the bottom. He had on a pair of red boots and a black cowboy hat that completely engulfed his head. He was peering out from under the brim of it, grinning broadly for the camera. Renee's grin matched his own, as the two of them stood arm in arm. A heavy sigh escaped him. It was true what they said about the innocence of youth.

Over the past year, he had noticed a distinct change in his sister's behavior towards him, and he suspected that she was jealous over the fact that their father had moved here to be with him. She never had any reason to feel that way though, because other than the monthly board meetings, and an occasional dinner set up by Jessica, he rarely saw him.

Renee had also become particularly aggressive towards Jessica, taking every opportunity she could to throw her affair in his face. She did it cunningly, maliciously, and without reservation - and he knew it was for the sole purpose of driving a wedge between them. He tossed the photo back in the box and took a last look around.

The sparseness of the bedroom fit his father's personality perfectly. It was who he was. He never did anything without a reason, and he never talked just for the sake of having a conversation. When he *did* speak, his tone was usually serious.

Ethan closed his eyes remembering one discussion in particular, after a board meeting at the hospital.

His father took him aside and waited for the room to clear. "How are things between you and Jessica?"

Ethan let his eyes drop to the floor. He had always figured that his father knew about her affair with Gavin, but this was the first time he had ever hinted that he did. "Things are fine," he answered.

His father tilted his head. "You can hide your feelings from most people, but I can tell by looking at you that things aren't fine."

Ethan sat down in one of the chairs, feeling defeated. He and Jessica had been back together for a few months now, yet he still found himself unable to forgive her. It had gotten to the point that he was thinking of divorcing her. But things had just become more complicated, as last night she'd told him that she was pregnant. A baby was the last thing they needed right now. How could they raise a child together, if he couldn't stand being in the same room with her?

Without warning, his father suddenly leaned forward and put his hand on his shoulder. "Son, do you love her?"

"Yes," he whispered.

"Then you do everything you can to make it work. Because nothing else matters. You have to go with your heart."

Ethan opened his eyes. He was ever so grateful to his father for speaking those words. At the time, it had all seemed so hopeless, but in reality, it was such a simple decision. It was a decision that he did not regret. He loved Jessica, and now they were a family.

~

Jessica was in the middle of giving Ryan a bath when she heard Ethan's footsteps. "Did you get everything taken care of?" she asked, looking over her shoulder.

He leaned against the doorway and nodded. "I brought home a few boxes. All the rest will go to the homeless shelter."

She opened the drain and lifted Ryan up, wrapping him in a fluffy blue towel before carrying him into their bedroom.

Ethan followed and stretched out on the bed beside him, watching as she dried him off.

Ryan's eyes wandered around the room, eventually stopping to rest on him.

Slipping his arm out from behind his head, he began to caress his chin.

Ryan wrapped his hand around his finger and smiled.

Ethan smiled back, but Jessica noticed the sadness in his eyes. "Are you feeling all right?" she asked tenderly.

He nodded as the smile faded from his lips. "I'm a little tired, that's all."

As she finished dressing Ryan, she saw two large books on top of the boxes he had brought home. "What are those?"

"Some photo albums."

She picked up the one on top and sat down on the bed next to him. The album itself seemed fairly new, but the photos inside appeared old and worn.

Ethan leaned back against the pillow with Ryan as he watched her slowly flipping through the pages.

"Is that Renee?"

He looked at the little girl in the picture and nodded.

Jessica shook her head in disbelief. "She's so little." She came to another one of her with her sitting in a woman's lap. "Is this your mother?"

"Yes," he answered, keeping his eyes on Ryan.

The woman in the photograph was young and beautiful with shoulder length black hair. Her eyes and smile were identical to Ethan's.

She guessed this was probably taken shortly before her death. Ethan rarely spoke about his mother, but she had learned from him that she had committed suicide when he was nine.

Sensing he was becoming uncomfortable, she closed the album and opened the other one. This one contained pictures of Ethan and Renee when they were older, along with a few of Everett. "Why are most of these in black and white?"

"Renee took those. She thought everything looked better that way."

She turned the page. "Did she take this one?"

"Mmm-hmm."

Jessica smiled. The black and white photo had been enlarged to an eight by ten. "How old were you here?"

He leaned over and studied it for a moment. "Sixteen."

Her fingers traced lightly over the photo. Shirtless, and wearing a pair of faded blue jeans, he stood proudly next to a tall black horse. Both he and the horse were looking right at the camera.

The sun was in the background, highlighting Ethan's upper body. His right arm was under the horse's neck, while his other one rested on his waist above his jeans. His hair was shorter and a little tousled. His muscles on his upper arms were small, but defined. His face was that of a boy, but just on the verge of becoming a man—and he was smiling. Something he rarely seemed to do anymore. "This is a beautiful picture. Would you mind if I framed it and hung it up?"

He shrugged. "If you like."

She finished looking through the album and set it aside. "Renee was a really good photographer."

"It was her major in college. I think she could have made a living out of it," he said with a hint of pride.

"Why didn't she?"

"She gave it up to work for my father."

A moment of silence fell around them.

"What are you going to do about the company?" she asked softly.

"I don't know," he said, rubbing his eyes. "I need to talk with Paul to find out my options."

She leaned over and kissed him on his cheek. "I'm going to let you get to sleep," she said, hearing the weariness in his voice. "Ryan and I are going to go have a bottle."

~

Jessica woke up to the sound of Ethan shouting in his sleep.

"No!"

She put her hand on his shoulder. "Ethan?"

He flinched at her touch as he flailed around in the bed. "Get them off me!"

Jessica gripped him by the arm and shook him hard. "Ethan?"

He sat up, drenched in sweat.

"It's okay," she said. "You were just having a bad dream."

He drew his knees up to his chest and leaned forward.

She stroked the back of his hair, trying to stop his trembling. For as long as Jessica could remember, Ethan had been haunted by the same nightmare, but it was something that he refused to talk about.

He threw the covers off and slipped out of bed. "I'll be back in a minute."

A feeble cry sounded from the nursery, making him stop.

"I'll get him," she said, motioning for him to go on. She hurried across the hall and looked in on Ryan. His eyes were still closed as he lay there fussing. Leaning against the rail of the crib, she ran her hand along the perimeter of the mattress until she found his pacifier. As she slipped it back into his mouth, she heard the familiar sound of the kitchen cabinet opening, followed by the clink of a glass.

Satisfied that Ryan had gone back to sleep, she tiptoed out of his room and headed down the stairs. Upon reaching the bottom, she could see Ethan in the living room. He was slumped against the sofa, staring blankly at the wall. A half-empty bottle of scotch sat on the coffee table.

Drawing a deep breath, she walked in. "It's late. Why don't you come back to bed?"

"I can't sleep," he said quietly.

"Are you worried about your father's company?" she asked, sitting down beside him.

The silence ticked by.

His refusal to confide in her only heightened the fact that he didn't trust her. "You know, Ethan, I never knew who my father was, and my mother died before I got a chance to make amends with her."

"This is different, Jess." His voice was soft.

She turned her question around. "Why do you think he left it to you?"

He shook his head. "I don't know."

Instinctively, she reached out and brushed the hair from his forehead. "Maybe he wanted to make things right."

A sigh fell from his lips, but he didn't say anything.

Jessica continued, letting her fingers intertwine around his dark locks. "I know you're hurting right now, Ethan, but getting drunk is not the answer."

He clenched his jaw and looked away.

"You're going to get through this."

"How do you know that?" he asked in a broken voice.

She paused as she chose her next words very carefully. "Because I'm going to help you."

Chapter Sixteen

Ethan sat back in the chair, halfway listening to what was being said. Phillip Martin had called a special meeting this afternoon to discuss potential candidates to take his father's place on the board. For the past half hour, names had been tossed back and forth, but they were still no closer to selecting one than when the meeting had started.

Phillip finally moved to adjourn, promising to pick this back up on their regular meeting.

Ethan couldn't help scowling, feeling that an hour of his time had just been wasted. He watched as Sarah, who seemed to be wearing the same look of disdain upon her face, hurried out of the room with Gavin close behind.

The other members filed out one by one, leaving only Phillip and Paul.

Ethan checked his watch. He was late for rounds, but he really wanted to talk to Paul. He had not been able to make an appointment with him due to his hectic schedule, and although he hated to discuss business with him here, he felt he had no choice. "Excuse me, Phillip," he said, walking up to them. "Would you mind if I spoke with Paul for a moment?"

"Of course not." Phillip gave Paul a slight nod as he turned to go. "Just stop by my office before you leave."

"Will do," he replied.

"I'm sorry for interrupting."

Paul shook his head and gave a laugh. "Actually, I'm indebted to you."

The two men found their way back over to the table and sat down.

"So what can I do for you?"

Ethan gave him a funny look, certain that he knew damn well what this was about. "Can we discuss my options regarding my father's company?" he asked, trying to hide his irritation.

Paul slipped off his glasses and tucked them in the holder attached to his shirt pocket. "I've been going over the legalities of the situation, and as I see it, you've got one option."

"Which is?"

"You can give a member of the board your proxy. With that, they can make the necessary decisions and vote on specific things at the board meetings."

"And if I do that, I won't have to be involved at all?"

"You'll be involved in name only."

Relief spread through him. "You're on the board, aren't you?"

"Yes," Paul answered. "Several people are, including your sister."

He shook his head. "No, I want you to have my proxy. I know you would run the company right, and not for your own personal gain."

Paul seemed startled. "Ethan, are you sure you want to do this?"

He stood up and extended his hand to him. "I'm not sure about anything, but I do know that I don't want to be president of Harrington Enterprises."

~

Sarah stepped onto the elevator and pushed the button for five.

"Hold the door, please."

Recognizing Gavin's voice, she continued jabbing the button.

He managed to squeeze through the doors just before they closed. "Thanks."

She gripped the rail behind her, refusing to look at him.

"I've left you three voice mails."

"I'm aware," she replied in a curt tone.

"We need to talk."

She held her hand up. "If it's about the other night, I don't want to hear it."

"No, I'm through talking about that. You made it very clear the other day how you felt."

The elevator opened up and she stepped out, not caring about which floor this was.

"Look, I know I screwed up," he said, following her on her heels. "And I know that you'll probably never forgive me for what I've done, but I was hoping that maybe we could still be friends."

She stopped and spun around. "What did you just say?"

He looked at her with his blue eyes. "I can't stand this distance between us. We may not be together anymore, but we can still have a friendship, can't we? I mean, there *are* going to be occasions when we're together, whether it's here at the hospital, or—"

"I can't think about this right now, Gavin."

"—or because of Ashley," he finished.

"You are asking a lot of me." She felt her voice trembling as she tried to stave off the tears. "I can't do this right now." She turned and hurried down the corridor.

~

That night Jessica awoke to sounds of thunder. She turned over to snuggle next to Ethan, but found he wasn't there. She sat up and looked around in the darkness of their bedroom. "Ethan?"

A strong draft, cold and wet, answered her. The door to the balcony was open.

She threw back the covers and hurried over to it, certain it was closed before they had gone to bed. She stepped halfway out, not wanting to get rained on. "Ethan?"

The rain was coming down so hard it was difficult for her to see. A flash of lightning suddenly lit up the backyard causing her eyes to widen. She stepped farther out and peered over the railing, waiting for the lightning to come again. A few moments later, it returned and confirmed what she had seen.

Jessica immediately turned and ran downstairs to the kitchen where she jerked open the back door. She began racing towards the pool, her bare feet smacking against the wet concrete.

Ethan was sitting on the pavement, dressed only in his pajama bottoms. His knees were drawn tight to his chest, his arms locked around them.

"Ethan? What are you doing out here?" she yelled over the noise of the rain.

His expression was blank as he stared off into the distance.

She shook his arm. "Ethan? What's wrong?" His skin was ice cold. His eyes still fixated on something that she could not see. She clasped both hands around his arm and pulled. "Ethan!"

He suddenly turned, and in an instant, had her by the shoulders.

A silent cry fell from her lips as he tightened his grip.

"Leave me alone," he said in an unrecognizable voice. He let go of her and returned his gaze into the darkness.

Jessica stood up and began backing away. Her damp nightgown clung to her as she ran back in the house and upstairs to call Grace. Picking up the phone, she strained to see if Ethan was still out there. Lightning lit up the sky and she quickly searched the ground. He wasn't there.

Thunder shook through the house, followed by another bolt of lightning. The flash was so bright it illuminated her reflection in the glass door—along with Ethan's.

She screamed and spun around.

The water dripped slowly down his hair and face as he stared at her.

A small cry came through the monitor.

If Ethan heard it, he didn't acknowledge it. Jessica was afraid to move. He was standing directly in front of her, blocking her way.

Ryan's cries soon became more volatile.

With her heart pounding, she stepped around him and ran to the door. Fear gripped her as she forced herself to look behind her.

Ethan had turned and was watching her, but made no motion to follow.

She hurried on across the hall and gathered Ryan in her arms. "Shh, it's okay." Her voice trembled as she kept an eye on the doorway. She paced the floor of the nursery with him until he finally relented and fell back asleep.

She stayed beside the crib for a long time, too afraid to leave him. As the minutes passed, she saw no movement in the hallway, meaning he was still in the bedroom.

Gathering her nerve, she silently went to the door and peered out. From where she stood, she could see Ethan lying in the bed; his eyes were closed, his breathing deep.

Her body shivered as she tiptoed into the room and pulled the door to the balcony shut. Then, dressing herself in a dry nightgown, she sat down in a chair beside the door and watched him sleep.

~

The next morning, Jessica stood in the kitchen pouring a liberal amount of cream into her coffee.

Ethan came up from behind and slipped his hands around her waist. "Good morning," he said, kissing her on the side of her neck.

She jumped at his touch, dropping the container of cream.

"I didn't mean to scare you," he said smiling.

"That's all right," she answered, looking at the mess in front of her.

He reached for a towel. "I'll get it."

She stepped away from the counter as he began wiping it up.

"Are you still upset about last night?" he asked, glancing over his shoulder.

She didn't answer. This morning, Ethan had no recollection of what he had done. When she'd told him what had happened, he began to deny that he had done any such thing, but had fallen silent when she'd pointed out his wet pajamas and sheets.

He tossed the towel in the sink and turned around. "Jess, I told you that it was nothing. I must have been sleepwalking. Don't let this bother you, okay?" He bent down and kissed her on the lips, pulling her close against him.

She drew back, knowing what he was trying to do.

A small sigh fell from him as he picked his keys up. "Do you want to ride with me to work?"

"No," she answered. "I've got a consult this afternoon that will probably run late."

"I'll see you later, then."

Jessica watched him go, unable to shake the incident from her mind. She found everything about it disturbing. When she had run through the kitchen last night, the back door was still locked. That meant he had either climbed, or jumped, down the balcony to get outside. A small shiver went through as she remembered how he had looked at her last night.

Chapter Seventeen

One early morning in June, Ethan found himself pacing the floor with Ryan, who was running a low-grade fever and had diarrhea. He held him in his arms, trying everything he could think of to calm him down.

"Shh, what's the matter, hmm? Do you miss Mommy?" Jessica was away attending a medical convention in Chicago.

Growing weary, he sat down with him in the rocking chair, and after lots of talking, singing, begging, and pleading, Ryan finally fell asleep.

He stood up and placed him in the crib, but his eyes popped opened as soon as the back of his head touched the mattress. He stuck the pacifier back in his mouth to try and stop his crying, but his quivering lips wouldn't even close around it.

Ethan picked him back up, and with him screaming in his ear, once more began pacing the floor. He glanced over at the clock on the changer. If he could hold out for a couple of more hours, he would call Dr. Nichols and have her meet them at the hospital.

Ryan suddenly coughed, sending a stream of vomit down Ethan's shoulder and arm. It was going to be a long two hours.

~

Dr. Nichols finished examining the baby under Ethan's watchful eye.

"What do you think?"

The doctor reached for her notepad and scrawled out a prescription. "I think he's just got a bug," she said, handing the paper to him. "But his right ear looks a little red inside, so I'm going to treat him for an ear infection as well."

As Ethan read the prescription, he saw her pull out a needle. "What are you going to do?"

Dr. Nichols peered at him through her glasses. "I'm just going to take a blood sample because of his history. I want to make sure we're not missing anything."

He placed his hand on the doctor's to stop her. "Um, is that really necessary?"

The woman laughed and slapped him on the back. "Don't worry, Ethan. I have a feeling this is going to be more painful for you than for him."

Ethan winced as she stuck the needle in Ryan's heel.

~

Sarah looked up from her chart when Ethan came into the office. He placed Ryan, who was nestled in his infant seat, on top of his desk. "How's he feeling?" she asked, standing up to have a look.

Ryan immediately started to cry.

He yawned and scratched his head. "There's your answer," he said, picking him up. The baby rubbed his face hard against Ethan's shirt. "He's more tired than anything."

Sarah watched as he comforted him, her maternal instincts longing to take over.

After a few moments, Ryan quieted down and fell asleep on Ethan's shoulder. He gently laid him back in his seat and covered him up.

"The poor little thing's exhausted."

"Mmm, so is Daddy," he answered, sighing.

Just then, the bell sounded in the other room, indicating there was a patient to see.

"I'll get this one," he said to her. "Mrs. Chambers should be by to pick him up in a few minutes. Do you mind to watch him until then?"

"Not at all."

He grabbed his stethoscope from off the coat rack and went through the door.

Sarah had no sooner returned to her paperwork, before Ryan woke and started to fuss. "Shh," she said, reaching in to pick him up. Tears inexplicably, and without warning, began to well up inside of her.

If her son had been born, he would have been eighteen months old next week. She swallowed the ache in her throat as she looked down at the baby. This was Gavin's son. Loss, coupled with anger, filled her soul.

"Sarah?"

She jerked her head up to find him standing beside the door. He was looking at her as if he knew what she was feeling.

"I heard one of the nurses say he was sick."

"It's nothing serious," she said, attempting to casually wipe her eyes.

Gavin reached out to take him from her. "Do you think I could hold him?"

She held Ryan away from his outstretched hands. "I don't think that would be such a good idea. Ethan's just in the other room."

He glanced at the door and then back at the baby. His eyes grew moist as he lightly ran one finger along the edge of Ryan's face before walking away.

Sarah watched him leave. Despite how much she hated him right now, she knew that it must be terrible for him not to be able to acknowledge his own son or even hold him.

Ryan yawned and rubbed his eye with his tiny fist.

She couldn't help but smile. "You know, you look just like your daddy," she whispered. "Yes, you do. You look just like your daddy."

"Do you think so?"

She jumped at the sound of Ethan's voice behind her. "Mmm-hmm," she mumbled.

He leaned over her shoulder to get a better look. "I really can't see it. I think he looks more like Jessica."

~

A few weeks later, Jessica stood in the shallow end of the pool, playing with Ryan. The baby laughed and giggled as she swirled him through the water. She laughed too. For the first time in a very long time, she was happy.

Ethan finally seemed to have come to terms with his father's death, telling her that perhaps Grace had been right; he had just needed some time. And there had been no more instances of him 'sleepwalking' since that night in May. Things were really good between them right now and she felt as if a huge burden had been lifted from her shoulders.

The kitchen door opened. "There you two are."

"Look, Ryan! Daddy's home!"

Ethan walked over to the edge of the pool and knelt down.

"You look miserable," she said, squinting at him.

"That's because I am. It was ninety today, and a hundred and two in my car. The air conditioner conked out." He grinned over at Ryan. "Did you have a good time playing with Mommy?"

The baby gurgled and slapped his hands against the water.

"It looks like you had a nice day off," he said, turning his attention back to her.

"I did. You ought to come on in and join us. The water's great."

"I think I will." Leaning forward, he placed his hands on the edge of the concrete and hopped in.

Jessica threw her head back and laughed. "I meant change your clothes first."

Ryan grinned toothlessly at his daddy, finding all of this very funny.

Ethan's tie floated on top of the water as he took him from Jessica. "Are you laughing at Daddy? Hmm? Are you laughing?" He kissed him on his ticklish spot below his ear.

Ryan kicked his feet as he squealed with delight.

Chapter Eighteen

Late one afternoon in August, Sarah sat in her office listening to Ethan tease her about the possibility of her dating a new doctor that had joined the staff.

"Ethan, would you please leave me alone? I am trying to get some work done," she said, pretending to be angry with him.

"All right, all right. I'm just trying to help. But if you don't want my help, that's fine," he replied, acting hurt.

Sarah rolled her eyes at him in mock disgust.

He grinned lopsidedly at her. "You know how much I like to irritate you, don't you?"

"Yes, and you are doing such a good job," she said, walking over to the filing cabinet by the door.

Things at the clinic had been slow today, allowing both of them to catch up on their paperwork.

Ethan had gotten through about half of his stack when he came across a lab report hidden underneath all the papers. Judging by the date stamped on it, it had been here for a while. He studied it for a moment and then picked up the phone.

"Lab."

"This is Dr. Harrington. I need you to pull a record for me. A blood test was performed on my son a few weeks ago, and I can't read it. The copy is smeared."

Sarah raised her head up from the files. *Oh, God.* She had no idea Dr. Nichols had done a blood test that day on Ryan. She fingered through the files in front of her, pretending to work, as she silently held her breath.

"What was Nichols' diagnosis?" Ethan listened as the lab technician read him his copy over the phone.

"...Bacterial infection," said the woman on the other end.

"What was his white cell count?"

"...WBC was normal."

"Thanks," he said, hanging up the phone. He folded the paper and started to stick it in his pocket, but stopped. He opened it back up, zeroing in on the bottom of the page. He could just make out the letters AB under blood type. This didn't make any sense. He and Jessica were both type O.

As he sat there trying to convince himself that the lab had made a mistake, he suddenly began to feel sick inside. "Sarah?"

"Hmm?" she replied, keeping her back to him.

He stood up and came around the desk. "What's Gavin's blood type?"

"I don't know," she said, certain that he heard the hesitation in her voice.

He brushed past her and jerked open the door.

"Ethan?"

He was already going up the stairs.

Sarah ran in the other direction to find Gavin.

~

Jessica smiled when Ethan walked through her door, but it quickly faded when she saw his face. "What's wrong?"

"I want you to look at this," he said, his voice trembling, "and I want you to tell me if it's true."

She tilted her head as she took the paper from him.

Ethan's eyes never left hers as she glanced over the report. He saw her expression turn from confusion to fear, confirming his suspicion. "It's smeared, but you can still make out the blood type."

She pushed her chair back and stood up. "Where did you get this?"

He was so angry he was shaking. "For once in your life, I want you to tell me the truth. Is Gavin his father?"

"Ethan—"

He slammed his fists down on her desk. *"Answer me, damn it!"*

"Yes," she cried, before clasping her hands over her mouth.

He turned away from her, fighting to control his rage.

"Ethan," she said, coming around the desk, "please listen to me."

"When did this happen?"

"Please…"

"*When?*" he said, grabbing her by the shoulders.

"It was when you were gone to New York."

He let go of her and clenched his fists.

"It was just one night. I swear, it didn't mean anything."

"When I took you back," he yelled, his accent becoming thick, "you *swore* to me, Jessica! You *swore* to me up and down that it was over!"

"It was! *Oh, God,* Ethan, I swear to you it was!"

The door suddenly opened.

He turned. "What the *hell* do you want?"

Gavin stood in the doorway with Sarah behind him. "Look, I know you're very angry, and you have every right to be. But let's just calm down and talk this through."

"You *son-of-a-bitch!*" Ethan said, grabbing him by his collar.

Gavin felt something in his jaw give as Ethan's knuckles collided with it. He went down, taking the filing cabinet with him. The coppery taste of blood swarmed in his mouth, as he lay sprawled on the floor.

Before he could move, Ethan straddled him and brought his fist down again, striking him on his left cheekbone.

Jessica began screaming for him to stop.

Gavin felt himself losing consciousness as he tried in vain to defend himself from Ethan's blows. A small gap between them suddenly opened as he drew his fist back again. Wasting no time, he stuck his foot in Ethan's stomach and shoved as hard as he could.

Ethan fell backwards against the fallen cabinet, feeling its sharp corner dig into his shoulder blade. Undeterred by the pain, he scrambled to his feet and started towards Gavin again.

Sarah hurriedly stepped in front of him and put her hands against his chest. "Ethan, please don't," she said, her voice shaking.

He looked at her with such anger that for a moment, she thought he was going to shove her against the floor as well. Then suddenly, he turned away, and placed his hands on top of his head.

The room grew very still, allowing Sarah to become aware of the crowd that had gathered outside the doorway. "Everything's under control," she said, closing the door on the curious onlookers.

Silence fell upon the four of them as she turned to survey the damage. Ethan was standing with his back towards her, but she could see the side of his face; his jaw was clenched and his eyes were closed. Blood was streaming from Gavin's mouth and nose as he struggled in vain to get to his feet. Jessica stood in the middle of the room with black tears streaming down her cheeks.

Without warning, Ethan spun around and jerked open the door. He did it with such force that it slammed into the wall, knocking a hole in the plaster.

"Ethan, please don't go!" Jessica called after him.

Sarah watched as he pushed his way through the crowd and disappeared around the corner.

Chapter Nineteen

Ethan felt the sand seeping into his shoes as he walked along the deserted beach. He wasn't sure how long he had been here, but he saw that the sun was coming up over the horizon. The sound of the waves pounding against the surf was making his head, and his ear, throb.

He shivered as the ocean's breeze circled him. He had left the hospital right after he had fought with Gavin, leaving the jacket to his suit behind in his office. Looking down, he noticed Gavin's blood on his shirt. He didn't know that he was capable of having that much rage inside him. He probably could have...or would have killed him if Sarah hadn't stepped in when she did.

He suddenly felt a strange sensation. His eyes started to sting and his throat began to ache, as images of Ryan played in his head over and over like a movie, but without the sound.

He swallowed hard and set his jaw, not wanting to give in to what was coming. He started to walk faster trying to stop it - but then it happened. The pain that was inside him came rushing out so fast he fought to catch his breath. He fell to his knees as a sob broke loose from his throat. His body shook as he tried to hold it in, but the force of it was too great. One by one, they rolled out of him, making his chest heave.

~

Trish Holloway stood behind the fifth floor nurses' station cleaning urine off the top of her shoe. Her day had already gotten off to a bad start and she'd only been on duty for an hour.

"Good morning."

She turned upon hearing Kellie Vandekamp's perky voice. "Weren't you supposed to work the seven o'clock shift with me?"

Kellie nodded as she stowed her purse under the counter. "I'm sorry I'm late."

Trish rolled her eyes, knowing that she really wasn't. It must be nice having your mom as the head nurse.

"Also, I have to leave early today for a meeting with the caterers."

"Fine," Trish snapped. "But you have to take care of Mr. Peters the next time he buzzes. He's already groped my ass twice this morning."

"Okay," she replied absently. "Hey, do you want to see my swatches for the bridesmaids' dresses?"

Trish bit down on her tongue. Kellie was engaged to a dermatologist who, according to her, was not only wealthy, and handsome, but good in bed as well. If she wasn't talking about him, she was talking about their upcoming wedding.

She nodded and grimaced at the same time as Kellie began showing her fifteen different colors of fuchsia.

"Hey, did you hear what happened yesterday between Dr. Harrington and Dr. Williams?"

"Which ones?"

"The *men*."

Trish shook her head.

Kellie gaped at her friend as she dropped the swatches on the counter. "I can't believe you haven't heard!"

"I was off yesterday, and I've been doing the job of *two* people this morning," she said, defending her ignorance.

"The two of them got into a fight in Jessica's office."

"What kind of fight?"

"A *fist* fight! Dr. Harrington beat the crap out of him!"

Trish thought back to earlier this morning. Dr. Harrington had bruises on his knuckles when he'd signed in.

"Do you think his wife is doing Dr. Williams again?"

"Shh!" Trish scolded her as Dr. Harrington passed by dangerously close to the station before rounding the corner to his office.

Just then, Dr. Williams came around the other way. He was sporting a black eye, as well as several cuts and contusions alongside his face. The two of them watched as he stopped and waited for Dr. Harrington to draw near.

"Can I speak to you for a second, Ethan?" It was an effort for him to talk as he had dislocated his jaw.

Ethan kept walking. "I have nothing to say to you."

Gavin grabbed his arm making him stop.

He jerked away. "Get your hands off me."

"Look, I know how you must feel—"

"You don't know a *damn* thing about how I *feel*."

"Look, we never meant to hurt you." Gavin kept his voice just above a whisper. "We were going to tell you the truth, but Jessica just wanted to give you some time. The affair was over with by the time she found out she was pregnant."

Ethan clenched his jaw. "I'm sure it was. Getting Jessica knocked up kind of complicated things, didn't it? Tell me something. Whose idea was it to lie about her due date? Was it yours, or did she think of that one all by herself?"

He stared at him for a moment. "I can see that you're not ready to listen to what I have to say."

Ethan watched him walking away as the anger churned inside him. "Gavin."

He stopped and turned around.

Ethan quickly closed the distance between them.

From the nurses' station, Trish and Kellie strained to hear what they were saying, but couldn't make out a single word. They watched breathlessly as Dr. Williams crossed his arms and stared up at Dr. Harrington, who was almost a head taller. It looked as if they were going to have another fight.

Ethan leaned into him until they almost touched. "Don't you for a second think this whole thing is just going to blow over," he said. "Because I'm not about to forgive...or *forget* what you've done."

Gavin didn't flinch. "Is that a threat, Ethan?"

"Take it any way you want," he said, before turning away.

~

Sarah hesitated outside her office door. She had seen Ethan's car in the parking lot and knew he was already here. Drawing a deep breath, she forced herself to go inside.

He was standing in front of the window holding a cup of coffee, but he turned slightly when he heard the door close.

She set her purse down on her desk, searching desperately for something to say.

"You knew…didn't you?" he asked, keeping his gaze locked on the window.

"Yes," she answered, overwhelmed with guilt.

His shoulders slumped forward as he let out a long sigh.

She walked over and laid her hand upon his forearm. "I'm so sorry—"

"Ethan?"

Sarah felt the muscles in his arm tense at the sound of Jessica's voice. She turned to look at her, but he remained where he was.

"Can I talk to you for a moment, please?"

He didn't answer.

Jessica folded her arms and looked expectantly at Sarah.

Without speaking, Sarah grabbed her stethoscope from the coat rack and brushed past her, wishing all the while that she would just go to hell.

Jessica waited for the door to close before walking up behind him. "Ethan, I'm so very sorry," she began. "I know you can't forgive me right now, but please, just let me explain."

There was nothing but silence.

"You have to believe me when I say that I never meant for this to happen, and if you'll just listen to me, I can –"

He suddenly spun around and slammed his cup down on the desk, spilling coffee everywhere. "*What?*" he shouted. "*What* could you possibly have to say to me that could justify what you've done?" Anger, mixed with anguish, consumed his face, turning his complexion dark. "My God, Jessica! How could you do this to me? How could you keep something like that from me?"

She fumbled for the words. A few minutes ago, she had everything she was going to say planned out in her head. "I swear, I was going to tell you the truth."

"When?" he asked, his accent growing thick. "When he turned *six* months old? When he started to look like Gavin? *When?*"

"I was scared," she said in a teary whisper.

He looked at her with disgust. "Quit crying, Jessica. Tears aren't going to work with me this time."

She wiped them away, only to have more take their place. "I didn't want to hurt you, Ethan." She grasped him by his arms, feeling the panic rising in her. "I'm so sorry. Please just say you forgive me."

He shook his head. "I cannot believe you have the nerve to stand in front of me and ask for my forgiveness!" He jerked his arms away and started towards the door.

"Where are you going?"

"I don't know."

"Please, just come home with me so we can talk."

He stopped and stared at her incredulously. "Do you honestly think that I'm going to stay with you?"

Her chin began to tremble. "What are you saying?"

"I'm saying don't look for me to come home tonight, or any other night."

"Ethan!" She grabbed his arm again as he stepped into the crowded hallway. "Don't do this!"

Several nurses and members of the staff had stopped what they were doing and were now watching the drama unfolding in front of them.

His fingers closed around her wrist as he lifted it off of him. "Get away from me," he said in a low voice, giving her a shove.

The hallway filled with gasps and whispers as she stumbled backwards. She reached out to the wall to catch herself. "Ethan, please! Please don't do this!"

He strode up to the nurses' station, leaving her sobbing in the corridor. "Trish, I'm going to be out for the rest of the day. If you need me, call me."

"Yes, sir."

~

"How long are you planning on hiding out in here?"

"Until everyone goes home."

"I don't think that's possible, considering that this is a hospital," Grace said, handing her a box of tissues.

Jessica wiped her nose and eyes. After her very public, and hysterical, exchange with Ethan this morning, she couldn't face anyone.

Grace leaned back against the sofa and crossed her legs, finding it hard to conjure up any sympathy for her. "You're going to have to go home eventually."

She crumpled the tissue between her fingers, hearing the indifference in her cousin's voice. "There's no reason to," she murmured. "He's not going to be there."

"Do you know where he went?"

"No," she replied, although she was fairly certain that wherever he was, it probably involved large quantities of alcohol.

"I understand that you want to try and make things right with him, but you need to take a step back and try and see things from his side."

She nodded. "I know."

"No, I'm not sure you do."

She looked over at Grace, hurt by her lack of compassion.

The older woman leaned forward. "My best advice to you, is to just leave him alone. He needs time to process what's happened, and your wanting to make things right with him this very second is only going to make it worse. Give him a few days to calm down."

Chapter Twenty

Sarah sat at her desk glumly going through another batch of invoices that had come in today's mail. The worst part of running this clinic was the heap of paperwork and reports that went along with it. She would normally talk to Ethan while she worked, making it fun, but at the moment, that wasn't exactly a word in his vocabulary.

She flicked her eyes in his direction. It had been a very grim atmosphere in here for the past few days, and she had avoided the subject of Jessica and the baby completely. But it was clear that he really needed to talk to someone. "Ethan? Can I ask you something?"

"Mmm-hmm," he answered, scribbling something in a chart.

"What are you going to do...about things?"

He stopped writing, and after a moment, looked up at her. "Honestly? I don't know."

The room grew still as she wrestled with what to say next.

Ethan laid his pen down. "Can I ask *you* something?"

"Of course."

"Did you divorce Gavin because of the baby?"

She clasped her hands together and propped her chin on them, trying to hide the fact that it was trembling. "Yes."

"When did you find out?"

Feelings that she had tucked away, began stirring inside of her. "He told me the night Ryan was born," she said in a shaky voice.

He looked at her with something that resembled pity, but she wasn't sure if it was for her or for him.

She cleared her throat and drew a deep breath. "Ethan, I know I'm the last person in the world that should be handing out marital advice, but there are two things that I think you should know."

"What's that?"

"Jessica didn't keep this a secret to lie to you. I think she was scared of losing you…the way Gavin lost me. She did it because she loves you."

He stood up and walked over to the filing cabinet beside the window.

"Do you still love her?"

He shook his head slightly. "I don't know," he answered, pulling open the top drawer. "The only thing I do know is that I thought I had a son and now I don't." His ulcer and his anger flared at the same time, making him slam the drawer shut.

Sarah watched him as he held his stomach and winced ever so slightly. He had come to her earlier in the year complaining of the pain. When she'd examined him, she had found a fairly large ulcer.

He placed his elbows on top of the filing cabinet and rested his head in his hands, waiting for the throbbing to subside. "Do you think you would have stayed with Gavin if he had told you the truth in the beginning?"

"I've asked myself that question a dozen times, and I really don't know if I would have or not. Looking at things now, I think we still would have ended up getting a divorce."

He raised his head and turned away from the cabinet, his face solemn.

"Please don't go by my actions, Ethan. Because there are still times that I regret leaving him."

"Are you still in love with him?"

"A part of me will always love him, I guess," she said softly. "But not as a husband. I think deep down, you still love Jessica. You two have this..." She paused, searching for the right words. "This chemistry between you. I've seen the way you look at each other. It's something that Gavin and I never really had."

He scratched his chin for a moment. "Is that the second thing?"

"Hmm?"

"Is that the second thing you wanted to tell me?"

"No," she replied, feeling her lips fold in on themselves.

He looked at her expectantly.

"You may not be Ryan's biological father, but you're still his father. You *have* to know that. If you can just accept it—"

"It's not that simple," he said, shaking his head. "I can't get past the fact that he's Gavin's son. For four months, Sarah, he was my son. *My* son! Now every time I think about him, all I can see is Jessica in bed with Gavin. Those two things intertwine in my mind, and I *cannot* turn it loose. It's like...it's..." He sighed and sat back down in his chair, giving up on trying to find the words to express how he felt. The truth was, he really didn't know.

Sarah walked around her desk and went to stand beside his chair. "It's all right," she said, placing her hand upon his shoulder. "I understand."

~

Later that evening, Ethan was in the locker room changing into his scrubs. Tonight was his turn to work in the ER, and although he really didn't feel like working a double shift, it did help to keep his mind off of things—as his hotel room didn't offer much in the form of entertainment.

He heard the door to his left swing open, followed by the sound of footsteps. When he saw who it was, he felt himself turn rigid.

Gavin edged past him and opened his locker, which was directly across the way. "Are you working ER tonight?"

He remained silent.

"You can't ignore me forever."

"It's working great so far," Ethan replied, unbuttoning his shirt.

Gavin turned his attention back to getting dressed. He could tell that his presence annoyed Ethan to no end, but frankly he didn't care. He had grown weary of having to walk on eggshells whenever he was in sight. "Are you going to try and work things out with Jessica?" he asked bluntly.

"That's none of your business."

Gavin slammed his locker and turned around. "No, *that's* where you're wrong. It *is* my business."

Ethan's jaw tightened. "What the *hell* does that mean?"

"Meaning, that whether you like it or not, Ryan is *my* son. And now that things are out in the open, I want to see him."

Rage, coupled with bitterness, caused his hands to clench. "I don't want you coming anywhere near him."

"Look, I'm sorry that we hurt you, but you're just going to have to get over it. *You* are Ryan's father, but he is *my* son. Now, I'm certainly not going to try and take your place, but I *am* going to be a part of his life."

Ethan suddenly stepped over the bench and shoved him against the lockers, just as Phillip Martin came through the door.

"What the *hell* is going on in here?"

As Phillip drew near, Ethan gave Gavin a small push before releasing his grip.

"I asked you a question."

Both men refused to answer as they stood less than a foot apart, glaring at one another.

"Does this have anything to do with the fight the two of you had a couple of weeks ago?"

The silence remained.

Phillip exhaled his anger. He was not a patient man. "Ethan?" he prompted.

"It's personal," he finally said in a low voice.

"Well then, if it's personal, I expect you to keep it out of this hospital. Understand?"

Gavin unruffled his shirt and turned back to his locker. Once he had finished dressing, he quickly left the room.

Ethan hung his shirt on the small hook and reached for his scrubs. He could feel Phillip's eyes on the back of him, and he knew he was about to receive a lecture.

"Ethan," he began, "I know that things are tough for you and Jessica right now."

He slid the shirt over his head and sighed. By now, everyone had heard that he and Jessica had separated. No one knew the reason why, but there was plenty of speculation.

"Did you know that my wife and I were married for thirty-five years?"

He shook his head. "That's a long time," he said, trying to imagine the possibility of being married to Jessica for that long.

"Yes, it is," Phillip said, sounding distant. "But my point is, marriage takes a lot of hard work. You know as well as I do, that it requires a lot of time and energy."

Ethan ran his fingers through his hair. "I know it does, Phillip," he said, closing his locker. "But I don't think I have enough energy left for this marriage...and I'm tired of trying."

~

The next afternoon, Jessica sat in the conference room staring blankly at the wall. They were forty-five minutes over what was supposed to have been a one-hour meeting.

These business meetings were held the first Tuesday of every month and, for the most part, were usually routine. Phillip would start it off, and then they would go around the room, with each person reporting on the figures and statistics of their department.

At the moment, Dr. Pearson was in the middle of giving his report. She checked her watch again and stifled a sigh. Between his fondness for pie charts and the obvious love he had for listening to himself talk, she knew this wasn't going to wrap up anytime soon.

She casually looked down the table at Ethan, who was leaning back in his chair with his arms folded, staring a hole through Dr. Pearson.

"Dr. Jessica Harrington report to CCU nurses' station," said a voice over the P.A.

Upon hearing her name, Ethan involuntarily glanced at her, but she had no sooner caught his gaze before he shifted it back to Dr. Pearson.

Dropping her shoulders forward in defeat, she gathered her things and stood to go. Almost two weeks had gone by since Ethan had learned the truth, and she'd decided to take Grace's advice and leave him alone. It was hard not running into him here at the hospital, but she had managed to give him a wide berth, telling Gavin to do the same.

"Cancel Dr. Harrington. Cancel Dr. Harrington," the voice said in a non-apologetic tone.

Jessica plopped herself back down, embarrassed. Throughout the rest of Dr. Pearson's monologue, she kept her eyes focused on the table as she went over an imaginary conversation in her mind with Ethan. At some point, she was going to have it with him, and she wanted to be prepared.

The sound of chairs scraping across the floor made her realize that the meeting had ended. She quickly stood up and began weaving her way towards Ethan, deciding that now was the right moment.

"Dr. Harrington, how are you?" Meredith Van Owen sidled up to him.

"I'm fine, Meredith. How are you?"

"Oh, I'm getting along," she said, batting her long, but clumpy, eyelashes at him.

Jessica felt the heat rising in her face as her footsteps faltered. Meredith was an outrageous flirt, who was obviously wasting no time in taking advantage of their separation.

"So tell me," she purred. "How's that little boy of yours?"

"He's fine."

She ran the tip of her fingernail along his tie as she smiled demurely. "I bet he's going to grow up to be just as handsome as his father."

Ethan's face fell as he nodded politely, before edging himself out the door.

~

Sarah listened to the clock ticking above the door. She usually couldn't hear it, but the silence that had enveloped the room since their return from the business meeting was making it sound like Gepetto's workshop.

She'd overheard what Meredith had said to Ethan, and he had not spoken one word since coming back. Opening her middle desk drawer, she pulled out two pencils and picked up the file in front of her. "Would you mind taking a look at this chart?"

He took the file from her and scanned it for a moment. "What do you want me to..." He stopped when he looked up. Sarah was sitting there, with a pencil hanging from each nostril.

"I need your opinion on this patient," she said, with the most serious expression on her face as the pencils dangled back and forth from her nose.

He grinned lopsidedly at her. "Sarah…"

"Hmm?"

He leaned back in his chair and began to laugh. "What are you doing?" He finally got the words out.

She took the pencils out of her nose. "Trying to get you to smile."

~

Jessica walked into the cafeteria and paid a large fortune for a small cup of tea. Her surgical consult that she had scheduled for the afternoon had canceled, leaving her with some spare time before she had to make rounds.

As she searched for an empty seat, she noticed Ethan sitting at a table in the far corner. It didn't appear that he had seen her, as he was busy poring over a medical chart.

Gathering up her nerve, she strode steadily over to his table. "Do you mind if I join you?"

He looked up, seeming a little startled.

Becoming aware that several of her colleagues and nurses were watching their exchange, it suddenly occurred to her that this was a stupid idea trying to talk to him in public. She had halfway turned to go, when he stood up and gestured for her to take a seat.

As she pulled out her chair, she saw a small carton of milk beside him. "So, we're drinking milk these days, huh?" she said nervously, trying to break the ice.

He held his tie against his chest as he sat back down. "Well, you know it does a body good."

Jessica clasped her hands together and pressed them against her lips, letting her elbows rest on the table. "Where have you been staying?"

He finished writing in the chart, and tucked his pen inside his shirt pocket. "In a hotel across town."

She waited for him to give her the specifics, but after a moment, it became clear that there wouldn't be any more details forthcoming. "I know you don't want to talk to me," she began, unlocking the words she had memorized, "but I just wanted to tell you that I'm sorry. And I know that sorry doesn't make it right, but I only did what I did to keep from hurting you."

He sat there silently as a hard edge formed along his jaw.

"Can I ask you something?"

"What?"

"Are you going to file for a divorce?"

Ethan put his elbows on the table, imitating her, and looked away. "I don't know," he said after a long silence.

The smallest of smiles found its way onto her lips. "I'm glad to hear you say that."

He looked back at her, confused.

"If you haven't filed for a divorce yet, that means you're not sure. And that tells me you still must think we can work things out."

"Jessica—"

"Please, Ethan, I know we can do this. I love you."

Ethan felt that people were starting to stare. He lowered his eyes, and his voice. "Jess, it's not that simple. This isn't just going to go away."

"I know, but things aren't going to get any better if we stay like this."

He took his hands away from his face and placed them on the table.

She reached out and laid her hand on top of his. "Will you at least think about coming home?" she asked softly.

Ethan looked at her hand, and then at her. He looked at her for the longest time.

She felt the tears welling up inside as he pushed his chair back and walked away.

~

Sarah ignored her growling stomach, wishing that she'd taken the time to eat lunch today, as she made her way along a corridor of the eighth floor towards Physical Therapy.

Stepping through the doors, she took a quick look around the deserted room and frowned. Therapists were never where they said they were going to be. Her feet were already moving as she turned to go, and by the time her eyes had caught up—it was too late. Her chest bumped against Ben Richards' hand, sending the cup of coffee in it tumbling.

He looked down at his shirt and let out a quivering breath. "H---ot. H---ot," he stuttered.

"I'm so sorry," she said, stepping forward to help. She swiped her hand across his shirt several times, trying to soak up the liquid with her palm.

"It's fine."

"I'm sorry," she repeated.

"I got that part," he said, repelling his chest away from her. "But you're just rubbing it in."

She stopped in mid-swipe and dropped her hand. "Sorry."

An impish smile spread across his lips. "Are you always this apologetic?"

Sarah wiped her hand on the pocket of her lab coat. "No…I mean…" She felt her face turning red. "I'm not usually this clumsy," she finally said.

He tossed his empty cup into a small wastebasket. "Glad to hear it." He looked down somewhat mournfully at the brown stain that was now smeared across his shirt.

"I'll pay to have it cleaned—"

"That's not necessary."

"—or I can buy you a new one."

He held up his hands. "Just stop," he said, shaking his head. "It's fine."

She cleared her throat, wishing that she could erase the last two minutes of her life.

"Is that for me?"

"Hmm?"

Ben pointed at the file she was clutching in her dry hand. "Is that for me?"

"Oh. Yes, I talked to you on the phone yesterday about Mr. Schultz."

"I remember."

"He'll be released in the morning," she continued, awkwardly thrusting the chart in front of his face, "and I'd like for him to start rehab as soon as possible."

"Shouldn't be a problem," he said, making a note on it.

"Thank you."

"No, thank *you*."

Finding his answer a little strange, she began edging herself towards the door. "Okay, then."

"Dr. Williams, would you like to have dinner with me sometime?"

Her mouth opened, but nothing came out.

"I wouldn't normally ask," he said, staring into her eyes, "but as I understand it you're back on the market, so to speak. Is that true?"

"Uh, yes, that's true. Mmm-hmm." Seeing that he was still staring at her, she nodded, just in case he hadn't understood.

His blue eyes twinkled, seeming to find it amusing that she was so flustered. "So, what do you say?"

"Um..."

"You don't have to give me an answer right now," he said, tucking the file underneath his arm, "but if you ever feel like going out, just give me a call." He gave her a small wink as he walked past her and out the door.

Sarah rolled her eyes and sighed to herself. *A nice man asks you out and all you can say is, 'Um?' God, you can be such a moron sometimes!*

Chapter Twenty-one

Jessica's whole body trembled as she slipped out of bed. Positive that she had heard something downstairs, she searched her bedroom quickly for some type of weapon. Spying her shoe, she picked it up and cautiously tiptoed down the hallway.

The sound of footsteps on the hardwood floor in the foyer made her stop at the top of the landing. She gripped her shoe with both hands and held it out in front of her. Her heart leapt into her throat when she saw the shadow of a man ascending the stairs.

Her mind told her to go lock herself in the nursery and call for help, but her feet refused to move. She was just about to scream as the intruder began to visualize. And then she saw his face. "*Goddamn it,* Ethan!" she said, breathing a sigh of relief. "You scared me to death!"

"Sorry. I didn't mean to," he replied, making his way up.

Her relief was short lived as she began to wonder why he was here at five in the morning.

He stopped on the next to the last stair. "Are you going to hit me with that?" he asked, gesturing towards the shoe that she had pointed at him.

She looked down at the black stiletto, not realizing she was still holding onto it. "I thought you were a burglar," she said, tossing it on the floor.

"I'm sorry. I should have called first." He rested his hand on the banister. "I know it's really early, but I was hoping that we could talk."

Apprehension surrounded her as they went down to the kitchen together. Having filled the coffee machine last night, she turned it on and sat down at the table.

He sat in the chair across from her, but didn't say anything.

Thinking that maybe he was waiting for her to start, she took a deep breath. "I know you're angry with me, Ethan. And I know I hurt you. There aren't enough words to tell you how sorry I am."

"Which are you sorry for? Sleeping with him again, or getting pregnant?"

She looked away.

He got up and walked over to the counter. He hadn't meant to sound so vindictive. "I just don't understand why you had to sleep with him again. We were trying to put the pieces back together."

Jessica pushed her chair back and slowly got to her feet. "Things hadn't been right between us for a long time *before* that, Ethan."

"We were trying."

"No, *I* was trying. You had given up."

"That's not true. I was trying my best."

"You stopped *touching* me. It had been over two months."

He gripped the edge of the granite.

"You didn't want me…Gavin did."

Ethan closed his eyes. "I know that hurt you, Jess. But that was no reason to do what you did."

"You're right, it was no excuse. But I swear to you it was only that one night when you were in New York. We both knew it was a mistake as soon as it happened."

He turned around to face her. "And then you decided to lie about it. How could you do that to me, Jessica? My God, all these months, you let me believe that he was mine!" His eyes filled with hurt as his voice started to break. "I fell in *love* with that little boy. He was my *son*, a life that you and I created together. How could you do that to me?"

She hugged herself tightly. "Because when I first told you I was pregnant, you were *less* than thrilled. I knew if I had told you the truth, you would have left me."

He began shaking his head.

"You would have left me. Don't you stand there and tell me you wouldn't have!"

"It doesn't matter what I would have done! What matters is that you should have told me from the beginning!"

Tears began to fall from her face. "I was scared of losing you."

He suddenly grasped her by the shoulders and shook her. "You had another man's baby and let me believe it was mine! How am I supposed to forgive you for that?"

His eyes were filled with so much pain that she couldn't even look at him. "I don't know," she cried. "I don't know." She slid to the floor and buried her face in her arms.

Ethan ran his fingers through his hair and sighed. He absolutely *could* not talk to her when she cried. Not knowing what else to do, he sat down beside her and leaned back against the cabinets.

The darkness in the room started to fade as the light from the sun began creeping across the floor.

Jessica watched it moving until it touched her bare feet. "I never meant for any of this to happen, Ethan. I swear to God, I didn't."

He drew his knees up to his chest and held his head in his hands.

"Please say that you forgive me," she begged, wiping at her eyes.

"It's not that easy, Jess. I can't just turn off what I'm feeling."

Her chin began to tremble. "Do you want a divorce?"

An agonizing moment of silence passed by.

He finally raised his head up. "No, that's not what I want," he whispered.

~

Sarah stood in one of the examination rooms filling the coffee pot up with water. Walking back into her office, she noticed her philodendron plant. It sat alone on top of the filing cabinet by the window, looking wilted and pathetic. Taking mercy on it, she gave it a good, long drink.

As the black soil soaked up the water, she let her eyes wander to the parking lot down below and saw Ethan standing beside his car, having what appeared to be a rather serious conversation with Jessica. Although she knew she shouldn't be watching, she also couldn't seem to tear herself away. The two of them stood talking for a long time, and then suddenly, Ethan bent down and kissed her.

Feeling like a pervert, Sarah turned away and finished the task of making the coffee, before attending to the matters on her desk.

A few minutes later, Ethan came through the door. "Good morning."

"Morning."

He started to pour himself a cup of coffee, but noticed it wasn't ready yet. When he turned around, he saw that Sarah was smiling at him. "What?"

"Nothing," she said, still smiling.

He looked down at himself to make sure everything was buttoned and zipped. "What is it?"

"Mmm, nothing," she chirped, turning back to her desk.

He sat down across from her and began sorting through his mail.

"So," she said, watching him closely. "Did you give Jessica a ride to work this morning?"

He looked up, resembling that of a deer caught in the headlights.

She arched her brow. "I saw you outside the window."

"Oh," he said, glancing in that direction. "No, I didn't give her a ride to work. But I did talk to her earlier this morning."

"*And?*"

A small smile formed on his face. "And we've decided to give it another go."

~

Ethan leaned against the doorway of the nursery, watching Ryan from a distance. Mrs. Chambers had left a few moments ago, and Jessica had phoned to tell him that she had an emergency surgery and was probably going to be late.

"Ba! Ba!"

He folded his arms across his chest and bowed his head. Tears fell like raindrops and collected at the bottom of his trembling chin. This was not how he'd expected his life to turn out. Everything that he knew and loved had been nothing but a lie.

"Ba!"

His legs shook as he walked across the room and peered into the crib. Ryan was lying there, chewing hungrily on his fist. Ethan gripped the rail, making it crackle.

The baby turned his head at the sound, and upon seeing his daddy, kicked his feet excitedly. "Ba!" he repeated.

Ethan's vision grew blurry as he looked at his son; his son who now belonged to another man. Abject grief began to pour from his heart, manufacturing a series of sobs that he could not control. Why had he taken Jessica back the first time? And why had he trusted her not to do it again?

Ryan gurgled softly and smiled.

It was at that moment that he felt something move inside him. He drew a deep breath, allowing it to continue. Reaching down, he gathered him in his arms. "Daddy's missed you," he whispered in a broken voice.

~

Sarah stood on the doorstep outside Gavin's apartment, waiting nervously.

"Uh, hi," Gavin said, sounding perplexed.

"I know I should've called first," she said, gripping the strap of her purse as it hung on her shoulder. "Is this a bad time?"

"No, of course not." He opened the door wider, allowing her to come inside.

Her feet had no sooner touched the hardwood when he suddenly cut in front of her and hurried towards the sofa - at least it looked like a sofa. The mound of newspapers and medical journals piled on top of it kept her from being certain.

"Here, have a seat," he said, shoving the papers to the floor.

Sarah sat down on the black leather square he had prepared for her.

"Can I get you some tea, or coffee?"

She shook her head. "I don't want you to go to any trouble."

"No, it's no trouble."

His sudden desire to please her made her feel more uncomfortable than she already was. "Tea would be fine."

"I'll be right back," he said, before scurrying into the kitchen.

The sound of dishes rattling and pots banging resonated through the doorway as she let her eyes wander around the room. His apartment was big and spacious, and seemed to be equipped with lots of nice amenities, including a flat screen TV that took up most of the wall in front of her.

As she set her purse by her feet, she couldn't help noticing that his most prized possession was proudly mounted on the wall next to it. A seven and a half pound largemouth bass with shiny scales and flipped out tail stared at her as it sat glued to a varnished piece of wood.

Sarah shivered, finding its bulging eyes and jagged teeth to be just as hideous as she had two years ago, when he'd brought it home one Sunday after a fishing excursion to Bar Harbor with Dr. Pearson. He'd ended up hanging it in the garage after she had refused to let him display it in their living room.

"Here you go."

She shifted her gaze from the creature to Gavin as he returned from the kitchen. "Thank you," she said, taking the cup from him.

He moved another stack of papers to the floor and then sat down next to her.

"Your apartment is very nice," she said, remaining perched on the edge of the cushion as he settled back.

"Thanks."

She looked down at her tea, feeling uncertain about how to start the conversation, and noticed that the liquid had little, to no steam, rising off of it. "I guess you heard about Jessica and Ethan."

He nodded. "Jessica told me this afternoon."

Of course she did. She set the lukewarm cup on the table, trying not to let her jealousy get the best of her.

He tilted his head. "Is there something wrong?"

"No," she answered, replacing her scowl with what she hoped resembled a smile. "I hope they're able to make it work."

He cleared his throat, but didn't say anything.

She tucked a strand of hair behind her ear and drew a silent breath. "Gavin, I've been thinking a lot about what you said a while back."

He stretched his arm across the top of the sofa and crossed his legs. "About what?" he asked in a smooth voice.

"About us being friends."

"And?"

"And if you're still willing, I think I'd like to be friends…or at least as close as we *can* be under the circumstances."

"I'd like that," he said, staring into her eyes.

She looked away and began digging through her purse. "Here. I brought you a housewarming gift."

There was a subtle change in his expression as he unwrapped a set of dishtowels.

"Thank you," he said flatly.

"From the looks of things," she replied, glancing around the disheveled room, "I think I should have hired a maid service for you, instead."

He chuckled as he surveyed his surroundings. "I guess it *is* a little messy."

"A *little?*"

They laughed out loud together.

~

Jessica scrambled out of her car and hurried across the floor of the garage. She had not intended for her and Ethan's first night back together to be spent apart.

The smell of tomato sauce, along with something burnt, greeted her as she came through the door.

Ethan's voice filtered from the nursery as she made her way up the stairs. Not wishing for him to see her in her sweat-stained scrubs, she tiptoed into their bedroom where she quickly changed into a pair of khakis and white sweater.

Ethan was pulling the door to the nursery closed when she came out.

"Hi," she said, trying to sound casual. "Is he asleep?"

"We'll see," he replied with a shrug. "Are you just now getting home?"

"A few minutes ago."

"Are you hungry?"

She felt a smile forming on her lips as she nodded. "Starving." She eagerly followed him back downstairs to the dining room where she saw that he had set the table.

"I made spaghetti for us. It'll just take a minute to warm up."

"Thanks, that was very nice of you."

"Don't thank me yet," he called over his shoulder, before disappearing into the kitchen. You haven't tasted it."

She laughed. Between the two of them, they could barely boil water.

~

Jessica took extra time that night getting ready for bed. Despite the encouraging start, dinner had been eaten mostly in silence, as they both had seemed at a loss for words.

When she emerged from the bathroom, he was sitting on his side of the bed, setting his alarm clock. She sat down next to him and began running her fingers along his back, gently tracing over the scars between his shoulder blades.

He turned suddenly, and looked into her eyes.

She brushed a lock of hair from his forehead and then leaned over to kiss him. Their lips had barely touched when he pulled away.

"I'm sorry," he said softly. "I just need some time."

"It's all right," she answered, concealing her hurt, as he turned out the light.

The silence that followed hung over them like a black cloud.

"I see that you've still got your cold feet," he said in the darkness.

She laughed in spite of herself. "You haven't been here to keep them warm."

He sighed loudly, pretending to be exasperated. "Well, bring them over here."

She cuddled up next to him and snuggled her toes between his legs. The moonlight outlined the edge of his face; his eyes were open, his jaw tight. "Ethan?"

"Hmm?"

"Everything's going to be all right. You'll see."

Chapter Twenty-two

Jessica stood gazing out the window of her office. She and Ethan had been back together for almost three weeks now, yet it felt as if they were just going through the motions of a marriage. Day in and day out it was always the same. He would come home, have a drink, and play with Ryan.

The two of them would then exchange polite conversation, which felt forced at times, before going to sleep. There was still a great deal of unspoken tension between them, and it was especially present in the bedroom.

Looking at her watch, she drew a deep breath and picked up the phone.

"Clinic, Dr. Williams."

"Sarah? May I speak to Ethan, please?"

There was a pause.

"It's Jessica," she heard her say.

"Hello?"

"Hi. I was wondering if you could meet me for lunch this afternoon," she said hopefully.

His sigh came through loud and clear. "Hang on a second."

Jessica held the phone against her ear and waited. His voice became distant as if he'd put his hand over the receiver, but she could still hear him talking.

"Sarah, would you mind if I went out for lunch?"

A faint reply sounded in the background.

"I can meet you in about half an hour," he said, his voice suddenly strong again.

"Okay, pick me up in my office."

~

A short while later Ethan stuck his head through the door. "Are you ready to go?"

"Almost." She stood up and walked around to the front of her desk. "Come in for a minute, though. There's something I want to show you."

He closed the door and turned to face her. "What?"

"This." She unbuttoned her lab coat and let it fall to the floor. She was wearing nothing but a skimpy red teddy that only covered as much of her body as it needed.

Ethan felt the blood leave his head.

Her red stilettos clicked softly upon the floor as she reached behind him to turn the lock.

Ethan could smell her perfume. Its scent was intoxicating to him, causing his thoughts to become entangled in his mind. He bent down to kiss her, but hesitated as the image of her and Gavin suddenly swirled in front of him.

Refusing to give up, she took his hand and placed it on her right breast, letting him feel her erect nipple.

The heat of the moment overcame him as he drew her closer and kissed her hard on the mouth.

She pressed against him, not wanting him to stop.

He pulled back and looked at her, his eyes filled with desire. "I've missed you so much," he whispered.

"Don't talk," she said, placing a finger over his lips. She traced the curve of his chin with it, letting it slide down his neck before unbuttoning his shirt. Her teeth grazed over his chest as she moved her hands down his torso to unbuckle his pants.

He led her over to the leather couch and lay down, pulling her on top of him as his fingers nimbly unfastened her teddy.

Their bodies became one as they moved up and down in unison, skin touching skin.

Jessica's flesh was hot to his touch as he slid his hands over the backs of her thighs. The leather underneath him became wet as their sweat-soaked bodies began to rise up and down more rapidly.

Jessica gasped as she dug her nails into his chest. With each breath Ethan drew, she took two as he thrust deep inside her. She closed her eyes, anticipating the moment, as he tightened his grip around her waist. She threw her head back and moaned as she felt her body fill with pleasure.

~

The afternoon sun slithered across the floor as she lay nestled in his arms.

"As much as I hate to," Ethan said, kissing the top of her head, "I have to go."

Jessica lifted his wrist and looked at his watch. It was with great reluctance that she got up and began to dress.

He finished buttoning his shirt and picked up her teddy from off the floor. "Would you wear this again for me sometime?" he asked, holding it out in front of him.

She leaned over and answered him with a warm and passionate kiss.

"You're making it hard to leave," he mumbled against her lips.

She drew back and grinned. "Sorry."

He got up from the sofa and went to unlock the door. "Let's do this again, very soon," he said, wrapping his arms around her.

"Absolutely." She grabbed him playfully by his tie, pulling his mouth towards hers once more.

He felt behind him for the doorknob. "I have to go now," he said with a laugh as he backed away from her lips.

"Ethan, wait. Let me fix your hair," she said, combing it with her fingers, "or Sarah's going to wonder what you've been doing."

He cradled her face in his hands and kissed her softly. "I'll see you tonight."

~

Jessica held her head and moaned as she squinted at the clock on the nightstand. With a lot of effort, she swung her legs over the side of the bed and pushed herself up. An empty bottle of wine lay turned over on the floor. She brushed the hair from her face and glanced back at Ethan. His head was stuffed under the pillow.

Stifling a groan, she shuffled into the bathroom and took some aspirin, vowing never to drink again. She'd met Ethan at the door last night with takeout and a glass of wine. The last thing she remembered was giggling profusely as she stumbled over to the bed with him.

Ethan had come out from underneath the pillow and was rubbing his eyes when she returned. "Well, don't *you* look sexy?"

She looked down at herself. "I'm not wearing anything."

He cocked his eyebrow and smiled. "Exactly."

"I have got one *hell* of a hangover," she said, tenderly rubbing her temples.

He threw the covers back and patted the mattress. "Why don't you come over here and let Dr. Ethan kiss it and make it better?"

"Tell me, Doctor," she said, straddling his thighs, "just how do you intend on making it better?"

"Mmm, come closer and find out."

Chapter Twenty-three

Grace was in Jessica's office enjoying a caramel latte. It was a guilty pleasure that she allowed herself to occasionally indulge in. She took a long sip, savoring its sweetness. "Since our husbands are playing golf together on Sunday, do you want to see a movie?"

"That sounds like fun. I'll ask Ellen if she can watch Ryan for a little while." Jessica usually tried to give her Sundays off, but felt she would probably make an exception.

Knock-knock.

A young man entered with a bouquet of yellow roses. "Dr. Harrington?"

"Yes?" she said, beaming.

"These are for you."

Grace leaned back in the chair and smiled as she watched her sign for the delivery. "Are they from Ethan?" she asked, after the man had left.

She read the card and pressed it against her heart. "Yes."

"They're beautiful," Grace said, honestly delighted for her. "So things are pretty good between the two of you right now?"

She placed the flowers on her desk and sighed contentedly. "These past few weeks have been wonderful."

Another knock sounded, making them both turn their heads.

Gavin's eyes went from Jessica to Grace. "Sorry to interrupt," he said, seeming startled to see her sitting there.

"It's all right," she replied, standing to go.

"Grace and I were actually in the middle of something," Jessica said with an edge in her voice. "Can you come back a little later?"

The muscle in the side of his jaw twitched as he turned towards the door. "I'll be waiting for you in my office."

Grace watched the exchange between them, feeling as if she were missing something. The smile Jessica had been wearing only moments ago, was now nowhere to be seen. "What was that all about?"

"Nothing," she replied, tucking a golden strand of hair behind her ear.

"It didn't *look* like nothing."

She stared at the roses and sighed. "Gavin wants to start seeing Ryan."

Grace sat back down in the chair. "What did Ethan say?"

She was silent for a long time. "I haven't told him yet," she finally said.

"Why not?"

"Why do you *think?*"

"Jessica, listen to me. Part of being married means that you take the good with the bad. Ethan knew this would probably happen when he came back to you. If you're afraid to tell him things, what's the point of being married?"

She shook her head, grappling for the words to explain her trepidation. "I wish you knew him the way I do, Grace. Deep down, I know that he's still hurting. I can see it in his face sometimes. I just don't want to make it any harder on him."

Grace pursed her lips, remembering the day Jessica had gone with Ethan on a spontaneous trip to Cancun. She had returned five days later, sporting a healthy tan and a ring upon her finger. It was the happiest she had ever seen her. Looking at her now, she found herself wondering how in God's name she had gotten herself into such a mess in the first place. "You're right," she said, after a moment. "It *is* going to be hard for him, but pushing it aside isn't going to help matters. Ultimately, it is going to have to be Ethan's choice to deal with it or not. You can't make that decision for him."

~

Ethan came out of the examining room rubbing the back of his neck. "Sarah, do you have the chart on Mr. Singleton? I can't find it anywhere."

She began thumbing through the folders on her desk. "Here it is."

"Thanks." He gave a small sigh as he sat down in his chair. It had been a long day and he knew he still had two to three hours left. He made a quick note in the chart and returned it to the pile.

Sarah picked it up and promptly dropped it back on his desk. "It doesn't go there."

"That's where I found it," he teased.

"No, that's where *I* found it. *You* couldn't find it because you put it in the wrong place."

Ethan thought of at least half a dozen remarks to make, but felt she wouldn't see the humor in any of them right now. Earlier this afternoon, he had seen Gavin outside the ICU talking to a nurse. His arm was outstretched against the wall as he leaned in close to her. The nurse, all twenty something years of her, was giggling shyly. It was around that same time that he noticed Sarah leaving the ICU nearly in tears.

"Have you heard from Ashley lately?" he asked, hoping to lighten her mood.

"I spoke to her last week. She's doing fine," she answered without bothering to look at him.

He scratched his head. "Why don't we grab a bite to eat?"

"No thanks."

"Oh, come on. Jessica's in surgery, and I can't think of anyone else I'd rather have dinner with."

Her eyes suddenly shot up. "Don't patronize me, Ethan."

"I'm not."

"I'm sorry," she said quietly. "I didn't mean to snap at you."

He leaned back in his chair, thinking carefully about what his next words would be. Although his feelings for Gavin were one-step below loathsome, he had to keep reminding himself that she used to be married to the man. He cared for her too much to say anything disrespectful about him in front of her. He also appreciated the fact that she had the same regard for him, when it came to Jessica. "I saw what happened today," he finally said.

"What do you mean?"

"I saw Gavin chatting up that nurse."

Her eyes darkened as they glowered at him. "If by *chatting up*, you mean flirting, I didn't notice."

"Then why are you letting it bother you so?"

Feeling the heat rising in her cheeks, she looked away.

Ethan reached across the desk and squeezed her hand. "I'm going to be honest with you right now, Sarah, because you've always played it straight with me. I am not patronizing you, or lying to you, when I say that you are too intelligent and beautiful of a woman to sit here and pine away for Gavin. He's not worth it."

~

The next morning, Gavin sat alone in the cafeteria having his third cup of coffee. He frowned as he checked his watch again. He had to get upstairs to surgery soon. Jessica was supposed to have met him over twenty minutes ago, and yet the longer he waited, the angrier he found himself becoming. Certain she had intentionally forfeited the meeting, he drained what was left in his cup and pushed his chair back to go. That was when he saw her heading his way.

She sat down quickly, grateful that he had chosen a table in the corner. "Sorry I'm late."

"Did you talk to him?"

"Yes."

"How did it go?" he asked, unable to hide his anxiousness.

She glanced around to make sure no one was listening. "He agreed that you could see him. *But,*" she said, "only once a week."

An expression of relief broke out over his face. "Thank you, Jessica."

She sighed and nodded.

"Was he upset when you asked him?"

"What do you think?" she said flatly.

~

Ethan gripped the pen tightly as he signed his name to some paperwork. He had been fit to be tied last night when Jessica had asked him if Gavin could spend time with the baby. They had argued about it until way after midnight, and had resumed it this morning. A sudden flash of anger went through him as he thought about Gavin touching Ryan.

"Good morning," Sarah sang out.

"Morning," he answered, pushing his thoughts to the back of his mind. He watched as she practically skipped over to the coffee machine.

She was wearing a bright red dress that nicely accented each and every one of her curves, and when she sat down across from him, he could not help but notice the amount of cleavage she was showing.

She began to hum as she sorted through her mail.

Ethan leaned back in his chair. "You seem to be in an awfully good mood this morning."

"That's because I am."

"Any particular reason?"

She grinned at him from behind her cup. "I have a date tonight."

"Anyone I know?"

"Ben Richards. He works in physical therapy."

"He seems like a nice guy," he said, nodding.

"He is, and I have you to thank for it."

"How's that?"

"Your words yesterday made me stop and think, and after a lot of soul-searching I came to realize that you were right."

Ethan managed a small smile for her personal victory, but secretly found himself wishing that his wife would heed his words as well as Sarah had done.

~

Gavin rushed around his apartment trying to straighten things up the best he could. He picked up the various assortments of dishes and glasses that littered the living room and crammed them in the dishwasher. He then bent over and gathered up all the newspapers and journals in his arms.

Ding-Dong!

Making a rash decision to hide the mess, he dropped to his knees and stuffed everything under the sofa. He then got to his feet and bounded over to the door. "Come in," he said, yanking it open.

Jessica entered, carrying Ryan in his infant seat.

"Is Ethan with you?" he asked, peering behind her.

"No." She placed the infant seat on the sofa. "I thought it would be for the best if I brought him here alone."

"You're probably right," he said, turning his attention to Ryan. Other than seeing him that day in Sarah's office, he had not had any contact with him whatsoever.

"Gavin, we're still in agreement that you won't take him out anywhere, right?"

He nodded his head, knowing that the last thing they needed was for people to start wondering what he was doing with her and Ethan's son. "Right."

She handed him a list of instructions. "This might help if he starts to fuss, and he'll be ready to eat again around seven. His bottle and food are in here," she said, pointing to the diaper bag on the floor.

Gavin listened intently as she went over the list.

"Okay, then. If all goes well tonight, you can start keeping him on your days off. I'll be back at nine to pick him up."

He walked her to the door. "Thank you, Jessica. You don't know how much this means to me."

"Yes, I do," she said, giving him a sad smile.

He tenderly reached out and touched her sleeve. "I'm sorry if this has caused more problems for you and Ethan."

"I'll be back at nine," she replied, giving him a look that said she didn't believe him.

Trying his best to hide his guilt, he watched her get in her car and drive away before closing the door.

Ryan stared curiously at him from his infant seat.

"Hi," he said, unbuckling him. After months of waiting and hoping, he was finally with his son. An overwhelming sense of joy surged through him as he lifted him into his arms. "I think it's time we got to know one another."

Ryan spit out his pacifier and began to cry.

Gavin's joy turned to panic as he began to walk around the living room. "It's okay, Ryan." He did his best to bounce and jiggle him, the way he had seen other people do their babies.

Ryan calmed down a little, but was still whimpering.

"Let's go in here," he said, carrying him into his bedroom. "I have something for you." He stepped over a pile of dirty clothes that lay by the door and pulled out a small sack from his top dresser drawer.

He sat down at the foot of the bed, with Ryan in his lap, and emptied its contents. A vinyl teething ring in the shape of a puppy fell onto the comforter. He picked it up and turned it over in his hand, remembering the day he had bought it. It was just after Sarah had told him they were going to have a boy. It was one of the happiest moments of his life. Swallowing hard, he handed it to Ryan.

The baby closed his tiny fingers around it, and immediately brought it to his mouth.

~

Ethan finished his rounds and stopped in his office to get his coat and lock up. "I thought you had gone already," he said to Sarah, who was busy studying herself in a mirror.

"Ben called and said he's running a few minutes late," she answered, dropping the compact in her purse. "He's going to meet me at the restaurant."

"Well, have a good time," he said, hanging his stethoscope on the peg.

"Ethan, can I get your honest opinion on something as a man?"

"Of course."

She pushed her chair back and got to her feet. "What do you think of this dress?"

"It's nice."

"Just nice?"

"Well, it's very pretty."

"Do you think it's sexy?"

He cocked his left eyebrow, making it disappear underneath his dark locks. "Yes, I do," he said, giving her a playful grin.

She put her hands on her hips and scowled. "I'm being serious."

"So am I."

"No, you're not. You're making fun of me."

"I swear, I'm not," he said, wiping the grin from his face. "Do you have any more questions?"

She looked down at herself for a moment. "Do you think it looks too promiscuous?"

Something that sounded like a snicker disguised as a cough came out of him.

"It's not funny, Ethan."

"I'm sorry," he said, laughing. "But I've never had to help you get ready for a date before."

Deciding that she was wasting precious time with him, she turned away and began fidgeting with the sleeve of her dress.

"Sarah, do you want my honest opinion?"

"Yes."

"You look gorgeous," he said, opening the door. "Ben Richards is a lucky guy."

She looked over her shoulder and smiled at him. "Thank you, Ethan."

He gave her a wink on his way out.

~

McKay's was a fairly nice bar and grill that catered mainly to white-collared businessmen. Ethan found it to be a place where he could relax and enjoy his drink without being bothered.

"Want a refill, Doc?"

"Thanks, Dave," he answered, holding out his glass. When he'd left the clinic tonight, he'd found that he had little desire to go home and be with Jessica—not when he knew what was taking place at this very moment. He felt his jaw tighten at the thought of Gavin holding Ryan. Although he knew this day was coming, he'd always thought that Jessica would see his side of things and not allow it.

He downed his drink and signaled for a refill. Gavin should walk away from this. He should just *walk* away.

~

Sarah took a deep breath as Ben pulled out her chair for her. This was her first date in over six years, and to say that she was nervous was an understatement.

"Is this place all right with you? If not, we can go somewhere else."

"No, this is fine," she said, searching the restaurant for the waiter. "I like *McKay's…*" Her voice faltered when she saw a very familiar face sitting at the bar. She didn't know if he had seen them or not, but she felt like crawling under the table right about now.

Ethan stole a sideways glance at Sarah as he finished his drink.

"Want another?" Dave asked.

He shook his head as he reached into his pocket to pay. "I better head for home," he said, not wanting to make his partner any more nervous than she already appeared to be.

Sarah let out her breath when she saw Ethan get up to leave.

"I hear their salmon is good."

She turned her attention back to Ben as he perused over the menu. His thin, sandy brown hair was combed neatly to the side as day old stubble outlined his face. And although she wasn't going to ask, she guessed him to be about the same age as herself, give or take a year or two.

After a glass of wine, she felt herself relax and the conversation started to flow. She learned that they had a lot in common. He was also divorced and had a fifteen-year-old son, and nineteen-year-old daughter who had just started college.

Ben kept the topics of discussion light, which she greatly appreciated. He was easy going and easy to talk to. The night flew by and before she knew it they were getting up to leave.

He casually put his arm around her waist as he walked her to her car.

"Thank you for dinner, Ben," she said, finding his touch somewhat exciting. "I had a nice time."

"Me too," he said, leaning against her car door. "Would you like to go out again sometime?"

"I'd love to."

He pushed himself away from her door and bent down to kiss her.

It was longer and harder than what she'd wanted, and she drew back when she felt his tongue.

He opened her door for her and smiled. "Goodnight."

~

Ethan stuck his hands in his coat pockets as he hurried across the parking lot. The weather this morning, which was dark and dreary, seemed to match his mood perfectly.

"Ethan, wait up!"

He turned around and stopped.

"Hi," Sarah said, catching up to him. "It's cold this morning, isn't it?"

He nodded as they walked up the steps to the hospital. "How was your date last night?" he asked, pretending that he hadn't seen her at *McKay's*.

"Fine."

"Are you going to see him again?"

"I think I am."

Chapter Twenty-four

The following Thursday, Ethan arrived home after eight. As he pulled into his driveway, he saw a blue sedan parked out front, and immediately recognized it as belonging to Gavin.

He went through the front door expecting to find them in the living room, but heard laughter coming from the upstairs. Feelings that he had done his best to bury, began stirring inside him.

Clenching his jaw, he silently went up the steps and stopped in the doorway of the nursery. Gavin was standing beside the crib with his wife, laughing. Jessica was laughing too, but fell silent when she saw him standing there.

"Ethan," she said, feeling her cheeks flush. "Gavin just brought Ryan home."

He leaned against the doorjamb and folded his arms as he flicked his eyes in Gavin's direction. "Well, if you've brought him home, I guess that means there's no reason for you to be here anymore, is there?"

Gavin cleared his throat. "No, I guess not."

"I'm sure you can show yourself out then," he said sarcastically.

Jessica looked at the floor, embarrassed by his behavior.

Gavin started to say goodbye to her, but thought better of it. Instead, he picked up his coat and went to the door.

Ethan hesitated for a moment, and then stepped aside to let him pass.

The sound of the front door closing echoed off the walls of the nursery as an uneasy silence settled in the room.

Not wanting to fight with him over what had just happened, Jessica leaned over the crib to tend to her son. When she turned back around, Ethan was still leaning against the doorway with his arms crossed, staring at her.

Keeping her eyes on the floor, she walked slowly towards him to leave. As she started across the hallway, he suddenly put his arm against the doorjamb, blocking her. She could smell the scotch on his breath as he leaned in close.

"I don't ever want to come home and find him in this house again."

She forced herself to look into those dark eyes of his; they were cold and hard...unrecognizable to her.

"Do I make myself clear?"

"Yes," she whispered.

He lowered his arm.

She hurried across the hall and swung the door to their bedroom closed. Something inside her made her turn the lock.

~

The next morning, Ethan was sitting on the bathroom floor unscrewing the trap beneath the sink.

Jessica came in carrying a large pan and a wire coat hanger.

"Thanks." He took the pipe off, allowing the water to spill into the pan.

She stood behind him, watching. This morning they had woken up to find the sink clogged, as well as a brownish, water-like substance standing in the tub.

"I swear," he muttered, twisting on the coat hanger, "I don't know what was going through my mind that day when I agreed to buy this house."

She remained silent, not in the mood to offer any assurance.

"Jess, is there something wrong?" he asked, poking the wire into the pipe.

"No," she answered, forcing a small smile.

"Are you certain? You've been awfully quiet."

"I'm going to go get dressed." She walked out, not giving him a chance to reply.

She slipped out of her robe, and pulled on a pair of jeans and a t-shirt before beginning the task of making the bed. She heard Ethan's footsteps behind her as she smoothed the lumps out of the comforter. "Did you have any luck?"

"Not this time. I'm going to have to call a plumber. Are you going anywhere today?"

"I have some errands to run, but I should be home by eleven."

"Okay, I'll see if I can get someone out here this afternoon."

"All right," she said, turning to go.

He caught her around the waist as she brushed past him. "Hey, what's your hurry?"

She felt herself stiffen as he drew her close.

"Hmm?" he asked, bending down to kiss her.

When he pulled back, she caught a glimpse of his eyes. They were warm and caring this morning. "No reason, I guess."

"How about if this evening, I take you out to dinner?"

Jessica stared at him blankly. He was either completely oblivious to his actions last night, or he was trying to apologize. She couldn't tell which.

~

That evening, Jessica hung up the phone and walked over to her bedroom window. It was eight-thirty. The hospital said that Ethan had left the clinic around six.

She went downstairs and into the living room where Mrs. Chambers sat playing with Ryan. "I'm sorry to have kept you so late, Ellen, but you can go now."

The older woman looked at her and frowned. "Are you not going out?"

"No, I'm afraid not. Ethan's still tied up at the hospital."

"I'm so sorry, dear," she said, patting her hand in a motherly fashion. "Maybe you two can go out tomorrow night."

"Yes, maybe," she answered, trying to smile.

~

Upon hearing the garage door open, Jessica turned over and glanced at the clock on the nightstand. It was after midnight. Slipping out of bed, she flipped on the light in the hall and made her way over to the stairs.

She watched from the top of the landing as Ethan tried several times, without success, to step over the baby gate that was latched at the bottom of the steps. "Do you have *any* idea what time it is?"

It took him a moment to find which direction her voice was coming from. "I'm sorry, Jess. I've been at the hospital."

She folded her arms against her chest. "Oh, for God's sake, Ethan! Give me a little bit of credit! I know *exactly* where you've been!"

He gripped the banister as he swayed. "I lost track of time. I'm sorry."

"Not half as sorry as I am," she said, turning on her heel. She stalked back into the bedroom and slammed the door.

~

Jessica hurriedly pulled her hair back into a ponytail and fastened the clip. The hospital had called a few moments ago to tell her that she was needed in surgery right away.

Ryan crawled past her, dragging her purse with him, as he headed into the bathroom.

Slipping on her shoes, she scooped him up before he made it and headed downstairs to the kitchen. In her haste to pull a clean bottle from the dishwasher, she managed to bring several more with it.

Ryan spit out his pacifier and laughed as they clattered against the tile floor.

She looked at him and smiled. "Did Mommy do something funny?" she asked, straddling the bottles.

Mrs. Chambers came in the back door.

"Oh, Ellen. Thank you for coming over here so quickly."

The older woman took off her coat and held her hands out to take Ryan from her. "That's all right, Dr. Harrington."

"'Bye, sweetie," she said, giving him a kiss on the cheek. Remembering that she had left her keys on the coffee table, she hurried into the living room.

Ethan was still asleep on the sofa.

She picked up a large book from off the shelf and let it fall from her hand. The sound of the hardback hitting the wood floor made a resounding thud.

He stirred and opened one eye. Seeing nothing but blinding light, he quickly closed it.

"Ethan."

He opened his eye again, but only as much as he had to. It focused on a pair of pants and moved upwards until he saw Jessica glowering down at him.

"I have an early surgery. It's six-thirty now, don't be late for work."

Before he could open his mouth to reply, she turned and disappeared through the door.

~

Gavin was waiting for Jessica when she came out of the OR.

"How did it go?"

"Pretty well, but I think we're looking at a bypass in the near future," she answered, peeling off her gloves and gown. "I'm going to talk to his wife in a few minutes."

He held the door open for her. "Would you like to join me for a cup of coffee?"

Hearing the kindness in his voice, Jessica wanted to say yes, but thought better of it. She didn't want it getting back to Ethan. The last thing she wanted today was to have another argument.

"Jessica?"

She returned her attention to him and saw that he was waiting for her answer. "I'm sorry, Gavin. Can I take a rain check?"

"Of course," he replied, walking her to the elevator.

As the doors slid open, an orderly and a nurse stepped off, leaving it empty for the two of them.

"Ethan seemed pretty angry with me the other night," he said, pushing the button for twelve.

She didn't answer.

"Is everything okay? Because if it's not, I can wait awhile before I see Ryan again."

She shook her head. "That wasn't why he was mad."

"What, then?"

"He was upset to find you upstairs...with me."

"Oh," he said quietly. "Is there anything I can do?"

"No, we worked things out. Everything's fine," she said, conjuring up the fake smile that she had been wearing for almost two weeks now.

~

Ethan came home from work that afternoon to find Jessica sitting on the foot of their bed. She was staring out the window, appearing to be deep in thought.

She turned at the sound of his footsteps. "You're home early for a Saturday."

"It was slow today," he replied, sitting down beside her. "Did the plumber show up yesterday?"

She nodded. "He was here thirty minutes and charged one hundred and eighty-five dollars."

He tilted his head but didn't say anything.

"Here," she said, reaching behind her. "I bought you a new dress shirt. I had to throw one of yours away the other day. It had blood on it that I couldn't get out."

He reached into the sack and pulled out a royal blue shirt along with a white and navy polka-dotted tie. "Thanks. This was very sweet of you."

She ran her fingers over the tie. "I thought you could wear it with your gray pants."

Guilt circled him as he put them back in the sack. "Jess, I'm sorry about last night. I just completely forgot. If Ellen would watch Ryan, we could go out to dinner tonight, and maybe see a movie."

Jessica fixed her gaze upon the floor, gathering her nerve. "I want you to promise me something, Ethan."

"What?"

"I want you to promise me you'll stop drinking."

"I promise." He nodded. "I won't come home in that condition again."

"No, Ethan," she said, realizing that he wasn't getting it. "I mean that I don't want you drinking...at *all*."

His jaw tightened as he got to his feet. "You're blowing this whole thing out of proportion."

"Am I?"

"Yes," he said, looking at her as if she were stupid.

"The past three nights you have come home drunk."

"Well, in case you hadn't noticed, or just plain don't care, I've been upset about Gavin seeing the baby."

She rose from the bed and folded her arms. "I don't think this is about Gavin. I think that's your excuse." Silence followed her statement. "Where *were* you last night?"

He slid his hands in his pockets. "*McKay's*."

"Why did you go there? You knew yesterday was my day off and that I was waiting at home for you."

Ryan stirred from his nap and began to whine through the monitor.

"I had a rough day yesterday. I just needed a couple of drinks before I came home," he said, raising his voice. "I forgot all about our dinner plans. It was a mistake. I'm sorry, all right?"

"No, it's not all right."

He held his arms out to his sides in frustration. "What else do you want me to say?"

Ryan's whines got louder and more persistent.

"I've got him," he said angrily.

Jessica followed and watched silently from the doorway.

Ethan took Ryan out of his crib and laid him on the changer, where he quickly stripped away his wet diaper and put a dry one underneath him.

Tears started to fall down Jessica's cheeks, shattering her silence. "Ethan?"

"What?" he asked, reaching for the powder.

"When you're drunk…you scare me."

His hands began to tremble as he finished putting the diaper on Ryan. "I never meant to scare you," he said after a moment.

She wiped at her eyes and shook her head. "Just promise me you'll stop." She shrugged her shoulders. "That's all I'm asking."

He picked Ryan up and walked over to where she stood. His face was taut as he reached out and put his arm around her. "I promise."

Chapter Twenty-five

Ben stretched, and put his arm behind Sarah's neck, pulling her towards him. This was their fifth date, and to be quite honest, he felt it was time. Leaning over, he kissed her longingly on the lips.

Sarah closed her eyes, trying to lose herself in the moment, but immediately tensed when she felt his hands on her breasts. "I'm sorry, Ben," she said, breaking away.

He sank back against the sofa and sighed. "Look, I know it's been a long time for you, but it's just like riding a bicycle."

"I remember how to *do* it, Ben. But I don't really even know you."

"Well, that's what I'm trying to change," he said, arching his eyebrows at her.

She giggled and leaned against him, letting her hand run along the crease in his pants.

"Did you know that the best way to get over your ex is to have revenge sex?"

"Is that a fact?"

"It *is*," he said, fingering the button on her blouse. "So, what do you say?"

She pushed herself up and looked into his eyes, wanting to explain herself. "I feel that sex should be a *plus*, not a *reason* for a relationship, Ben. I'd just like to take things a bit slower."

The grin on his face faded as he glanced at his watch. "Well, it's getting late and I've got an early day," he said, rising from the couch.

She followed him to the door and gave him a kiss.

"I'll call you," he said, walking out.

Sarah watched him get into his car and drive away, knowing that would be the last she saw of him.

~

Jessica stood in the hallway by the attic stairs, looking at the opening in the ceiling. "Did you find it?"

"Not yet," Ethan called to her.

She slid her hands up and down her arms in an effort to take the chill away. When it didn't work, she walked to the end of the hall and turned the knob on the thermostat until she heard a click.

With a huge groan, the old furnace kicked on.

She could hear the ceiling creaking above her with each step Ethan took. Suddenly, there was a big thud.

"Ow!"

"Are you all right?"

"I found it!" he answered.

A minute later, he appeared at the opening with the box, and began making his way down the steps. "Is that everything?"

Jessica surveyed the pile of Christmas decorations that now lined the hallway. "I think that's it," she answered, picking a cobweb out of his hair.

"Good, because it's really cold up there."

She stood back as he folded the stairs up and made them disappear into the ceiling.

The two of them then carried everything downstairs and into the living room.

Jessica sat down on the floor and began sorting through the cartons. It was the Tuesday before Thanksgiving, and she wanted to get all the decorations put up beforehand, because Paul and Grace were coming over for dinner that day. Grace had volunteered to help her with the cooking, which in reality meant, that she would do everything and Jessica could watch.

This year, she and Ethan had decided to put the tree right in front of the French doors that led to the front patio. This way, it could be seen from the road. He had bought some lights this afternoon to put up outside. She couldn't wait to see how everything looked when it was all finished.

Her brows furrowed together as she pulled out a string of lights. Every year she promised herself she would pack them away neatly, yet here they were, in one big, knotted glob.

"What would you liked for Christmas this year?"

She smiled as she worked on untangling the cords. "Surprise me."

"All right. A toaster oven it is."

Jessica giggled and turned around. "You know that Christmas falls on a Friday this year," she said, hoping to take advantage of his good mood.

"Mmm-hmm," he answered, straightening one of the tree's artificial branches.

"Well, that gives us a long weekend, and I thought that maybe Gavin could have Ryan the Sunday after." She cringed, waiting for his reply.

"No," he said flatly.

"It would just be for one day. We would have him on Christmas Eve and Christmas," she said, knowing that she was trying his patience.

"Look," he said, standing up. "I don't want Gavin to have him on Christmas weekend. That's all there is to it."

She dropped the lights and walked towards him. "You know, Ethan," she said, playing with the chest hairs that were peeking out of the top of his shirt, "there could be an advantage to letting Gavin have him. We would be all alone."

He pushed her hand away. "Don't patronize me."

"Why do you always have to be so difficult?" she snapped, hurt by his sudden rejection.

"Why do you even have to *ask* when it comes to Gavin?"

She crossed her arms. "Ethan, I am so tired of arguing with you over Gavin seeing him."

"I agreed to let him see him every Thursday, didn't I? *That* was the agreement. I don't think *I'm* the one being difficult."

"Tell me something. What's the difference if he sees him on Thursday, or the holidays?"

"There *is* no difference, Jessica," he said through clenched teeth. "The point is that I don't want Gavin spending any more time with him than he already does. And if I had my way, he wouldn't be seeing him at all."

"So that's it? The mighty Ethan has spoken," she said sarcastically. "I think I should be allowed to have a say in this."

He let the branch fall back into the box. "Meaning, that since I'm not his father, I shouldn't be making any decisions where he's concerned."

"That is *not* what I meant, and you *know* it," she said, rolling her eyes.

"That's not the way it sounded."

"Look, Ethan. You don't know how much I wish that Ryan were your son. I know that all of this has been very painful for you, and I'm sorry. But you're just going to have to learn to deal with it, because it's never going to get any easier for you if you don't."

"Well, I'm sorry if I just can't quite come to terms with the fact that you had another man's *baby!*"

Feeling her face flush with anger, she turned and walked out of the room.

Ethan followed her. "Or would you rather I deal with it the way you did for nine months, and just pretend everything's *fine!*"

She walked up the stairs, pretending not to hear him.

"Is that what you want?" he shouted after her. *"Is it?"*

Jessica made her way into the bathroom and splashed some cold water on her face. This was supposed to have been a fun night. She hadn't meant to get into an argument with him.

When she came out, Ethan was sitting on the bed, looking contrite. "Jess, I'm sorry. I shouldn't have said those things to you," he said softly.

She sat down next to him and sighed. "Ethan, we can't keep doing this. I hate fighting with you."

He let himself fall backwards on the bed. "Why can't we just keep things the way they are?" he asked, rubbing his eyes.

She looked over her shoulder at him. "Because it's not working. Every time Gavin comes to pick him up, or bring him home, you get angry."

"I just can't pretend that this is normal. What's going to happen when Ryan turns five or six and starts to wonder why this other man is spending time with him?"

"I don't know," she answered quietly. "We're just going to have to deal with it when the time comes."

He suddenly sat up and clenched his jaw. "What's he going to call himself? *Uncle Gavin?*"

"Ethan—"

He got to his feet and stalked out.

Jessica remained on the bed. After a few moments, she heard him slam the kitchen cabinet.

She made her way down to the living room. She stared at the half-put together tree and felt the enthusiasm for tonight fading quickly.

Her eyes rested upon a small paper sack on the coffee table. She leaned forward and opened it, knowing what it was.

Pulling out the ornament, she turned it over carefully in her hands. Two white Persian cats sat under a Christmas tree in a background of red. One had a black bow tied around its neck, while the other one had long, beautiful eyelashes. 'Our third Christmas together', was written in cursive on the other side of it, along with the date. She already had the first and second year ornaments from the last two Christmases and had bought this a few weeks ago.

She went over and hung it on the tree, but it did nothing to lift the darkness that had settled in the house.

~

"A penny for your thoughts," Ethan said, handing Sarah a cup of coffee.

"Is that all I get?" she asked glumly, staring out the window of their office.

"Well, okay…fifty cents, then."

"I talked to my daughter last night. She told me that they wouldn't be coming home for Christmas."

"I'm sorry. Did she say why?"

"With tuition and everything, their money has been tight. I offered to pay for their tickets, but she refused." She shook her head and sighed. "Too independent, I guess."

"Well, maybe you can get her to change her mind."

She smiled half-heartedly at him. "Maybe. So, how was your Thanksgiving?"

"It was fine," he answered, but the truth was, it had been very tense. There were times it seemed to him as if Jessica felt that ignoring the problem was the solution. He didn't know if she was just blind to his feelings, or if she truly thought that if they carried on about their duties everything would work itself out.

He took a sip of his coffee and glanced at Sarah. "How was yours?" he asked, realizing it was his turn to speak.

"It was nice. I enjoyed having the time off."

Ethan heard the sadness in her voice and couldn't help feeling sorry for her. He knew how hard it was to be alone. It was something he never wanted to do again.

~

Saturday evening, Jessica stood in her kitchen peeling some carrots for a roast she was attempting to cook, but she was so mad at Ethan right now, she could barely see straight. He hadn't come home last night until after eleven, and she knew *damn* well he hadn't been at the hospital. Not wanting to provoke another argument, she hadn't said anything to him, but this evening, he was already halfway through a bottle of vodka.

"Hi," he said, walking in. "Something smells good."

She drew a deep breath and began chopping on the vegetable.

"Is there something wrong?" he asked, munching on a carrot.

"No." He didn't say anything back to her, and she turned around to see if he was still there.

He was busy taking a long swallow from the glass in his hand. He caught her gaze when he was finished and shrugged his shoulders. "*What?*"

She wiped her hand on the dishtowel. "I thought we had an agreement."

"An agreement about what?"

Her eyes went from him to the glass in his hands.

He let out a long sigh. "It's just one drink. Come on, Jessica, I'm not drunk."

She turned back around and laid another carrot on the cutting board. This had been going on for some time now. She would say something about his drinking, and he would say exactly what he had just told her. "That's your fourth in less than an hour, Ethan."

"Are you counting now?"

She turned to look at him. "You promised me you'd stop!" she said, surprised at the sudden rage in her voice.

He poured the liquid into the sink. "There! Are you happy now?"

She returned her attention to the cutting board.

Ethan tossed the glass in the sink, shattering it.

Jessica kept her back to him, continuing to chop at the now mutilated vegetable. She suddenly felt his hands around her waist.

"Do you know that you're very sexy when you're angry?" he said, kissing her ear.

She let go of the knife and gripped the edge of the granite as he pushed against her. The more she resisted, the harder he tried to persuade her. She felt his tongue roaming along the back of her neck. His hands, strong and sure, began touching her in all the right places. She turned around and met his warm lips with a fiery passion of her own.

Ethan cleared the counter behind her, sending the carrots and knife clattering to the floor.

~

Monday evening, Jessica sat in the living room watching Ryan play. His game at the moment, was to crawl from the chair to her, and then back again. Each time he came up to her, he would laugh. She pretended to laugh, glad that he was too young to understand the difference.

She was still very angry with Ethan over what had happened Saturday, but angrier with herself for having had sex with him; because in *his* mind, she knew that he thought it made everything okay.

The sound of the garage door opening vibrated through the wall.

Ryan stopped crawling and looked at her. "Ba!"

"Yes," she whispered, getting to her feet, "Daddy's home." She picked him up and went into the kitchen to find Ethan rummaging through the cabinets. "You won't find any."

He spun around.

"I poured all of it down the sink."

He knelt back down and began looking again, thinking she was joking. After a minute, he slammed the cabinet shut. "Why the *hell* did you do that?"

"Because I'm *sick* of it, Ethan! I'm *sick* of it! I'm not going to allow you to drink anymore in this house! Understand?"

He walked around the island and over to where she stood. "My God, Jess, you're insane! Do you know that?"

Ryan began to cry.

She lowered her voice. "You're not going to drink in this house anymore."

The muscle in his jaw twitched as his eyes darkened. "Fine!" He grabbed his keys from off the counter and turned towards the door.

She followed on his heels. "Ethan, if you leave this house, don't you *dare* bother coming upstairs when you get home!"

He slammed the door in her face.

"Do you hear me?" she screamed after him.

Chapter Twenty-six

Two days later, Jessica was upstairs changing Ryan when she heard footsteps on the hardwood downstairs. Glancing at the clock, she saw it was six forty-five. She placed Ryan on the floor, and threw the wet diaper in the trash.

"Hi," she heard Ethan say.

Ryan saw his daddy and crawled over to see him.

Ethan grinned as he bent down to pick him up.

Jessica stole a glance at him as she put the wipes away. By his movements, she could tell he'd been drinking. "Come on, sweetie," she said, taking Ryan out of his arms, "let's get your clothes on."

Ethan stuck his hands in his pockets and leaned against the doorjamb. "Why? I think he looks cute in just his diaper."

She laid him down on the changing table. "I have to get him ready for Gavin."

His mood changed abruptly. "He's not supposed to have him until tomorrow."

"He has a surgery scheduled for tomorrow."

"Well, thanks for telling me."

She took a deep breath and counted to three. "I discussed this with you last night."

Ethan thought back. He vaguely remembered the conversation, but didn't acknowledge it out loud to her.

The doorbell sounded as she slid the shirt over the baby's head. Out of the corner of her eye, she noticed that Ethan made no motion to answer it. Ryan was making it nearly impossible for her to dress him quickly, as he kept flopping over and trying to crawl away.

The doorbell rang again.

"Ethan would you please go let him in?"

He left the nursery, taking his time as he went down the stairs.

"Ethan," Gavin said, nodding. He stuck his hands in his coat pockets as the wind whipped about his face. The current temperature was twenty-nine with a wind-chill of eighteen.

Ethan kept his hand on the door, making no offer for him to come inside.

"Thanks for letting me switch nights. I really appreciate it."

"Jessica will be down in a minute," he said coldly.

It was the longest minute Gavin had ever known, and he was relieved when she finally appeared at the door.

She exchanged a subtle glance with Ethan, mentally telling him to move his arm.

He reluctantly stepped back, allowing her to hand the baby to him. His stomach began to churn as he watched Gavin take him in his arms. He turned away with his hands clenched and stalked into the living room.

"I'm sorry," Jessica said, shaking her head.

"It's all right," he answered. "I'd probably feel the same way if the situation was reversed."

She closed the door behind him and went into the kitchen, bypassing Ethan in the living room. These past couple of days they had barely spoken to one another, and it looked as if tonight was shaping up to be no different.

Peering into the refrigerator, she realized that the choices for dinner were slim. She stood with the door ajar for a few seconds more before deciding upon a peanut butter and jelly sandwich. She thought about making one for Ethan, but knew he wouldn't eat it. The only thing he wanted was his scotch.

The telephone rang as she hunted in the drawer for a butter knife. She could tell by its ring that it was the hospital calling. They had to have two phone lines because of the constant calls for either herself or Ethan. "Hello?"

"Dr. Harrington. This is Bonnie calling from ICU. I have a patient of your husband's that's just been admitted by the attending."

"He's not home yet, Bonnie, but I'll have him call you as soon as he gets here." She hung up the phone quickly before the nurse could reply.

"Was that for me?"

She glanced over her shoulder. Ethan was standing behind her. "Yes."

"Why did you say I wasn't home?"

"Because," she said, walking back over to the counter.

"Because why?"

"Because you're too drunk to be making any medical decisions."

He grabbed her roughly by the arm and spun her around to face him. "Don't you *ever* do that again! Do you understand me?"

"You're hurting me," she said, trying to pull away.

His grip tightened. "Answer me."

Jessica felt her breath catch in her throat as his hand fell across her face.

He immediately let her go.

A cry fell from her lips as she began backing away.

"Jess—"

She turned and ran up the stairs.

His cell phone began to vibrate, making it walk across the countertop. With trembling fingers, he picked it up. "Dr. Harrington," he whispered.

~

Ethan sat at the top of the stairs with his head in his hands, listening to his wife sobbing. He had tried several times during the past three hours to talk to her, but she refused to open the door.

He closed his eyes as the incident played over and over again in his mind. He remembered the sudden burst of rage he'd felt just before it happened, but by the time he had gained control, it was too late.

Ding-dong!

He got to his feet and sighed, knowing it was Gavin.

"Thanks again for letting me see him tonight," he said, handing him Ryan, along with the diaper bag.

Ethan's eyes were expressionless as he closed the door in his face.

~

Jessica hugged herself tightly as she watched the headlights of Gavin's car back out of the driveway. No matter how hard she tried, she could not stop herself from shaking. Never in a million years did she ever think that Ethan would hit her.

An uncontrollable shiver went down her, making her stomach hurt. She had never been more terrified in her life.

Curling up on the bed, she drew her pillow against her as the sobs started all over again.

~

The next morning, Ethan stood at the counter in the kitchen mixing up some cereal for Ryan, who, at the moment, was sitting on the floor having a fit. "Daddy's hurrying as fast as he can," he said, adding the hot water to the bowl.

Ryan crawled across the floor and grabbed onto his leg, raising his screaming another decibel.

Ethan closed his eyes as his shrieking pierced his ears. His back hurt from sleeping on the couch last night, and he had a terrible headache. "Come here," he said, bending down to scoop him up. Figuring it would be quicker to feed him in his lap, he decided to forgo the highchair.

Ryan pushed the back of his head against Ethan's chest as he continued to scream.

Ethan shoved the spoon into the bowl and brought it to his lips. "Shh…here you go."

It was instant gratification.

He sighed, wishing that his own problems could be fixed with a bowl of cereal.

Jessica came down the stairs and stopped just short of the doorway. Her movements made Ethan turn his head. His eyes, full of remorse, locked with hers briefly, before looking away.

She went up to the table and sat down across from him.

He gave Ryan the last spoonful of cereal and wiped his mouth. "I'm sorry," he said to her quietly as he placed him on the floor.

Jessica felt her lips start to tremble. "How could you do that to me?"

He slid out of his chair and knelt in front of her. "You've got to believe me when I tell you that I didn't mean to do it. It just happened," he said, reaching for her hand.

"It *happened* because you were drunk." She stood up and went over to the sink.

He got up from where he had been kneeling and turned around. He watched as Ryan crawled over to her and whined. "You're right," he said, walking up to her. "I was drunk. But it will *never* happen again. I promise."

Jessica held her breath as she began to cry. Silent tears rolled down her face.

Ethan saw her shoulders shaking and went to put his arms around them.

"Don't," she said, shrugging him off.

"Jess...come here."

"No."

"Come here," he said again, pulling her close. "I can't stand it when you cry." He pressed his cheek against hers as he stroked the back of her hair. "I'm sorry. I am so very sorry. Please tell me that you forgive me."

"Promise me that you won't drink anymore," she murmured into his shoulder.

"I promise," he whispered.

She lifted her head up and looked into his eyes, desperately wanting to believe him.

He brushed her tears away with his thumb and nodded. "I promise."

~

Jessica lingered by her locker, waiting until the room was empty. Staring at the small mirror that was adhered to the inside of the metal door, she looked solemnly at her face. There was no evidence that Ethan had struck her, but there were dark bruises forming on her upper arms where he had held her. She pulled her scrub shirt off and slipped the cable-knit sweater over her head.

"Jessica?"

She spun around. "Grace. How long have you been standing there?"

"I'm sorry, I didn't mean to startle you."

"It's all right," she replied, quickly slipping her arms through the sleeves.

"I think I'm headed out to do some Christmas shopping," Grace said, grabbing her purse from her locker. "Do you want to come along? We could stop and eat at the new Chinese place."

"I'd love to, but I think I'm just going to head home and sink into a hot bath."

"Is everything okay?"

"Of course," she said in the most enthusiastic voice she could find. "Why do you ask?"

"I don't know. You just act like something's bothering you."

"And you know this based on what?" she asked curtly as she grabbed her coat from her locker. "Your background in psychology?"

Grace tilted her head, giving her a hurtful look. "No…based on our friendship."

"I'm sorry," she said miserably, sitting down on the bench.

"What's wrong?"

"Ethan and I have been arguing a lot lately."

"About what?"

"Everything," she said with a sigh. "But mostly about his drinking."

The older woman thought back for a moment. She remembered seeing him at Paul's birthday party earlier in the year. He had put away four glasses of scotch and was unscathed.

"You know, Grace, he's always drank…I mean for as long as I've known him, but I've never really given it much thought until now."

"And why now?" she asked softly.

Jessica felt the sting of tears. "Because lately, he doesn't stop until he's drunk."

"Have you tried talking to him about it?"

She tucked her hair behind her ears and nodded. "Several times. We had another long talk about it this morning, and he promised me that he would stop."

"Do you not believe him?"

"I don't know," she said bitterly.

~

Ethan jockeyed for position at the jewelry counter in the department store. The mall was full of angry, tired adults and screaming children.

"Can I help you, sir?" asked the young woman behind the counter.

"Um...yes. Can I see those, please?" He pointed to a pair of earrings displayed underneath the glass.

The sales clerk unlocked the door and reached in to retrieve them. "These are one and a half carat with twenty-four carat gold backings," she said in a voice that told him she was ready to go home.

He held the small box in his hand and turned it towards the light. The diamonds sparkled brightly. A faint smile formed on his lips as he pictured Jessica wearing them. Perhaps he was buying them more out of guilt than love, but he *did* love her, and he wanted to show her how much. He handed them back to the clerk and nodded. "I'll take them."

~

Jessica woke up and glanced around the room. The sun was just beginning to filter through the curtains, telling her it was still early. She pressed her head further into her pillow and yawned, reflecting on the dream she'd had about Everett last night.

It was summertime, and he was playing with Ryan on the swing set—except Ryan wasn't a baby anymore. He was about three or four years old. She recalled how his beautiful black hair tossed about as Everett pushed him on the swing.

He was giggling with delight and kept yelling, "Higher, Grandpa! Higher!"

Every now and then Everett would throw his head back and laugh.

Jessica turned her head into the pillow as a tear rolled down her cheek. She guessed he must have been on her mind with the holidays coming up. Perhaps he had been on Ethan's mind as well. Maybe that was why he had been drinking so much.

Last night had been nice. They had spent a quiet evening eating pizza in front of the television. There had been no arguments or accusations, and for the first time in a very long time, he hadn't come home smelling of liquor.

She stretched and turned over, knowing that Ryan was going to wake up any minute.

Ethan instinctively snuggled up behind her and threw his arm across her. "Love you," he mumbled.

Jessica settled against his chest as she held onto his arm, remembering that Ryan had Ethan's eyes and hair in her dream. "Me too," she whispered.

~

Ethan was pouring himself a cup of coffee when Sarah arrived.

"Good morning!"

"Morning."

"Guess what?"

He took a sip of his coffee before answering, finding that she was way too chipper for him. "What?"

She clasped her hands together and took a deep breath. "Ashley called me yesterday to tell me that she and Ted are coming home after all."

"That's great!" he said grinning. "But I thought they couldn't afford it."

She shook her head, making her red locks bounce softly upon her shoulders. "They couldn't, but she told me that they won two free tickets to anywhere in the U.S."

"You're kidding."

"The airline called them and said that their name had been randomly selected by the computer, and that it was part of their promotion for the holidays." She paused a moment to catch her breath. "It was something about them being on a list of U.S. citizens. Each year the airline gives away dozens of tickets so people can fly home." Her smile covered her entire face. "Isn't that wonderful?"

"Absolutely."

"They'll be here on Christmas Eve and stay until the fifth or sixth. So would you mind if I took off those days?"

"No, of course not. You deserve it."

"Well, I hate leaving you to fend for yourself. It's always a mad house around here over the holidays."

"Sarah, you're the only one I know who feels guilty about taking vacations."

She opened her mouth to defend herself but the telephone interrupted her. "Clinic. Dr. –"

"Sarah, it's Gavin. Do you have a few minutes? I really need to talk to you."

"Um, I guess so. I can stop by after I make my rounds."

"Can you do your rounds after? This is really important, and I've got surgery in an hour."

"All right," she said, hearing the urgency in his voice.

"Thanks."

Sarah grabbed her stethoscope and then hurried upstairs to Gavin's office.

"Thanks for coming," he said, closing the door behind her.

She sat down in one of the chairs across from his desk and let her eyes wander for a moment. She had forgotten just how huge his office was—and the furniture in it hadn't come out of the storage room in the hospital basement, either. His desk was mahogany, and was the size of hers and Ethan's put together. A pair of matching bookcases, with very expensive knick-knacks adorning them, lined the wall behind it. She had always been slightly envious of him, thinking it unfair that he got whatever he wanted from the board just because he was head of cardiology.

Gavin leaned forward in his chair and cleared his throat, drawing her attention. "I don't really know where to start."

She shoved her jealousy to the side when she saw the expression on his face. "What's wrong?"

"I asked Jessica if I could have Ryan the Sunday after Christmas, but she told me no," he said. "I know it's because Ethan was the one who refused. And I know that I have no right to ask you this, but I was wondering since you're such good friends, if maybe you could try to talk to him." He finished and looked at her hopefully.

She felt her blood pressure starting to rise.

Gavin began to cringe.

"This? This was what was so *damned* important?" She stood up and walked around the chair. "God! I can't believe you, Gavin!"

"Look, I just thought—"

"Thought what? That I would put in a good word for you?

"Ethan listens to you. I thought you could get him to change his mind."

She walked directly up to him and pointed a finger at his chest. "This is *your* problem. *You* were the one that had the affair, and he's *your* son. None of this has to do with me. And don't you *ever* ask me again to take advantage of my friendship with Ethan just so you can get your way!"

~

Jessica stretched languorously on the sofa as the afternoon sun spilled into the room. There was a reason Sundays were lazy. This was the only day of the week that she and Ethan were off at the same time, and except for the occasional emergency at the hospital, they usually spent it together. She buried her toes under the afghan and took a sip of her coffee as she turned the page of the newspaper.

Ethan was sitting on the floor with the camcorder stuck in Ryan's face. "Ryan, can you say 'Dadda'? Hmm? Come on, say it for me," he pleaded.

"Ethan, you're going to make him blind," she teased.

Ryan reached out and touched the lens. "Ba!"

"That's close. Now, say 'Dadda'."

Jessica rolled her eyes and chuckled as she picked the newspaper back up. He had been trying to get him to say that for over a week now. A second or two later, she saw the light from the camcorder shining her way.

"Let's see what Mommy's doing."

"Ethan, don't. I look terrible."

He walked towards her, viewing her through the lens, oblivious to the coffee table in front of him.

She threw the afghan over her head. "Ethan, please."

His shin suddenly found the corner of the table. "Ow!" he exclaimed, falling backwards into the chair.

She uncovered her head and began to giggle.

He turned the camera off and rubbed his shin.

"Serves you right," she said, still snickering.

"That's not very nice. I'm probably bleeding, and you're sitting there laughing," he said, pretending to be hurt. "Ryan, can you believe Mommy? She's laughing at me."

Ryan looked at him and smiled. "Dadda."

Ethan's eyes grew big. "Did you hear him? He said it! He said 'Dadda'!"

She got off the sofa and picked him up. "You said it, didn't you?" she cooed.

He turned on the camcorder again. "Okay, Ryan. Say it once more for Daddy. Please...say 'Dadda'."

Jessica smiled as she turned Ryan towards the camera.

~

Monday morning, Sarah stood outside her office rummaging in her purse for the keys when she saw Gavin walking towards her.

"Can I speak to you for a moment?"

She unlocked the door and flipped on the lights. "What do you want?" she asked, tossing her purse on the desk.

"I owe you an apology for the other day."

She crossed her arms and looked at him expectantly. "I'm listening."

"I'm sorry. It was wrong of me to ask you to talk to Ethan."

"Yes, it *was* wrong of you. It was also selfish and rude." She paused for a moment, not wanting to lose her temper with him again. "Letting you see Ryan is a very delicate subject with Ethan, and as far as I'm concerned, it's between him and Jessica. I'm not about to try and convince him otherwise."

The door swung open and Ethan walked in grinning from ear to ear. "Sarah, guess what Ryan said yester—" He stopped short when he saw Gavin standing there. "I'm sorry. I didn't mean to interrupt."

"Oh, you're not," she said quickly. "I was just telling Gavin about Ashley coming home."

Gavin slid his hands in his pockets, choosing to remain silent.

She cleared her throat as if to eradicate the tension that had settled in the room. "So tell me, what did Ryan say yesterday?"

"It was nothing," Ethan said, seeming to have lost his enthusiasm.

Gavin turned to her with a bitter expression upon his face. "I'll talk to you later about Ashley."

Sarah gave him a nod and waited for the door to close behind him before turning her attention back to Ethan. "What did Ryan say?" she prompted him again.

He began sorting through the mail on his desk. "It doesn't matter," he replied, clearly wanting to drop it.

~

That night Jessica was upstairs trying in vain to get Ryan to sleep. He was cutting another tooth, which was making both of them miserable. She patted him gently while rocking him back and forth, and noted with relief that he had finally started to close his eyes.

It was then that she heard the phone ringing in their bedroom. The sound of it told her it wasn't the hospital, so she opted to let the machine answer it in order to avoid getting Ryan roused up again.

The baby's eyes opened and closed with the motion of the rocking chair as he twisted the ends of her hair around his tiny fingers.

Eventually his eyes closed for good and she felt him go limp. She rocked him for another five minutes or so for good measure before putting him down in his crib. Warmth, coupled with sadness, flooded her as she watched him sleeping. It wasn't going to be long before he was walking and talking. Time had never moved so fast.

She turned off the light and went downstairs to the kitchen to see who had called earlier.

The machine beeped before playing back the message.

"Hi, sweetheart, it's me. I'm tied up here at the hospital. I'll try to be home as soon as I can, but it's probably going to be late when I get in. Love you."

She walked over to the table and sat down, feeling her stomach begin to knot.

~

Jessica woke up to the sound of water running. Rolling over, she squinted at the clock on the nightstand and saw that it was just past six.

Ethan was standing over the sink getting ready to shave when she came in. "Hi," he said, lathering his face.

She crossed her arms. "Would you like to tell me where you were last night?"

"Didn't you get my message?"

She took a deep breath, trying to control her anger. "Don't you stand there and lie to me. I *called* the hospital. You left around eight."

He drew the razor across his face. "Are you checking up on me now?"

"What were you doing until one o'clock this morning?"

"Well, I wasn't out *screwing* around if that's what you're worried about."

She shook her head in disbelief and turned to go, but suddenly stopped. "You know what? I wish you *were*. Because I could deal with another woman...but not this."

He laid the razor on the sink and looked at her reflection in the mirror.

Storming out, she walked across the bedroom and jerked open the closet to get dressed for work. As she let her nightgown fall to the floor, Ethan's hands were suddenly upon her. He held her from behind, kissing the back of her neck and shoulders, his bare chest warm against her. She pushed his hands away, still upset.

He turned her around to face him. "Please don't be mad," he whispered, bending down to kiss her on the lips. His hands slipped inside her panties, caressing her buttocks.

Jessica stopped resisting and let him make love to her. It was the only way she could be close to him—if only for a little while. During this brief moment, he was hers, and she was the only thing that mattered to him. She closed her eyes and breathed him in. She loved him. She loved him more than he would ever know.

Chapter Twenty-seven

Ethan's cell phone rang as he downed his drink at *McKay's.* He picked it up from off the bar and looked at the screen. It was Jessica again. She had called three times in the past hour. He turned it off and signaled the bartender for another. This afternoon, they'd had yet another argument at the hospital, leaving him with no desire to go home anytime soon.

"There you go, Doc." Dave finished pouring him his drink, before moving to answer the phone. "*McKay's.*"

"Yes, I'm looking for Ethan Harrington. Sometimes he stops in there?" Jessica held the phone against her ear. This was the sixth bar she was calling.

"Hang on a second and I'll check, okay?" Dave held the receiver against his chest. "Has anyone seen Doc Harrington?" he called out loud enough for her to hear him.

Ethan shook his head.

"I'm sorry, ma'am, he's not here."

"Thank you," she said quietly before hanging up.

~

The next morning, Ethan was in one of the examination rooms going over the inventory. He and Sarah were busy compiling the budget request for next year.

"How many?" she called to him from the office.

"Eight dozen," he answered, closing the cabinet.

Sarah punched in the numbers on her calculator, subtracting what they still had in inventory versus how much they had purchased for this year.

She and Ethan were only halfway finished, yet she already knew they were going to have to ask for more money than last year. She also knew that it would not sit well with Phillip.

The door swung open, making her turn to see who it was.

Jessica marched in, her eyes searching the room until she found her husband.

Ethan looked over when he saw her, but didn't say anything.

"Are you going to come home tonight at a decent hour?" she asked, walking into the examining room.

"Don't start," he said in a low voice.

"I'm not starting anything. I just want to know if you're going to come home *sober* tonight."

Ethan glanced into the other room, locking eyes with Sarah, before closing the door.

"What's the matter? You don't want Sarah to know that you stay out all hours of the night drinking?"

"I am *not* going to argue with you right here. Can we discuss this later, please?"

Jessica put her hand on her hip. "And just when might that be? The only time I see you is here at the hospital."

Sarah sat at her desk with her back to the door, trying to go about her business, but the shouting that was going on behind it was making it difficult.

A minute or two later, the door jerked open, revealing Ethan's voice in mid-sentence. "...else to you want me to say?"

"Nothing!" answered Jessica, stalking out. She crossed the small hallway and then turned back around. "You *better* be home tonight by seven, and you *better* be sober—or don't bother coming home at all."

Ethan clenched and unclenched his jaw as he watched her disappear through the door. He was embarrassed by her behavior just now, and angry that it had happened in front of Sarah.

After a moment, he walked out and began leafing through the papers on top of his desk. "Sorry about that."

Sarah stopped pretending to be studying the figures and looked up. "Is everything okay?" she asked quietly.

Ethan rubbed his chin, avoiding her gaze. "She's just overreacting."

~

Grace stuck her head in Jessica's office later that afternoon. "Ready for a coffee break?"

She closed the chart in front of her and nodded wearily. "Absolutely."

The older woman placed a Styrofoam cup on her desk and sat down. "What a day," she said with an exaggerated sigh.

"You too, huh?"

"There's nothing like the holidays to bring the weirdoes out of the woodwork. I am so looking forward to having some time off for Christmas. How about you?"

Jessica forced a smile, not wanting to burden Grace with her problems.

"I was thinking that the four of us could ride together to the party tomorrow night," she said, taking a sip of her coffee.

"That would be nice."

"Have you gotten your Christmas shopping all done?"

Jessica struggled to maintain her smile as she talked with her friend. "Yeah. Now I just have to wrap all of it," she answered. "How about you?"

"Yes, and as usual Paul told me that I'd spent way too much on our granddaughters."

"Well, what's the point of having grandchildren if you can't spoil them?"

Grace shook her head and laughed. "That's *exactly* what I told him!"

Jessica sometimes wondered how her cousin put up with Paul. He was quite the tightwad.

"What did you finally decide to get for Ethan?"

"I got him a new five-iron that he's been wanting."

"Well, I got Paul something that he's going to hate."

"That's nice," she said absently.

Grace eyed her curiously. "How are things right now between you and Ethan?"

She swallowed hard and looked away, feeling that if she spoke, everything was going to come tumbling out. "Not good," she answered after a moment.

"Is he still drinking?"

"You know, Grace, I thought if I got rid of it all, he would know that I was serious and stop. So a few weeks ago I poured every bottle we had down the sink, and told him he couldn't drink in the house anymore." She tilted her head. "Of course, that didn't work out the way I'd planned."

"What do you mean?"

"He's going to the bars to do it, and not coming home until one or two in the morning. It's not just occasionally anymore, Grace—it's four or five nights a week. I swear to God, I don't know how he manages to drive himself home, he's so drunk."

Grace was silent for a long time. When she did speak, her voice was as delicate as it was serious. "Have you tried talking to him about Alcoholics Anonymous?"

Something that sounded like a cross between a laugh and a cry came out of her. "There is no way that I could get Ethan to attend an AA meeting."

"Well, the first step is getting him to admit that he has a problem."

"According to him, he doesn't have one." She held her hands up in the air. *"He can handle his drinking just fine!"* she said, mocking him.

Grace's mind quickly churned. "Well, I do have one more alternative."

"What is it?" she asked hopefully.

"Maybe I can get Paul to talk to him."

~

Ethan hurried into the nursery and flipped on the light, momentarily blinding both him and Ryan. "Hey, what's the matter?" he said, making his way over to the crib.

Ryan held his arms out as tears streamed down his face.

He picked him up and gave him a kiss as he felt of his diaper. "Are you wet? No? Did you have a bad dream?" He leaned over and retrieved his pacifier from the crib. "Let's go over here," he said, making his way to the rocking chair.

Ethan snuggled him against his chest as he began to rock him. "You're getting so big. You're going to be grown before I'm ready to let you go," he whispered.

Ryan sucked on his pacifier, seeming content to be in his arms. Ethan smiled down at him. "The first thing Daddy's going to teach you how to do is play catch. And then, I'm going to show you how to ride a bicycle. I'm going to take you to baseball games and the circus. I *have* to take you to the circus. And if you're really good..." he said, tickling him on his neck, "I'll buy you a puppy. Because all little boys have to have a puppy. I think it's a rule."

A small sigh suddenly fell from his lips. "Then one day, you're going to outgrow your tricycle, and your bicycle, and I'll have to buy you a car. *But,*" he said, shaking his head, "it's not going to be a fast one. I don't want you getting hurt."

Ryan looked at him with those painfully innocent eyes of his.

"All right, I'll *think* about a sports car..."

~

Jessica silently tiptoed past the nursery and slipped into the bedroom.

"How was your surgery?" Ethan asked in the darkness.

"What are you doing awake?" She had been more than a little surprised to find his car in the garage.

"Ryan woke up. I just got him back to sleep."

Jessica heard the edge in his voice as he spoke. She knew he was still mad over what she had said to him this morning. Too exhausted to take a shower, she felt her way over to the bed and sat down to undress.

She heard the covers rustling behind her and then the touch of Ethan's hands upon her shoulders. "That feels good," she said, feeling the tension drain from her body as he rubbed the area just below her neck.

She could smell his aftershave as he brushed her hair away from her shoulders. Turning around, she placed her hand upon the side of his face and leaned over to kiss him. His lips were warm and tasted of scotch.

Ethan settled back against the pillow and held his arm out to her.

She stretched out beside him, laying her head upon his chest. "I'm sorry about today."

He was silent for a long time. "I did what you asked," he finally said. "I'm home...and I'm sober."

She sighed inwardly. His definition of sober and hers were obviously not the same. Feelings of hopelessness began to surround her.

"Jess?"

"What?" she answered, trying to swallow the ache in her throat.

"I don't want Gavin to see the baby anymore. You and I are going to raise him together *without* his interference...or I'm going to leave."

Chapter Twenty-eight

The next afternoon, Sarah was at her computer typing up the budget report for the clinic. She was a fairly good typist when it came to words, but had to hunt and peck for the numbers on the keyboard.

"Do you think you'll be done typing that before the Christmas party tonight?" Ethan asked with a smirk upon his face.

"I type faster than *you,*" she retorted.

He closed the file in front of him and stood up.

"So, what time are you and Jessica going to be there tonight?"

"I don't know," he answered with a groan as he walked over to get his coat. "Have I told you how much I'm looking forward to this evening?"

"Only about fifty times." He was referring to the annual Christmas party that was held for the members of the board and its contributors. It was sort of a way to thank those who had donated money to the hospital, as well as secure their funding for the coming year. Of course, the latter involved some major brown-nosing. "Are you heading home?"

"I've got to stop by Paul Cumming's office and sign some papers first, but I'll see you tonight."

~

Paul sat across from Ethan, explaining the various documents that he was putting his signature on regarding his father's company. There was quite a stack to sign as things were getting pushed through before the end of the year.

Ethan flipped the page and checked his watch.

"I promise you'll be out of here in time for the party."

"Honestly, I'd rather stay here and sign papers."

"I know what you mean. I'm probably going to get stuck talking with Phillip all night."

"I'll trade you Meredith for Phillip any day." Ethan grinned, scrawling his signature on the form.

"Maybe we can work out a deal, then," Paul said with a chuckle as he struggled with what to say to him next. He absolutely hated getting involved in his and Jessica's personal problems, but he also did not want to be on the receiving end of Grace's wrath.

He had learned a long time ago that it was better to have your wife on your side over your best friend. "You know," he said, clearing his throat, "I saw you the other day."

"Where was that?"

"I passed you in your car on Third Street. It looked like you were turning into *McKay's*."

"Yeah, I probably was," he answered, flipping over to the next page.

"It seems like I've seen you there a lot lately."

"Have you?"

Paul was silent.

Ethan looked up from the paper, feeling a surge of anger. "Did Jessica put you up to this?"

Paul hesitated. "She asked me if I would talk to you, yes."

"I don't believe this," he said, shaking his head.

"She's very concerned about you."

He stood up. "Look, Paul, I think I know where this conversation is headed, and it's pointless."

"Why are you getting so defensive?"

"I'm not."

He leaned back in his chair trying not to intimidate him any further. "Jessica told Grace you've been coming home drunk."

"My wife has a tendency to exaggerate."

"She said that it's happened more than once."

"Come on, Paul," he said, trying to reason with him. "After working all day, I just need to unwind. You know what that's like, don't you?"

He nodded. "I do."

"So I have a few drinks. What's the harm in that?"

"Nothing. As long as it doesn't become your primary source for relaxing."

He pushed the papers across the desk. "I have to go."

"I'm not judging you, Ethan. I'm just looking out for a friend, okay?" He put his hand on his shoulder as he walked him to the door. "Are we still on for tonight?"

"Yeah," he muttered, reaching for his coat.

"All right, we'll pick you up around seven."

Ethan left the office, embarrassed and angry.

~

Jessica was in the bathroom fixing her hair when she heard him come in. "You're late," she called.

He tossed his jacket down on the bed. "You can blame Paul for that."

"I stopped on my way home and picked up your long black coat from the cleaners."

He muttered something under his breath as he began to change.

She walked into the bedroom. "Is there something wrong?"

"Oh, don't play dumb with me, Jessica!" he said, throwing his shirt on the floor. "You know what you did!"

"Well, forgive me for caring about you, Ethan!"

He grabbed a fresh shirt out of the drawer. "You had no right to talk to him. No right whatsoever."

"I had *every* right, Ethan. And it's not like I went behind your back. I have tried talking to you about this, but you won't even listen."

"Well, maybe that's because you sound like a broken record."

"I really don't think you understand how serious this is," she said, folding her arms across her. "When was the last time you spent an evening home with me? How long has it been?"

"Has it ever occurred to you, "he said, slipping his tie through his collar, "that I might spend more time with you if you weren't such a nag?"

Her face flushed. "You are *not* the same man I married, and certainly *not* the same man that I fell in love with!"

"I think you've got me confused with Gavin."

"Don't you *dare* bring him into this! Every time we fight, you just *have* to drag all that up!"

He sat down and slipped on his shoes.

"I don't want you drinking tonight."

"It's a fundraiser, Jessica," he said with a sigh. "Everyone there is going to be drinking."

"Well, I don't want *you* doing it, okay?"

He walked over to the dresser and slid open the top drawer.

"I asked you a question."

The side of Ethan's jaw grew rigid as he slammed the drawer shut. "You know, I'm beginning to think that I made a big mistake with you."

"Meaning what?"

"Meaning, that maybe I never should have come back!"

Jessica looked at him, her eyes full of hurt. "Maybe you're right."

The silence that followed was deafening, and was only cut short by the sound of the doorbell.

~

Sarah picked up her glass of wine at the bar and meandered across the room, chiding herself for being punctual. There were only about a dozen or so people here, none of whom she really knew except for Meredith. She shivered at the thought of having to make conversation with her, and was relieved when she saw Gavin walk in.

He was looking very dapper in his dark suit. It was quite a contrast to his khaki pants and sport coat; his main wardrobe. She also couldn't help noticing that he had come alone.

Upon spotting Sarah, he handed the attendant his coat and made his way over to her. "Hi," he said. "You look nice."

"Thank you." She was wearing a royal blue dress that was cut modestly low in the front and back.

Their conversation faltered as quickly as it had started.

"You know that Ashley and Ted are coming in," she said, grasping for something to say.

"I'm looking forward to seeing them," he replied with a nod.

"She told me that she would really like for you to join us for Christmas dinner."

Gavin hesitated. "I don't want to make things uncomfortable for you."

"I'm okay with it. Unless, you have other plans."

He gave her a small smile. "I don't."

She smiled back at him, feeling as if a barrier had been broken.

"Can I bring anything?"

"Well, you could bring some wine if you want."

"Red or white?" he asked absently.

"White…" She noticed as she spoke that he was no longer looking at her. Turning slightly, she followed his gaze across the room. The Harringtons had just arrived. Jessica was wearing a tight, red cocktail dress that accented her petite figure enviably. "White would be lovely," she said, trying to draw his attention.

"Excuse me," he said, brushing past her.

Sarah watched as he cut a path towards Jessica, discarding her like an ugly, useless thing.

~

Paul and Ethan were talking quietly at the bar when they heard the unmistakable shrill voice of Meredith Van Owen. Both men turned at the same time to face her.

"Paul, Ethan, it's so nice to see the both of you," she said, squeezing in between them.

"Meredith. You look radiant," Ethan said, feigning interest in her.

She touched the bun in the back of her frosted hair and smiled. "Oh, thank you."

"It looks like we're going to have quite a turnout," Paul said.

Her eyes sparkled brightly. "Yes, it certainly looks that way doesn't it?"

If there was one truth to be told about Meredith, it was that she thrived on parties—especially ones of a social nature.

"Oh! There's someone over there that I must say hello to. Now, both of you promise me a dance later, all right?"

As she scurried off to her next victim, Paul and Ethan looked at each other and sighed.

Ethan made it a point not to finish his drink and excused himself from the bar. Although Paul had not said anything else to him, he felt as if he were being scrutinized. He saw Sarah across the way and headed towards her.

The Christmas party was being held this year at the Sidebrook Inn, a posh restaurant on the north side of town. It had a large room in the back that could be used for parties, seminars, or receptions, and came complete with a wet bar and live band.

Of course, all the members of the band looked to Sarah as if they should be in a nursing home. None of them, all wearing matching green blazers, appeared to be under the age of seventy. The sound of the clarinets and other woodwind instruments grated over her nerves like fingernails on a chalkboard.

In the distance, she noticed Ethan approaching and smiled.

"There she is, still wearing that smile. How many more days is it?"

She threw her head back and laughed. "Two more. But who's counting?" He was, of course, referring to Ashley's coming home.

"You look very pretty tonight," he said, gesturing towards her with his hand.

"Thank you." She noticed he looked more handsome than usual. The blue shirt he was wearing played off his dark hair and eyes.

He glanced casually around the room. "So, have you hit anybody up yet for a donation?"

She looked around at the crowd of people. "Mmm, I just spoke to Donald Freeman." She nodded her head at the heavy-set man standing on the other side of the room. "He might be interested."

Ethan looked in the direction she was staring. "I don't think I've met him before."

"Well, he seemed very impressed with our work. Come on, I'll introduce you."

~

Grace felt someone tap her on the shoulder as she stood talking with Jessica and Gavin.

"Excuse me," Paul said smiling. "But I couldn't help noticing how beautiful you are, and was wondering if your husband wouldn't mind, if you would care to dance."

"I would love to," she said, taking his outstretched hand.

Jessica watched the two of them walk over to the dance floor. After nearly twenty-five years of marriage, they still had the romance.

"Can I get you a drink?"

She turned to Gavin, having forgotten he was there. "Maybe later."

"I don't guess Ethan has changed his mind about this weekend."

She shook her head. "No, I'm sorry."

"It's all right," he said with a shrug.

~

Around ten o'clock the party was in full swing. Everyone was drinking, dancing, or laughing; some were doing all three at the same time.

Ethan stood next to Sarah as Phillip Martin introduced a gentleman to them. "This is Daniel Preston, of Preston Lines."

Ethan knew of his company. He owned a fleet of cargo vessels, and was a self-made millionaire several times over. "Nice to meet you," he said, switching his drink to his left hand so he could shake with him.

For the next twenty minutes or so, they worked on him with Sarah taking the lead. She told him in a very charming and eloquent manner all the wonderful services that the clinic provided, as well as what they hoped to offer in the near future.

As she spoke, Ethan noticed Jessica talking with Gavin at the bar. They were sitting close together, side by side. He turned his attention back to Mr. Preston, who at the moment, seemed to be far more interested in Sarah, than anything to do with him or the clinic.

"Would you like to dance?" Preston asked her.

A startled look came over Sarah. "I'd love to," she said, giving Ethan a subtle glance.

They went out to the dance floor, and as he turned her around to face him, she held up five fingers to Ethan.

He winked at her in understanding, before heading over to the bar. He set his drink down, forcing himself between Jessica and Gavin. "Don't you have somewhere else to go?" he asked, locking eyes with him.

Gavin clenched his jaw and stood up. "Excuse me."

Ethan watched him leave before taking his seat.

"Do you think you could have been any ruder?"

"Well, actually," he said, checking his watch, "I thought I showed a great deal of restraint."

Jessica stared darkly at her glass of wine. The tension between them right now was unbearable as the words that had been spoken in their bedroom still followed them.

Ethan finished his drink and sighed quietly. "Would you like to dance?"

She took his arm as they walked over to the dance floor. The band was playing a very slow and depressing tune—at least it sounded that way to her. Feeling the unsteadiness in Ethan's feet as he drew her close, she laid her head upon his shoulder, searching for some semblance of comfort.

He stumbled slightly and stepped on her foot. "Sorry."

She shook her head as she pulled away from him. "I have to go to the ladies room."

"What's wrong?"

"You know what's wrong," she whispered, before disappearing into the crowd.

~

Sarah's face hurt from wearing her frozen smile as she danced with Daniel. He was a short, rotund little man with a scraggly beard and mustache. When he walked, it reminded her somewhat of an ape taking a stroll through the jungle.

"So, are you married?"

"Divorced," she answered, finding it a little embarrassing that she had to look down at him. "And you?"

"Me? Never been married. I just haven't found the right woman yet," he said, staring into her eyes.

Sarah felt his hand inching its way lower and lower down her back until his fingers were resting on her left buttock. She breathed a sigh of relief when she saw Ethan coming to her rescue with Meredith draped over his arm.

"Excuse me, Daniel, but I don't think you've met our hostess for this evening." And that was all he needed to say. Meredith took over from there.

Ethan and Sarah gradually inched away from them until they were lost in the crowd.

~

Jessica wet a paper towel and dabbed at her eyes, trying to wipe away the mascara runs. She shouldn't have had Paul talk to Ethan tonight. It had only made matters worse, and now she was faced with the task of trying to repair yet another tear in their relationship.

The door to the ladies' room opened and she glanced in the mirror. Seeing Sarah's reflection behind her, she reached for another paper towel, ignoring her.

Sarah stepped two sinks to the left and opened her purse. Two could play this game.

Jessica hurriedly got rid of the black smudges and turned to leave when a wave of dizziness came over her. She grabbed hold of the vanity as the room began to spin.

"Are you all right?"

"I'm fine. I just got a little lightheaded for a second."

"Do you want me to get Ethan?" asked Sarah, noticing how pale she was. "I think he's right outside."

"No, I'm fine," she said curtly. She knew it was probably too much wine on an empty stomach, but was irritated that it had happened in front of Sarah.

~

Paul stood off to the side of the bar speaking with Phillip about the issues for the upcoming board meeting. Paul genuinely liked him, but Phillip only had one channel. He only talked business, and seemed incapable of carrying on a social conversation. He also had the unfortunate ability to take a casual discussion and turn it into something business related.

"I'd like to go over those papers with you before the holidays, if possible," Phillip continued.

He sighed inwardly. "Sure, I'll try to stop by after work tomorrow or the next day."

Phillip caught Ethan's attention and waved him over. "Have you gotten a good read on the donations tonight?"

Ethan nodded. "I think we're going to get a sizable one from Mr. Preston," he said, gesturing with his hand.

Paul and Phillip both glanced over in the direction he had pointed. Daniel Preston seemed to be in a deep discussion with Sarah.

"I think he's smitten with my partner," Ethan said grinning.

Paul chuckled. "Poor woman." As he turned his attention back to Phillip, he noticed that he was staring at Ethan who, along with his eyes being glazed over, was leaning a little to the right.

Phillip's smile folded inward, making a straight line across his face.

Paul tapped Ethan on his shoulder. "Why don't you join me for a cup of coffee?"

He looked at him and shook his head. "No, I don't think so," he replied in what sounded like a very crass tone.

~

"Are you tired, Grace?" Jessica asked as she watched her stifle a yawn.

She nodded and gave her a weary smile. "It's way past my bedtime. And my feet are killing me."

The two of them sat at a quiet table near the back, out of the way of the crowd.

Jessica casually glanced in Ethan's direction. He was on the other side of the room talking with Sarah. His head was tilted to the left, so he could hear with his good ear whatever it was she was whispering into it. He kept nodding his head and smiling, and then he laughed. She looked down at the table, wishing he would laugh with her that way.

"Paul told me about his meeting with Ethan," Grace said, just loud enough to be heard over the chatter.

"Well, as you can probably tell, we had an argument about it when he got home."

"I'm sorry it didn't go very well."

"I think tonight he's just drinking to be spiteful."

Grace had been watching Ethan on and off for most of the evening, and began to feel that he had a very serious problem. She also saw just how much this was tearing her cousin apart. "Jessica, what if you and Ethan had some counseling together?"

"What? You mean marriage counseling?"

"It does a world of good for some couples. I can recommend someone to you."

"I don't know. Right now, I'd be willing to try almost anything, but I doubt if Ethan would ever agree to it."

She patted her hand reassuringly. "Well, we'll just have to work on him, then."

Jessica forced a smile and stood up. "I think I'm going to get a cup of coffee. Can I get you anything?"

"No, thank you. I think I'm going to go find Paul and persuade him to leave. Are you ready to go?"

"I'm ready whenever you two are," she answered over her shoulder.

"What can I get for you?" asked the bartender as she drew near.

She sat down dejectedly on the stool. "Coffee, please."

"Tired?"

She looked to her right. Gavin was standing beside her.

"It's been a long day."

He signaled to the bartender. "Can I get a beer, please?"

Jessica waited until the bartender had brought them their respective drinks before speaking. "I have a favor to ask of you, Gavin."

"What's that?"

She poured the cream into her cup and stirred it for a moment, trying to answer. "I need for you to stop seeing Ryan for a while."

"Why?" he asked, taking a sip of his beer. "Is Ethan still having problems with it?"

She heard the callousness in his voice and bit her tongue. He could be extremely arrogant when he wanted to be. "We're having some issues," she finally said. "And this thing with Ryan is just escalating them."

"You know he's never going to come to terms with this," he said bitterly.

She tucked her hair behind her ear and nodded. "You're probably right, Gavin, but I really need for you to stop seeing him for a while. Please?"

~

Ethan still sat at the table with Sarah. The last few minutes his mood had grown somber as he watched his wife talking with Gavin.

"Did you see Dr. Pearson dancing earlier?" Sarah asked, hoping to draw his attention away from them. "He looked like a bird trying to take flight."

"No," he answered, keeping his eyes trained on the bar. It was just about then, that Gavin reached over and laid his hand on Jessica's arm. A surge of anger tore through Ethan's blood opening up old wounds.

He pushed his chair back and strode over to Gavin. "Get your hands off my wife!" he said, grabbing hold of his wrist.

Gavin jerked free of his grasp and turned to face him. "*What* is your problem?"

Jessica felt her cheeks beginning to burn. "Ethan, please don't."

"*You* are my problem!" he said, ignoring her. "Why can't you find some other woman to spend your pathetic life with? Preferably one that isn't *married!*"

Gavin set his drink down on the bar and stood up. "You know, I have had it up to *here* with you!" he said, making a motion with his hand.

By this time, they had the entire attention of everyone there.

Ethan shoved him. "What are you going to do about it?"

Gavin returned the gesture, making him take a step backwards to keep his balance.

Ethan seized him by his tie and cocked his fist back, but before he could let it loose, someone grabbed him from behind.

"That's enough, Ethan! Just calm down!" Paul said.

Phillip and another man stepped in front of Gavin and pushed him away.

~

Jessica gave Grace a short wave as she and Paul backed out of the driveway. The ride home had been long, miserable, and silent.

Mrs. Chambers greeted them in the foyer. "How was the party?"

"It was nice," she said, turning to Ellen. "Did Ryan give you any trouble?"

"Oh, he was good as gold. He went down about ten o'clock," she replied, reaching for her coat.

Jessica accompanied her to the kitchen, trying to make small talk along the way. "Are you all packed for San Diego?"

The older woman's eyes lit up as she grinned. "Yes, I can't wait!"

"Well, I'll be home early tomorrow afternoon, so you'll have plenty of time to make it to the airport," she said, opening the door for her.

"Thank you, Dr. Harrington. Goodnight."

"Goodnight." Jessica's smile faded the instant Ellen had turned away. She watched her walking across the backyard until she disappeared in the shadows. A moment or two later, she saw the lights in the guesthouse come on.

Ethan slung his jacket over the chair and sat down on the sofa with a glass of scotch. He leaned his head against the back of the cushion and closed his eyes.

Jessica's heels clicked across the hardwood. "Oh, by all means, have yourself another drink!"

"Don't start," he said, sighing.

"Where did you get that?" she asked, gesturing at the bottle that sat on the table.

He didn't answer.

Jessica clenched her teeth as she walked over to the Christmas tree and bent down to unplug the lights. "I just want you to know," she said, crossing her arms as she straightened up, "that I have never been so embarrassed and humiliated in my entire life as I was by you tonight!"

He got to his feet. "Oh, *you* were embarrassed? I think you've got it backwards! You were the one embarrassing *me*!" He walked around the sofa. "Do you know how it looked tonight? Nearly everyone there knew that you and Gavin had slept together, and there—"

She turned away and began shaking her head.

He grabbed her by the arm, making her look at him. "—and there the two of you were tonight, all over each other!"

"You are so paranoid!"

"What were you talking about with him?"

"Nothing," she said, prying his fingers off her arm.

"How do you think that made me feel, seeing you laughing and carrying on with him like that?"

"You know, Ethan, I could say the same thing about you. You spent practically the whole night talking with Sarah."

"I didn't have an *affair* with Sarah!" He turned and hurled his drink across the room, shattering the glass against the wall.

Jessica shuddered and took a step back, but her sudden retreat only seemed to intensify his anger. In an instant, he had his hands locked around both of her wrists.

"I want you to tell me what you were talking about!" he said, jerking her towards him.

"Stop it."

"Tell me!"

"I was asking him not to see Ryan for a while," she said, banging against his chest with her fists. "Now, let go of me!"

Ethan suddenly released his grip, causing her to stumble backwards into the tree.

She heard the sickening sound of glass hitting the floor. Turning around, she saw the fragmented remains of a red and white ornament. Tears began to fill her eyes as she bent down to pick one of the jagged pieces up. The smiling face of a cat stared at her.

"I'm sorry," he said in a low voice.

She let the piece fall through her fingers before marching out of the room.

Ethan looked down at the broken ornament and sighed. It seemed that the only way the two of them could communicate anymore was by screaming at each other.

He walked across the foyer and started up the steps, trying to form an acceptable apology in his mind.

When he got to the door, he reached for the knob only to find it locked. "Jess, open up, I want to talk to you."

She didn't answer.

He became enraged as he tried the knob again. "Jessica, open this door!" Bringing his foot up, he kicked it hard, sending it slamming against the bedroom wall.

Jessica stood in the middle of the room, her face ashen.

He walked slowly in. His eyes went from her, to the open suitcase lying on the bed. "Are you leaving me?"

Ryan's cries flowed through the monitor as she began backing up. Seeing that the safety of the bathroom was just a few feet away, she darted in and swung the door closed.

He turned the knob before she could lock it and forced it open, grabbing her by the shoulders. "I will *never* let you leave me!" he said, pushing her up against the vanity.

"Ethan"—her voice shook—"please don't." His eyes were not his own. They were steely black, like that of a shark attacking its prey. They were relentless, uncaring, and showed no mercy. The force of his fist knocked her to the floor.

Ethan fought through the blinding rage that had engulfed him, trying to gain control as his hand raised again. He could hear nothing but a deafening roar, and then the faint sounds of cries.

Jessica lay crumpled at his feet, sobbing, with her hands over her head.

He dropped to his knees and gathered her in his arms. "Jess, I'm sorry."

She let him touch her, too afraid not to.

Brushing her hair from her face, he saw that her upper lip was cut and bleeding. "I'm sorry," he whispered again. He closed the lid to the toilet and helped her up.

She numbly sat on the seat and watched as he pulled a washcloth from the drawer. Her body trembled as he pressed it gently against the cut.

"Please...please, just stay right here," he said in a quivering voice. "I'll go get some ice."

Jessica waited until he had gone downstairs before crossing the hall into the nursery.

Ryan was standing in his crib, his little face red and streaky. "Shh," she said, picking him up. "It's all right."

She went to the landing at the top of the steps and peered around the corner. Ethan was still in the kitchen. Her legs shook as she hurried down the stairs and slipped out the front door. The cold wind bit into her bare arms as she buckled Ryan in his infant seat.

"Jessica!"

She whirled around to see Ethan running towards her. Panic struck her as she opened her own door and got in. She fumbled alongside the panel for the lock just as he reached the car.

"Jessica, open up!" He pulled on the handle. "You can't leave me!"

Her hands were trembling so badly, she dropped the keys on the floorboard beneath her.

Ethan kicked the door. "Jessica! Unlock this door!"

The whole car rocked as the assault continued.

Ryan was screaming in the back seat, holding out his hands for her to take him.

"God, help me," she prayed, picking up the keys. Her fingers clumsily slid the key into the ignition and turned it. The engine roared to life as she shifted it into reverse.

As she began to back out, he struck his fist hard against the window. Jessica turned her head as the glass shattered, but managed to keep her foot on the accelerator.

~

"I'm exhausted," Grace said, sitting down on the bed next to Paul.

"Me too," he replied with a heavy sigh. "It was a nice evening…up until the end."

She nodded as she reached up to take off her earrings.

Paul ran his finger along the buttons of her dress. "Did I tell you how beautiful you looked tonight?"

"You did," she said, smiling.

"Well, it bears repeating." He leaned over and kissed her softly on the lips.

The sound of tires squealing into their driveway made Grace pull back. It was immediately followed by a car horn. She hurried into the living room and opened the front door. "It's Jessica," she called over her shoulder as she ran out.

Jessica got out of the car clutching Ryan in her arms. "Help me, Grace, please!"

"My God! What happened?" she asked, drawing near.

Paul flipped the porch light on and met them on the sidewalk. "What's wrong?" he asked, but then he saw. He cupped Jessica's chin in his hand and turned it towards the light. "That *son-of-a-bitch.*"

The gunning of an engine and bright headlights was suddenly upon them as Ethan's car skidded into their driveway.

"Get inside and lock the door," Paul said in a low voice.

Grace ushered Jessica and the baby inside just as Ethan began to approach the house.

Paul shoved him backwards. "Don't come any closer, Ethan."

"I want to see her."

"Well, she doesn't want to see you. You've done enough damage for one night."

Grace took Jessica and Ryan into her bedroom and told her to lock the door. She had to get back outside, fearful of what Ethan might try to do. She could hear his voice, loud and uneven, as she stepped out onto the porch.

"Get back inside, Grace." Paul's jaw was clenched.

The two men stood a few feet apart on the front lawn, as if there was a battle line drawn between them.

Ethan started towards the house again.

Paul grabbed him and held him by his arms. "Look at me, Ethan! I am *not* going to let you inside! Understand?"

"I just want to tell her I'm sorry," he said, looking past him to plead with Grace.

He tightened his grip. "You need to calm down. She's not going to listen to anything you have to say right now." He shook him to get his attention. "Do you hear me?"

Ethan stopped pushing. "I *need* to see her."

"You can see her tomorrow." He turned his head slightly. "Grace, let me have his keys."

She stepped down off the porch and hurried over to Ethan's car, retrieving them from the ignition.

Ethan began to struggle, trying to get loose, and Paul could feel that he was losing his grip on him. Fearful that he was going to break free and head for the house, he shoved him as hard as he could, hoping to put enough distance between them that he could stop him if he tried.

His plan worked. Ethan lost his footing and fell backwards against the hood of his car.

As Grace stood watching, she noticed that her husband's shirt was smeared with blood. She shifted her eyes to Ethan and saw that his right hand was covered in it.

Paul felt a sense of relief when he made no motion to get up. "Come on," he said to him, taking the keys from Grace. "I'll drive you home."

Ethan pushed himself away from the car. "I can drive myself home."

"You're too drunk."

"Give me back the keys, Paul." Ethan's breath came out in white clouds.

"You can't drive in the condition you're in."

"Give me the keys," he repeated, trying to snatch them from his hand.

Paul stuck them in his pants pocket.

Ethan clenched his jaw. "Give me the *goddamn* keys, Paul!"

"No."

Ethan took a step back and swung his fist at Paul's head.

He easily ducked and landed a blow of his own squarely on Ethan's mouth, knocking him to the ground. "*That's* for what you did to Jessica!" he said, grabbing him by his shirt and straddling him. He raised his fist and hit him again. "And *that's* for being such a jackass!"

"Paul, stop it! You're hurting him!"

He got off him. "I didn't *hurt* him, honey," he said, rubbing his knuckles. "I promise you, he didn't feel a *thing*. Isn't that right, Ethan?"

Ethan turned over on his side and coughed. He slowly got to his feet, and placed his hand on the hood of his car to steady himself. Blood trickled from his left nostril as he glared at Paul. "Go to *hell*."

Grace clasped her hands around Paul's arm as they watched him stumble across the yard. "You can't let him walk home."

"What the *hell* am I supposed to do? He won't let me drive him."

"He's *hurt,* Paul. And it's freezing out here. He doesn't even have a coat."

Paul went inside and grabbed his jacket. "Lock the door behind me. If he comes back, call the police. Understand?"

~

Jessica paced back and forth trying to get Ryan to calm down, but it was of no use. He was upset because she was upset.

There was a short knock.

"It's me," Grace called.

She unlocked the door.

"It's all right, he's gone," she said, taking Ryan from her. "Shh…shh…it's okay." After a few moments, he stopped crying and laid his head upon her shoulder. She turned her attention to Jessica. "Let's get you out of that dress and into something warm."

Jessica turned her back to her, allowing her to unzip her. The dress immediately fell from her shoulders.

"I should have never left you alone tonight," Grace said, staring at the purple marks that had begun to form on her arms. "I'm so sorry."

"It's not your fault, Grace," she said, pulling on her cousin's bathrobe. "I lit into him as soon as we got home. It turned into a big fight." She sat down on the bed and drew a shaky breath. "I should have known better."

Grace cradled the back of Ryan's head as she sat down beside her. "What do you mean, you should have known better? Has he hit you before?"

She looked away and wiped her eyes, too embarrassed to answer.

"Oh, Jessica," she said in a voice that was full of both anger and hurt. "Why didn't you say anything?"

Chapter Twenty-nine

Sarah picked her way carefully across the parking lot of the hospital. Snow had fallen late last night, depositing about three inches on the ground. The maintenance crews had not spread salt down as of yet, making her trek up the steps treacherous.

Once she reached the safety of the lobby, she took the elevator to the fifth floor and then made her way down the corridor. Glancing at her watch as she unlocked her office, she determined that she had just enough time for a cup of coffee before having to go over the budget request with Phillip.

Walking inside, she flipped on the lights and immediately jumped at the sight of a man sleeping on her couch. A scream started to escape her lips until she realized it was Ethan.

She dropped her purse on her desk and waited for her heart to return to its normal rhythm. It wasn't that unusual for her, or Ethan, to sleep here if they'd handled an emergency during the night, but *last* night, neither one of them had been on call.

Leaning over him, she saw that there were several cuts and gashes across the knuckles of his right hand. The blood appeared dried, and had caked around the wounds. Wanting to see it better, she picked it up for a closer inspection.

Ethan jerked his hand away and cursed at the sudden pain that was traveling up his arm.

"Sorry."

He glanced around the room trying to get his eyes to focus, confused as to where he was.

"What happened?"

He looked down at his hand for a moment, and then remembered everything. After he had left Paul's house last night, he had walked here. The hospital was seven blocks away. Seven very cold blocks. He had been half-frozen by the time he'd made it through the front entrance.

"What happened to your hand?" she repeated.

Ethan carefully sat up, trying not to provoke his throbbing head.

"Are you all right?" Sarah asked, kneeling in front of him.

He nodded slowly as he set his feet on the floor. She reached for his hand again, but he held it away from her, drawing it tight against his stomach, instead.

A sigh fell from her as she stood to go. "I have to meet with Phillip in about five minutes to go over the budget. Why don't you go on down to X-ray, and then I'll look at it when I get back, all right?"

He cleared his throat, trying to erase the dryness in it. "It's not that bad," he croaked.

"I think it's probably broken. Don't make me drag you down there," she said, knowing how obstinate he could be sometimes.

He leaned forward and held his head with his other hand. At the moment, he didn't know which one hurt worse.

~

Phillip Martin slowly flipped through the pages of the report as Sarah read the figures to him from the copy in her lap. When she had finished, he nodded his head. "Well, everything seems to be in order, and you aren't asking for an enormous amount of money."

"I think we're being very reasonable," she said in earnest.

He closed the file and took off his glasses. "I appreciate you taking the time to show it to me."

Sarah bit her tongue. She knew what his response meant. Come January first, she and Ethan would get their standard budget—slashed by ten percent. It was the same as last year, and the year before.

"Well," she heard herself say, "I wanted to go over it with you now, since I'm going to be off for the next couple of weeks."

"Oh, that's right. Your daughter's coming in, isn't she?"

She pursed her lips in order to keep her smile hidden. "Tomorrow."

"Have a nice time."

"Thank you."

"Have you seen Ethan this morning?"

"Not yet," she lied.

He started to say something, but was interrupted by his telephone. "Excuse me just a moment," he said, picking up the receiver. "Dr. Martin."

Sarah stood to go, but he held up one finger to her. Stifling a sigh, she sat back down and waited. It was very quiet in his office, and although she didn't mean to, she could hear the voice on the phone loud and clear. She toyed with her pen as she listened to Jessica talk.

"I need to have the next couple of weeks off, starting today."

"I see," replied Phillip.

"I'm sorry that it's such short notice, but I wouldn't ask if it wasn't important."

"Is there anything the matter?"

There was a long pause, and Sarah found herself holding her breath to hear what she was going to say next.

"Ethan and I have separated…and I need some time to find a place to live."

Phillip rubbed his thick eyebrows with an even thicker finger. "I'm sorry to hear that."

"Thank you. I'll be staying at Dr. Cummings' house for a few days until I can get settled."

"All right, I'll speak to Gavin about your caseload. Let me know if there's anything I can do."

"Thank you, Phillip."

A troubled look came upon him as he hung up the receiver. "I'm sorry to keep you waiting."

"That's all right," she said, putting on her best poker face. "Did you have a question about the budget?"

"No," he said, shoving the folder to the side. "Please tell Ethan that I want to see him as soon as he gets in this morning."

~

Paul's boots crunched on the freshly fallen snow as he walked around Jessica's car. There was a medium-sized hole in the middle of the driver's side window where the impact had been. The rest of the glass looked like a spider web where it had shattered, but not broken. There were several dents that ran alongside the bottom of the door.

He set about putting a piece of cardboard over the window. He felt his jaw tighten as he placed strips of duct tape along the edges. He could not—and would not—ever understand why some men felt it necessary to hit a woman. He had always thought of Ethan as one of his closest friends, but how he could do this to Jessica, his own wife, was beyond him. He should have phoned the police last night and had him arrested for battery.

He looked over at Ethan's car. It was parked halfway in the driveway and halfway in their front yard. Paul had searched for the better part of an hour for him last night, but had never found him. He didn't know where the hell he had disappeared to.

~

Grace was sitting in the kitchen holding Ryan when Jessica came out of the guest bedroom. "How are you feeling?"

"All right, I guess."

Grace got a good look at her upper lip as she bent down to give the baby a kiss. The left side of it was swollen and bruised, and harbored a deep cut that had closed itself during the night.

"Where did you get that?" she asked, referring to the bottle Grace was giving him. She hadn't even had time to wrap Ryan in a blanket last night, let alone bring any food or diapers for him.

"Paul went to the convenience store this morning and bought him a few necessities."

Jessica glanced at the clock on the microwave. It was still early. "He must have gotten up at the crack of dawn."

"Well, I think he was up anyway. He didn't sleep much, *if any*, last night."

"That was very sweet of him," Jessica said in a quiet voice.

"Can I get you something to eat?"

"Uh, no. I think I'll just have some coffee."

Ryan held out his hands and cried for her to take him.

"Come here, sweetheart," she said, pulling him into her lap as she sat down. A cool gust of wind made her shiver as the front door opened and closed.

"It looks like we got about three or four inches last night," Paul said, shaking the snow from his boots. He walked across the floor and bent down to see Ryan. "Hi there," he said, tickling him with his fingers.

The baby pushed back against Jessica as he laughed.

Paul's fingers went from Ryan to the side of her face. "How are you?" he asked softly.

"I'm fine," she answered, avoiding his gaze.

Grace set a steaming cup down in front of her. "Here you go."

Jessica grasped the handle of it and took a small sip, wincing as the hot liquid bit into her cut.

Grace looked at her sympathetically. "Do you want some ice to put on it?"

"No, it's all right," she replied, wishing that they would both stop staring at her.

Paul poured himself a cup of coffee and sat down at the table across from her.

Jessica pressed the side of her face against Ryan's cheek. She needed to call Mrs. Chambers this morning before she came over to the house. She also needed to call the sitter service that was replacing her and cancel.

There was a lot to take care of, but at the moment, all she wanted to do was cry. She took another sip of the coffee, hoping the discomfort of it touching her lip would be enough to thwart her tears.

~

"I'm going to give you a shot of Lidocaine for the pain," Sarah said, inserting a syringe into the small vial she held between her fingers.

Ethan flinched as he felt the sting of the needle going into his hand.

Sarah readjusted the overhead lamp and began cleaning the dried blood away with an antiseptic wipe. After a minute or two, his hand relaxed and became limp, telling her that the shot was working.

She pressed gently on the wounds, trying to see the extent of the damage. Deep inside the gashes were several pieces of something that resembled glitter. She immediately swiveled her stool around, and pulled out a set of tweezers along with a magnifying lens from the drawer beside her.

Ethan watched as she attached the lens to the mechanical arm that slid out from underneath the table.

Sarah peered through the lens for a long time, probing the wounds. "Are you going to tell me how this happened?"

He remained silent, as he had done for most of the morning.

With a sigh, she set about removing the slivers of glass one by one.

Knock-knock.

The door opened and a technician leaned in to hand her a large folder.

"Thanks," she said, slipping the X-rays out and placing them on the overhead. She put her hands on her hips as she studied the films. After a moment, she pointed to the fractures. "It's broken in two places."

Ethan looked at the X-rays, and then rubbed his eyes, too tired to care.

Sarah sat back down to the task of removing the slivers. As she worked, she noticed that besides having blood on his sleeve, he had a small amount of it on his collar. There was also a light bruise on the left side of his mouth. It made her wonder if he and Gavin had continued their fight in the parking lot last night. "You're going to need a few stitches," she said, laying the tweezers aside.

Ethan watched as her fingers nimbly began suturing the gashes closed. "Have you heard from Ashley?" he asked quietly. At the moment, he really didn't care if she had or not. He just wanted the attention off of him.

She nodded. "Her flight gets in tomorrow afternoon."

"You must be excited."

"I am, but right now, I'm more concerned about you." She put the last suture in and looked up. "I was in Phillip's office when he took a call from Jessica. I overheard her telling him that the two of you had separated."

He swallowed hard before casting his eyes downward.

"I'm so sorry. Is there anything I can do?"

He drew in a deep breath and let it out slowly. "No," he whispered.

~

A little while later, Sarah stood over the sink washing the plaster off her hands. "How does that feel?"

"Fine," he answered, looking at the cast. He hopped off the table and went across the small hallway into their office. Once there, he poured himself a cup of coffee and took two pain relievers.

Sarah finished cleaning up the examining room and joined him a few minutes later. "I hate to be the bearer of more bad news," she said, pouring some coffee into her own mug, "but Phillip wants to see you in his office first thing."

"Great," he muttered.

She slipped a shirt and tie off the coat rack and held them out to him. "Why don't you clean up a little first?"

~

Gavin sat in Phillip's office discussing Jessica's caseload. He thought Phillip had asked him in here to admonish him on his behavior last night. He hadn't expected this.

"Do you think you can handle her patients along with yours for a couple of weeks?"

"I don't think it'll be a problem. Did she say why she needed the time off?"

Phillip hesitated. "I'm sure she'll call you later on to explain."

There was a knock upon the door.

"Come in."

Gavin sighed inwardly when he saw Ethan. This was not going to be good.

"Have a seat," Phillip said.

Ethan closed the door and sat down in the chair next to Gavin.

Phillip gestured towards his hand when he saw the cast. "What happened?"

"It's nothing."

He eyed him closely for a moment before taking off his glasses and rubbing his forehead.

Ethan watched the vein near Phillip's right temple. It was usually a good way to judge how mad he was.

"I guess you both know why you're here. If not, let me clarify things for you," he said, walking around to the side of his desk. "Your behavior last night was abominable. The two of you carried on like two adolescent school boys."

Gavin shifted uncomfortably in his seat.

"It seems lately, that every time I turn around, the two of you are at each other's throats. Do you know how much you embarrassed yourselves, *and* this hospital last night? Two grown men carrying on like children."

Ethan noticed the vein was now protruding through Phillip's skin. It reminded him of a lightning bolt.

"I want the two of you to listen to me very closely, because I'm only going to say this once. From this moment on, at this hospital, and at any other hospital function, you will *never* pull another stunt like you did last night. Now, I know the history that you two share, and I don't expect you to be friends. But you *will* treat each other with some respect and common courtesy. Do I make myself clear?"

It was Ethan's turn to shift in his seat.

"Well, *do* I?"

"Yes," they answered in unison.

"I'm sorry, Phillip. I had a little too much to drink last night," Gavin offered.

"I'm sorry too, Phillip," Ethan said, echoing his words.

He nodded, accepting their apologies. "That's all I have to say," he said, returning to his seat behind the desk.

The two of them took that as their cue to leave and stood to go.

"Ethan? I'd like to talk to you alone for a moment."

Ethan let out a small sigh as Gavin disappeared through the door. He should have known Phillip wasn't going to let him off so easily. He slowly turned and reluctantly sat back down in the chair.

"Jessica called me this morning and told me that the two of you had separated," he said bluntly, but not without compassion. "I'm sorry. I know it's tough. It's been a rough year with your father's passing…and now this."

Ethan propped his elbow up on the arm of the chair, trying to ease the pain as he pretended to listen.

"I also know that running the clinic can be stressful at times, and that you and Sarah have the biggest caseloads in this hospital."

He suddenly raised his head up, having heard his last words. "I can handle it," he said earnestly.

Phillip nodded and held his hands up. "I know you can. You're a good doctor, Ethan. A *damn* good one. But every doctor has his breaking point."

"What are you saying?" he asked warily.

"That maybe you've got a little too much on your shoulders right now."

"I can handle my work, Phillip."

"Ethan, you know as well as I, that drinking can be stress related."

"Oh, come on, Phillip. Practically everyone there last night had a little too much to drink."

"Last night wasn't the first night I've seen you drunk. There have been other times, at other engagements. It's starting to become a pattern with you, and quite frankly, I'm a little concerned." He leaned forward. "Look, Ethan, all I'm saying is that maybe we should lighten your caseload a little bit."

"I can handle my caseload," he insisted as he got to his feet. "I promise that something like this will never happen again."

Phillip looked at him for a long time before answering. "All right, Ethan. But this is your only warning. There won't be any more chances."

~

Sarah was gone when Ethan returned to their office. He immediately picked up the phone and dialed Grace's home number.

"Hello?"

"Grace, can I talk to Jessica, please?"

There was a long pause.

"Ethan, I'm sorry, but she doesn't want to talk to you right now."

"Can you please put her on, so I can hear her say that herself?"

"I'm sorry," she said, hanging up.

He slammed the receiver down just as Sarah came through the door.

"How did it go?"

He looked at her blankly before realizing she was referring to his meeting with Phillip. He shook his head and sighed. "My ears are still ringing."

~

Jessica knelt on the floor of the nursery, solemnly putting some of Ryan's toys into a bag. Paul had already taken the playpen and highchair out to the car. They'd intended to take the crib, but after determining it wouldn't fit in Paul's hatch, they'd decided to take the mattress only. Grace was on the other side of the room packing some of his clothes for her.

She couldn't begin to thank them enough for what they were doing, as they both had taken the day off to help her.

Paul returned from his last trip out to the car, his cheeks red from the cold. "Is there anything else you want me to take down?"

She looked around the room. "I guess that's it," she said, handing him the bag with the toys in it. "I just need to get some of my things and then I'll be ready."

He scooped Ryan up from the floor. "Take your time. I'll take him downstairs with me."

Jessica followed him out of the nursery and started to go across the hall when she remembered something. "Paul? Don't let Ryan go in the living room."

"Why?" he asked, giving her a puzzled look.

"There's broken glass on the floor," she said quietly.

A moment of silence passed before he answered. "All right."

Something crunched underneath Grace's foot as she walked from the nursery into the bedroom. Looking down, she saw that it was a large splinter of wood. Her eyes moved upwards to the door and saw that it was leaning partially against the wall, its top two hinges broken and twisted.

Jessica stepped around her cousin, ignoring the horrified look upon her face, and silently crossed over to her dresser. Not wishing to be in here any longer than she had to, she quickly pulled out a pair of jeans and a sweatshirt. Grace had lent her some clothes to wear this morning, but the older woman had a good two inches in height on her, making her have to cuff the pants at the bottom.

"Why is your suitcase on the bed?" asked Grace in a half-whisper.

She slipped her arms inside her sweatshirt, refusing to look at her. "I was leaving him."

~

Ethan saw his car sitting in his driveway, along with Paul's SUV. He paid the cab driver and grimaced as he started up the sidewalk. He was in no mood for another confrontation with Paul. He had specifically left the hospital early because he'd wanted to clean himself up before going over to try and speak with Jessica.

Paul was standing in the foyer when he came through the door. "We're just here to get a few things," he said, walking over to the staircase as if to protect it.

Ethan came around to the front of the stairs. "Is she up there?" he asked calmly.

"Yes, but I can't let you go up."

He felt his jaw twitch. "This is my house," he seethed. "And I can do whatever I *damn* well please."

"Dadda."

Looking behind him, he saw Ryan crawling towards him, his little hands slapping against the hardwood floor as he moved across it. He bent down and picked him up as Paul continued his vigil by the stairs.

Both men turned, however, when they heard voices coming from the top of the landing.

Jessica froze when she saw Ethan. She had come over here early thinking he would still be at the clinic. She suddenly felt Grace's hand on her back, gently prodding her to move her feet.

Paul took the suitcases from her when she reached the bottom, and carried them over to the front door.

Ethan stood motionless as she followed him across the floor and put her coat on.

"Is that everything?" Paul asked in a low voice.

She nodded, avoiding Ethan's gaze.

Grace slipped her own coat on, and then walked up to Ethan. She looked at him apologetically as she held out her hands.

He gave Ryan a kiss. "Daddy loves you," he whispered, before handing him to her. He felt his throat tightening as he watched them leave. "Jess?"

She stopped and looked over her shoulder.

Tears began to trickle down his face. "Can I talk to you for a moment?" he asked. He turned his head, ashamed for Paul and Grace to see him.

Jessica exchanged a silent glance with her cousin.

"We'll wait for you outside," she said, wiping tears from her own eyes.

When Ethan heard the door close, he turned around, and for the first time, saw the damage that he had inflicted upon her. His breath came out all of a sudden, making it sound like a sob. "I'm sorry," he said, walking up to embrace her.

She took a step backwards. "Don't."

He stopped in his tracks and held his hands up. "Please don't leave me…I'll quit drinking, I swear."

"You've said that before."

"This time, I promise. I'll never touch another drop as long as I live." His chin trembled as he spoke. "Please don't leave me."

"I have heard you say those words so many times." Her mouth twisted in agony, wanting so very much to believe him.

"I mean it this time." His breath grew ragged as he fought to convince her. "I swear, I do."

She brought her hands to her face and shook her head. "I can't do this anymore, Ethan," she said as her tears seeped through her fingers.

"Jess—"

She opened the door and stepped out onto the porch, intending to leave.

He caught her by the arm and spun her towards him. "Jess, I can't live without you," he whispered.

"Ethan," she cried, "please don't make this any harder than it is."

"I love you," he said, pulling her close. "Look me in the eyes and tell me that you don't love me."

"Please stop…"

"Tell me!" He put his hands on the sides of her face. "Tell me," he said in a soft voice as he leaned in and kissed her tenderly.

She broke away from his lips and bowed her head.

He rested his forehead against hers as he struggled to breathe. "Tell me."

Her shoulders began to shake. "I can't do this, Ethan. I'm sorry," she said tearfully as she turned and ran towards the car.

He stepped off the porch. "Jessica!"

Paul got out and opened the door for her as she drew near.

"Jessica, please don't go!" Ethan dropped to his knees as they slowly backed out of the driveway.

~

Jessica fell back into bed and pulled the covers up around her. It was the second time tonight that she had thrown up. Uncertain if it was a stomach virus or a compilation of what had happened over the last twenty-four hours, she turned over on her side and prayed for sleep to come.

The image of Ethan sobbing on his knees in the snow this afternoon kept replaying over and over in her mind, refusing to allow her any rest. In all the years she had been with him, this was the first time that she had ever seen him cry.

Tears fell from her cheeks and dropped one by one onto the pillow. Guilt seemed to consume her over one constant thought. Was it her fault? She wondered if things would have been different if Ryan had been Ethan's.

Chapter Thirty

Sarah sat in her office watching the minute hand on the clock. The afternoon was dragging by. It was still some four hours before Ashley and Ted would be here.

"Staring at the clock is only going to make it go slower."

"I can't help it," she said with a sigh.

The corners of Ethan's mouth twitched as he continued to write in the chart in front of him. "Why don't you go on home? I can handle things here."

"Because I'd probably just climb the walls."

"And...the difference would be?" he said, sounding irritated.

Guilt began to swarm her as she watched him scribbling in the chart. She had no right to be so happy when she knew what a terrible time he was having. "I noticed that you're working a double tomorrow."

"Mmm-hmm."

"You have seniority over Jackson. Why are you working?"

He shrugged. "Jackson's got two kids and so does Marcus. They should be able to spend Christmas Day with their families. Besides," he said, reaching across his desk for the letter opener. "I don't have any plans."

"You know, you're more than welcome to have Christmas dinner with me and my family."

"Sarah," he said, sliding the letter opener inside his cast to relieve an itch, "the last thing I would want to do, is intrude on your time with Ashley."

"You wouldn't be intruding. I would love to have you over."

"I thank you, Sarah, from the bottom of my heart. But I'll be fine, really."

Sensing that he wanted to wallow in his misery alone, she gave him a small nod and dropped the issue.

"Mom?"

She spun around in her chair.

Ashley stood at the door.

Sarah jumped to her feet and threw her arms around her. "What are you doing here? I wasn't supposed to pick you up until five!"

"We got an earlier flight."

"Why didn't you call and let me know?"

She stepped back and grinned. "I wanted to surprise you."

"Well," Sarah said through her tears, "you did. Where's Ted?"

"He's downstairs waiting in the lobby."

"Ethan," said Sarah, as she wiped her eyes and sniffed. "Look who it is."

He laughed. "I can see," he said, coming around the desk. Ashley was about Sarah's height with long, thick hair that fell down her back. It had a slight auburn tint to it, but wasn't as bold as Sarah's. She definitely had her mother's eyes, though. They were green and vibrant.

"Hi, Dr. Harrington."

He cocked his head to one side and looked at her quizzically. "Is this the same Ashley?"

"It's me."

"This couldn't be the same little girl who left. You're all grown up.

"Thank you," she said, blushing slightly. She turned to Sarah. "Mom, if you don't mind, I'm going to go see Dad for a minute."

"That's fine. I'll get my things and meet you in the lobby."

Just as she was going out, a young man wearing blue jeans and a brown leather jacket came through the door. "Dr. Harrington?"

"That's me."

He held a clipboard out to him. "I have a registered letter for you."

Ethan scrawled his name as best as he could on the signature line.

"Have a Merry Christmas," the man said, handing him the letter.

"You too," he answered, staring at the envelope. He waited for him to leave, before turning it over in his hand. It was from Paul's office. He slowly tore the seal and slid the contents out. He felt his insides go numb as he read the opening paragraph.

"Is everything all right?"

He looked up, having forgotten that Sarah was still in the room. He folded the papers and stuffed them back inside the envelope. "It's just something concerning my father's company."

"Well, I guess I'm out of here," she said, pulling on her coat.

He reached for his stethoscope. "I'll walk you to the elevator. I've got to make my rounds."

"You know, the invitation still stands if you change your mind."

"Thanks," he said, giving her a meager smile.

Ashley met them as they rounded the corner. "Are you ready to go?"

"That was fast," Sarah remarked.

She shrugged. "Dad's in a consult."

Sarah turned to Ethan as she began buttoning her coat. "Are you sure you don't mind me taking off? Because, if you'd rather be off...I would understand."

He put his arm around her as they walked down the hall. "Ashley? Would you do me a favor?"

"I'll try, Dr. Harrington," she answered, walking on the other side of Sarah.

"Would you please take your mother home and get her out of my hair? Because I don't want to see her again until next year."

She laughed. "I'll do my best."

Ethan drew Sarah close to him and kissed her on top of her head. "Merry Christmas."

Before she could reply, he turned her loose and disappeared down the corridor. She stifled a sigh and pressed the button for the elevator. As she waited, she took a moment to look down at herself. Something didn't feel right. "Darn it!"

"What's wrong, Mom?"

"I forgot my purse. I'll be right back," she called over her shoulder as she started back around the corner towards her office.

Once inside, she pulled her purse out from underneath her desk and turned to go.

Ring-ring!

She stopped and pursed her lips. There was something inside of her that refused to ignore a ringing telephone; it caused her lots of grief, especially when it came to telemarketers. "Clinic, Dr. Williams."

"May I speak to Dr. Harrington?"

"I'm sorry, he's stepped away for a moment. Can I take a message?"

"Sure. This is John from Australian Airlines. I was just calling to make sure that his friends got in from Sydney okay."

Sarah was speechless.

"Hello?"

She shook her head slightly as if to clear it. "Yes, um...I can tell you that they just got in."

"Great. Just tell Ethan that I called and Merry Christmas."

"Merry Christmas," she repeated.

~

Grace was in her office taking care of some last minute details when Paul poked his head in the door. "Are you ready to go home?"

"Absolutely. Just let me grab my coat." He had given her a ride to work this morning in case Jessica needed to use Grace's car. He'd said that he didn't want her driving her own with the window busted.

She locked her office and they walked down the corridor arm in arm. It was still fairly early in the afternoon, but the hospital had already grown quiet, leaving only the unfortunate souls who ranked low in seniority to man the stations for the holidays.

Paul glanced around nervously as he picked up his pace.

"Why are we walking so fast?"

"I'm trying to avoid Phillip. If he sees me, we won't be home until New Year's." He suddenly stopped and scowled.

The doors to the elevator were propped open with a ladder inside.

"Let's walk down, shall we?"

"That's eight floors!"

Grace pulled on his arm. "Oh, come on! It'll do you good."

They started down the stairwell with Paul moaning and groaning. By the time they had gone down a few flights, he was puffing hard.

"Let's stop here and catch the elevator," he said, panting.

"It will take us to the south side of the parking lot."

"I don't care," he puffed.

She looked at her red-faced husband and smiled inwardly, knowing that this year she had chosen her present for him wisely. Tomorrow, he would receive a treadmill. "All right," she said, reaching for the door.

They began making their way down the dimly-lit hall towards the elevators on the opposite side.

Grace noticed the light coming from underneath the door of Ethan's office and paused.

"What are you stopping for?"

"Let me talk to Ethan for just a minute, all right?"

He gave her his aggravated look.

"Paul, please don't act this way," she said in a low voice.

"I'm not acting *any* way. I just don't care to see him. And I can assure you that he does not want to see *me* right now."

"Ethan is one of your best friends."

He shook his head slowly. "Not anymore."

"How can you say that?"

"I don't want to fight with you on this, sweetheart."

"He needs our support right now, just as much as Jessica does."

"Don't you dare ask me to feel sorry for him."

"I'm not. I'm just asking you to try and understand him."

"Understand him?" He rolled his eyes. "Don't bring your Ph.D. into this. There is *no* justification for what he did."

"I'm not condoning what he did, Paul. But it's obvious he has a problem. You just can't turn your back on him."

He stared at her defiantly.

Realizing that she wasn't going to be able to reason with him, she knocked on the door and went inside.

Ethan looked up from his paperwork.

"Hello, Ethan."

"Grace," he said standing up. Behind her, he could see Paul out in the hallway. "How's Jessica?" he asked softly.

"Well...she's doing all right, under the circumstances. How are you doing?"

He shrugged, not knowing how to answer.

Out of the corner of her eye, Grace saw her husband shift his weight to his other leg. "You know, Ethan, Jessica is like a daughter to me and I care about what happens to her. But I also care about you."

"I appreciate that," he mumbled, but his words lacked conviction.

"Well, I guess I better be getting home. Merry Christmas." She immediately bit her tongue. Those last two words had come out by force of habit from having said it dozens of times over these past few days. She realized how terribly inconsiderate it must have sounded to him.

~

That evening, Ethan was on his way upstairs to take a shower when his doorbell rang. He trotted down the steps and hurried across the foyer to answer it. "Sarah."

"Can I come in?"

"Sure," he said, stepping aside. "But why are you here?"

She walked in carrying a big grocery bag. "Well, Ashley and Ted were invited to a Christmas party at his brother's house," she said as he took the bag from her. "Thanks." She unbuttoned her coat, revealing blue jeans and a sweater.

"And?"

She took the bag back from him and shrugged. "Well, I couldn't see letting this dinner go to waste. You haven't eaten, have you?"

"No."

"Good. Let's go to the kitchen."

She set the bag down on the island and pulled a silver five-quart pan from it.

The aroma made Ethan's mouth water. "Mmm, smells good. What is it?" he asked, peeking under the lid.

"Chicken and dumplings. I have some rolls, too. Do you have a baking sheet?"

He opened the cabinet underneath the sink. "I'm sorry you didn't get to spend any time with Ashley tonight."

"That's okay. I told myself that I'm going to have her all to myself for the next two weeks. By the way," she said, sliding the rolls out of the bag, "before I left the hospital this afternoon, I took a message for you."

"From who?" he asked, scouring the shelves.

She watched him closely as she spoke. "John from Australian Airlines. He wanted to know if your passengers had gotten in all right."

He was silent as he turned around and set the pan on the counter. "You weren't supposed to find out," he said after a moment.

Sarah's eyes brimmed with tears as she wiped her hands on a towel. "How did you arrange all this?"

"John is a friend of mine, and he owed me a favor, so..."

She shook her head slightly and sniffed. "Did you pay for it?"

He looked at his shoes and shrugged.

"Why did you do this?"

"Because I saw the look on your face when you found out she wasn't coming. It about broke my heart—"

She suddenly threw her arms around his neck. "Thank you! That's the nicest thing anyone has ever done for me in my life."

"Well then," he said, winking at her, "you've had a hard life."

~

After dinner, Ethan made a pot of coffee and they went into the living room to talk. Sarah noticed that his guard was up when it came to Jessica, and he went to great lengths to avoid questions about her. She tried her best to keep the conversation light, steering it mainly towards Ashley and Ted.

The phone rang.

"I need to get that," he said, standing up. "I'm on call tonight."

She leaned back against the couch and sipped her coffee as she waited for him to finish. Her eyes wandered slowly around the room taking in all of the Christmas decorations. It was very tastefully done in warm colors of silver and gold, the eloquence of which, made Sarah's light up lawn Santa and reindeer seem cheesy.

As she went to set her coffee down, she spied a set of papers that were lying open on the table. Without thinking, she picked them up and began to read. It was only then that she noticed the room had grown quiet. Looking up, she saw that Ethan had hung up the phone and was now staring at her. Her cheeks began to burn. "I'm sorry."

"It's all right," he said, waving his hand as if it didn't matter.

She placed the papers back on the table. "This was what that courier delivered to you this afternoon, wasn't it?"

He sat down beside her.

"Ethan, I'm so sorry."

"Paul must have stayed up all night to get these delivered to me today," he said with an edge in his voice.

She leaned over and squeezed his hand. "Ethan, I know it looks like your world has just ended, but I'm here to tell you that it does get easier."

Her words were met with silence.

She frantically searched in her mind for something else to say. "Oh, I almost forgot."

"What?"

She got up and scurried into the foyer, returning a moment later with two small boxes wrapped in red foil. "With all the excitement this afternoon, I forgot to give these to you today," she said, handing him the first one.

He took the box from her and tore at the paper. Enclosed was a silver pen. He lifted it out of its casing and saw that his name was engraved along the side of it. "This is just what I needed. Thank you."

"Now you have no excuse for taking mine."

"No, I guess not," he said, laughing.

"Here, open the next one."

The second box contained a tie with a bunch of Santas printed on it. He held it up against his shirt and smiled.

"I thought you could wear it to work tomorrow."

He leaned forward and kissed her on the cheek. "Thanks." He set the boxes on the table and stood up. "I have one for you, too." With everything that had happened, he had forgotten to take it to work today.

Sarah peered over the back of the couch and noticed that there were only three presents under the tree, making it look sad and desolate.

Ethan knelt down and picked up one of them.

"You've already given me a wonderful present," she said.

"Well, you're allowed to have two."

She tore at the wrapping and lifted a bottle of perfume out of the box. "How did you know I wanted this?" she asked, sounding startled.

He gave her his lopsided grin as he sat back down. "Because you were scratching and sniffing it in a magazine the other day."

"I was *not!*" She thought for a moment and then threw her head back and laughed. *"Was I?"* She took the cap off and squirted a tiny amount on her wrist. The fragrance was divine. "It smells nice, see?"

He sniffed her wrist as she held it out to him. "Mmm-hmm."

The grandfather clock in the foyer began to chime, telling Sarah it was time to leave. "Well, it's getting late, and I know you have to be at the hospital early tomorrow," she said, standing to go.

"Wait a minute," he replied, walking towards the kitchen, "don't forget your leftovers."

"You can keep them and return the pan later."

"Well, that's fine," he said, helping her with her coat, "but I hope that's not your favorite pan."

~

Jessica sat on the floor rubbing Ryan's back in an attempt to get him to sleep. He wasn't taking to his new surroundings very well, and every night had become a chore when it came time for bed.

Finally, his eyes closed and his pacifier grew lax in his mouth. Placing her hand against the nightstand for leverage, she got to her feet and slipped out the door.

The smell of a pumpkin pie baking in the oven immediately assaulted her nose, making her stomach roll. Grace had been in the kitchen most of the evening, doing what she loved.

Jessica couldn't help smiling as she watched from the doorway. Her cousin stood hunched over the counter, contentedly rolling out dough for another pie. Flour and empty mixing bowls littered the area around her.

She looked up when she saw her standing there. "Is he asleep?"

"Finally," Jessica answered, swallowing the bout of nausea that was circling inside her.

Grace laid the rolling pin aside and picked up the flattened dough. "You know that you and Ryan are more than welcome to come with us tomorrow."

She folded her arms across her stomach as if that would somehow stop the bile from churning. "I know."

"I'm sure that Will and the girls would love to see you again."

She was referring to her and Paul's son. He lived two hours away with his wife and their twin daughters. "I appreciate the offer, Grace. I really do, but I think Ryan and I will just spend a quiet day here."

A small sigh fell from her cousin's lips as she pressed the dough inside a baking dish. "I don't like leaving you here alone," she said, cutting off the excess with a knife. "I really think it would be best if you came with us."

"I'll be fine, Grace. But you and Paul go and enjoy those grandkids of yours."

"Well, you know I will," she said with a chuckle as she began to scrape the pie filling into the dish. "I can't wait to see them open their presents."

The queasiness inside her grew, causing her to cover her mouth with her hand.

"Are you still nauseous?"

She nodded, unable to answer at the moment.

"There's a stomach virus going around. Do you want me to call you in a prescription? The drugstore around the corner is open 'til nine."

She took her hand away and drew a deep breath. "It's not a virus."

Grace looked up from the pan, startled. Her lips opened and closed several times before anything came out of them. "Are you pregnant?"

Jessica's eyes flooded with tears.
"How far along are you?" she whispered.
"Almost six weeks."

Chapter Thirty-one

Sarah leaned over the sink, rinsing the plates off one by one. All things considered, Christmas dinner had gone pretty well. She and Gavin had managed to make polite conversation when they'd had to, and kept their distance the rest of the time.

She went back out into the dining room to get the last of the dishes and noticed that Gavin had Ted cornered. Her son-in-law was a small, wiry young man, with a tinny voice to match. His eyes darted nervously back and forth as Gavin grilled him about his studies.

Laughing softly to herself, Sarah returned to the kitchen.

"What's so funny?"

"I think you need to go rescue your husband. He's turning pale."

Ashley smiled, revealing a perfect set of teeth. "I think I'll let him suffer for a bit." She flipped her long, auburn hair over her shoulder as she loaded the plates into the dishwasher. "Mom, yesterday when I went up to see Dad, I overheard two nurses talking in the elevator."

"And?" she asked, placing the stack of dishes on the counter beside her.

"They were talking about Dr. Harrington and his wife, saying how they had separated. Is that true?"

Sarah pursed her lips a moment before answering. "Yes."

"That's too bad. Their little boy is only what…eight months old?"

She nodded, painfully aware of his age.

Ashley rinsed the plate she was holding twice. "Mom? Do you think Dad and Jessica are seeing each other again?"

"Why would you ask such a thing?" she asked, cramming a fork into the dishwasher caddy.

"Because I also overheard the nurses saying that Dad and Dr. Harrington had gotten into a fight at the Christmas party."

Sarah felt her face start to tingle as she reached for another fork.

"So, do you think they are?"

"No," she said, giving her an absurd look.

"Did you see them fight?"

Sarah straightened up and placed a hand on her hip. "First of all, it wasn't a *fight*. They had some words. The two of them had a little too much to drink, that's all."

Ashley nodded, seeming to accept her explanation.

"Sweetheart, I've got to go," Gavin said, coming through the doorway. "I've got to make my rounds."

Ashley dried her hands off and gave him a hug. "Thanks for coming, Dad. I'll see you on Thursday…right?"

"Absolutely."

"Don't forget your leftovers."

He glanced in Sarah's direction and then at the kitchen table. "Oh, right," he said, reaching for a plate wrapped in foil.

Sarah picked up a glass of wine from off the counter and finished it, not caring whose it was. "I'll see you out," she said, clearing her throat.

They walked silently out of the kitchen and through the front door.

"Thanks for having me over."

"You're welcome."

He opened his car door and slid the plate of leftovers in the front seat.

"Gavin? After you left the party the other night, did you and Ethan fight outside?"

"No. Why?"

"No reason," she said, shaking her head. "Have you talked to Jessica?"

"I've been meaning to give her a call, but I wanted to wait a few days. Why are you asking all these questions?"

She shivered and bundled her coat around her. "I just wondered if she'd said anything to you about what had happened."

"I haven't spoken to her since the morning after the party. She called to tell me that she had left Ethan and needed some time off. That's all she said."

She searched his eyes for any hidden message.

He cocked his head. "What?"

"Are you seeing her again?"

He leaned against his car. "Why would you even *think* that?" he asked angrily.

"Because your daughter heard about your confrontation with Ethan from someone at the hospital, and *asked* me if you were."

"What did you tell her?"

"Nothing. I told her that it was a misunderstanding and that you weren't having an affair."

"Did she believe you?"

"I think so," she said, nodding. "But I just felt you should know what she was thinking."

"And what about you? What do you think?"

She crossed her arms, picking up on his tone. "It doesn't really matter what I think, does it?"

He turned and jerked open his door. "Not anymore."

~

Sunday afternoon, Jessica stood in front of the bathroom mirror staring at her lip. The bruise had faded, but the cut was still there. She applied a heavy amount of foundation on her mouth, and then covered it with a dark shade of lipstick.

"Jessica? Gavin's here," Grace said, pushing the door open.

She continued to stare at herself in the mirror. "Grace? Can you tell?"

She stood behind her and looked at her reflection. "No, sweetheart."

Gavin was in the living room with Ryan when she walked in. "Thank you for letting me have him today. You don't know how much I appreciate this."

She hid behind her smile. "You two have a good time."

"How have you been?"

"Well, I guess I've been better," she said, trying to laugh.

He shook his head. That had come out wrong. "Is there anything I can do to help?"

"No, but I'll be all right," she replied, hoping she sounded confident.

He switched Ryan to his other arm. "Jessica, do you mind if I ask you a personal question?"

"You want to know why I left him," she stated.

His face flushed.

She sat down on the sofa and folded her hands in her lap.

"Was it because of what happened at the party?"

"This has been coming for a long time. The party just brought it all to a head," she said softly.

Gavin started to say something but stopped.

"What?"

"I know this is the last thing you need to hear right now, but some people at the hospital, my ex-wife included, think that you and I are seeing each other again."

She sighed.

"I didn't mean to upset you. I just thought you should know before you went back to work."

~

Later that day, Jessica stood alongside Grace on the front steps of a house that was for rent. As the realtor unlocked the door for them, she took a moment to look around the outside of it. It had cream-colored aluminum siding, and a covered porch. There was also a white picket fence set around the front yard; perfect for Ryan to play in.

Walking through the door, she noticed that the inside was not nearly as small as it appeared to be. The living room was a good size with light colored walls and carpeting, and just off to the right, there was a large den with an attached bathroom. Jessica thought that Mrs. Chambers could make that her bedroom. Upstairs, there were two more bedrooms as well as another bathroom.

"Would you like to see the backyard?" the agent asked.

"I'd like to take another look around up here first, if you don't mind."

"Not at all. I'll be downstairs if you need me," she said eagerly.

Jessica walked over to one of the windows. She had not intended to get a house, but the rent was the same as most of the apartments she had already looked at this morning. This particular house came with the option to buy later on.

"What do you think?" Grace asked, meandering around the room.

She shook her head and sighed. "I don't know."

~

Jessica sat at the kitchen table that evening, biting her nails. For the past hour she had done nothing but think about buying that house. It was a scary prospect, especially when she considered all the responsibilities that came with it.

She was still deep in thought when the doorbell rang. Expecting it to be Gavin, she got up and opened the door.

Ethan stood on the other side.

Feelings of fear, surprise, and hope came over her all at once, leaving her speechless.

"I'm sorry. I know I should have called first, but you won't talk to me on the phone. Can I come in for a moment?"

She hesitated. Grace had gone to the grocery, and Paul was out having dinner with a client. She really wasn't keen on being in the house alone with him.

"Please?"

She widened the door and stepped back, allowing him to come inside. She noticed he was carrying a rather large package under his arm with a smaller one resting on top of it. He set them down on the floor and took off his coat.

"Have a seat," she said, gesturing towards the chair.

"Thanks."

An agonizing moment of silence dragged by.

"Where's Ryan?"

"He's not here. He's out...with Gavin." There was no point in lying to him.

Ethan nodded. The fact that Gavin had gotten his way seemed of little importance to him right now. Sitting forward in the chair, he drew a deep breath and said what he'd come to say. "I'm sorry for hitting you, Jess."

"Are you?"

A look of surprise came across him. "*Yes.*"

She shook her head as if she didn't believe him.

He reached for her hand and held it tight. "I swear to God that it will never happen again."

She stared into those beautiful eyes of his. They were the ones she had fallen in love with so long ago.

He let go of her hand and went to touch the side of her face.

"Don't, Ethan," she said, drawing back.

"Jess...can you please just give me another chance?" he half-whispered. "I gave *you* one."

She looked at him for the longest time before answering. "No, you didn't. You held it over my head every chance you could. I know how badly I hurt you, Ethan...but I also know it's something that you just can't quite forgive me for."

He cast his gaze on the floor.

"I see it in your eyes when you look at me sometimes, and I hear it in your voice when we argue. I'm tired of feeling guilty over something I can't change."

"It won't be like that anymore. I promise, I'll never bring it up again. Things will be different this time, Jess. I'll quit drinking."

She wiped at the tears that were forming in her eyes. "Don't make promises you can't keep," she said quietly.

"I'll stop. You have to believe me, I haven't had a drink since that night."

She rose from the couch and began shaking her head. "Do you think this is all just going to go away because you *say* it's going to be different?"

He got to his feet. "What do I have to do to make you believe me?"

Jessica folded her arms against her chest and swallowed hard. With all her heart and soul she wanted to tell him that she was pregnant, but she knew it would only bring more empty promises from him.

"I'll do anything. Anything you say," he begged.

She suddenly looked at him, feeling hopeful. "Will you go to an AA meeting?"

He locked onto her eyes. "No."

It was her turn to plead. "I'll go with you."

"Haven't you been *listening* to me? I have not had a drink since that night."

"And just how long has that been, Ethan? Five whole days? Don't you see what this has done to *you?* What it's done to *us?* You need help. And you need to get it before it's too late."

"I am not an alcoholic!" he yelled, clenching his fists.

She visibly recoiled from him.

Frustrated, he turned his back on her and put his hands on his hips. "I'm not," he said, lowering his voice.

"Fine. Let's talk about your temper, then."

He turned.

"We *both* know what a bad temper you have, Ethan, and when you're drunk, you can't control it. What if next time you take it out on Ryan?"

"How can you even think that? I would *never...ever* hit Ryan."

Her chin began to tremble. "What would you have done to me if you had gotten my car door open?"

It was an emotional blow. He looked away, not knowing how to answer.

She sat down on the couch and buried her face in her hands as her shoulders began to shake. She couldn't hold it in any longer. It was over. It was over and she had no idea what she was going to do.

Ethan watched her as she cried, but made no attempt to comfort her this time.

~

Jessica finished giving Ryan his bottle and laid him in his playpen, finding that he seemed to sleep better in it. She picked up the present Ethan had brought by today. It was a very large mechanical puppy that told nursery rhymes and bedtime stories. She selected a disc and inserted it in the hidden compartment in the puppy's back. Placing it beside Ryan, she turned it on. The puppy made a whirring noise and came to life. Its tail wagged back and forth as its mouth opened and closed.

Ryan turned over on his stomach and watched intently. He was utterly fascinated. He kept trying to catch the puppy's eyes as they winked at him.

She sat down on the bed and picked up the present Ethan had left for her. A broken breath fell from her lips as she placed it back on the nightstand and slipped under the covers. She laid her head against the pillow and closed her eyes, letting the soft, hushed tone of the puppy's voice lull her to sleep.

~

Ethan sat in the darkness in his living room. The only light came from the fire that was crackling softly in the fireplace. He rested his head on the back of the cushion and sighed. There was an unopened bottle of scotch on the table that he had been staring at for some time. The orange flames danced wildly upon the side of it, seeming to give it a life of its own.

He could faintly hear a shutter banging on the backside of the house as the wind howled. He listened to its haunting wail as he continued to stare at the amber colored liquid. Maybe there were times that he drank too much, he thought to himself, but he certainly wasn't an alcoholic.

He leaned forward and unscrewed the cap off the bottle. Its aroma was strong as he brought it to his lips. He stopped and rested it on his leg. Looking down, he noticed that his left hand was trembling ever so slightly. How had he gotten to this point in his life? His whole world seemed to be crumbling.

He took a long swallow from the bottle and breathed in sharply as the heat surged through him. After a moment, his trembling stopped.

Ethan cradled the bottle in his arms as he let the alcohol comfort him. It was a true friend indeed. It knew his sorrows, but never left him. It never betrayed him, or hurt him. It knew all his dark secrets that he had hidden in his soul, but never judged him. It knew his every fear, but never taunted him. It anticipated his pain, and offered him solace. He never had to explain himself to it, or hide his feelings from it. It just wanted to help him. And like a lover, it held out its arms to embrace him unconditionally. He turned the bottle up and drank until the darkness engulfed him.

Chapter Thirty-two

Jessica sat on the kitchen floor of her new home unpacking one of the boxes. She looked around, dismayed by all the cartons and sacks that were strewn about. She had rented a small moving truck this morning, and she and Grace, along with Paul, had collected the rest of the things from her house.

"Why don't you take a break?" Grace asked, sitting down beside her.

"I'm all right. I just want to get this done."

"You know, you need your rest," she said in a motherly tone. "You have to take care of yourself...and the baby."

"I know," she said, sifting through the objects in the box. She pulled out a silver picture frame and turned it over. Her eyes immediately began to water. "You know, Grace, I thought I would be married to him forever."

"I know, sweetheart."

She wiped at her eyes. "I keep thinking that if I had been a better wife to him..." She stopped and shook her head. "If I hadn't slept with Gavin, maybe he wouldn't be so bitter, and he wouldn't drink so much."

Grace placed her hand under Jessica's chin and forced it up. "*Don't* make excuses for him. You could have been the most perfect wife in the world, and he would *still* be an alcoholic. There is absolutely nothing you did. Absolutely nothing."

"I don't think I can do this," she whispered.

"You are a lot stronger than you think." Grace's tone of voice relaxed as she patted her hand. "It's a new year; a time for fresh starts and new beginnings. And just remember that Paul and I are only a phone call away."

Ding-dong!

"Oh, that must be the pizza guy," she said, standing up. "I don't know about you, but I'm starving."

As Grace hurried to answer the door, Paul came down the stairs and wandered in to wash his hands in the sink.

"Here you go." Jessica got to her feet and handed him a paper towel.

"Thanks."

"Paul, thank you for all that you've done for me and Ryan. Words cannot express how truly grateful I am."

He smiled. "I was glad that I could help."

"Well, I'm sure the both of you will be happy to have the house back to yourselves again. No more crying baby…no more annoying guest…"

Paul put his arm around her shoulder and sighed. "You know, now that you're gone, she's going to make me start using that *damn* treadmill."

~

Ethan stood in the doorway of the nursery, his jaw clenched. She had taken everything. The room was barren except for a few stuffed animals that lay scattered about on the floor.

He stalked into their bedroom and jerked open the closet door. Seeing that all of her things were gone, he struck out at the first thing he could. Their wedding picture went crashing to the floor.

He fell back against the door and closed his eyes, fighting the tears that wanted to come out. Desiring the one thing that would stop them, he opened his eyes and started to head downstairs. That's when he noticed something shiny on the nightstand.

Walking over, he saw that she had left the keys to the house. Beside them, sat a small box. A bitter sigh fell from him as he sat down on the bed. He recognized the box as Jessica's Christmas present. It had not been opened.

~

The sunlight spilled through the big bay window in the kitchen casting a warm glow about the room. Jessica finished unpacking the last of the boxes and closed the cupboard. She stretched for a moment and began rubbing the back of her neck. She was starting to feel the effects of having been up since dawn.

A growl from her stomach made her remember that she definitely had to go to the grocery today. Sitting down at the kitchen table, she began to compile a list. As she wrote, she listened for any sounds of life from her son on the monitor a few feet away.

"Good morning."

She looked up from her paper. "I hope I didn't wake you," she said apologetically.

"Oh, no," Mrs. Chambers said, waving her hand in the air. "I wanted to get up early and go get the rest of my belongings from the guesthouse."

Jessica nodded. When she had phoned her to tell her about her new living arrangements, the older woman had not seemed surprised. She knew that she had heard them arguing on occasion, not to mention Ethan's absence most nights.

"You know, Ellen, I can't thank you enough for moving in here with us. I know that you're giving up a great deal of your privacy."

"I'll let you in on a little secret, dear," she said, sitting down across from her. "I was pretty lonely in that guesthouse. I don't mind being here at all."

Jessica smiled. "I'm so glad you feel that way."

She covered her mouth as a yawn escaped from it. "Excuse me," she said with a chuckle. "I'm still running on California time. I think I'll fix some coffee. Would you like a cup?"

"No, I can't have any." Jessica pursed her lips, immediately regretting her words.

The older woman turned. "Why not?"

She knew she was going to have to tell her sooner or later, as she was certain she'd heard her throwing up earlier. "I'm pregnant," she said quietly.

A broad grin spread across Ellen's face making the lines around her eyes crinkle. "Oh, that's wonderful!" Her grin collapsed in on itself as quickly as it had come. "I'm sorry. I mean—"

"It's all right, really. To tell you the truth, I'm not even sure how I feel about it, yet. I just found out myself a week ago...after Ethan and I had separated. I haven't told him yet, so I would appreciate it if you wouldn't say anything to him."

"Of course," Ellen said sympathetically.

~

Sarah and Ethan sat in the hospital cafeteria having breakfast. It was nearly deserted except for the two of them.

"Did you have a nice vacation?" he asked, taking a sip of his coffee.

"It was wonderful," she answered, reaching for the pepper in front of her.

"Are Ashley and Ted gone?"

"They went back yesterday morning."

"I'm glad you got to see her."

She nodded as she blackened her eggs. "I'm going to visit them this summer."

"Well, that will give you something to look forward to," he said, rubbing the sleep from his eyes. He had been called to the hospital around three-thirty this morning. One of his patients, a woman with terminal cancer, had taken a turn for the worse. The only thing he could do for her now was make her as comfortable as possible, and let her family say goodbye.

"Were things very hectic in the clinic while I was away?"

"It wasn't too bad."

"And how are things with you?" she asked, lowering her voice.

"The same," he said, not really wanting to elaborate.

~

Later that morning, Ethan stood over the bed in the darkened room of Mrs. Grayson, the woman dying of cancer. He had given her another gram of morphine to make her pain subside and she was now resting comfortably. A few milligrams more and he knew she would die peacefully in her sleep. He ran his fingers through his hair and sighed. It was a fine line that doctors walked between easing someone's pain, and committing euthanasia.

Six months ago, Mrs. Grayson was a healthy, happy woman with a true zest for life. Now, there was nothing left of her but her soul. He could see her skeleton showing through her skin.

As he went silently out the door, he saw her family off to the left in a small waiting room. The woman's son stood up when he saw him approaching. There were two young girls, whom Ethan figured were her grandchildren, asleep on the sofa.

The son, who looked to be in his late thirties, rubbed his bleary eyes. "How is she?"

"It probably won't be much longer. She's not in any pain right now, and we're going to try and make her as comfortable as we can," Ethan said, feeling somewhat frustrated at his answer. With all the technology this hospital had, and all of the training and medical skills he had been given, there was nothing else he could do to save her.

The man looked away for a moment and nodded his head.

Ethan made his way down the corridor. It was an awful thing to watch someone you love die a slow and agonizing death. It was a death that had no dignity.

As he neared the elevator, he noticed Gavin standing by the nurses' station.

"Ethan," he said, nodding.

He would have ignored him if Phillip hadn't been watching the exchange on the other side of the hall. He gave him a curt nod and pushed the button on the wall. As he waited for the doors to open, he could feel Phillip's disapproving eyes on his back.

~

Jessica sat in her office that morning reviewing her caseload. Gavin had already gone over the charts with her earlier, giving her an update. A few moments from now, she would start her rounds and try to pretend that everything was normal, but she cringed at the thought of having to leave her office.

She took a sip of coffee and shivered at its foul taste. She knew some women had strange cravings during pregnancy, but the only thing she really longed for was caffeine. Her hand inadvertently slid over her flat stomach as her thoughts turned to the baby again. She wasn't sure she was up to raising another child on her own, and she had scheduled an appointment for later today to speak with Dr. Cali about an abortion.

~

Ethan watched the snow from his office window. The large flakes fell from the sky, covering the ground in a fine white powder. He stared intently at his car down below and found himself wondering how long it would take before it blanketed his windshield.

"Ethan?"

He turned at the sound of Jessica's voice.

She stood by his desk, her face expressionless as she held a piece of paper out to him. "That's my new address and phone number."

He studied the address silently for a moment before folding the paper and tucking it in his shirt pocket.

Having accomplished the difficult task of seeing him, she turned quickly to go.

"Jess?"

She stopped but didn't look back.

"Can I come by tonight and see Ryan?"

She drew a deep breath and held it. Paul had set the legal paperwork in motion asking that she have sole custody. It was something that Ethan knew nothing about.

Once he had been served with the papers, there would be a meeting with the judge to decide temporary custody until the case had been heard. But Paul had warned her that, at least for the next couple of weeks, she had to let Ethan see him. There was nothing they could do legally, and furthermore, it would probably be best if he didn't suspect anything.

~

Ethan drove slowly down Meridian Street looking for the address Jessica had given him. He passed house after house looking for the number 1024, but most of the mailboxes were covered with snow. Before long, he came to the end of the street.

He turned his car around and went back, driving even slower this time. His windshield wipers squeaked back and forth as he searched. A few yards ahead, he finally spotted Jessica's car parked out in front of a house with the porch light on.

Mrs. Chambers greeted him at the door. "Dr. Harrington, how are you?"

"I'm fine," he said, wiping his feet before coming in. "Did you have a nice Christmas with your daughter?"

The older woman smiled. "I had a wonderful time."

"How was California?"

"A lot warmer!" she said with a laugh. "Here, let me take your coat."

"Thank you."

"What happened?" she asked when she saw the cast on his hand.

"I had a little accident."

"Dadda!" Ryan was inching towards him in his walker.

Ethan knelt down and picked him up. "Hi there," he said, giving him a big hug.

Ellen hung up his coat and excused herself from the room.

"How's my big boy? Did you miss Daddy?"

Ryan touched his face and grinned.

Ethan kissed him on the ticklish spot of his neck, sending him into a spasm of giggles.

Jessica hesitantly came down the stairs. "Did you just get off work?"

"Yes."

"How are the roads?"

"Getting slick. I think if it's all right with you, I'll just stay here and visit."

"That's fine," she said, not wanting to jeopardize Ryan's safety. She walked over and sat down on her new sofa. She had purchased the beige piece of furniture yesterday, along with two matching chairs.

Ethan followed silently and sat on the opposite end of it. He bounced Ryan up and down on his knee as he took a moment to look around. "This is a nice house. Are you renting?"

"For now." She watched as Ryan began climbing up his chest.

"What are you...a monkey?" he asked, holding onto his legs to keep him from falling.

Jessica swallowed hard. If it weren't for the underlying tension in the room, one would never guess that there was anything wrong between them. Her hormones were wreaking havoc on her body, making it increasingly difficult for her to refrain from bursting into tears.

"He's really grown," he said, more to himself than to her.

She cleared her throat, hoping it would dissolve the lump that was building up. "It's about time for his dinner. Do you want to feed him?"

He drew Ryan close to him. "Are you hungry?"

Ryan placed his hands around Ethan's neck and leaned into his cheek with his mouth open.

"What was that?" he asked, laughing as he wiped the slobber from his face.

"I think that's his idea of kissing," she said, turning towards the kitchen so he wouldn't see that her chin was trembling. "He just started that last week."

He followed her into the kitchen and placed Ryan in his highchair.

She opened a jar of baby food and held it out to him. As Ethan took it from her, she suppressed a shudder. The sight of the cast on his hand brought back images she would just as soon forget. "I'll leave you two alone."

"You don't have to go," he said, sounding hopeful as he fastened Ryan's bib.

"I've got some paperwork that I really need to get through." She hurried out the door before he could persuade her to stay. She was feeling very vulnerable at the moment and didn't want to leave herself open to him.

Chapter Thirty-three

Ethan stuffed the last of the Christmas decorations into a box and taped it shut. A tired sigh fell from his lips as he looked at all the cartons sitting on the floor. Finding that he was not in the mood to lug them up the attic stairs right now, he went over and sat down on the sofa, promising himself that he'd do it tomorrow.

Grabbing his drink from off the table, he leaned back against the cushion and began sorting through his mail. He looked at each piece before tossing it aside. Water bill...phone bill...junk...he stopped when he came to the next one. It was from Paul's office.

He hesitated before opening it, knowing it was regarding the divorce. He hadn't even gotten himself an attorney yet. After finishing his drink, he opened the envelope and began to read.

'From Paul Cummings, Attorney at Law...regarding dissolution of marriage...on the twenty-fifth day of January...there will be a hearing...temporary custody.'

Ethan sat forward and tore the letter in half. There was no way in *hell* she was going to do this to him.

~

Jessica sat on the lid of the toilet seat watching Ellen give Ryan a bath. She normally liked doing it herself but was not feeling well. Her morning sickness had eased up, but she had felt nauseous and dizzy for most of the day.

The doorbell sounded below.

"I'll get it." She glanced at the clock on the wall as she hurried down the stairs. It was almost nine. Approaching the door, she cautiously peered through the peephole.

Ethan stood on the other side.

She started to unlock the door, but hesitated. She knew he had gotten the papers today.

He impatiently rang the bell again.

Drawing a deep breath to steel herself, she opened the door and took a step back.

Ethan's eyes were smoldering as he walked inside. "Why did you file for sole custody?"

"I think you know the answer to that," she said evenly.

"*No,* I don't *know,* Jessica. That's why I'm here."

She crossed her arms. "If we shared joint custody of him, I would be scared to death you would hurt him."

He began to shake his head. "I can't believe this."

"I know you wouldn't hurt him intentionally, Ethan. I'm talking specifically about your need to drink yourself into a *stupor* and then drive home."

"You can't be serious!"

"Play it down all you want," she said, pointing her finger at him, "but I'm not *about* to let that happen." An onslaught of dizziness made her forget what else she was going to say.

His temper flared. "You *cannot* keep me from seeing my son!"

Jessica saw the hardwood hurtling towards her.

Ethan reached out and caught her in his arms. "What's wrong?" he asked, easing her down onto the floor.

Before she could say anything else, a sharp, stabbing pain traveled through her abdomen.

"What's the matter?"

Mrs. Chambers came running down the stairs with Ryan. "What happened?"

She cried out as another pain tore through her.

"Jess, what's wrong?" he asked, trying to pull her hands away from her stomach so he could look.

Ellen knelt on the other side of her. "Is it the baby?"

A startled silence suddenly came over Ethan, making him withdraw his hands. His eyes filled with hurt as he looked at her.

Jessica turned her head away.

After a moment, he leaned over and scooped her up. "I need to get her to the hospital."

Mrs. Chambers hurried in front of him to open the door.

Jessica curled herself up in the front seat, letting her head rest against his shoulder, as he sped towards the hospital.

He reached for his cell phone. "This is Dr. Harrington. I need to know if Dr. Cali is in the building."

Jessica closed her eyes as he gave instructions on the phone. His voice sounded muffled to her.

He tossed the phone on the dashboard and reached for her hand. "Everything's going to be fine," he said, trying to sound calm.

When he pulled up to the emergency room entrance, a nurse and orderly were waiting with a stretcher. As they helped her onto it, Ethan noticed the blood on her pants.

"Dr. Cali is here, she's finishing up with a delivery and will be down shortly," the nurse said to him.

Once inside the cubicle, the nurses helped Jessica with her pants and underwear before covering her with a sheet.

After a few moments, Dr. Cali appeared around the curtain. She took one look at Jessica and turned to the nurse. "Let's do a vaginal ultrasound."

Ethan watched as the nurses slid her feet into the stirrups.

Dr. Cali sat down on the stool and studied the monitor beside her as she guided the instrument inside Jessica. She leaned over and whispered something to the nurse, who nodded and left the room.

Ethan looked at the monitor and could see the fetus, but he couldn't see the heartbeat.

"I'm sorry," Dr. Cali said. "I'm going to have to do a D and C to stop the bleeding."

"All right," he heard himself say.

The nurse came back in carrying a covered tray.

Jessica cried out again in pain.

He immediately took a step towards her, but Dr. Cali put her hand against his chest and backed him away. "Ethan," she said evenly, "I think it would be best if you waited outside."

Before he could answer, the nurse drew the curtain separating him from her.

Time seemed to move in slow motion as he waited. Overwhelmed with guilt, he began pacing the floor.

Twenty minutes later, Dr. Cali finally came out.

"How is she?"

"She's fine. I'm going to keep her overnight for monitoring because of the amount of blood she lost, but I don't anticipate any problems." The doctor placed a hand upon his shoulder. "I'm sorry."

He gave her a brief nod as she turned to go. "Kate?" he said, stopping her. "I don't want anyone, who doesn't have to, to know about this. Can we keep this as discreet as possible?"

"I'll do my best. You can see her now if you like."

When he stepped through the curtain, Jessica was lying on her side with her knees slightly bent. Her blonde hair was tangled and matted as it gathered around the pillow. "Why didn't you tell me?"

"I'm sorry," she whispered.

He clenched his jaw at her answer. "How far along were you?"

She kept her eyes focused on her I.V. "Nine weeks."

Anger churned in him, but he realized that this was neither the time nor place to display it. "Do you want me to call Grace?"

She nodded, the movement of her head shaking loose the tears that had pooled in her eyes.

Ethan watched as they rapidly fell down her cheeks. After a moment, he turned and walked towards the curtain. "Jess?" he said, looking back. "I'm sorr—" He stopped and drew a deep breath. After a moment, it became clear that he was not going to be able to finish. His lips quivered as he parted the curtain and left.

~

Jessica stared blankly out the window from her hospital bed. The sun was just beginning to rise, bringing the city out of its slumber. It had been a long night without sleep and she wished Grace would hurry back with her change of clothes. She wanted to be ready to leave when Dr. Cali discharged her.

The anxiety inside her grew when she looked at the clock on the wall. She'd hoped to be gone before the next shift change—before any of her colleagues arrived. Today happened to be Friday, her regular day off, and she figured that she would spend the weekend recuperating and then be back at work Monday without anyone realizing what had happened. Dr. Cali had admitted her under her maiden name in order to help.

She absently brushed her hand over her stomach. It was a gesture that immediately sent a surge of guilt through her as she remembered how she had felt when she'd found out she was pregnant. She had not wanted this baby.

The sound of a man's footsteps approaching made her cringe. Grace had told her that Ethan had been waiting outside all night, and she knew it was just a matter of time before he came in.

He stood just off to the side, keeping a distance. The anger he'd held in his eyes last night had long since faded.

She gripped the sheets tightly, dreading the conversation that was about to come forth.

He looked at her and shook his head. "Why didn't you tell me?"

"Because I needed some time to sort things out."

"I had a right to know," he said quietly.

"It was my body."

His jaw tightened. "You still should have told me. Things would have been different."

"Different in what way?" She held back her tears. "Your knowing wouldn't have changed anything, Ethan. It wasn't going to magically reconcile us. I couldn't come back to you. *Not* when I was pregnant...and *not* now."

~

Sarah held her arms underneath the sink, rinsing the vomit from them. Her lab coat had taken the brunt of it, but there was still plenty to wash off her skin. Her head hurt, her feet hurt, and now she smelled.

She walked out of the examination room thinking that her day couldn't possibly get any worse.

"Hello, Dr. Williams."

She was wrong.

"Renee, it's nice to see you again," she said, summoning a pretend smile. "How are you?"

"I'm doing well, thank you," she answered. "And you?"

"Busy."

She arched her eyebrow and gave her a quick glance that was not meant to be subtle. "Yes, I can see that."

Sarah could feel her cheeks burning. Today of all days, she was wearing her scrubs and tennis shoes. They could hardly compare to what Renee had on which, she gathered, had certainly not come from any department store. "Ethan is with a patient right now," she said. "He'll probably be a little while."

She smiled sweetly at her. "I'll wait."

"All right," Sarah said, gesturing towards the couch. "You can wait over there..."

Renee sauntered over and sat down in Ethan's chair. She threw her purse on top of the desk and crossed her silk-stockinged legs.

Sarah dropped her hand and bit her tongue. She guessed this would do nothing to improve Ethan's mood. He had been in a dark one all day.

As if on cue, he came out of the other examination room and stopped in his tracks. "Renee," he said, half-smiling.

She kissed him lightly on his cheek.

"What brings you here?"

"A business meeting," she replied, reaching up to wipe her lipstick off his face. "And I had a few hours to kill before my flight, so I thought we might be able to have a late lunch."

Ethan checked his watch. He should have had lunch two hours ago. "I'm really sorry, but I don't think I can get away. How about a cup of coffee, though?"

~

They walked silently along the snow-covered sidewalk in the park. It was deserted except for the pigeons pecking through the snow for some morsel of food.

As he took a sip of his coffee, he noticed Renee looking at his cast.

"What happened?"

"Nothing," he said, sticking it in his coat pocket.

Renee noticed the weariness in his eyes. The boyish quality he used to possess was no longer there. He had a man's face now…and it looked as troubled as it did sad. "How's Jessica?" she asked, watching him closely.

"Fine."

"I heard that the two of you are getting divorced."

He kept walking.

"Is that true?" she asked, half-running to keep up with him.

"Yes."

"Can I ask why?"

Ethan shook his head. There was not even the slightest hint of sympathy in her tone. "That's between me and Jessica."

"Well," she said, taking a sip of her coffee, "she must have done something terrible this time. I mean, *more* terrible than having an affair."

He set his jaw, refusing to play along with her mind games today.

"How's Ryan?"

"Fine," he muttered.

"So who does he look like most? You or Jessica?"

He stopped walking. "What do you want, Renee?" he asked with an edge in his voice.

She smiled, knowing she had struck a nerve.

Ethan looked at the smirk she was wearing, and suddenly realized that he had fallen right into her trap. He immediately turned and began walking again.

"I think you know why I'm here," she said when she had caught up to him.

"Sorry. You'll have to enlighten me."

An exasperated sigh fell from her. "I'm not going to pretend that I wasn't hurt when you gave Paul Cummings your proxy."

He tossed his empty cup into a nearby trashcan. "I did what I thought was best."

Renee slowed her pace, unable to be angry and walk at the same time. "You know that those shares belong to me!" she called out.

He stopped and turned around. "What do you mean?" he asked warily.

She closed the distance between them and laid down her trump card. "We both know that Ryan is Gavin's son."

Her remark clearly caught him off-guard, but he hid it well. "You're insane, Renee."

"Am I? Maybe I should go talk to Jessica."

He grabbed her by the wrist and jerked her towards him. "You stay the *hell* away from her."

"Let go of me," she said, certain he could hear the tremble in her voice.

He tightened his grip on her before letting her go.

She took a step back and rubbed her wrist. "We both know the truth, Ethan. You can't hide it forever."

An uneasiness settled inside him as he watched her turn and hurry away.

~

Ethan stood over the bathroom sink soaking his cast. He couldn't stand the sight of it any longer. After a few minutes, the plaster became pliable enough for him to cut it off with a pair of scissors. As he let the warm water run over his knuckles, he couldn't help but stare at his reflection.

Besides the obvious signs of fatigue displayed upon his face, he also noticed that his eyes appeared empty; devoid of life. Jessica's words to him this morning had only solidified the fact that his marriage was over. It was a concept that was as devastating as it was surreal.

The pale moon shown through the curtains casting small shadows at the foot of the bed as he slipped under the covers. He closed his eyes trying to forget the last twenty-four hours, but was unable to do so.

His conversation with Renee this afternoon had left him deeply disturbed. He had greatly underestimated her cunningness. Although legally he knew she couldn't do anything until the two years were up, he was afraid that she would start rumors, and they could be far more damaging.

He began to think that maybe he should give her his proxy in order to pacify her. He rolled over and sighed. Doing that would just make her believe she was right about Ryan, and she would probably only push harder. Reaching out, he drew Jessica's pillow close, wishing that she were here with him.

Chapter Thirty-four

Jessica sat outside the courtroom with Paul waiting for their turn. It was near the end of February and today was the first day of the custody hearing. Last month, the judge had awarded temporary custody to her, allowing Ethan to have Ryan every other weekend. This had not gone over well with him, and she knew, or rather feared, what today would bring.

Paul had warned her that it would probably get nasty by the time it was all over. He had also informed her that if she wanted to win sole custody, they were going to have to prove that Ethan was an unfit father. In order to do that, some painful things were going to have to be told. She consented to his plan, but made him promise not to reveal that Ethan had hit her. He had reluctantly agreed.

~

Ethan made his way up the tile-covered steps of the courthouse. The building was over one hundred and fifty years old, and he honestly didn't know how it was still standing. A few years ago it had caught fire and had nearly burnt to the ground. You could still see the black marks around the windows outside.

His footsteps echoed as made his way down the enormous hall. Rounding the corner, he spotted his attorney waiting for him outside the room. "Joseph," he said, extending his hand.

"Ethan."

Joseph Davies was an older gentleman, distinguished in his years. He had a reputation for being the best when it came to custody suits, and that was all Ethan needed to know.

The two of them made their way into the courtroom.

Jessica and Ethan did not look at each other as their attorneys shook hands.

After a few minutes of waiting, the judge came out of his chambers and reviewed the papers in front of him. He looked up. "Mr. Cummings? You're first."

Paul stood up and called Jessica to the stand.

Her stomach began to churn as she made her way over.

Paul placed his hand on the banister and smiled at her reassuringly. "Would you please state your name for the record?"

"Dr. Jessica Harrington," she said in a meek voice.

"How long have you and your husband been married?"

"Three and a half years."

"And how old is your son?"

She relaxed slightly. "Ten months."

"Now that your marriage is ending, why don't you want your husband to have custody of your son?"

"Because...he drinks too much."

Paul looked back at Ethan. "By drinking, you mean *alcohol*."

"Yes."

"Dr. Harrington, when you say he drinks too much, what exactly do you mean?"

Everything Paul was asking her had been rehearsed. "Four or five nights a week, he would come home drunk."

"Dr. Harrington, do you think your husband is an alcoholic?"

Ethan's attorney suddenly stood up. "Objection, Your Honor. The witness is being asked to speculate."

"On the contrary, Your Honor. My client is a doctor, and I am asking for her opinion as such."

The silver-haired judge peered down at Paul over his black-rimmed glasses. "I'll allow it if you restate the question."

He turned back to Jessica. "Dr. Harrington, in your professional medical opinion, is your husband an alcoholic?"

"Yes."

Paul paused a second or two, for effect. "No further questions, Your Honor," he said, returning to his seat.

Jessica remained, wishing that she could go back to her seat as well. She curled her fingers inside her palms when Ethan's attorney stood up.

He didn't say anything right away. He appeared to be busy reading something on his legal pad. "Dr. Harrington?" he said after a moment. "Is your husband the biological father of your son?"

Jessica cleared her throat. She knew the question was going to be asked, and it was for that reason Paul had asked for a closed hearing, meaning that no one else would be allowed in the courtroom during testimony.

The attorney stood waiting for her answer.

"No, he's not," she said evenly.

"Who *is* the father?" he asked, walking around the table he was sharing with Ethan.

"Gavin Williams."

"Did you have an affair with this man?"

"Yes."

"And when you found out that you were carrying his baby, did you tell your husband?"

Jessica looked over at Paul, but the attorney stepped in her line of vision, forcing her to look at him instead. "I told him I was pregnant," she stated.

"That's not what I asked. Did you tell your husband that it was Gavin Williams' baby?"

"No," she answered, feeling her face turning red.

"No," Mr. Davies repeated, pursing his lips. "In fact, you never told your husband the truth at all, did you? He had to find out from a blood test. Isn't that right?"

"Yes."

"What did your husband do when he found out the truth?"

"He left me."

The attorney nodded his head as if agreeing with her. "He left probably because he was devastated and hurt, wouldn't you say?"

She glanced over at Ethan. He was sitting there showing no emotion whatsoever. "Yes."

"Isn't it also true that after a few weeks had gone by, your husband came back and said he wanted to work things out?"

"Yes."

"My client came back to you and wanted to make the marriage work, even though he knew he wasn't the father of your child. Is that correct?"

"Yes."

"Dr. Harrington, have you witnessed any instances in which your husband has treated your child in a bad way, or differently, since he has learned the truth?"

"No."

He leaned in close to her. "Would you say that he loves your little boy?"

"He loves him very much," she said, looking at Paul apologetically. There was no question in her mind whether Ethan loved him or not.

Mr. Davies smiled at her. "What is your relationship with Gavin Williams currently?"

"We work together at the hospital."

Paul gripped his pen tightly as he listened, fearful of where this was headed.

"Before you got pregnant, had you slept with him before?"

Paul stood up. "Objection."

Mr. Davies shook his head. "Your Honor, I am merely trying to establish a point."

"Then make it...quickly," the judge said. "Overruled."

"Answer the question, please," Mr. Davies said to Jessica.

"Yes," she said, bowing her head.

"So the affair that resulted in your pregnancy was not the *first* with him, was it?"

"No."

"No. In fact, you had relations with him throughout your marriage to Dr. Harrington, didn't you?

"Yes." Her voice was barely audible.

"Do you like having affairs, Dr. Harrington?"

"Objection, Your Honor," Paul said again.

"Sustained."

"No further questions, Your Honor," Mr. Davies replied, walking back to his chair.

"You may step down," the judge said kindly to her.

Jessica, on the verge of tears, hurried across the room and took her seat next to Paul.

Ethan's eyes, full of remorse, followed her. He leaned over to his attorney. "Was that necessary?" he whispered angrily.

Joseph looked at him. "Do you remember the question that I asked you before we began all this?"

Ethan looked at him for a moment and then leaned back in his chair. When he had first gone to Mr. Davies, he had asked him how much he loved his son, and how badly did he want custody of him.

~

The rain drizzled lightly down the window of Ethan's office as he sat at his desk. He was trying to get some paperwork out of the way before heading to court this morning. The custody hearing had been going on for two weeks now, and it seemed to him that it had become a case of one-upmanship between the attorneys, instead of a custody trial.

Today was probably going to be the last day of testimony and Mr. Davies had told him that it was looking pretty good for him. He warned him, however, that if Paul introduced the fact that he had been abusive to her, they could lose the case.

Ethan rubbed the back of his neck and closed his eyes. During its course, the hearing seemed only to have succeeded in turning him and Jessica into enemies. Yesterday, they had argued bitterly with each other in her office over certain things that had been said in the courtroom.

The telephone interrupted his thoughts.

"Clinic, Dr. Harrington."

"Ethan?" a raspy voice sounded into the receiver.

"Sarah?"

"I can't make it in today."

"What's wrong?" he asked, looking at his watch. He was due in court at nine.

"I've been vomiting since early this morning. I think it's a stomach flu," she wheezed. "I'm sorry."

"There's nothing to be sorry about. You just stay home and rest. I'll take care of things here."

"Are you sure?"

"No worries. Do you need anything?"

"No, I'll be fine."

The bell went off indicating there was a patient to see. "Okay, but call me if you do."

The rest of the day was absolutely hectic; there was standing room only in the tiny waiting room of the clinic. Ethan had been able to corral a nurse away from her normal duties to help him. She pulled the files and got the patients ready for him to see, which helped to move things along.

He was in the middle of examining an elderly man when there was a knock upon the door.

Jessica came halfway in. "Can I speak to you? It's important."

He looked at Jessica and then his patient. "I'll be right back, Mr. Anderson."

Once they were in his office, she turned on him. "Why did you cancel the hearing this morning?"

"Because Sarah is sick and I had no choice," he said, crossing his arms. "Why should you care?"

"I specifically rearranged my surgical schedule, not to mention my patients," she said angrily. "Now, I've got to rearrange it all over again."

He gave a nod towards the examining room. "In case you hadn't noticed, I'm just a little busy myself, and I'm sure if Sarah could be here, she would."

She glared at him for a moment before opening the door.

Ethan slammed it shut before she could get out. His eyes flickered as he leaned in close to her. "Don't you *ever* come in here again and interrupt me while I am with a patient."

She pulled on the knob, but he kept his hand against the door. She looked up at him. His eyes held nothing but pure hatred for her.

He slowly took his hand away and jerked the door open.

~

Sarah leaned against the wall as she made her way downstairs. That had been her seventh trip to the bathroom today; she couldn't remember a time when she had thrown up so much. She was almost over to the sofa when she heard the doorbell.

"Ethan?" she said, gathering her robe around her. "What are you doing here?"

He came in carrying his medical bag and a small white sack. "I was worried about you."

She turned and followed him over to the sofa, embarrassed by her appearance. She was wearing an old, terry cloth housecoat over her nightgown, and a pair of Gavin's sweat socks that he had left behind. Not to mention the fact, that she hadn't even combed her hair or brushed her teeth.

Ethan took off his coat and sat down beside her. "How do you feel?"

"Terrible."

He reached into his bag and retrieved his stethoscope and thermometer. "That's why I'm here," he said, checking her temperature.

"How were things at the clinic today?"

He warmed his stethoscope in his palm before placing it inside her robe. "Not too bad."

She remained quiet as he listened to her heart, and then had her cough. "It's probably a stomach bug."

He nodded. "I must have treated at least a dozen patients today complaining of the same symptoms."

"I thought you said that you weren't busy."

"*No,* I said it wasn't too bad," he answered, putting his stethoscope away. "I gave most of them a shot of Compazine."

She shook her head. "I don't need a shot."

His mouth twitched. "I called you in a prescription of Phenergan," he said, pulling the bottle out of his pocket. "But it works best on a full stomach. Have you been able to keep anything down?"

"No."

"I brought you some chicken soup and Jell-O from the cafeteria. Do you think you could eat?"

The very idea of food made her want to gag, but she nodded anyway, not wanting to hurt his feelings.

He disappeared into her kitchen and returned a few minutes later. "Here you go," he said, setting the steaming bowl of soup in front of her.

"Thank you."

He sat down in the chair beside the sofa and watched her eat. "By the way..." he said, reaching behind him for his coat, "this little guy followed me here."

Sarah looked up to see what he was talking about. A white, stuffed bunny rabbit with long, floppy ears was peeking out of his coat.

Ethan made it wave to her.

She broke into a smile. "Thank you, Ethan."

"You're welcome," he said, returning the smile. He knew she liked rabbits, whether stuffed or ceramic.

A familiar rolling in her stomach made her spit out her third spoonful of soup. "Excuse me," she said, running up the stairs.

The back of her throat burned as she heaved into the toilet. Before she could take a breath, her gag reflex kicked in bringing more of the yellowish bile up. When she had finished, she sat back on her knees and wiped her mouth.

"Do you need anything?"

She looked over her shoulder to find him standing in the doorway with his back to her. "I'm fine," she answered, flushing the toilet.

He turned around to face her and took her by the elbow. "I wish you'd let me give you the Compazine," he said, helping her over to the bed.

"Let me try the Phenergan."

He sighed and went downstairs. He returned a minute later carrying a glass of water and the bottle of pills. "Here you go."

"Thank you."

He sat down in a pink, overstuffed chair and watched her.

"Ethan," she said, setting the glass on the nightstand, "you don't have to stay here. I'll be fine."

"I don't mind. Besides, I'm enjoying your company."

She laughed. "Well, you must be pretty hard up to be enjoying *me* right now."

He grinned lopsidedly at her. "I see you still have your sense of humor."

~

Ethan cleaned up Sarah's dishes from the living room and carried them into the kitchen. As he was putting things away, he spied a bottle of vodka in the cabinet underneath the sink. He looked at it long and hard before closing the door and heading back upstairs.

As he watched Sarah sleep, his mind kept going back to the vodka. He bent down and picked up a book from off the floor. The cover of it was black except for a pair of red, animal-like eyes. Opening it up, he began to read, and as the night wore on, he became somewhat absorbed in its pages.

Sarah suddenly woke up and took a deep breath. "Gavin! There's someone downstairs!"

Ethan went quickly to her side. "Shh, it's okay," he said softly. "You were just dreaming."

She looked confused for a moment, and then sighed as she fell back against the pillow.

He felt of her cheek. "Your fever's supposed to be going down, not up." He went into the bathroom and returned with a wet washcloth.

She closed her eyes as he laid the cold rag on her forehead. "That feels good, thank you."

"You're welcome."

Her eyes jerked open. "I called out for Gavin a minute ago, didn't I?"

He sat down on the edge of the bed and gave her a sympathetic smile.

She shook her head, disgusted with herself.

"It's all right. Sometimes, I wake up in the morning thinking Jessica's left for an early surgery before I remember she's—"

She sat up and pushed against him.

"What?"

"I have to get up."

He quickly got off the bed.

Sarah ran into the bathroom and sank to her knees, hugging the seat of the toilet. When she was through, she felt Ethan's hands under her arms. He helped her back into bed and covered her up.

She threw her forearm across her face and let out a long, miserable sigh. "I think I'm dying." When he didn't answer, she looked across the room and found him digging through his medical bag. Her eyes widened when she saw him pull a small vial out. "I already told you, I don't need a shot."

"Well, that's too bad," he said, drawing the medicine out of the vial with a syringe, "because I'm going to give you one." He walked around the bed and knelt beside her.

"Ethan," she protested.

He sighed as he tore open a package containing an antiseptic wipe. "Sarah, your fever is up, and you are well on your way to becoming dehydrated. Now if you don't let me give you this, I will take you to the hospital and start you on an I.V."

She looked at him solemnly for a moment. "I'm embarrassed," she said finally. "You've never seen me...there before."

He cocked an eyebrow at her. "I won't look, I promise. Now, come on." He gestured for her to turn over.

She begrudgingly turned away from him and raised her nightgown up over her hip. She felt her face flush when he pulled her underwear down slightly. A second or two passed, and then she felt a sharp sting.

"All done."

She rolled over onto her back as he sat down beside her.

"You know," he said, smiling at her, "you probably wouldn't have those nightmares if you wouldn't read those scary books."

"I like them," she said defensively. "They're good."

He rolled his eyes and nodded at the book in the chair. "I hadn't even gotten through the first three pages when some poor camper got disemboweled by the hideous beast."

"It's entertaining," she said, laughing.

"Obviously." He leaned over her to retrieve the washcloth that was lying on the other pillow. As he did, his tie fell across her face.

She picked it up and studied its paisley pattern. "What time is it?"

He looked at his watch. "Almost midnight."

"Oh, Ethan. You need to get home. I don't want you here looking after me all night."

"Well, I'm not going to leave you here on your deathbed." He laid the cloth against her forehead and winked. "I'll be right back.

A few minutes later, he returned with some Jell-O for her and a glass of milk for himself.

She took a bite of the bright red food and found that it tasted better than she thought it would.

"How is it?"

"Good." She suddenly put the spoon down, remembering something. "You were supposed to be in court today, weren't you?"

He finished his milk and nodded.

"I'm so sorry you missed it because of me."

"I know you didn't do it on purpose. We rescheduled for Friday."

She set the dish on her nightstand. "How does it look?"

He glanced away for a moment. "It could go either way."

~

Sarah woke up as the sun pilfered through the curtains in her bedroom. The bunny rabbit Ethan had bought for her was sitting next to her on the pillow with a note pinned to its chest.

Sarah, call me and let me know how you're feeling. There's still some Jell-O in the fridge. Don't come to the hospital today unless you want to be admitted.

Ethan

Chapter Thirty-five

Thursday afternoon, Jessica was sitting in Paul's office downtown. They had been going over which points to make, and not to make, in front of the judge tomorrow. She didn't like what she was hearing.

"I'm going to be truthful with you, Jessica. Right now, I think Ethan has a chance at winning custody."

"How much of a chance?"

He leaned forward, placing his elbows on the desk. "An *excellent* chance."

She breathed in deeply feeling the fear creep in.

"Let me bring it out that he hit you."

She opened her mouth to protest, but he held his hand up.

"Now, I know that's not what you want, but it's our only option. We have a judge who has a reputation for being sympathetic towards women who have been abused."

She shook her head. "I don't know, Paul."

"Look, just think about it tonight and let me know your decision in the morning."

~

Ethan held his empty glass up at the bartender and nodded. *McKay's* was slowly beginning to fill with customers as the dinner hour approached. He didn't really like the crowd, but he couldn't face going home to an empty house tonight, either.

From where he was seated at the bar, he saw Paul and Grace come in. He stared darkly at his glass. Paul, whom he'd once considered to be a good friend, was now a thorn in his side.

The hearing would probably be over with by tomorrow and he figured his chances at gaining custody were good; of course, that was as long as his violent history wasn't brought up.

~

"Paul, please stop staring," Grace said quietly.

He shifted his attention to her. "Sorry."

"I swear, I will be so glad when tomorrow is over," she said, sounding irritated.

"We all will, sweetheart," he said, opening up the menu.

"Are you sure about that?"

He looked up. "What do you mean?"

She saw Ethan pay for his drink and then get up to leave. "I mean that I think you are enjoying this just a little too much."

He dropped the menu on the table and leaned forward. "Why would you say that?"

"Because I think you're enjoying putting the screws to Ethan. It's like you have a score to settle with him."

"That's nonsense. I'm just helping Jessica out."

"Paul, you haven't handled a divorce case in years. You're a corporate attorney."

He set his glass of wine down in frustration. "She asked me to handle it."

"You could have recommended someone else."

"Would you please lower your voice?"

She stopped and glanced around. They were getting a few stares. When she spoke again, her voice was just above a whisper. "What you do tomorrow is going to affect both of them. You're playing *God* just because you can, and I think you're wrong."

"You don't think Jessica should have full custody?"

Grace shook her head. "No, and neither did she until you talked her into it."

"What about what he did? Have you forgotten?"

"No, I haven't, but this isn't about him and Jessica. It's about custody of that baby. And that little boy is all that he has left right now."

He looked at her solemnly for a moment. "It's a boy that's not his."

Grace pushed her chair back and stood up. "I can't believe you just said that." She threw her napkin on the table and stormed off to the ladies room.

~

Jessica busied herself folding a basket of laundry, as Mrs. Chambers and Ryan played a rousing game of peek-a-boo. The two of them seemed as if they could go at it all night, but she was growing weary of listening to it.

There was a sudden pounding on her front door that made her heart lurch.

"Jessica?" Ethan's voice was loud and angry.

She rose from the sofa. "Ellen, would you please take Ryan upstairs?"

"Do you want me to call the police?" she asked, gathering Ryan in her arms.

"No, I'll do it," she said, picking up the phone.

Ethan continued to bang on the door. "Jessica?"

With a trembling hand, she opened it, being careful to keep the storm door locked.

"Can I come in?"

"No."

"Please?"

She shook her head. "I've called the police. I want you to go home before they get here."

He pressed his hands against the glass. "I don't want this divorce, Jess." He closed his eyes and sighed. "I love you, and I love Ryan."

"Ethan..."

"I can't be away from you anymore," he said with a quiver in his voice.

"You're drunk. Please go home."

Something flickered in his eyes. "I don't *have* a home!" he screamed. "You and Ryan were *it* for me! Don't you get that?"

Jessica backed up, startled by his anger.

He ran his fingers through his hair and sighed. "I'm sorry," he said quietly. "Can I see him?"

"No."

Another burst of anger tore through him as he kicked at the door. "Why are you doing this to me?"

Jessica saw the red and blue flashing lights on the police car as it pulled into her driveway.

He turned around to see what she was looking at.

The officer got out of the squad car and made his way up the sidewalk. "Good evening, folks. What seems to be the problem?"

Ethan looked back at Jessica, his face unreadable.

The officer approached the bottom step. "Sir? Can you come down here for a moment?" His attitude was nice, but his tone carried authority.

Ethan stepped down off the porch and stood in front of the officer, who looked to be about his age.

"What's your name, sir?"

"Ethan Harrington."

"Do you live here, Mr. Harrington?"

"No."

"It's pretty late. Why are you here?"

Jessica glanced across the street. Every porch light on the block had come on. Several of her neighbors had come outside of their homes, curious as to what was happening.

The officer reached for his flashlight that was clipped to his belt. "Why are you here, sir?" he repeated.

He turned his head away from the light. "I'm here to see my son."

"Can I see your driver's license?"

Ethan sighed angrily as he reached into his coat.

The policeman studied his license under the light for a moment. "How much have you had to drink tonight, Mr. Harrington?"

"A couple."

"It looks to me like you've had more than a couple," he said flatly. He looked over his shoulder and pointed at the car parked on the side of the street. "Is that your car over there?"

"No," he answered quickly, realizing the consequences if he said yes.

"That's not your car? How did you get here, then?"

"I walked."

"Walked from where?" The officer's patience was wearing thin.

He jerked his head. "There's a bar a few blocks that way."

"So you're telling me that you walked here and that's not your car parked over there."

"That's right."

"And if I were to run that license plate, they would tell me it belonged to somebody else?"

"Yes."

The officer clipped the light back on his belt. "Mr. Harrington, I'm going to ask you to step over to my car, please."

He didn't move.

"This way, sir."

Ethan slowly walked over to the squad car.

Jessica felt the lump rising in her throat as she watched the officer reach behind him for his cuffs.

"Turn around and place your hands on the hood of the car."

"I haven't done anything," he said, refusing.

"We can do this the easy way or the hard way, Mr. Harrington." He was in no mood to deal with a drunk tonight.

Ethan glared at him for a moment and then turned and placed his hands on the car. He clenched his jaw as he felt the cold metal clamp around his wrist.

The officer turned him around and leaned him against the car. "Stay right here," he said, opening the door.

As the officer ran a check against his license, Ethan glanced at the house. Jessica stood at her front door wearing a look that resembled a cross between pity and contempt.

"Okay, Mr. Harrington, I'm going to go talk to this lady, and I don't want you to move. Understand?"

"Yes," he muttered.

The officer walked up the steps and nodded at her. "Good evening, ma'am. Can I get your name, please?"

"Jessica Harrington," she said meekly.

"Is this your husband?"

"We're in the process of a divorce."

"What happened tonight?"

"He just showed up banging on the door and screaming."

"He told me he wants to see his son. Does he live here with you?"

"I have custody of him right—"

"*Temporary!*" Ethan yelled. "You have *temporary* custody!"

The officer turned. "Mr. Harrington, I'm only going to ask you once to stay quiet."

He leaned back against the hood, his eyes dark.

Jessica tucked her hair behind her ears. "I've been granted temporary custody until the judge decides."

"Did he threaten you or try to hurt you tonight?"

"No."

He scratched his head. "I can take him to jail, Mrs. Harrington. I can't get him on DUI, but I *can* get him on drunk and disorderly."

"No, I don't want you to arrest him. I just want him to leave."

"Are you sure?"

"Yes."

"All right, but I can't guarantee you that he won't come back. The only way to be sure is for me to arrest him," he said, trying to reason with her. "You should consider filing a restraining order."

"I'll think about it, thank you," she said.

He trotted down the steps and walked back to his car. "Mr. Harrington, I'm going to let you go. If it were up to me, you would be on your way to jail, but your wife doesn't want that to happen." He took Ethan by his arm and turned him so he could take the handcuffs off. "I'm going to call you a cab, and I don't want to see you back here again. Do you understand?"

"I have a right to see my son."

"She has temporary custody of him. Now, that means you are just going to have to wait until the judge makes his decision. There's nothing you can do until then. My suggestion is that you go home and sober up."

Jessica stepped inside and turned off the porch light in hopes that the crowd of onlookers would disperse.

Ethan looked at her through the door.

The officer stepped in his line of sight. "Mr. Harrington, I'm serious when I say that I don't want you back over here. Because next time you *will* go to jail, understand?"

He nodded his head in defeat.

~

The next morning, Ethan sat on the witness stand as his attorney tried to score a few last points.

Joseph Davies scratched his silver beard. "Dr. Harrington, do you love your son?"

"Yes."

"Even though you are not his biological father?"

"It doesn't matter."

"Did you want this divorce?"

He flicked his eyes in Jessica's direction. He was truly ashamed of his behavior last night. She must hate him. "No, I didn't," he said softly.

"Do you still love your wife, despite her transgressions?"

Paul leaned forward. "Objection. May I remind Mr. Davies that this is a custody hearing, and not a divorce hearing?"

"No further questions, Your Honor," Joseph said, returning to his seat.

Jessica looked over at Paul. His eyes silently asked her what she wanted him to do. She gave him a subtle nod.

He stood up and walked over to the witness stand. "Dr. Harrington, can you tell me what happened on August eleventh of last year?"

Ethan didn't answer him right away. "I found out I wasn't Ryan's father."

"And afterwards on that same day, did you have an altercation with Gavin Williams?"

"Yes."

"Did you strike him several times in the face?"

"I was angry."

"And you were so angry, that you felt the need to dislocate his jaw?"

Mr. Davies stood up. "Objection."

"Sustained." The judge looked down at Paul. "Keep your personal comments to yourself, Mr. Cummings."

"I'll rephrase the question," he said, turning back to Ethan. "Did you dislocate Dr. William's jaw?"

Ethan glared at him. "Yes."

Paul stepped away from the stand and walked over to his table. "Dr. Harrington, would you say that you have a temper?"

"Objection."

Paul looked at the judge. "I think Dr. Harrington can tell me if he thinks he has a temper or not, Your Honor."

The judge leaned back in his chair. "I presume you are going somewhere with this, Mr. Cummings?"

"Yes, Your Honor."

"I'll allow it. Objection overruled."

Paul held up a white envelope as he made his way over to Ethan. "*Do* you have a temper?"

"Sometimes."

"On December twenty-second of last year did you attend a Christmas party with your wife?"

"Yes." Ethan felt his stomach start to churn. Paul was going to crucify him.

"Would it be fair to say that, while at the party, you consumed a rather large amount of alcohol?"

"I had a few drinks."

"And later that same evening, did you have to be restrained from throwing a punch at Gavin Williams?"

"Yes."

Paul placed his hands on the wooden railing. "Why?"

"Because he was coming on to my wife," he said flatly.

"How did you come to that conclusion?"

"Because I saw him," he said, accenting each word.

"Was he kissing her, or touching her inappropriately?"

"No."

"Then how did you know he was coming on to her?"

"He was talking to her the whole night."

Paul nodded. "I see. So, the fact that he was talking to her meant he was coming on to her. Well, that's a rational observation."

Ethan's face darkened.

"What happened between you and your wife after you left the party and went home?"

"We argued."

"I'd like to remind you, Dr. Harrington that you're still under oath." He paused for a long moment. "What happened after the argument?"

"I went upstairs to apologize."

"Did you?"

"I tried."

"Yes or no, please."

He swallowed hard. "No."

"No. Because instead of apologizing you kicked in the bedroom door and struck her in the face. Isn't that right?"

Ethan looked over at Jessica. Her head was bowed with her hand over her mouth. Tears ran down her face. He looked at the floor, admitting his guilt. "Yes," he whispered.

Paul decided to go for it all. "Your wife then tried to flee in her car with her son, but before she could," he said, holding a finger up in his face, "you threw your fist against the driver's side window. Isn't that also true?"

He closed his eyes briefly as the image surfaced. "Yes."

Paul slid two photos out of the envelope he had been holding. "Your Honor, I submit as evidence a picture of my client's car showing the window shattered, as well as a photo of the bedroom door which Dr. Harrington has admitted to kicking in. I have no more questions."

Ethan stepped down from the witness stand knowing it was all over.

Two hours later, the judge returned with his decision. Jessica was granted sole custody with Ethan being allowed to visit him every other Sunday.

Chapter Thirty-six

Sarah opened the blinds, allowing the sun to come through the window in her office. The month of April had brought a warm breeze and budding trees. It had been an unusually long and cold winter, and after several false starts, it seemed that spring had finally arrived.

It was a year ago this week that she had learned what had transpired between Jessica and Gavin. The memory of that night was still vivid in her mind and would automatically play for her from time to time without her consent. She began to wonder if she would grow to hate the spring because of what it represented to her.

She heard Ethan come out of the examining room. "Are there any more patients to see?"

"That's it for now," he replied, sitting down at his desk.

She pulled herself away from the window and sat down across from him. She was tired, hungry, and looking forward to what was waiting for her at home in the crock-pot. "I think I'm going to call it a day."

"That's fine," he said, scrawling something in a chart.

Sarah stole a sideways glance at him as she began tidying up her desk. The change in his mood over the past few weeks had been drastic. He had become extremely withdrawn, almost to the point of alienating himself from everyone, including her.

She had also seen him lose his temper on a few occasions. One was with Dr. Pearson regarding the treatment of a patient, and another was with Phillip over funding for the clinic. Phillip had not been amused.

It was for this reason that she handed him a sealed envelope with trepidation.

"What's this?"

"A courier delivered it about fifteen minutes ago." She had seen it was from the office of Paul Cummings.

Ethan tore it open and stared at the papers for a long time before laying them aside.

"Bad news?"

He shrugged. "Depends on how you look at it. Our divorce is final." He closed the chart in front of him and looked up at her. "Let's go celebrate. What do you say?"

"What did you have in mind?"

"I don't know," he said, getting to his feet. "How about having a couple of drinks with me?"

"Mmm, I don't think I'm up to it."

"Well," he said, opening the door, "you don't know what you're missing. But if you change your mind, I'll be at the *Happy Parrot*."

Before she could say anything else, he was gone.

~

Sarah sat in the parking lot outside the *Happy Parrot*. It was a bar situated on the east side of town, and had a reputation for hookers, drugs, and fights. A sign stating that it was two for one night blinked continuously in the darkened window.

She reluctantly got out of the car and made her way across the parking lot. She hated bars in general, never understanding the draw that some people had to them.

She went through the door and was immediately overwhelmed by cigarette smoke; it circled the ceiling like a thick fog. The bar itself was decorated in a nautical theme that included a roughly hewn, wooden plank floor. Its walls were embellished with pictures of pirates and old ships. Several statues of women, whose clothes had been strategically ripped, were scattered throughout the place. It reminded Sarah of a sadistic version of the Pirates of the Caribbean ride at Disney.

Several men looked at her as she walked across the room. An older man, covered in tattoos, stared particularly hard at her, making her regret her decision to come here.

After a lot of searching, she finally spied Ethan. He was at a table in the far corner of the room with two women. As she drew nearer, she realized that using the word, *women,* was a polite term for what they were.

A blonde was sitting on his lap. The other, a brunette, sat next to him with her arm draped across his neck.

Ethan leaned over and whispered something in the blonde's ear. She listened intensely for a second and then threw her head back and laughed, exposing a set of large, firm breasts housed only in a halter-top. He grinned back at her as he lifted his glass.

Sarah cleared her throat to get his attention. "Hi, Ethan," she said, loud enough to be heard over the crowd.

"Sarah! I'm glad you came. Um, this is..." he said, pointing to the woman in his lap.

"Tory," answered the blonde, laughing.

"Right, Tory," he said. "And this is Karen." He nodded at the woman next to him.

"Carrie," she corrected him in a husky voice.

"Ladies, this is Sarah Williams, a very good friend of mine."

The brunette took a long drag on her cigarette, as she looked her up and down.

"Have a seat." He gestured with his hand.

Sarah sat down not knowing what else to do. The table was littered with empty shot glasses.

The blonde glanced at Sarah before leaning over and whispering something in Ethan's ear.

As he listened, a smile broke out over his face. "Maybe," he said, grinning.

The brunette kept running her fingers through his hair as he flirted with her, making it obvious to Sarah that he was enjoying the attention. Tonight, he was brash and assertive, almost to the point of being cocky. It was a far cry from the man she had developed such a close friendship with, and she began to deny in her heart that his behavior was hurting her.

Ethan drained his glass. "Well, I could use another. How about you ladies?"

The woman he introduced as Tory hopped off his lap so he could get up. "I'll have another."

"Sarah?"

"Uh...white wine, please," she answered.

"I'll be right back." He headed towards the bar, leaving her at their mercy.

The blonde watched him walking away and then flicked her big blue eyes over to Sarah. "Ethan is such a great guy. He's so funny!"

The brunette brought the cigarette to her lips again.

Sarah watched the tip of it turn bright orange as she inhaled.

She blew the smoke in her direction. "Are you his girlfriend?"

"No," Sarah answered, searching the room for Ethan.

She held the cigarette over the ashtray and tapped it with a black fingernail. "His mistress?"

Having had enough, Sarah stood up and made her way over to the bar. She found Ethan standing at the counter waiting for their drinks. "Let's get out of here."

He tapped his ear. "What?"

Sarah put her hand on his shoulder and tiptoed to talk in his good ear. "Let me take you home."

"Why?" he asked, sounding confused.

She searched quickly for an answer. "Because I really need to talk to you."

He looked at her for a moment. The alcohol seemed to slow his thought process down immensely. "All right."

They made their way back over to the table. "Well, ladies, I'm going to call it a night."

The brunette stood up and grabbed him playfully by his tie. "Come on, Ethan, the night is still young," she said, rubbing up against him.

Sarah left him to say goodbye and waited for him over by the exit. She watched as the blonde kissed him long and hard on the lips before slipping a card into his shirt pocket. *Her business card no doubt.*

~

Twenty minutes later, Sarah pulled into Ethan's driveway.

She waited impatiently as he fumbled with the lock. "Here, why don't you let me?" she said, taking the keys from him.

He leaned against the doorbell, setting off an unending series of ding-dongs.

Once inside, she took him by the arm and steered him towards the stairs.

"Where are we going?" he asked, reaching for the banister. "I thought you wanted to talk."

"I think you need to go to bed and sleep it off."

He jerked his arm away from her, nearly losing his balance. "I'm not tired," he said, stumbling into the living room.

Sarah reluctantly followed.

There was a half-empty bottle of scotch on the table beside the sofa. He grabbed it and fell back onto the cushion. "Would you like one?"

"No. Thank you." She watched as he poured himself a glass. "Ethan, do you know what those two women in the bar were?"

He laughed. "Mmm-hmm."

"Well, do you do that sort of thing often?"

"*What* thing?"

She raised her eyebrows. "Frequent with *hookers*."

He laughed again and shook his head. "I was celebrating!"

~

Sarah rang Ethan's doorbell for the third time as she stood waiting on his front porch. She had left him last night passed out on his sofa after watching him finish off the bottle of scotch. She rang the bell again and checked her watch. She was already late for rounds.

Ethan opened the door and squinted against the sunlight. "Would you please *stop?*" he whispered.

"Sorry," she said, brushing past him as she stepped inside. "I came to give you a ride to pick up your car."

"My car?"

"It's at the *Happy Parrot*. I drove you home last night." She tilted her head at him. "Don't you remember?"

"I don't remember very much of last night, to tell you the truth," he said, rubbing his eyes.

"Do you remember Tory and Carrie?"

"Who?"

She reached into his shirt pocket and pulled out the card.

He looked at it for a moment and then sighed. He had a vague recollection of last night, which had involved multiple shots of tequila. His stomach felt as if it was on fire.

"Why don't you take a shower, and I'll make you some coffee."

Half an hour later, they were on their way into town.

Ethan took a sip of his coffee that she had made for him and leaned his head against the back of the seat.

"How do you feel?"

"Terrible."

"It serves you right."

He looked over at her, surprised.

"What you did last night was really stupid."

"Well, *thank you* for pointing that out," he said sarcastically.

"I'm being serious, Ethan," she said, stopping at a light. "Those women could have robbed you or worse. Not to mention the fact that you could have wound up in jail."

He took another sip of his coffee. "The light's green."

She looked up at the light and pressed on the accelerator. "I don't mean to sound angry, but it's only because I care about you."

He sighed. "I know. And I know what I did was stupid. I just had a little too much to drink last night and got carried away."

She put her blinker on and turned into the parking lot of the *Happy Parrot*. She pulled up next to his car and shut off the engine. "Ethan," she said, turning to him, "I think you need to quit pining away over Jessica. I know it's hard, but it's time to move on."

"You know..." he said, looking over at his car, "I seem to remember someone a few months back who was moping around because of *her* divorce."

Sarah's mouth opened to protest. "I wasn't *moping.*"

He cocked his head. "No? What would you call it then?"

"I...was feeling a little sorry for myself—"

Ethan began to nod.

"—but I wasn't *moping.*"

"Okay, whatever you say," he said with a smirk.

She smiled in spite of herself. "Listen to me. You gave me some very good advice a while back. You told me that I should forget about Gavin, because he wasn't worth it. I think you should do the same."

"But I don't like Gavin," he said, grinning at her.

"You know what I mean." Her tone was serious. "I think it's time that you let Jessica go."

Ethan's smile left him as he opened his door. "Thanks for the ride. I'll see you at the hospital."

Chapter Thirty-seven

The month of May, in all its glorious splendor, embraced Jessica as she drove to work. Summer was just around the corner, and for the first time in many months, she felt good about herself. She hummed softly as she got out of her car.

Ethan pulled up alongside of her. "Jessica, can I talk to you for a minute?" he said, opening his door.

She looked at her watch. "What about?"

"I would really like to keep Ryan this Saturday and bring him back to you on Sunday night." He waited patiently as she thought it over.

"I don't think it would be a good idea," she finally said.

He looked away for a moment. "I promise, I won't drink." His words were clipped.

She knew this was hard on him, but she wasn't going to put Ryan in jeopardy just to appease him. "I'm sorry," she said, turning to go inside.

~

Ethan hurriedly added the figures in his head before scribbling them on the report in front of him. It was his and Sarah's turn to work in the ER tonight, and he still had a lot to do before six o'clock, including finishing his report on the clinic's caseload for the board meeting tomorrow.

Sarah came through the door carrying a large folder. "Here are the X-rays you were waiting for. I picked them up along with mine."

"Thanks."

"Do you want to grab some dinner tonight before we go on shift?"

"Sure." He held the film up to the light.

Sarah plopped down in her chair and began going through a stack of invoices. "What is today? The fifth?" she asked, flipping through the pages on her calendar, which was still showing April.

"The sixth," Ethan answered, walking over to the filing cabinet.

She studied the date for a moment. "Hey! Did you know that this coming Saturday will be the fourth anniversary that we became partners in the clinic?"

He pulled open the top drawer and began rifling through it. "Really?" he said, trying to sound interested.

Sarah watched him for a long time before she spoke again. "Well, I think it's cause to celebrate. How about dinner this Saturday?"

Ethan found the file he was looking for and yanked it out. Somehow, he figured she was taking pity on him. "I thought you were seeing that guy you stitched up," he said, pausing to make a note in the file.

She had treated a man involved in a motorcycle accident a couple of weeks ago. In return, he had asked her out. "We've gone out a few times, but he's a little too conceited for me," she said, shrugging. "So, what about you?"

"What *about* me?"

"Are you thinking about dating again?"

Ethan quit writing and looked up at her, startled by the question. "I don't know."

"Well, when you decide it's time, let me know. Because I can fix you up."

"Yeah, right," he said, returning his attention to the file.

"No, really. I can."

He closed the drawer and sat back down. "Who would want to go out with *me?*"

She looked at him incredulously. "Oh, come on, Ethan! I can name at least half a dozen nurses who would love to go out with you."

He cocked his eyebrow at her. "I don't think anyone in their right mind would want to go on a date with me."

She leaned back in her chair and crossed her arms. "What's not to like about you? You're kind, considerate, handsome..."

Ethan's face suddenly turned a bright red.

"I don't believe it. You're blushing!"

"No, I'm not."

"Yes, you are. Hasn't anyone ever told you that you were handsome before?"

His mouth twitched. "Only my mother, and she was biased."

"Well, you *are* very handsome and any woman would be lucky to have you." She grinned as she watched him turn a deeper shade of red.

"Don't you have any patients to bother?"

"Mmm, yes. But this is more fun."

"Well, I'm glad you're enjoying yourself."

She stood up and walked towards the door not wanting to embarrass him any further. "I'm going to go change. Are you ready?"

"I need to finish this first. Why don't I meet you in the cafeteria in about twenty minutes?"

"Okay, but you let me know about this dating thing, all right?"

He scowled at her, but the corners of his mouth were turned up. "Goodbye."

"'Bye." She went out the door smiling.

He turned back to his work.

She popped her head back in. "I'm serious about fixing you up."

"Sarah..." he said in a warning tone.

"I'm going."

He waited a few moments for her to come back. When she didn't, he finished the caseload report and closed the folder. He leaned back in his chair and rubbed his eyes. It had been a long day for him already, and it was only half over.

He pulled open the bottom right hand drawer of his desk and felt in the very back of it. His hands soon found what they were looking for. He glanced up to make sure that the door was still closed.

The small pint of whiskey fit in the palm of his hand. A grateful patient who worked at the local distillery, had given it to him as a gift. Instead of taking it home, Ethan had stuck it in his desk, forgetting about it until today.

He wrestled with his emotions for a long time. He shouldn't even have a drink, knowing he was about to go on duty in ER, but there was another part of him that told him it was okay. It was the part of him that trembled inside. He unscrewed the cap and took a drink. The fire traveled through his veins and silenced his shaking.

~

Sarah sighed to herself as she took the next chart from Trish. "What do we have?"

"Seven-year-old with an eraser stuck up his nose."

So far this evening, Sarah had been kicked, thrown up on, and called a dirty name; and it wasn't even nine o'clock yet.

A redheaded boy with matching freckles sat on the stretcher as his mother stood beside him.

"Hello, Cody. My name is Dr. Williams," she said, sitting down on the stool in front of him. "Why did you put an eraser in your nose?"

The little boy looked at her with painfully innocent brown eyes and shrugged. "I just wanted to see if it would fit up there."

~

Ethan was suturing up a man who had been involved in a bar fight. He had been hit in the back of the head with a pool stick. The man had been rambling on in an incoherent manner for the past fifteen minutes. Eventually, he passed out, leaving him in peace to put the final sutures in.

The wailing scream of the sirens meant another victim was coming in.

Sarah met them at the door.

"We've got a twenty-one-year-old male with a knife wound to the abdomen," the paramedic said as they hurried down the corridor.

"Let's take him into two," she said.

"B.P.'s one twenty over sixty, pulse ninety."

Sarah stood on the other side of the stretcher preparing to move him onto the bed. "On my count. One, two, three."

The man groaned as they lifted him. "Leave me the *fuck* alone!"

"He's also higher than a kite," the paramedic said, heading out the door.

"Let's start another line and call X-ray. Tell them we'll be bringing him up shortly," Sarah said to Denise.

Trish hung up the phone. "I have OR standing by."

Sarah examined the wound. "It doesn't look that deep."

"God, it hurts!" the man screamed. "I need something for the pain!"

Denise sighed. "I can't find a vein." He had needle tracks up and down both arms.

The man grasped Sarah's sleeve. "Didn't you hear me? I said I need something for the pain!"

She looked into the man's eyes; his pupils were the size of dimes. "Sir, I can't give you anything until I know the extent of your injury and you tell me what kind of drug you've been doing."

He suddenly jumped off the stretcher and pulled a knife out of his pocket.

Sarah tried to back up but he held her by the arm.

"We need some help over here!" Trish shouted.

"Shut the *hell* up!" the man barked.

Ethan stepped around the curtain wondering what all the commotion was about.

When the man saw him, he grabbed Sarah around the neck and got behind her. "Back off, or I swear I'll slit her throat."

Ethan held his hands out in a non-threatening manner. "What do you want?" he said, taking a step towards him.

Sarah's eyes could only focus on the steel blade that he held against her throat. She could feel the tip of it as he pushed it against her.

The man backed away from Ethan dragging her with him. "Don't come any closer!"

Ethan's heart pounded. Denise and Trish stood in the opposite corner of the room looking about as helpless as he felt. "Tell me what you want," he repeated in a calm voice.

The man jerked his head towards the cabinet beside him. "I want some Oxy."

"Okay. Let her go and I'll—"

"No! You give me the Oxy and *then* I'll let her go."

Sarah could feel him shaking as he held her; his breath was hot and shallow against the side of her face.

Ethan held out his hand to Denise. "Give me the keys."

The brown-haired nurse, small in stature and voice, pulled them from her pocket.

Ethan quickly unlocked the cabinet and took a small bottle off one of the shelves. "Okay," he said, turning to face him, "let her go."

Sarah felt him tighten his grip around her neck.

Ethan set the bottle down on the stretcher. "Let her go and you can have it."

"Hand it to me."

"No," he answered, seeing the desperation in his eyes. "Just turn her loose and it's yours."

The man looked at Ethan and then the bottle. He pushed Sarah away from him and lunged for it, but before he could grasp his fingers around it, a spasm of pain shot through him causing him to stumble.

Ethan stepped forward and caught him in his arms.

The man immediately began to struggle, shoving Ethan against the cabinet. Its glass doors shattered as they both fell to the floor.

Ethan scrambled to gain control, but the younger man was quicker. By the time he saw the knife coming at him, it was too late. He felt a burning sensation in his shoulder as he wrestled to get the knife out of his hands. In an act of desperation, he shoved his left arm under the man's chin as hard as he could.

The man's face went pale as he gasped for air.

Ethan took hold of his wrist and slammed it against the floor, sending the knife sliding across the room. "Get me a sedative!" he yelled, struggling to hold down his arms.

Trish, Denise, and a burly orderly came to his aid. The three of them held him still long enough for Ethan to inject the sedative.

The man stopped flailing and went limp.

Ethan checked his vitals as they loaded him onto the stretcher. "Get him to X-ray," he said, nodding to Trish, "and be sure and take an orderly with you."

Sarah stared down at the broken glass strewn about and felt a warm hand upon her shoulder.

"Are you all right?" Ethan asked, looking into her eyes.

"I think so."

He lifted her chin up and checked her throat to make sure he hadn't cut her. When he was satisfied that he hadn't, he slipped his arm around her waist and led her over to a stool. "Here, just sit down and catch your breath for a minute, okay? I'll get you some water."

Sarah took a deep breath and felt of her throat; she could still feel the coldness of the blade.

Denise smiled sympathetically at her. "Are you okay?"

She took a sip of the water and nodded. "I'll be fine. I just need a minute," she said, trying to stop her hands from shaking.

Ethan leaned against the counter as he watched her with concern.

Denise noticed a good amount of blood dripping from his right shoulder. "You're bleeding, Dr. Harrington."

He looked down at himself, not realizing that the cut was so deep.

Sarah quickly got to her feet and lifted the sleeve of his scrub shirt. "You're going to need stitches."

Ethan glanced over at Denise and winked. "I don't know," he said, shaking his head, "you might have to amputate."

Sarah let herself smile as she moved the stool over to the counter with her foot. "Have a seat," she said, slipping on a pair of gloves. "When was the last time you had a Tetanus shot?"

He shrugged. "I'm sure it's been within the last five years."

"Denise, why don't you check Dr. Harrington's medical file and see if he's due one."

Trish stepped over the shards of glass upon her return. "I thought you might like to know that the guy is in radiology handcuffed to his stretcher. They'll be bringing him back down in a few minutes."

"Well, I don't know about you, but I can't wait," Sarah said sarcastically as she put the last suture in Ethan's arm.

Denise came back into the room with his file in hand.

"What did you find out?" asked Sarah.

The nurse looked at him and smiled. "Well, it looks as if he's due."

"That's got to be a mistake," he said, shaking his head.

Denise prepared the syringe and handed it to Sarah.

"I think you are all enjoying this way too much," he complained.

Sarah smiled as she brought the needle closer.

"Wait a minute," he said, holding his arm back, "I'm not ready."

She arched her eyebrows. "Okay, tell me when you're ready."

He paused a moment and took a deep breath. "I'm ready."

She poked the needle into his skin.

"Ow!"

"Oh, come on, now…that didn't hurt, did it?" she asked, throwing the syringe away.

"*Yes,* it did!" he answered, rubbing his shoulder.

She turned to Trish. "Do we have any suckers?"

"Sorry, we're all out."

"Well, I'll tell you what," Sarah said, reaching into the drawer beside him. "Because you were such a good boy, I'm going to give you a Superman Band-Aid."

Ethan watched her place the colorful bandage where she had administered the shot. "You know what?"

"What?"

"You give lousy shots."

The sound of sirens made them turn their heads.

The doors to the emergency room slid open as two paramedics hurried in with a stretcher.

Ethan hopped off the stool and ran to meet them. "What do we have?"

"We've got a nine-year-old male with a GSW to the chest. He was playing with his father's gun."

Sarah appeared on the other side of the stretcher.

"Okay...one, two, three," Ethan said, as they lifted him onto the bed.

"Pupils are blown," Sarah said.

Trish came through the door. "There's a hit and run coming in with possible head trauma."

They could hear the sirens.

Ethan nodded at Sarah. "I've got this, go on."

Sarah hurried out of the room to meet the ambulance.

Denise was by Ethan's side seeming to anticipate his orders before he gave them.

"Let's get an airway going." He took the scope from her and tilted the boy's head back. With quick precision, he guided the tube down into his throat. As he waited to hear the first beep on the monitor, he took a moment to look at the boy. He lay there lifeless and pale, his hair spattered with blood and fragments of flesh.

Two more nurses came in to help.

The beeps finally came, but were irregular.

Ethan worked frantically trying to stop the bleeding and get him stabilized.

Suddenly, the monitor exploded with a series of beeps.

"He's crashing!"

"Set it on sixty!" he said, reaching for the paddles. "Charging...okay, clear!" He placed the paddles on the boy. His small body jerked and convulsed.

Across the hall, Sarah had her own hands full. Her patient was bleeding from her ears and nose, and had suffered multiple fractures, including two broken vertebrae.

"OR's ready for her," Trish said.

Sarah worked to stabilize her, and then took her up to the operating room where she briefed the surgeon on call.

When she returned to the ER, Ethan was still trying to resuscitate the boy. She could see the hesitation in the nurses each time he gave the order to charge the machine again.

After the last time, he threw the paddles down and did it with his hands, but he had no sooner started before he stopped and backed away. "Call it," he said hoarsely. "Time of death...eleven twenty eight." He stripped off his gloves and walked over to the counter.

Denise covered the boy's face with a sheet and turned off the monitor. "His parents are waiting outside," she said quietly.

Ethan nodded but didn't turn around.

She waited for him to follow her, but he remained motionless.

He suddenly slammed his fist against the counter.

Sarah walked silently in and nodded at Denise.

The nurse nodded back and left the room.

Sarah moved around the stretcher where the boy still lay. "Do you want me to tell them?" she asked softly.

He turned around at the sound of her voice. "No," he said, wiping the sweat from his face with the sleeve of his shirt. "I'll tell them."

A moment later, Sarah could hear the cries of the mother. They were the type of cries that nothing or no one could comfort.

~

Ethan sat alone in the locker room. The wails of the boy's mother still traveled through him.

There was a quick knock upon the door.

"Attention, woman entering the men's locker room. Repeat. Woman entering the men's locker room." Sarah appeared around the door with one hand over her eyes. "Are you decent?" she asked, talking to a row of lockers.

He looked down at himself. He was still in his scrubs. "Well, *physically* I am."

She took her hand away and smiled. "You know," she said, sitting down on the bench beside him, "I never got a chance to thank you for what you did for me tonight."

"Not necessary," he said.

Sarah nudged him in an affectionate manner. "You could have been killed."

He sighed and started to say something, but she cut him off.

"It was very brave of you, and you probably saved my life. So, thanks for being my hero."

Ethan smiled at her and then looked back down at the floor. "I don't feel like much of a hero."

"You did everything you could."

He nodded and rubbed his tired eyes. "That doesn't make it any easier, though."

"I know."

A heavy sigh fell from him as he stood up. "Give me a minute to change, and I'll walk you out."

Chapter Thirty-eight

The small conference room began to fill with soft murmurs and quiet conversation as the members of the board straggled in one by one.

Sarah made her way over to the coffee machine in dire need of caffeine.

Gavin stood off to the side stirring cream into his cup. "Morning."

"Good morning." She dispensed the brown liquid into her mug and glanced at the clock above her. It was a few minutes before seven. Ethan should have been here by now.

"I understand that there was some excitement in the ER last night," Phillip said, coming up behind her.

"What happened?" Gavin asked.

As a crowd gathered round her, Sarah recounted the events that had unfolded last night.

~

Ethan sat up in his bed and fumbled with the clock. His lips formed an obscenity as he stumbled over to the closet and pulled on a pair of dark pants. The board meeting had already started, and today of all days he was supposed to make a presentation to the members.

He scoured the closet for a clean shirt but couldn't find one. His right arm was sore and throbbing, more from the tetanus shot than the wound itself. He picked up a shirt from off the floor that didn't look too wrinkled and held it to his nose; it would have to do.

Mrs. Raines, his cleaning lady, probably hated him, he thought as he made his way over to the nightstand to look for his wallet. His eyes searched for it, but only saw an empty bottle of scotch. He quickly hunted for his pants he had worn last night. Spying them, he felt in the back pocket and pulled the leather billfold out. In an instant, he was flying down the stairs.

~

Phillip was going over some announcements and promotions when Ethan came through the door. All heads turned to see who was coming in.

"Sorry I'm late," he said, taking the chair next to Grace.

"Well, if it isn't the man of the hour," said Phillip. "Would you like us to call you Ethan, or Slugger, now?"

A small round of laughter went around the room.

"I'll get back to you on that one," he answered with a smile. He glanced down the table at Sarah and saw that his report was in front of her.

Phillip turned his attention back to the announcements.

Jessica watched Ethan out of the corner of her eye and wondered if it was as obvious to everyone else as it was to her that he was suffering from a hangover.

After the meeting, Ethan and Sarah returned to their office.

"What happened to you this morning?"

He rubbed his eyes and sat down in his chair. "I overslept. I forgot to set the alarm."

She grabbed her stethoscope from its peg.

"Thank you for going over my report at the meeting."

She hung the instrument around her neck and nodded. "Buy me breakfast and we'll call it even."

"Deal."

"I'll meet you in the cafeteria after rounds," she said, opening the door.

Ethan leaned his head back against the chair and rubbed his temples. A few minutes went by before his attention was drawn to his bottom desk drawer. He swallowed hard trying to banish the thought from his mind, but he couldn't do it. He opened the drawer and pulled out the bottle with trembling fingers. Unscrewing the cap, he brought it to his lips and took a long drink.

He closed his eyes feeling a calmness surround him. When he opened them, Phillip was standing in front of him.

"I'll take that," he said, grabbing the bottle out of his hands.

Ethan could not get his thoughts together quickly enough to say anything.

Phillip didn't speak for a long time. He quietly twisted the cap back on the bottle and slid it into the pocket of his lab coat. "How long has this been going on?"

"This is the first time, I swear."

"And you feel it's necessary to take a drink at eight-thirty in the morning?"

He stammered as he searched for the words. "It isn't what you think, Phillip."

"Ethan, you do realize that I could fire you right now for this."

He nodded and dropped his head.

"You've got a problem and I think it's time you admitted it."

He rose to his feet. "I don't have a problem," he said defensively.

"Then why did I find you hunched over this bottle a few moments ago?"

Ethan took a deep breath and cursed himself for not being able to come up with any excuse. "It was just a small sip," he said finally. "What's the big deal?"

Phillip's temple began to throb. "It is a *very* big deal, when we're talking about the welfare of the patients in this hospital. And what worries me the most, is this cavalier attitude you have towards it."

"Look, Phillip, I know I screwed up. But I promise it won't happen again."

"I want you to go to an AA meeting."

"You can't be serious."

"I'm *very* serious."

He turned away and began to shake his head.

Phillip grabbed him by his arm making him look at him. "In a matter of months, I have watched you go from a brilliant and respected doctor to *this*. You're lying if you say you don't have a problem."

"I *don't,*" he said, jerking his arm away from him.

"Look at yourself, Ethan. You've got a hangover right now."

He remained silent.

Phillip took a deep breath. "So you're telling me that you won't go to an AA meeting?"

Ethan suppressed the anger that was building up inside him. "I won't go, because I don't need to."

"Then I have no choice but to suspend you for two weeks. Your reinstatement will be pending upon a review by the board."

He felt his chest begin to tighten. "Phillip, please don't do this to me."

"You either go to AA, and get the help you need, or take the suspension."

"You're not *listening* to me!" he yelled. "I don't have a problem!"

Phillip turned and went to the door. "You're suspended, Ethan. You have fifteen minutes to leave before I have security escort you out."

~

Sarah pulled into Ethan's driveway and sat for a long time. She was still in disbelief. Phillip had caught her during her morning rounds and told her what had happened.

She numbly got out of her car and walked up the sidewalk. There weren't any lights on in the house, but she thought she saw movement through the window as she rang the bell.

The porch light came on and the door opened slightly.

"Hi," she said.

Ethan widened the door and stepped back. "Hi."

"I wasn't sure if you were home."

"I was out on the patio."

She followed him through the house and out to the backyard where he sat down in a sling back chair. Her gaze went from him to the glass of scotch that sat beside him on the concrete. "I tried to think of something to say on my way over here…" she said, sitting down in a matching chair, "but the truth is, I don't know what to say."

Ethan stared at the ground, too ashamed to look at her. "Does everyone know?"

"Phillip made a formal announcement to the board this afternoon."

His jaw twitched.

Sarah crossed her legs as an uneasy silence settled around them.

"Aren't you going to ask me *the* question?" he said, sounding bitter.

"What question?"

He shook his head. Sometimes her lack of curiosity amazed him. "Never mind."

The sun slowly began to sink behind the guesthouse.

Ethan leaned against the back of the chair and sighed. "I'm sorry I left you in such a bind at the clinic."

She tilted her head. "I think you're apologizing for the wrong thing, aren't you?"

He looked over at her.

She waved her hand in the air as if to dismiss the question. "I need to be getting home."

"What's wrong?" he asked, standing up.

She rose from the chair and put her hands on her hips. She had expected to come over here and have him explain to her that it was all a mistake, but she could tell by the look in his eyes that he'd been drinking. "You know what?" she said, reaching down to get her purse. "It's late. I think it would be best if I talked to you tomorrow."

Chapter Thirty-nine

Sunday evening, Jessica sat on her sofa leafing through the newspaper. Mrs. Chambers had gone to church, and Ryan was upstairs taking a much-needed nap. She had kept him awake for most of the afternoon thinking that Ethan would be coming by to pick him up, but so far she hadn't heard from him. It was unlike him to miss his visitation.

She laid the paper aside and tucked her hair behind her ear. When Phillip had told everyone on the board that he had suspended him, she had not been surprised. She knew that it would only be a matter of time before he carried his drinking into his professional life. As tragic as she knew this was for him, a small part of her was glad that it had happened. She hoped that this would finally force him to get help.

~

Ethan stood outside on his balcony staring at nothing in particular. It had been five days since his suspension, and he had not seen or talked to anyone from the hospital during that time. In fact, with the exception of making a run to the liquor store, he had not left his house.

He emptied the last of the scotch into his glass and tilted his head back. A wave of dizziness suddenly struck him, causing the glass to slip from his fingers. A second later, he heard it shatter on the patio below.

He leaned heavily against the railing and looked down. In the dimness of the night, he could see the swimming pool; its blue tarp was covered with dirty water and leaves. He should have opened it by now, but there was really no point. Jessica and the baby weren't here to enjoy it.

Fixing his gaze on the red bricks that made up the patio, he could faintly make out the shards of glass as they lay scattered about. Their edges glistened from the light seeping out of the kitchen window. As he looked at the broken pieces, he began to wonder how far of a fall it would be from the balcony. The longer he stared, the more entranced he became with the thought. It was quickly diminished, however, as the desire for another drink consumed him.

He stumbled out of the bedroom and down the stairs to the kitchen where an unopened bottle sat waiting for him. He tore at the seal and brought it to his lips, bypassing the need for a glass. A small shudder went through him as the liquid heat traveled downwards.

He did not know how much he had drunk today, but knew it had been more than usual. The numbness he longed for refused to come, making the pain inside him hurt that much more.

Setting the bottle down, he caught sight of his beeper lying on the counter. His chest rose and fell, bringing forth a heavy sigh. He had worked so hard to become a doctor, fighting his father over it tooth and nail. And now, he had gone and fucked it up as well. It was the one thing…the only thing…he had left.

~

Jessica awoke from a deep sleep and fumbled for the phone. "Hello," she whispered, reaching out to turn on the light.

Ethan sat on the edge of the sofa with the phone in his left hand, and a .22 revolver in the other.

"Hello?" she repeated.

"It's me," he spoke into the receiver.

She glanced at the clock. "What do you want?"

There was a long pause.

She sat up and swung her legs over the side of the bed.

"I want to tell Ryan goodnight."

"It's three o'clock in the morning," she said, feeling the anger creeping inside her.

Ethan pressed the side of the pistol against his cheek. Its cold steel felt good against his skin. "Please," he whispered.

"You're drunk."

He closed his eyes and swallowed hard. "Will you kiss him goodnight for me...and tell him that I love him with all my heart?"

She took a deep breath and held it a moment before answering. "Yes."

"It's important"—his voice broke—"that you tell him. Do you promise?"

Jessica hung up, not wanting to hear anymore.

Ethan wiped at his eyes as he laid the phone down. He pointed the gun at his chest and pulled the trigger.

Chapter Forty

Renee stood alone in the cemetery, weeping. Why had Ethan done this? Why? It was a question that she had asked herself a thousand times, but had no answer. She knelt down in front of the tombstone and placed her hand on its gray marble.

Her mind became engulfed in memories of her and Ethan when they were growing up. She remembered back to when he used to take her riding with him. He would lift her high upon the horse and then climb into the saddle behind her. In an instant, they would be off, riding hard and fast. She remembered how she used to look back at their house. She would watch it grow farther and farther away as they rode until it was just a tiny speck in the distance. His arms would be wrapped tightly around her making her feel safe. Every now and then, he would look down at her and smile.

Renee let her fingers trace over the letters engraved in the stone. Feelings of guilt overwhelmed her as she thought back to her last meeting with him. She was sorry she had treated him so badly. How she wished she had told him how much she loved him. She used to tell him all the time when they were kids.

She wiped at her eyes and stood up, dusting the blades of grass from her knees. "Goodbye, Daddy." She turned and walked down the winding path to her car. She had never gotten the chance to tell her father that she loved him before he died, but she was going to tell Ethan. She started the engine and drove towards the hospital.

~

In the dimness of the room, Jessica stood over Ethan's lifeless body. His skin was paler than the sheets, his dark brown eyes closed and still. He had shot himself in the heart. The bullet had lodged itself in his right ventricle, which had created a left to right shunt. This meant that the blood was not flowing from the left ventricle of his heart to the right ventricle, and was not re-circulating through the pulmonary artery or lungs.

Jessica had been able to remove the bullet and repair the shunt, but how much damage had been done remained to be seen. She knew he would have died within seconds if the bullet had gone half an inch in any other direction.

A series of beeps brought her attention to the monitor. His heartbeat was slow and irregular, but that sound was the only thing that showed he was alive. His condition was listed as critical, and he showed no signs of improvement.

"Excuse me, Dr. Harrington?"

"Yes?"

"Dr. Harrington's sister is here."

Jessica nodded at the nurse and followed her out. This was something that she had been dreading.

~

Sarah waited quietly in Jessica's office, grateful to be alone for the moment. She had just spent the last two hours talking with the police. This morning, for a reason still unknown to her, she had decided to stop by Ethan's house and bring him breakfast. She felt bad about the way she'd left things when she had seen him last week, and hoped to make amends.

When he didn't answer the door she had started to leave, but noticed his car was still in the garage. Thinking he might be out on the patio, she went around back and found the door unlocked. The house was strangely quiet as she walked through the kitchen and into the foyer. Guessing he was probably asleep upstairs, she turned on her heel to go back out the way she came. That's when she saw him.

He was lying facedown on the floor in the living room. Hurrying over to him, she shoved the coffee table out of the way and turned him over. His upper chest was covered in blood. As she tore open his shirt to locate the source of the bleeding, she noticed the gun lying near his shoulder.

With trembling fingers, she checked for a pulse; it was barely there. She called an ambulance and tried to stanch the bleeding. By the time he arrived at the hospital he was in v-fib.

The sound of the door opening made her turn around.

Jessica hesitated before coming in.

Sarah wiped her eyes. "I was waiting to talk with you."

"There hasn't been any change," she said, walking over to her desk.

Sarah noticed the envelope she held under her arm. "Are those his X-rays?"

Without answering, Jessica slid the film out of the envelope and placed it on the board in front of her. "These were just taken," she said, flipping on the lights. There was a soft flicker and then a hum as the black film illuminated. She pointed to a gray mass on the X-ray. "We got all of the bullet. There were no fragments. But you can see the damage that it did to his heart...there."

Sarah came up behind her to see. "How bad is it?"

"It's too soon to tell." She placed another X-ray on the board. "He also has a fairly large ulcer."

Sarah studied the film. It had almost doubled in size since she had first examined him.

Jessica glanced over her shoulder. "Did you know about this?"

"I've been treating him for it for just over a year."

She swallowed her anger. "Did you also know about *this?*" She thrust a piece of paper at her. "We did an ultrasound because his CBC count showed the enzymes in his liver were abnormally high."

Sarah looked down at the small picture. "Cirrhosis," she said numbly.

Jessica nodded. "It's in the early stages."

The numbness traveled from Sarah's mouth to her feet as she headed towards the door.

"That's why I left him."

She stopped and turned.

Jessica was staring at her. "Contrary to the popular opinion of this hospital, and whatever Ethan may have told you...I didn't leave him because of Gavin. I left him because he is an alcoholic, and I couldn't deal with it any longer."

Sarah looked at her for a long time before speaking. "I'm sorry," she whispered.

Jessica coldly turned her attention back to the X-rays. After a moment, she heard Sarah's heels clicking across the floor and then the sound of the door closing. She placed her hands on the credenza in front of her and bowed her head. Her whole body shook as she began to cry.

Suddenly, someone's hands were on her shoulders; they were strong, familiar, and comforting. She turned and fell into Gavin's arms. "When did you get back?"

"Just now. I caught the first plane I could."

He had been in Baltimore attending a seminar when he'd received a call from Phillip. He had hoped to make it back in time to do the surgery, but Jessica had decided they couldn't wait any longer.

"I'm sorry that you went through this alone. I know it must have been hard." He held her tightly against him. "I've seen his chart. You did an excellent job. It's exactly what I would have done," he said softly.

She lifted her head up and wiped her eyes. "I don't think it was good enough."

~

Renee sat beside Ethan's bed, her hands knitted together in her lap. He lay there unmoving with machines and tubes hooked up to him. His face still wore that troubled look she had seen that day in the park.

She leaned forward and caressed the side of his cheek. When they were younger, Ethan had always been there for her. He was her big brother, her protector, her confidante, and her friend. A silent sob escaped from her lips. It had been all too easy with the lifestyle she had chosen to forget what was important.

Jessica watched Renee as she sat stoically beside Ethan, keeping a vigil. She had prepared herself for her former sister-in-law's brutal accusations, and acrid tongue, but had received none of it. Renee seemed unusually quiet.

There was suddenly an explosion of beeps on the heart monitor, followed by a long tone.

"What is it?" Renee asked, getting to her feet.

Nurses and doctors came rushing in, causing her to retreat to the corner of the room.

Gavin seemed to appear out of nowhere. He stepped in and took the paddles from Jessica. "Set it to two hundred," he said, rubbing them together. "Clear!"

Ethan's chest rose and fell.

"Nothing," said one of the nurses.

Renee covered her mouth with her hands as she sank against the wall.

~

Sarah ran down the corridor to CCU. She had been upstairs trying to sleep when she heard the code blue over the P.A. She hurried through the door and ran straight into Gavin. "I heard the code!" she said, trying to go around him.

He held her by her arms. "Hold on," he said, refusing to let her go in.

Sarah looked up at him with tears streaming down her face.

"We got his heart started again," he said tenderly.

She tried to thank him, but a sob replaced her words. He drew her close as she buried her face in his shoulder.

A few feet away, Jessica stood outside the station instructing the nurses on what she wanted done. She was sure they heard the trembling in her voice.

Grace was waiting for her when she came out. "Come on," she said, leading her over to a small waiting area just around the corner.

She brought her hand to her mouth as her legs buckled underneath her. "He called me last night, Grace." Tears spilled from her eyes as she began to tell her cousin the story of what had happened. "If I hadn't of hung up on him, maybe he wouldn't have done this."

"Jessica, that is not true." She lifted her chin up. "Now, listen to me. When Ethan called you, he had already made up his mind to do this—"

She shook her head.

"—that's why he was calling. He wanted to say goodbye."

"Why did he do this, Grace?"

The older woman put her arm across her shoulder as her own lips began to waver. "I don't know, sweetheart. I don't know."

Chapter Forty-one

Four days later, Ethan still remained unconscious. He had developed an infection from the bullet. Gavin was treating him with large doses of antibiotics, but they didn't seem to be helping. His blood pressure had dropped to ninety over forty.

Jessica stood over him listening to his heart. She remembered how she used to listen to it beating after they had made love. She would lie there, with her head resting lightly on his chest, and let the sound lull her to sleep.

She slid her stethoscope along his torso and listened for a moment. His lungs were congested. The infection was spreading.

~

The next morning, Sarah came out of the examining room in the clinic and fell into her chair. The pain in her neck told her that she had spent one too many nights on the sofa in her office.

Her eyes involuntarily wandered over to Ethan's chair. She stared at it for the longest time, wishing that it were empty because he was making rounds. She knew that everyone at one point in their life, herself included, had thoughts of suicide, but it was usually a fleeting thought in a moment of self-pity. For someone to actually go through with it, knowing they were going to end their life, was difficult for her to understand.

A knock on the door interrupted her thoughts.

"Hi," Gavin said quietly.

She swiveled around in the chair as he crossed over to the sofa and sat down. A feeling of alarm surged through her. "Has something happened?"

He held up his hands to calm her. "He's okay. I thought you might like to know that his blood pressure has come up some. It's not a significant improvement, but it's the first sign we've seen that the antibiotics are fighting off the infection."

She saw the fatigue in his eyes and knew that he had gotten little, if any, sleep these past few days. "Thank you for coming up here to tell me."

He shrugged. "I knew that you were anxious about him, so..."

Sarah gave him a small smile as he stood to go.

~

Jessica paid for her coffee and headed for an empty table by the window. The past twenty-four hours Ethan's vitals had slowly improved. He would occasionally move his fingers which was a good sign that he might be waking up soon.

It was only three in the afternoon, but the storm clouds gathering outside made it seem much later. As she brought the cup to her lips, she became very much aware of the number of people that were staring at her. Some were casual—others blatant. She set the cup down, feeling her cheeks burning. If she hadn't been so tired, she would have gotten up and left.

These past few days had been a blur for her with no differentiation between the ending of one, and the beginning of another. She stared out the window, letting her mind drift. It unfortunately went to the same spot it always did—her last conversation with Ethan. Guilt, coupled with grief, swarmed her. She should have picked up on the desperation in his voice but was too busy being angry.

The sound of her beeper going off jarred her. She glanced down at the number displayed on the tiny screen and saw that it was CCU. Shoving her chair away from the table, she ran for the stairs.

Gavin was already there by the time she arrived.

"What's happened?" she asked, pushing her way through the nurses.

Ethan's eyes were still closed, but his head moved from side to side as he tossed about in the bed.

Gavin was leaning over him putting his arms in restraints to keep him from hurting himself.

"What is it, Gavin?"

"I'm not sure. His blood pressure's one forty over eighty, pulse one twenty."

Jessica's mind began to run down the possibilities for his sudden change.

Ethan's body strained against the leather straps that now bound him to the bed. "Get them off me!"

She reached into her lab coat and pulled out her penlight. His pupils did not respond when she lifted his eyelids.

"Make them go away!" Ethan pleaded as his whole body began to tremble.

Jessica exchanged glances with Gavin.

He turned to the nurse. "Let's start another I.V. with fifty percent glucose."

"Yes, Doctor."

He noticed Renee looking through the glass as the nurse hurried out of the room. "Do you want me to talk to her?"

Jessica nodded. She seemed to take things better when they came from Gavin.

"What's wrong with him? Why is he doing that?" Renee asked, as he met her at the door.

He motioned for her to follow him.

They went outside CCU and stood in the corridor.

"Your brother is suffering from Delirium Tremens. Do you know what that is?"

She shook her head. "No, not really."

"This condition is caused when a person's body is going through withdrawal...from alcohol. This causes Delirium Tremens or D.T.'s. It makes them hallucinate and have nightmares," he said delicately.

Renee stared at him for the longest time. "Are you telling me that he's an alcoholic?"

Gavin nodded.

She looked away for a moment, her mind denying what he had just said. "He seemed to be doing better. Is this going to make him worse again?"

"This *could* be dangerous to him, yes. Especially after the type of surgery he's had. But we're going to treat him with glucose, which should take care of it. And we're going to monitor him very closely."

~

Jessica gently swept the hair from Ethan's forehead. It had been a long, hard night for him, but he was finally resting. The glucose had worked, eventually bringing an end to his nightmares, and his blood pressure had stabilized.

Her breath quivered as she drew it in. The man who had once walked a mile in the rain to find her lost cell phone, had surprised her with a dozen pink roses on her last birthday, and had whisked her away to a sandy beach in Mexico, where he'd made love to her underneath the moonlight…now lay shackled to a hospital bed.

"Dr. Harrington?"

"Yes?" she said, pushing her memories aside as she turned to the nurse.

"The lab called and said they have the latest results ready."

"Thank you." She stretched and walked over to the doorway looking for Renee, thinking that perhaps she would want to sit with him. But as her eyes scanned the empty waiting room, it suddenly occurred to her that her former sister-in-law had not been seen since Gavin had spoken with her yesterday.

"Jess?"

She spun around. Ethan remained still. He had called out for her several times during the night. Convinced that's all it was this time, she turned to go, but a low groan made her stop.

His eyes slowly fluttered open.

She hurried to his side. "Ethan?"

Ethan tried to find his way through the black haze that surrounded him. After a moment, shadows began to take shape and Jessica's face appeared. "What happened?" he asked in a voice that was as dry as it was hoarse.

"Get some rest," she said. "We'll talk in a little bit."

Finding her answer strange, he went to sit up but couldn't. It suddenly felt as if his chest were being crushed. Panic surged through him as he fought to breathe.

Jessica placed her hands on his shoulders and forced him back down. "Ethan, you need to lie still. I know you feel like you can't breathe, but you're fine. Take short breaths. Do you hear me? Just short breaths."

He stopped struggling and did as she instructed. After a few seconds, the feeling in his chest subsided.

"See?" she said, offering him a small smile. "You're okay."

"What happened?" he repeated.

"We'll talk later, I promise." Seeing him awake and talking was an answer to her prayers, but she had no idea what to say to him and felt it would probably be best if Grace handled it.

His eyes darted about the room. "Why am I here? What happened?"

She looked at him solemnly for a moment. "You sustained a gunshot wound to your heart..."

He closed his eyes as he heard her words. Everything came rushing back, making his head hurt.

~

Ethan pulled against the restraints with all his strength as he watched Jessica speaking with Grace outside his room. The two of them seemed to be having a long discussion at his expense.

After what seemed an eternity, Grace finally came through the doorway. "Hello, Ethan," she said in a soothing tone.

"Grace, get these things off me!"

The corners of her mouth turned down slightly. "I will, Ethan, I promise. But I think I'm going to wait for a little while, all right?"

"I want these things *off!*"

"Ethan—"

He clenched his jaw and swallowed hard, trying to calm down. "Who found me?" he asked in a low voice.

She leaned forward. "What?"

He sighed. "Who found me?" he repeated.

Grace hesitated before answering him. "Sarah."

He turned his head, trying to bury it in the pillow. "Please...just leave me alone," he said bitterly.

Chapter Forty-two

The next day, Grace sat in Phillip's office along with Jessica and Gavin. The four of them were discussing Ethan, and what would be the best option for him.

"Right now," Grace said, looking around the room at her colleagues, "he's not saying much of anything to anyone. I'd like to begin counseling him, but we all know he would never agree to it."

Phillip took off his glasses and rubbed the bridge of his nose. "Under state law, he could be admitted to the psychiatric ward of this hospital for a maximum of thirty days by his next of kin."

Jessica nodded. "That's true, but I'm not sure if forcing him would be such a good idea."

"Well, it's either that or nothing."

Jessica looked over her shoulder. Gavin was leaning against the wall with his arms folded against him. He had remained quiet up until now.

Phillip sat forward in his chair. "What's his medical condition?"

"He's doing better every day," Jessica replied. "If he continues to improve, I'll probably release him in a week."

"Do you think we could talk Renee into admitting him?" Grace's question was directed at Jessica.

"I honestly don't know."

"Do you want to try talking to her?" Phillip asked.

She shook her head. "Renee doesn't want to listen to anything I have to say. Maybe it would be better coming from you."

They all agreed that Phillip would be the one to talk to her.

On their way out, Gavin gently brushed Jessica's arm. "You know, I was thinking how hard this is on you, and I wanted to tell you that I would take over Ethan's case if you don't feel up to it."

They walked together in silence as she mulled it over. It was true that she dreaded going in to see Ethan, let alone examine him. There was so much tension and bitterness between them, that it made it extremely difficult. "I appreciate the offer, Gavin," she finally said, "but I don't think he would react very well to your being his doctor."

He accompanied her to the elevator and pressed the button. "You're probably right."

~

Ethan stared out the window watching the rain coming down. Sometimes the drops would get very big and cover the pane so that he couldn't see through it. Other times it would slow down to just a pitter-patter. He struggled to turn over on his side, but the restraints on his wrists held him immobile.

The sound of heels clicking across the floor made him cringe. It was most likely Grace or Jessica, and he did not want to see either one of them.

"Ethan?"

He clenched his jaw upon hearing Sarah's voice.

She came around the side of the bed so she could see him and was immediately taken aback by his appearance. His hair was disheveled and he had about a week's growth of beard on his face and neck. There was dark bruising on the skin underneath his eyes. Wanting to comfort him, she reached out and laid her hand upon his forearm.

He flinched at her touch, and began pulling at the restraints that held him.

"Is there anything that I can get you?" she asked, blinking back her tears.

He kept his eyes away from her. "Would you please get these things off of me?"

"I can't do that. I'm sorry."

His breath quivered as he exhaled.

She took a step closer and reached out for him again. "Ethan, I—"

He turned his head towards the opposite wall, taking as much of his upper body with it as he could.

Sarah folded her arms across her chest and swallowed the ache in her throat. Grace had told her earlier that she could visit him, but had also cautioned her that he was extremely agitated.

Although she was thankful to Grace for making her aware, she had casually dismissed her warning, surmising that even if Ethan were acting in that manner, he certainly wouldn't behave that way with her. They *were* best friends after all.

Her heart sank as she watched him struggling against the restraints. His fists were clenched as he pulled at them until his body shook. A silent sob fell from her lips and she quickly brought her fingers to her mouth. "Well, I'll leave you alone," she said, clearing her throat. "I know you're tired."

~

That afternoon, Ethan was sitting upright in his bed. He was no longer bound by the restraints, but felt he may as well have been; as for the better part of an hour, he'd had to endure having the nurse outside stare at him.

"Ethan?"

He looked over and saw Renee standing in the middle of the room. "What are you doing here?"

"Well, that's a rather silly question now, isn't it?" she asked, kissing him on the side of his face.

The smell of her perfume lingered heavily around him even after she had pulled away.

She sat down in a green plastic chair and crossed her legs.

The room grew quiet, catching both of them off-guard.

He couldn't help noticing that she was tapping her fingers impatiently on her knee; it was a habit their mother used to do.

"Is there anything I can bring you from your home?"

"No."

Her fingers fell silent as her eyes searched his face. "Gavin tells me that you're an alcoholic."

"Well, Gavin's an *idiot*."

She suddenly leaned forward and clutched his hand in her own. "Is there anything I can do to help?"

He picked up on the sincerity in her voice; it was unusual and completely out of character for his sister. "Why are you really here, Renee?" he asked, pulling out of her grasp.

She gave him an odd look. "Because I care about you."

He raised an eyebrow at her.

"You don't believe me, do you?" she asked, sounding hurt.

He didn't answer.

She sucked in her breath and rose from the chair. The moisture in her eyes immediately dried up as a bitter expression formed in them. "Have you talked with Dr. Cummings?"

"Yes."

"Did you know that she, along with your ex-wife, would like to admit you to the psychiatric ward?"

He remained silent. He had figured as much, but he also knew that legally they couldn't—. He jerked his eyes towards her.

Her face now wore the thinnest of smirks.

"You can't do this to me, Renee."

"I think you need help," she said innocently.

"What do you want?"

"What do you mean?"

"Don't play games with me! What do you *want?*"

She moved closer to him. "I want your proxy. You sign it over to me, and I won't admit you. It's that simple."

He clenched his jaw. "You're sick."

"Oh, no, Ethan," she said, leaning over him. "You have it backwards. You see *you're* the one who is sick, and *I'm* the one who is holding your future. Now, whether or not you want to spend it in a loony bin is up to you." She let him think it over for a minute. "Do we have a deal?"

"Yes," he answered spitefully.

"Good. I'll be back in a couple of hours with a notary."

~

Paul sat behind his desk reviewing a case that was about to go to court. He had hoped to avoid a trial altogether, but unfortunately, neither side was willing to budge.

His intercom chimed. "Mr. Cummings? Mrs. Westcott is here to see you."

He closed the file and leaned forward. "Send her in, please," he said, feeling the hairs on the back of his neck beginning to prickle.

The oak door to his office swung open as she strode in.

He rose to his feet. "Renee, it's good to see you."

"Hello, Paul," she said in that arrogant tone she used sometimes.

"Please, sit down."

"Thank you."

"What can I do for you?"

She opened a small attaché case that she had brought in with her. "It's concerning my brother, and his interests in Harrington Enterprises," she said, pulling out a white piece of paper.

Paul took the document from her and scanned it. After a moment, he laid the paper aside and looked up. "May I ask why Ethan signed his proxy over to you?"

She sighed as if his question was of little importance to her. "I'm just looking out for my brother's welfare, and I don't feel as if you have his best interests at heart. He knows that I do."

Paul bit his tongue.

"This document revokes the original proxy that he gave you."

"Yes. I do know a little about the law." He picked up the document again and checked Ethan's signature. "He willingly signed this over to you?"

She smiled smugly. "Of course."

~

Jessica removed her stethoscope from Ethan's chest and straightened up. "There's still some congestion in your left lung, but the antibiotics should clear it up," she said, slipping the instrument around her neck. "Do you have any questions?" A few moments ago, she had explained, in great detail, about the damage done to his heart.

"No," he replied, looking in any direction but hers.

The tension between them was making it impossible for her to talk to him in any way other than matter of fact. "We also ran some tests on your liver because your CBC count was so high. You are in the early stages of Cirrhosis."

She held the picture of the ultrasound up for him to see. "I know you understand the seriousness of this, Ethan, but I'm going to tell you anyway. You are going to have to stop drinking."

His expression remained blank. "When are you going to release me?"

She hesitated a moment. "Well, if your tests we took this morning show no signs of infection, then possibly tomorrow or the day after."

"I'd like to take a shower."

"If you feel up to it," she said, making a note in his chart.

He scratched at his face. "And shave."

"I'll have a male nurse come in and do that for you after you've showered."

Chapter Forty-three

Ethan opened his eyes and squinted at the bright sunlight. He felt very groggy as he brought his hand to his face and wiped the sleep away. Once his eyes had focused, he noticed that he was in a completely different room. There was no furniture in here at all; no chair, no dresser, no nightstand—just his hospital bed.

He pushed the covers back and stumbled over to the window. The glass was encased with wire mesh. He turned and looked at the door. It was the same way. His chest began to tighten as he hurried over to it.

Peering through it, he could see the nurses' station. Renee was standing near it talking with Phillip.

A sense of relief came over him. She must be here to get him out. He went to turn the knob, but found it locked. "Hey!" he shouted, pounding his fist against the door.

Phillip glanced over at him and then said something to Renee, who nodded.

Ethan took a step back as the door swung open. "Why do you have me in here?" he demanded.

Phillip stuck his hands in the pockets of his lab coat and pursed his lips. "You're going to be in here for a while, Ethan."

"On whose authority?" he asked, knowing that he couldn't do this.

"Renee signed the papers admitting you this morning. For the next thirty days you will be under Dr. Cummings' care."

He jerked his head towards Renee, who remained out in the hall.

"This is going to be difficult for you," Phillip continued, "and I know—"

Ethan brushed past him and out the door. "We had a deal," he said, pointing his finger at her.

She crossed her arms. "I don't know what you're talking about."

"Let's not make this any harder, Ethan."

He spun around to face Phillip. "You can't keep me here."

"Ethan?"

He looked over his shoulder to find Grace. Two burly orderlies stood behind her. She gestured for him to return to his room. "Let's go inside and talk, all right?"

He shook his head. "I don't have anything to say to you." He turned back towards Renee. "This isn't funny. Tell them!"

Grace signaled the men that had accompanied her.

Before Ethan could do anything else, the orderlies had him on his knees with his arms pinned behind his back. "You can't do this!" he yelled, trying to get to his feet.

They half-dragged, half-carried him into his room where they forced him onto the bed.

Grace held up a syringe. "This is just to calm you."

He struggled, but could not move under their weight. He felt the sting of the needle, and then a cloud of darkness swept over him.

~

Jessica walked briskly down the north hall of the psychiatric ward. She had happily released Ethan from her care two days ago, being more than ready to let Grace take over. But she had gotten a call from her this afternoon asking if she would check on him. She paused outside his room for a moment and counted to three before going in.

Ethan lay on his side with his back to the door.

"Ethan," she said, coming around the bed, "I need to examine you."

"There's nothing wrong with me."

She opened his chart and began flipping through the pages. "Well, you're running a temperature and you haven't eaten or drunk anything in the last two days. There must be something wrong. Come on." She motioned for him to turn over.

He begrudgingly rolled onto his back, allowing her to check his incision and listen to his heart. His emotions churned inside him as her fingers swept along his chest.

"Everything looks good," she said, hanging the stethoscope around her neck. "But I'm going to order a blood test just to be safe. In the meantime, I'd like for you to eat something."

"Why?" he asked in a voice laced with bitterness.

Her left eyebrow shot up. "You don't want to be forced do you?"

He turned back over onto his side, hoping she would go away.

Chapter Forty-four

Sarah felt the warmth of the sun on her shoulders as she knelt in her backyard. She dug her fingers into the rich black soil noting how good it felt to get her hands dirty. She reached beside her and carefully took the small begonia out of its tray and placed it in the hole she had dug. She loved her garden. This was her sanctuary.

The creeping phlox she had planted last spring were now in full bloom; their brilliant purple petals spilled over each other as they encircled the base of her maple tree. Just in front of her lay rows upon rows of pink roses and purple irises. She lovingly spread the soil around the begonia and gave it a small drink of water.

She wiped a bead of sweat from her cheek with the sleeve of her shirt. They were just a few days into the month of June, but it was already plenty hot. Today was Saturday, and normally she would have been at the clinic, but after nearly five weeks of working every day, she had to stop; she was emotionally and physically exhausted.

This was also the week that she had planned to visit Ashley in Sydney, but there wasn't any way she could leave the clinic now.

When she had called to tell her, Ashley had given her some news of her own. She was pregnant. Sarah had tried to sound happy, but was sure her daughter heard the disappointment in her voice. She couldn't help feeling that this was a huge mistake. Ashley and Ted hadn't been married all that long, and she was barely twenty years old.

A heavy sigh fell from her as she reached for another begonia. She only wanted what was best for her daughter and had always hoped that she would have been older and more settled in her marriage before having a child.

~

Jessica stood beside Ethan's bed going over his blood work from the lab. With the exception of his CBC count, everything looked normal. She closed the chart and looked at him. "Still not hungry?" she asked, gesturing at the breakfast tray in front of him.

He was sitting up with his arms folded tightly against his chest. His jaw was clenched; his face dark.

She slid the tray towards him. "I know the food can be lousy in here sometimes, but this doesn't look too bad."

He suddenly grabbed the plate and slung it across the room.

She took a step back as a familiar fear surrounded her.

Ethan's eyes grew from dark to black as he took the tray cart and shoved it. It went skittering across the room on its wheels before flipping over.

Jessica took a deep breath and forced herself to take control. "I'll be right back." Her feet carried her swiftly out the door as she went to speak with Grace.

A few minutes later, an orderly came in and began cleaning up the mess.

Ethan watched, feeling ashamed. "I'm sorry about that."

The man shook his head. "No problem." He set the cart back up and made a quick job of mopping the floor. "Take it easy now," he said heading towards the door.

Jessica stepped to the side to let him pass and then walked in. Two nurses; one female and the other, an able-bodied male, followed her.

Ethan looked at what she held in her hands. "You're *not* going to give me that."

The male nurse stepped forward and leaned all his weight on Ethan's upper body, making it impossible for him to move. He watched helplessly as the nurse put his hands and feet in the restraints.

"Hold his head still," Jessica said, sliding the tube out of its wrapping.

He struggled harder as he felt the tube go inside his nose. It wasn't long before he started to cough.

Jessica continued pushing the tube. "I need you to swallow, Ethan. It'll be easier if you just let it go down."

Grace stood silently watching from the doorway. It wasn't the first time a patient of hers had to have this done, but she didn't like it. She found it to be a double-edged sword. It was the humane thing to do, yet it was done in the most inhumane way.

The entire process took about an hour. Ethan's eyes were still dark, but fortunately for Jessica, he had stopped struggling a while ago. "Okay," she said, preparing to remove the tube. "I need you to take a deep breath."

He stared at the far wall, refusing to acknowledge her.

In one quick motion she pulled.

Ethan coughed and sputtered as it came up his throat.

The nurses undid the restraints and left, leaving Jessica alone with him. As she peeled off her gloves, she noticed a bit of blood trickling from his nostril. Grabbing a tissue, she leaned over him to wipe it.

He pushed her hand away.

Jessica sighed and dropped the tissue in his lap. "You're only hurting yourself, Ethan."

~

Gavin set the cup of tea in front of Jessica and perched himself on the edge of his desk.

"Thank you," she said, reaching out to take it.

"The blood tests showed no trace of infection?"

"His refusing to eat isn't physical," she answered.

"Well, he's obviously upset about being transferred to the psych ward."

She nodded in agreement. "But I don't know what to do."

Gavin could see the toll that this whole ordeal had taken on her; her face was thin and gaunt, her eyes sunken. She looked like she hadn't had a good night's sleep in weeks. "I think you should let me take over."

"I can't. It will just make things worse."

"How much worse could I make it? I think he would endure the pain of another feeding tube just because he knows it would bother you to do it. He would not get the same satisfaction if I did it, because it wouldn't bother me in the *least*. That alone would probably make him eat."

Jessica stared at him in disbelief.

He held out his hands. "I'm sorry. But I can't stand seeing you this way."

She knew she was going to have to think of a different approach.

~

Sunday afternoon, Ethan lay on his side looking out the window. From his bed, there was really nothing to see but sky, but it was better than staring at four walls. He heard the door open and then the sound of a familiar little voice.

He quickly turned over.

"Can you say 'hi' to Daddy?" Jessica stood by his bed with Ryan on her hip.

Ryan was chewing on his fingers smiling at him.

She leaned over and deposited him in Ethan's lap. "I'll be back in a little while."

~

Sarah returned the vacuum cleaner to the closet and tossed the last load of laundry in the dryer. She had made a promise to herself this weekend that she wasn't going to think about the clinic or Ethan. The result had left her with a lot of nervous energy. This morning she had gone to the grocery, cleaned her house from top to bottom, and done all the laundry.

The growl in her stomach told her it was time for lunch. As she pulled the sack of bread out of the pantry, her cell phone chimed. Picking it up, she frowned when she saw the caller id. She knew what this was going to be about. "Hello?"

"Have you talked to Ashley this week?" Gavin started right in.

"Yes. I gather you just spoke with her."

"She called to wish me a happy Father's Day and then told me she was *pregnant*."

Sarah leaned against the kitchen counter as she held the phone to her ear.

"She's too young to be having a baby," he continued.

"I agree."

"You need to talk to her."

She rolled her eyes. "And tell her what, Gavin?"

"I don't know. You're her mother. Just talk some sense into her."

"She and Ted are *married*. And whether we like it or not, this is between the two of them. I can't tell her what to do. You know how well it worked out the last time we tried that."

There was a long pause.

"Well, I think if you'd tried a little harder we wouldn't be having this discussion at all."

Sarah felt her anger rising. "What do you mean by that?"

"*You* are the one that gave in and told her she could marry him. If you had just supported me on my decision she never would have left!"

"You know what? I'm done talking to you." She pushed the button on her cell and dropped it on the counter. She exhaled loudly for no one's benefit but her own. She should have known he would try and make this all her fault.

~

Ethan sat on the floor with Ryan, playing with the wooden blocks that Jessica had stuffed inside the diaper bag.

He shook his head in silent wonder as he watched him. It was amazing how much he'd changed over the past few weeks. The tiny baby that he used to hold in his arms was no longer present; his hair had gone from light blond to brown, and his face was becoming that of a little boy.

"Dadda, Dadda." Ryan held a block up and said something incomprehensible.

Ethan smiled and took the wooden cube from him, stacking it neatly on top of the other one. He heard the sound of a click and looked over at the door.

Jessica walked inside and bent down. "Hi, Ry-Ry. Did you have a nice time playing with Daddy?"

Ryan grinned, allowing a big line of slobber to come rolling out of his mouth.

"He must be cutting another tooth."

Jessica nodded. "He's got two coming in the back." She knelt down and began putting the blocks inside the diaper bag. "I'm sorry he can't stay longer, but I don't want to get Grace into trouble."

"I understand," he said, knowing that visitors under the age of fourteen were prohibited on the psychiatric ward. He helped her with the blocks and got to his feet, scooping Ryan up along with him. He gave him a kiss before handing him to Jessica.

"Did you tell Daddy what we practiced?" she asked, balancing him on her hip.

Ryan responded in gibberish.

Jessica threw her head back and laughed. "Well, that's his way of saying it." She reached into her purse and handed him a card.

"What's this?"

"Happy Father's Day."

He slid the card out of its envelope and opened it. Ryan's handprint, done in red, was inside. It immediately brought a smile to his face. "Thank you, Jess."

"You can thank me by eating, okay?" Her voice was as serious as it was pleading.

He closed the card, finding it awkward to have to give her an answer.

She looked down at Ryan. "Wave bye-bye to Daddy," she said, making the gesture with her own hand.

Ryan waved, imitating her.

~

Grace sat at the foot of Ethan's bed. A small tape recorder lay beside her. She preferred it to a pad and pencil as it enabled her to truly listen and see her patients as they talked to her. Then later, she could go over every word and study their tone of voice. Of course, with Ethan, the only voice she had been studying was her own.

"I can't believe how big Ryan is getting. Did you see all the teeth he had?" She stifled a sigh and crossed her legs at the impending silence. She was trying every avenue she knew to get him to talk but was having no success. He had, at least, eaten something, which for now gave her some indication that he didn't want to die.

She soldiered on, hoping to get something out of him other than a blank stare. "I can't get over how much he's talking now. He's quite the little chatterbox."

Ethan rolled his eyes. "Grace, please don't patronize me."

"Well, you *can* talk after all."

He glowered at her for a moment before returning his gaze to the window.

"You know, Ethan, I'm here to help you. But it's kind of hard when you won't talk to me."

"I don't need any help."

"I'm looking at a man who was so distraught that he tried to take his own life...I think you *do* need help."

He snapped his eyes back to look at her. "Do you have *any* idea how embarrassing this is for me?"

"I can see why you would feel that way, Ethan, but I can assure you that everyone here is very concerned about you."

"I want to talk to Renee."

"She's already gone back to D.C., remember?"

"Then let me borrow your cell phone for a minute."

"I'm sorry, Ethan, but I can't allow that."

He pushed the covers back and swung his legs over the side of the bed.

"Look, I get that you don't want to be here. But you're stuck with me for the next few weeks, so we might as well pass the time by talking."

He stared out the window, but she knew he was listening.

"We can talk about anything you want. About Ryan...or the weather, your job, Jessica— "

"Why would I want to talk about *her?*"

"I don't know. Why *don't* you want to talk about her?"

Ethan felt his jaw tighten. He really resented her being here and the way she turned his words against him.

"Why don't you want to talk about Jessica?" she repeated.

"Because I'm not married to her anymore."

"Do you wish you still were?"

"I didn't want the divorce. You know that."

"Why did she divorce you?"

"Oh, come on, Grace," he said, sighing. "You were there."

"I know that," she said, nodding. "But I'm asking you what you think."

Ethan fell silent once more and Grace knew her window of opportunity had closed.

Chapter Forty-five

Grace sat in her office taking notes as she listened to the recording of her last session with Ethan. She had been counseling him for almost two weeks now, but felt she had made little headway.

"Can you tell me how you felt when you found out that Ryan was not your son?"

There was a long pause on the tape.

"How do you *think* I felt?"

"I don't know. That's why I'm asking."

"I was angry and hurt."

Another moment of silence passed as she waited for him to continue, but he didn't. Grace snapped the recorder off and rubbed her eyes. Ethan had kept his guard up with her every single moment.

A heavy sigh fell from her as she pushed her chair back and left the office. She climbed three flights of stairs in mere seconds and stopped just outside a large door. This was the entrance to the psychiatric ward, and no one was allowed in or out without an access code. She swiped her card into the small black box that was mounted on the wall and waited.

A loud buzzer sounded as the door unlocked.

Grace walked on down the corridor and past the recreation area where there were about a dozen or so men and women milling about.

An older man, who was seated at a table playing solitaire, gave her an enthusiastic wave. "Hi, Dr. Cummings."

"Hello, Virgil."

He got up and shuffled over to her. "Did you come to see me?" he asked eagerly.

"I've already spoken with you today, remember?"

Virgil nodded as the light faded from his eyes.

Grace couldn't help but feel sorry for him. Loneliness was a compounding factor for those who suffered from a mental disorder. "I'll stop by and see you later, all right?"

The smile returned to his troubled face. "Okay."

She continued down the hall and stepped cautiously around a ladder with a maintenance man's legs on it. The rest of him had disappeared through a hole in the ceiling. She got to the end of the corridor and made a left, stopping to peer through the first door.

Ethan sat on his bed, shirtless, flipping half-heartedly through a magazine. He refused to associate with any of the other patients on the ward, and he would not go to the AA meetings that were provided at the hospital as a service. Instead, he remained in his room, silent and withdrawn.

"Hello, Ethan," she said, closing the door behind her. The room was stifling. "I'm sorry it's so hot in here, but they're working on it."

He closed the magazine and set it aside.

"So, how are we doing today?"

"*We're* fine," he said, reaching for his t-shirt.

She sat down on the edge of his bed and flipped on the recorder.

As Ethan turned away to put his shirt on, the sunlight engulfed him, highlighting three very prominent scars on his back.

She immediately decided to switch gears. "I thought if it's all right with you, we'd talk about something different today."

He shrugged.

"I'd like for you to tell me a little about your childhood."

"Why?"

"Sometimes it helps me to start from the beginning of a person's life. What were you like growing up for example? What were some of the things you liked to do?"

He crossed his arms and began to pace the floor.

"Well, I for one think it's fascinating that you grew up in England. I've never been there, but I'd love to go sometime."

Still nothing.

"Jessica told me once that your mother had committed suicide when you were little. Is that right?"

He made a motion with his head that resembled a nod.

"That must have been very hard on you and Renee."

He turned and went over to the window.

Grace knew whenever he went over to that damn window he was done talking, but she kept trying. "What was she like?"

"I don't really remember much," he said after a moment.

"What was your father like?"

"*You* met him."

"Yes, but what was he like when you were growing up? It must have been hard on him after your mother's death."

"I guess."

"Was he a good father?"

"Yes."

"Did you have a good relationship?"

He pushed himself away from the window and spun around. "*Yes.* I loved him very much. Is that what you're getting at?"

~

Grace turned over and looked at the clock. Between Paul's snoring and her inability to shut her mind off, she gave up on trying to sleep. Slipping out of bed, she ambled into the kitchen where she set about making herself a cup of tea.

Her thoughts turned to Ethan as she filled the kettle with water. Yesterday afternoon, she had listened carefully to the session they'd had together, and as the recorder played, she picked up on a tiny inflection in Ethan's voice when he'd answered the questions about his father.

She pulled his case file out of her bag and sat down at the kitchen table. Her tired eyes scanned every line of her notes hoping to find something that would help her. She was running out of time with him. The thirty days were almost up.

Every session she'd had with him led to a brick wall, but the one yesterday bothered her greatly. When she had asked him if he had a good relationship with his father, he had gotten an odd look in his eyes. The closest word she could use to describe it, was conflict.

~

Sarah stood outside Ethan's room watching him. He was leaning against the wall staring out the window, seeming to be a million miles away.

The click of the latch made him turn his head. He smiled slightly upon seeing her. "Hi."

Feeling encouraged, she stepped into the room. "How are you?"

"Fine, I guess," he answered with a shrug.

"I brought you the latest medical journal."

Ethan eagerly took the magazine from her and studied its cover for a moment. "What is today?" he asked, noting it was the July edition.

"It's Wednesday, the twenty eighth."

"Of *June?*"

"Mmm-hmm."

He sighed. It was hard keeping up with the days in this place.

Sarah looked around uneasily, not knowing what else to say to him.

"So, what's been going on with you?" he asked, picking up on her nervousness.

A small smile formed on her lips as she remembered her news.

"What?"

"Well, I'm going to be a grandmother."

He broke into a wide grin. "Hey! That's wonderful!" He tilted his head when she didn't share in his enthusiasm. "Isn't it?"

"I'm still getting used to the idea."

"You think she's too young."

"Among other things."

He stepped forward and gave her a hug. "You raised a good daughter, Sarah. Have a little faith in her, okay?" he said, giving her a wink.

She smiled back. For just a brief moment, he was his old self once more...and then the room grew quiet again.

Ethan let his eyes wander back to the window. He could not begin to describe how ridiculous he felt standing in front of his colleague and best friend wearing these damn pajamas. Blue bottoms and a white t-shirt were standard issue on the psych ward, along with a bright red ID bracelet made of plastic that would not come off. Over the years, the hospital had a few patients walk out of the ward unnoticed. This was their solution—along with heavily locked doors.

"Is there anything I can bring you from home? Or anything I can get for you?" The look in her eyes was as sincere as her voice.

"Not unless you can spring me from this place."

Although Sarah knew he meant that as a joke, it only added to the tension that surrounded them.

He folded his arms against his chest and sighed, seeming to feel it as well. "How are things in the clinic?"

"Busy," she answered, "but it's—" Her beeper suddenly went off.

Ethan instinctively moved his hand to his waist.

Sarah's heart fell for him as she silenced the pager on her hip.

He saw the pity in her eyes and it made him angry. "Force of habit," he said quietly.

Silence rolled in, getting tangled up in the tension. It was a suffocating combination.

Chapter Forty-six

David Straithan was pouring himself a cup of coffee when his telephone rang. "Hello?"

"Yes, I'm trying to reach a Dr. David Straithan."

"Speaking."

"My name is Dr. Grace Cummings. I'm calling from a hospital in Maine. I'm sorry for disturbing you at home, but I'm desperately trying to locate some information on a person that I believe used to be a patient of yours a long time ago."

He splashed a dab of cream into his coffee and began to stir it with his spoon. "Let me give you the number to my office and they can check for you."

"I've already spoken with your office *and* your answering service. They told me that there's no record of this patient; however, your name appears as his physician." Grace tried to sound as polite as she could, but she was growing tired of the runaround.

"Well, if it was a few years ago the files are probably in storage. Give me the name and I'll have someone check on it for you and call you back," he said, reaching for a pen.

"All right," she replied wearily, doubting that this was going to get her anywhere. "The patient's name is Ethan Harrington."

Dr. Straithan stopped writing.

"He would have seen you about twenty years ago, or so." There was a long pause on the other end, making Grace think she'd lost the connection. "Are you still there?"

He shook his head as if to clear it. "Yes, um…how do you—I'm sorry, what did you say your name was again?"

"My name is Dr. Cummings. I'm calling from Serenity Harbor Hospital in Maine."

"Is Ethan all right?"

It was Grace's turn to pause. "Do you remember him?"

"Yes, he's a good friend of mine," he answered, sounding frustrated. "Has something happened?"

Grace heard the panic in his voice and pressed the phone tighter to her ear. "I'm sorry to be the one to tell you this…but Ethan tried to kill himself."

~

The sky grew from dark to black as angry clouds silently rolled in. Ethan watched the rain begin to fall as they opened up. It started down lightly at first but within seconds became a downpour. A bright bolt of lightning struck out over the ocean, followed by a tremendous roar of thunder. He could feel the floor beneath his feet quivering.

This type of storm was what the locals referred to as a summer squall. It would come out of nowhere and be upon you so fast that it would take you completely by surprise. And then, just as quickly as it had come, it would disappear.

He pressed his hands against the window and sighed as he watched the swells in the ocean rise and fall. Five more days. Just five more days and he would be going home.

"Hello, Ethan."

"Grace," he answered, seeing her reflection in the pane of glass.

She set the recorder on the tray. "So, how are you today?"

"Fine."

"Yesterday, we talked a little bit about your father. I'd like to pick up on where we left off."

Ethan turned away from the window and folded his arms, his mental barriers rising up around him like a defensive shield.

~

Grace waited anxiously outside the corridor, resisting the urge to pace.

The doors to the south elevator finally slid open and a tall, thin man with round, wire-framed glasses stepped off.

"Dr. Straithan?"

He offered her a firm handshake. "Dr. Cummings."

"Thank you so much for coming here," she said, showing him to her office. "You must be tired from your flight."

"Well, as I told you over the phone, some things are better explained in person."

"Can I get you anything before we get started?"

"No, thank you," he said, sitting down.

"You said that you and Ethan were friends. Can you tell me how you know one another?" she asked, getting right to the point.

David looked at her. He wasn't sure if he liked her or not. "First, may I see his chart, please?"

"Of course."

His face grew pale as he began to read over it. "He's lucky to be alive," he said softly.

"Yes, he is," she answered.

"Dr. Cummings, forgive my asking but why do you want to know his medical history from so long ago?"

Grace folded her hands on top of one another. "I believe Ethan's father abused him as a child."

There was a slight hesitation in Dr. Straithan's voice as he answered. "Why do you think that?"

"The way he speaks when I ask him about his father. It's the things he says...or rather doesn't say. I've been doing this long enough to recognize the telltale signs. That, along with some scars on his shoulders that appear to have been made by a belt or whip of some kind."

David cleared his throat and adjusted his glasses. "Those are very astute observations, Dr. Cummings."

"Well, I was hoping I was wrong."

He didn't say anything for a moment.

"Doctor, can I please see his file now?"

"Call me David, and yes, you can see it. But first, please tell me how knowing these details is going to help him?"

Grace felt as if he were stonewalling her. "Someone that suffers great trauma as a child can sometimes have a reaction to it later on in life. In Ethan's case, his father dying last year most likely unlocked those memories and brought them to the surface. I'm guessing that he's never told anyone, which means he's never really learned how to cope with it."

He reached down and pulled a folder out of his briefcase. "Dr. Cummings, these records are not public. They have always been with me, and I wish them to remain private. I *will* be leaving with them."

She nodded slightly. "I understand."

As she read over the file, David continued. "I first met Ethan when he was six. His father had hit him in the head with…something. I don't know what. The injury resulted in him losing part of the hearing in his right ear."

She flipped through the pages. "There aren't very many entries."

He adjusted his glasses again. "These are the ones severe enough to warrant medical attention. I know there were many more times. Ethan usually had old bruises under fresh ones."

She closed the file and looked at its front for a moment. "Forgive me for asking this, but why didn't you contact the authorities if you knew this was happening?"

He shook his head slightly. "Dr. Cummings, I have been asking myself that same question for almost thirty years now…and I don't have a good answer. Everett Harrington called me up out of the blue one night. I had never met him before then, and I had never dealt with anything like that. But I remember him being very sorry. He told me he'd been drinking, and that it was an accident. I let it go. Three years passed before I saw Ethan again."

"After his mother died."

He cleared his throat. "The calls became more frequent after her death, yes."

"And you still felt it wasn't necessary to contact the authorities?"

He looked away. "Dr. Cummings, the truth is I was green, fresh out of internship, and desperate to establish a practice. Everett paid me well and always seemed genuinely sorry." He stopped and adjusted his glasses. "We've all done things were not proud of, and I would appreciate it if you wouldn't judge me for it."

There was a long silence.

"Did Ethan ever talk to you about it?"

"Most children don't want to dwell on bad things."

Grace paused to make some notes in her file. "How did you get to be such close friends?"

"When he got older, he would help me out in my clinic sometimes after school. We got to know each other quite well."

She looked up at him.

David adjusted his glasses again. He didn't mind her looking at him, but it was the look itself that was making him uncomfortable. "Can I please see him now?"

"Of course."

The two of them made their way to the eleventh floor.

"When was the last time you saw him?" she asked, swiping her card.

"It's been a few years. It was when he was interning in Detroit."

"You care a great deal for him."

"Yes," he said without hesitation.

"When was the last time the two of you spoke?"

"About three months ago. I called him on his birthday."

"And how did he seem then?"

"He seemed okay, but I think he was still having a hard time over his divorce."

They walked down the corridor and stopped outside Ethan's room.

"I'll wait for you in my office. Just tell the nurse at the station when you're ready to go and she'll buzz you out."

"Thank you," he said politely, before pushing open the door.

Ethan immediately turned. "David!"

David embraced him and held him tight. After a moment, he relaxed his arms and brought his hands to his face. "Are you all right?"

"I am now," he said, swallowing hard.

David smiled and shook his head. "It's been way too long."

Ethan smiled back. Except for some gray hair around the edges, David still looked the same; the years had been kind to him. A feeling of bewilderment suddenly came over him. "How did you know I was here?"

"Dr. Cummings was looking for your medical history. The paper trail led her to me."

The smile ran away from Ethan's face. "Did you tell her?"

"I didn't have to," he said. "She already suspected it."

A heavy sigh escaped from his lips as he sat down on the edge of the bed.

"You know, Ethan, Dr. Cummings just wants to help."

He looked away, feeling extremely ashamed of the whole situation that had unfolded. "Are you disappointed with me, David?"

He sat down next to him. "Of course not. There is *nothing* you could *ever* do that could make me feel that way." He paused. "But I *am* very worried about you."

"How's Joanne?" Ethan asked, hoping to change the subject.

"She's fine. She sends you her love, *and* her prayers."

The corners of his mouth turned up slightly as he gave him an abrupt nod.

David remembered him doing that often as a boy, and had determined it to be a sign of embarrassment. He could still vividly recall seeing him when he was younger; his little body bloodied and bruised at times. He would be as gentle as he could with him, and afterwards he would always ask him if he was all right. Ethan would look at him and give him that small nod.

A tightening began to form in his throat. Ethan wasn't a little boy anymore, and although he could see that his wounds had all physically healed, he knew that emotionally they were still raw.

"It's all right, David," Ethan replied, noticing that his eyes were brimming with tears.

"No"—his voice broke—"it's not all right. I wish I had done the right thing the first time I ever saw you, Ethan. I think your life would have been *immensely* different." The tears began to fall down his face. "I'm so sorry."

Ethan hadn't realized that he had been carrying this guilt all these years. "It's not your fault, David." He shook his head. "It's *not.* All those days I got to spend with you…those were happy times for me. I loved helping you in the clinic. Don't you get it?" he continued. "Those days spent with you meant more to me than anything, and I wouldn't trade them for the world."

He wiped at his eyes and fixed his gaze upon the window. "I wish you would have called me, Ethan."

Ethan didn't speak for a long time. "I can't really explain why I did it, David," he finally said. "I don't really understand it myself."

They sat side by side, looking out the window that was now encased in darkness.

David cleared his throat. "I read your medical chart."

"Well, I'm sure that made for some interesting reading," he said, wanting to lighten the mood.

"Mmm," David replied, raising his eyebrows. "It looks like you need to stop drinking."

Ethan remained silent.

He nudged him with his shoulder. "Don't you think?"

Ethan raised his eyebrows, mimicking him. "Mmm," he answered back.

~

Grace finished making her notes in the file and put her pen down. Dr. Straithan had shed a lot of light on Ethan's childhood for her, but she couldn't help but lay the blame squarely at his feet.

She had watched their exchange when he had first gone into the room. He had hugged him the way a father would hug his child, and she guessed that he probably viewed himself as a father figure to Ethan. In his mind, he felt like he was protecting him.

~

That night Ethan lay in his bed staring at the ceiling. He wished he were at home, and away from the watchful eyes of this place.

As sleep surrounded him, he saw himself when he was sixteen. The smell of fresh straw lingered heavily about him as he stood in the stable brushing down his horse. He was laughing at something Renee had just told him...

"That's a corny joke, Renee."

"It's supposed to be corny," she explained. "That's why it's a joke."

"Ethan?"

They both turned around to see their father walking in.

"Hi, Dad." Renee ran up and gave him a hug.

"I need to speak to your brother for a moment. Go on up to the house and help Greta with dinner, all right?"

Ethan put the brush away as he watched Renee leave. His father strode over to the horse's side and raised his hand. "Go on," he said, swatting him on the rump.

The horse whinnied and took off out of the barn.

His father quickly closed the gap between them, and Ethan felt himself begin to tremble. His father was tall, strong, and endowed with a deep baritone voice. His eyes were dark, and he always smelled of scotch.

"I just came from a school board meeting and had the pleasure of talking to your math teacher, Mr. Andrews."

A queasiness formed in his stomach.

"He informed me that you were failing this grading period and wanted my permission to tutor you after school. I told him that it wasn't necessary and that you just needed to work harder."

He nodded emphatically. "I will. I promise."

His father looked at him. "I have no doubt. But I'm not finished. Your teacher reminded me that you had barely passed the last grading period which indicated to him that you were not understanding the material."

He reached into his shirt pocket and pulled out a small white card. "Now, I honestly don't remember you getting a D last time." He turned it over and held it up for him to see. "It looks like my signature, but I didn't sign it. Did you?"

Ethan lowered his eyes, struggling for his answer.

"Answer me, damn it!"

"Yes – " The back of his father's hand fell across his face. He blinked back the tears as blood pooled in his mouth.

"Did you think that I wouldn't find this out?" He grabbed him by his collar. "Did you think you were just going to lie and get away with it?"

Ethan shut his eyes as his father raised his hand again. Seconds passed and then he felt himself being shoved backwards. He opened his eyes and wondered why he had not followed through.

His father was pacing the floor like a rabid animal. "I swear, I don't know what I'm going to do with you. It's obvious the belt doesn't work anymore. I have half a mind to sell that damn horse!"

"I'm sorry."

"You're sixteen years old, Ethan. How in the hell are you going to get into college with grades like these?"

"I'll try harder next time."

He stopped pacing and began to roll up his sleeves. "You're damn right you will." He began to unbuckle his belt but stopped. His jaw grew rigid as he walked over to the back wall and jerked the riding crop from off its nail.

"Dad – "

"Take off your shirt," he said, sliding the crop up and down in his fingers.

Ethan did as he was told.

In an instant, his father grabbed him by his arm and turned him around, pushing him against the stall door. "You are going to think twice before you ever lie to me again."

"Please, Dad," he whispered. The first lash brought tears to him as he held onto the stall. The force of the second blow brought him to his knees. He cried out as he felt the leather lay open the skin between his shoulders.

"Get up!"

As he tried to get to his feet, he struck him again. A sob fell from his lips as it tore another place in his skin. His cries only made his father bring the crop down harder.

Ethan woke up fighting for his breath. He sat up and swung his legs over the side of the bed, but the dream stayed with him. He held his head tightly as he rocked himself back and forth; his hands trembled for what they could not have.

He lifted up the bottom of his shirt and wiped the sweat from his face, wishing that Grace would have left things alone. It may have been enlightening for her, but it only brought back pain to him. Pain that he thought he'd left behind a long time ago.

Chapter Forty-seven

Renee could see the lights from the Capitol as she stood in her living room staring out her bay window. Her husband, James, was away this evening on business. That was the excuse he had given her anyway, but she knew *bloody* well what he was doing, and whom he was doing it with.

In a more vulnerable time in her life, she might have been hurt by his actions, but as long as he was discreet, she didn't care who he slept with. She couldn't afford to let personal feelings get in the way of her ambitions.

"Excuse me."

She turned around. "What is it, Maria?"

"Dr. Sutton is here."

"Show him in, please."

The dark-haired maid hurried out of the room.

A moment later, an older man appeared in the doorway. "Mrs. Westcott," he said, taking her hand.

"Hello, Kenneth. It's lovely to see you again." She had met the doctor at a political fundraiser a couple of weeks ago. "Would you like a glass of brandy?"

"Thank you."

"I guess you're probably wondering why I've asked you here."

"Well, I assume it's concerning your brother, whom you spoke of at the fundraiser," he said, taking the glass from her.

"Please, sit down and make yourself comfortable."

Dr. Sutton took a sip of the brandy and looked at her expectantly.

"I would like for you to commit my brother to a sanitarium," she said pointedly.

The doctor stroked his beard. "Well, I would have to evaluate him first, to see if he needs to be."

"My brother is very sick, Kenneth."

He cleared his throat. "I'm sure he is. But as I said, I need to see him first and then make my decision."

Renee crossed her legs. "I know that you are one of the most prominent psychiatrists in D.C. I also know how busy you are, so I would be willing to make this visit worth your while."

He narrowed his eyes.

She knew she had his full attention now. "How does fifty thousand sound?"

The doctor set his glass down and stood up. "I think you've misunderstood me. I don't take bribes."

"I'm not offering you one," she said simply. "I am just paying you for what I think your time is worth." Renee rose from her seat. "Once you have evaluated him, I will pay you another fifty thousand."

A troubled smile formed on his round face. "I'll clear my schedule."

Dr. Sutton was one of the top physicians in his field, but Renee had learned that he had a bit of a gambling problem. "Kenneth," she said, walking him towards the door, "I trust you'll make the *correct* evaluation."

The doctor tilted his head. "Of course."

~

Ethan stood outside on the hospital grounds talking quietly with David. This morning Grace had brought him some clothes and had allowed him to accompany her to say goodbye to him.

The engine of the taxi sputtered loudly, making Ethan's anxiety grow. "I wish you didn't have to go," he said.

"I know. And I'm sorry, but I've got to get back to my practice." David put his arm across his shoulders. "Please let Dr. Cummings help you, okay?"

Ethan glanced over in her direction. She was standing about ten yards away, keeping a close eye on him. *Where did she think he was going to go?*

"When you get released, promise me that you'll come for a visit. Joanne would love to see you." David smiled and touched the sides of his face. "We could go fishing."

His voice faltered as he went to answer him. "Okay."

David wiped at his eyes before slipping into the cab.

Ethan felt Grace's hand upon him as he watched him pulling away.

"Let's take a walk," she said.

The heat from the sun made his skin tingle as they walked around the path that encircled part of the hospital.

"Are you angry at me for contacting David?"

"No," he said, shaking his head.

"He seems like a good friend."

"He is. I wouldn't be a doctor if it hadn't been for him."

"How so?"

"My father had always said medical school was a waste of time and money, and he had me set to go to college for a business management degree. Then shortly after my seventeenth birthday, I got a letter from a law firm regarding my mother. She had apparently left me some money. It wasn't a lot, but it was enough to get me on my way. I never told my father about it."

He stepped off the path and made his way over to a nearby park bench. "David helped me set it up with a bank. Then when the time was right, I walked away."

The sun beat down relentlessly as Grace joined him on the bench. She could feel the sweat running down the back of her knees and found herself longing for the comfort of her air-conditioned office. "Why do you think your mother left you the money?"

"I really don't know. It was strange receiving it after all those years." He ran his fingers through his hair. "She had arranged all of it two days before she died."

"Ethan, are you angry at your mother for killing herself?"

He looked at her, seeming startled by the question. "No," he said after a moment.

"How did she die?"

He took a deep breath that quivered as he let it go. "She hung herself."

"Do you remember her being depressed at all?"

"She used to cry a lot. Then other times she would be happy." He smiled slightly. "...*silly* happy. And then there were days she wouldn't get out of bed." He shook his head. "It used to frustrate my father to no end. Looking back now, I think she was probably bi-polar."

"Did your father drink a lot?"

"Sometimes," he said, squinting against the sun.

"Did he drink more after she died?"

He stared off into the distance. "I think he was doing the best he could to cope with her death and raise us on his own," he said definitively.

"Ethan, how old were you when you first started to drink?"

He leaned back against the bench and folded his arms. "It really doesn't matter, does it?"

She spoke her next words softly. "Do you know that most victims of child abuse become abusers themselves, as do children of alcoholics?"

His eyes suddenly filled with hurt. "Is that all you see when you look at me? An alcoholic and a wife beater?"

"No, of course not."

"Well, what *do* you think?"

"Why don't you *tell* me what I think?"

"Grace, please don't turn it around."

"No, I'm curious. Tell me what you think."

"Fine," he said with a sigh. "You think I'm nothing more than a drunk who can't get past the fact that his wife had an affair. You *don't* like me. You only tolerate me because I married Jessica."

She waited for him to go on but it appeared that he was finished. "That's very interesting. Now, would you like to know what I really think?"

"I can't wait," he said flatly.

She crossed her legs and sat forward. "You are a brilliant doctor, as well as a kind, warm and compassionate human being. You're thoughtful and very polite...a true gentleman. *That's* what I think. But just underneath the surface, I see a troubled man who suffered as a boy at the hands of his father. It has left you hurt, angry, and emotionally scarred. And you have kept all these emotions and memories locked away. You learned early on that alcohol kept them in check. Then the sudden death of your father...your tormentor, unlocked all those memories. You began to struggle to keep them under control. I think you started to drink more thinking it would help. But it was a daily fight. The breaking point came when you found out Jessica had lied to you. Everything came flooding to the top, and it sent you into a tailspin, causing you to do things you wouldn't normally do."

He seemed stunned. "Wow...you're really good."

She laughed softly. "It's okay to be angry at your father. It is a perfectly normal reaction," she said, reaching for his hand. "And I do *like* you, Ethan. I care very deeply for you."

He wiped a bead of sweat from his upper lip. The back of his shirt clung to him as he got to his feet.

Grace stood up as well and checked her watch. "Is it time to go back?"

"Yes, but we can walk a little more if you want," she said smiling.

~

"Am I interrupting?"

Sarah looked up from her paperwork. "Hi, Phillip," she said wearily.

He sat down in Ethan's chair. "How are things going up here?"

"Busy."

"Well, that's what I'm here to talk to you about."

She saw the papers in his hand and began shaking her head. "We've been through this."

"I know we have," he said. "But you can't keep on like this. I know how hard it is for two people to run the clinic, let alone just one."

"It's not going to be for much longer. Ethan's going to be released in a few days and then he'll be back."

Silence followed her statement.

"You *do* realize that he still has to appear before the board on my suspending him."

"What are you saying, Phillip? That they're going to fire him?"

"Let's not jump to any conclusions," he said, pushing the chair back. "I'll just leave these resumes of interns on your desk. And if you feel like looking at them, go ahead."

Chapter Forty-eight

Monday morning, Grace walked briskly down the corridor of the third floor. She had been summoned to Phillip's office.

"Grace, thank you for coming so quickly." Phillip rose to his feet as she came inside.

Before she could answer him, another man stood up.

"This is Dr. Kenneth Sutton. He's a psychiatrist from D.C."

He extended his hand to her. "Dr. Cummings, it's a pleasure."

"Dr. Sutton," she said, shaking his hand.

"Dr. Sutton is here to evaluate Ethan Harrington."

She turned to Phillip to protest, but the grim expression he wore made her keep silent.

"His sister asked me to come," Dr. Sutton interjected. "Dr. Martin, if you don't mind, I would like to see him as soon as possible. I'm on a fairly tight schedule."

Phillip nodded. "Of course. Grace, would you please escort Dr. Sutton to the psychiatric ward?"

"If you'll wait outside, I'll take you to him," she said in her best diplomatic voice.

"Thank you."

Once the door had closed, she turned on Phillip. "What the *hell* is going on?"

He walked around his desk intercepting her anger. "Now Grace," he said, "my hands are tied on this."

She put her hands on her hips. "I don't like this, Phillip."

"Neither do I; however, Renee has called him in for a second opinion, and we have to abide by her wishes."

She shook her head and started to say something, but Phillip held his hands up. "Grace, I can't do anything. Turn over your files to Dr. Sutton," he said, opening the door for her.

She refused to move.

"Please?"

~

Ethan stared down at the parking lot below, watching Sarah walk across it. Her visits to him were becoming less and less frequent.

"Hello, Ethan."

He turned from the window. "Grace."

"I need to talk to you for a moment and I don't want you to get upset by what I'm about to say."

"What's wrong?"

"Renee has asked another doctor to see you. His name is Kenneth Sutton and he's—"

"What the *hell* is she doing?"

She grabbed him by his arm. "Ethan, listen to me. *Listen,*" she said in a low voice. "You have got to stay calm and rational. This isn't the time to fly into a rage. He's right outside."

He glanced at the door and quickly turned away. "Grace, you can't tell him anything. *Anything* that we've discussed," he whispered.

She remained silent.

"Grace," he pleaded, "you *can't* tell him."

Under the oath she had taken as a doctor, she was obligated to hand over all of her notes and findings to Dr. Sutton. But she also knew how damaging it would be if Renee found out the truth about Ryan. Looking at Ethan right now, with his voice and eyes full of panic, she decided that her obligation was to him. She took him by his hand. "I promise."

Ethan watched as she opened the door. A tall man with a silver and black beard walked in.

"Ethan, this is Dr. Kenneth Sutton."

The doctor stepped forward. "Hello, Ethan." His tone of voice was condescending.

"Dr. Sutton," he said politely.

"I can take it from here, Dr. Cummings. Thank you," he said, looking over his shoulder.

Grace exchanged a subtle glance with Ethan before leaving the room.

~

Two hours later, Grace and Phillip met with Renee in Grace's office. Dr. Sutton was present also.

Renee sat down in the chair and crossed her legs. "Well, as you both are aware, I am deeply concerned about my brother's welfare. I want to make sure he is getting the best treatment that he possibly can." She looked over at Grace. "It's nothing personal. Please don't take offense."

Grace folded her hands together. "None taken."

"And after hearing what Kenneth had to say," she continued. "I think it would be best if my brother were to be under his care."

Phillip and Grace exchanged glances.

"What was your diagnosis, Dr. Sutton?" Phillip asked with concern.

The doctor cleared his throat. "Upon observing Dr. Harrington this afternoon, it became very clear that he is a severe manic-depressive with suicidal tendencies. And in my opinion, he would be better off at the Willow Tree Sanitarium in D.C. under my care."

"Dr. Sutton, I'm sorry, but how could you have come to that conclusion? I have spent nearly a month with him and not once has he ever exhibited any signs of being a manic-depressive."

"That is your opinion, Doctor, and you are entitled to it. But the man I visited with today was nothing like what you wrote in your observations."

Grace leaned forward, her knuckles pressing against the wood of her desk. "Such as?"

He looked down and began flipping through the pages of her file.

She watched him. She had been careful to delete anything concerning their conversations about Ryan's paternity. She had also held back all of the recordings.

"Well, for example, you wrote down, and I quote...'Patient was extremely despondent when first admitted, but the past few days has become more involved with a fairly healthy attitude for the future.'" He stopped reading and looked up.

Grace nodded. "That is true."

"I'm sorry, I just didn't see that. Dr. Harrington was moody, agitated, and very withdrawn with me."

"I find that very hard to believe," Grace snapped.

Dr. Sutton began to stroke his beard. "Obviously."

Phillip stood up. "Renee, I can appreciate your concern for Ethan. I know that you want him to get better. We all do. But I think moving him to a private sanitarium would not be the best thing for him."

Grace folded her arms. "I agree."

Renee rose from her chair and gave a deep sigh. "I thank you both for your concern. But I'm going to go with Kenneth's decision."

Dr. Sutton opened the door for her. "I'll make the arrangements for him to be transferred to Willow Tree this Friday."

~

Renee sat in the small waiting room reapplying her lipstick. When she noticed Grace approaching, she slipped the tube back into her purse and stood up. "Did you tell him?"

"He wants to see you," she said flatly.

She followed Grace down the hall and made a right. Peering through the door, she saw her brother pacing the room with his hands clenched.

"You'll have to leave your purse outside."

"Very well," she said, leaving it with Grace.

Grace unlocked the door and pushed it open for her.

"Hello, Ethan," she said walking inside.

He stopped pacing and strode up to her. "Why are you doing this?"

"I am doing this for your own good," she said innocently.

"This is my *life* you're playing with, Renee. It's not a business deal!"

"*Christ,* Ethan!" she said, rolling her eyes. "Don't be so bloody melodramatic. Why can't you believe me when I say that I'm doing this because I care about you?"

The words had barely gotten out of her throat before Ethan's hands were on her shoulders, pinning her against the wall. "Because every word that has spewed forth from your filthy mouth has never been anything but a *lie,*" he shouted. "How much did you pay that doctor of yours, hmm? *How much?"*

"Get your hands off of me, or I swear to *God,* you'll never see the light of day again."

He clenched his jaw as he let her go. "What do you want from me?"

Renee smoothed her jacket. "I want the company," she said evenly.

"I can't do anything about that," he replied, spreading his hands out. "You've already got my proxy."

"That's true."

"Then why are you doing this to me?"

"Call it an insurance policy if you will. Because I have no doubt that the minute you walk out of here you're going to revoke the proxy." She studied her fingernails for a moment. "There is an important deal that I am trying to push through next month."

"So?"

Renee looked at him as if he were stupid. "*So*, thanks to *you* Paul Cummings will have controlling interest of the company again. I know him. He's much too conservative to vote my way. So, I've got a new deal for you. You promise to let me keep your proxy until next May, and I'll change my mind about Dr. Sutton."

Ethan stared at his sister, completely amazed by her lack of emotion for him.

"Well?"

"You know, Renee, it takes more than just the word of Dr. Sutton to commit me. I can fight you on this. We can go to court."

She slowly shook her head. When she spoke her eyes and voice were full of pity. "You don't get it do you? Don't you think I'm capable of having more than one doctor testify against you? If you want to fight me, go ahead. But let me remind you of this. You'll have to stay in the custody of the psychiatric ward until a decision has been reached." She arched her eyebrows at him. "That might take a while."

His face darkened. "Why just until May?"

"Because come May, your two years will be up and I will prove that you are not Ryan's father. Then the company will be mine...by default."

"Ryan *is* my son," he said in a low voice.

"So you say," she said, picking a piece of lint off of her lapel. "If you want to keep up that little charade, that's fine. Just promise me that you'll let me keep the proxy, and you're a free man."

He shook his head. "I want out of here first."

"How do I know you'll keep your word?"

"You mean like the way you kept yours?"

She turned and started walking towards the door.

"Renee, wait."

She stopped.

He clenched his jaw. "You have my word."

A thin smile formed on her lips. "I'll tell Dr. Cummings I've changed my mind."

He saw the twisted pleasure on her face and shook his head. "My *God,* Renee, what did I ever do to you to make you hate me so much?"

Her smile suddenly faded. "What did you do? What did you *do*?" Her face contorted as her lips folded in on themselves. "You *left* me! You *left* me, Ethan! And you didn't even say goodbye! You don't have a clue what those years without you were like. Do you?"

Guilt flooded him.

"I don't think he was ever sober for even a day after you left! It was like you had gone and *died* the way he mourned for you!" She pointed a finger at her chest. "I was invisible to him. He didn't want anything to do with me, let alone be his partner in the company."

"Why would you have wanted to? You were so good at photography, Renee. Why didn't you stay with that?"

"Because I wanted him to love me. *Really* love me. And just once tell me how proud he was of me. But he never did." She looked at him with contempt. "I guess it was because I didn't come equipped with a penis!"

"I'm sorry," he said quietly.

She turned away and struggled to compose herself. "Then one summer he asked me to come work for him. And you know what, Ethan? I was good at it. I was *so* good I changed my major to business. I wasn't invisible anymore—or so I thought." She spun back around. "But then he goes and *dies,* and just hands his company over to *you,* the prodigal son."

Chapter Forty-nine

The following Tuesday, Ethan was waiting for Grace in her office. He was studying her diplomas on the wall to occupy his time.

"Sorry to keep you waiting," she said rushing in.

He stood up. "It's no problem."

"Please, sit back down," she said, taking the seat behind her desk.

"You know what, Grace?" he said, looking around. "You have a very nice office. It's much nicer than mine."

She smiled at him. His spirits were definitely up. "So tell me, are you glad to be at home?"

"Yes."

She flipped on the recorder and glanced at her notes. "What have you been up to?"

"Paying bills, doing things around the house, things like that. I thought I might play a round of golf later this afternoon."

"Your hearing is on Monday. How do you feel about it?"

He shrugged. "How would you feel if it were *your* head on the chopping block?"

"Is that how you perceive it?" she asked, noticing his abrupt change in mood.

"Phillip is going for my blood."

"I'd like for you to tell me about the day he suspended you."

"I'm sure he's told you everything."

She toyed with the pen in her hand. "I'd like to hear your side."

He remained silent.

"*Were* you drinking that morning in your office?"

"Yes."

"Why—"

"I don't know *why*, Grace!" He stood up and walked around the chair.

"Do you think that you may have a drinking problem?"

There was a long pause.

"No," he answered.

"Ethan, I'd like to give you some advice...off the record."

He turned around and looked at her expectantly.

"The fact is, that you were caught drinking while on duty by the chief of staff of this hospital. Now, you can play that any way you want, but it doesn't sound good."

"What are you saying?"

"I think you should make it a point to attend an AA meeting. The members of the board would probably be more understanding if you did."

He jerked open the door, his face red with anger. "I'm not an alcoholic, Grace."

~

Sunday evening, Ethan sat on the floor in his living room playing with Ryan as Jessica watched from a nearby chair. Feeling apprehensive about leaving Ryan alone with him, she had offered to bring him over and stay for the duration of the visit; and although she was certain Ethan knew the underlying reasons as to why, he didn't seem to care. In fact, for the first time in months, there wasn't any tension between them at all. It was a sensation that she found to be as strange as it was refreshing.

She casually glanced at her watch and saw that it was past time for Ryan to be in bed.

"Do you need to go?"

Looking over, she saw that Ethan was staring at her. "We probably should be getting on home," she said apologetically.

Without speaking, he picked Ryan up and escorted her into the foyer.

"Come on, sweetheart," she said, lifting him from Ethan's arms.

"Before you leave, I've got some things of yours."

"What things?"

"I was going through the attic the other day and found some boxes that belong to you."

Before she could say anything else, he had stepped over the baby gate and was jogging up the stairs. He disappeared once he reached the top, but returned a few moments later with three boxes piled under his chin.

"What is all that?" she asked curiously.

"It's just some odds and ends," he replied. As he started down, the box on top slipped from its perch and fell, spilling its contents down the staircase.

Jessica placed Ryan on the floor and went to help, picking up the items as she climbed the steps.

"Sorry about that."

"That's okay," she said, meeting him at the top of the landing. A smile crossed her face as she looked at what was in her hands. Loose photographs of her and Grace when they were younger, along with a few of her aunt and uncle, stared back at her. "I forgot I even had these."

Ethan nodded at the one on top. "I think you could probably blackmail her with that one."

She laughed at the picture she held of Grace; it was an experimentation in hair color gone wrong. "You're probably right."

He took the items from her and placed them back inside the box.

"Thank you."

"You're welcome."

She waited for him to pick up the boxes and take them downstairs, but he made no motion to do so. "Are you nervous about the hearing tomorrow?" she asked, figuring it must be weighing heavily upon him.

"A little."

"Well, I'm sure everything will be all right," she said, turning to go downstairs in hopes that he would follow.

"Jess, can I talk to you before you go?"

She stopped and turned around. "It's getting late."

He sat down on the top step. "It will only take a minute."

With reluctance, she climbed back up the stairs and sat rigidly beside him.

Ryan stood at the bottom of the steps with his hands wrapped around the bars of the gate as he tried his best to open it.

Ethan cleared his throat. "There's two things," he said nervously. "First of all, I wanted to thank you for everything you did for me while I was in the hospital. I know I wasn't exactly an ideal patient."

"It's all right. I've had worse, believe me."

"Well, I'm grateful anyway."

She kept an eye on Ryan down below making sure he didn't wander into the kitchen.

"The second thing, is that I wanted to apologize to you for ever having hurt you…for hitting you."

She looked away as the memory from that night slammed in front of her. "It's okay," she replied after a moment.

"No." He shook his head. "It's not okay. I am so sorry for hurting you. If I could take it all back, I would."

"I know you would," she answered in a soft voice.

"Mommy…"

She shifted her gaze to Ryan, who was still trying to open the gate. It wouldn't be long, she determined, before he figured it out. Out of the corner of her eye, she noticed Ethan twisting his wedding ring around his finger. Guilt and embarrassment swarmed her as she slowly covered her left hand with her right. She had not worn her ring since the beginning of the year.

"Anyway," he said with a sigh, "I'm sorry I made your life so miserable these past three years."

She glanced over at him. "You know, Ethan, they weren't *all* bad. Believe it or not, I *do* have some good memories."

"You do?"

"Yes."

"Like what?"

"Mmm, like the time when we were first married and had that apartment over on Maple. I remember that one night I was going to make you dinner…" She began to laugh.

"I remember that," he said smiling. "You made me macaroni and cheese."

"Yes, but it was terrible! The noodles were burnt and the cheese was all clumpy. I didn't have a clue on how to cook." She shook her head. "I *still* don't. But I'll never forget the look on your face when you took a bite."

He cocked his eyebrow. "It had a definite taste to it."

"You were such a brave man for eating it, and I don't think I ever told you how sweet it was of you." She paused a moment. "I also remember the day we bought this house. It was a happy day."

"Do you remember?" he said, getting caught up in her enthusiasm. "We sat right here and planned where we were going to put everything, and how we were going to decorate it."

"We were going to fill the house with kids," she said, nudging him. "You told me you wanted at least ten."

"Well, that way we would have had enough for our own little league team."

Jessica giggled.

Ethan smiled at her as something inside him began to stir. "Do you think you have enough of those memories to give me another chance?" The words tumbled from his lips in a panicked whisper.

Her smile disappeared.

"I still love you, Jess," he said, placing his hand upon the side of her cheek.

"Ethan..."

"Please give me another chance. I've changed, I swear I have."

She looked deep into his eyes, feeling her mouth being drawn to his. "I can't," she said, pulling back.

He slowly removed his hand.

"I'll always love you, Ethan. But I can't love you in that way anymore. I've finally gotten my life back together, and I can't put myself through that again."

His face was expressionless.

"I'm sorry."

"It's okay," he said, looking down.

A terrible silence drifted in.

Chapter Fifty

Ethan sat at the end of the long table in the conference room. Meredith was at the opposite end, talking in a low whisper with some of the other board members. For the first time he could ever recall, she hadn't flirted with him. It struck him as being truly amazing at how people were reacting to what he had done. You would have thought that attempted suicide was contagious by the way they kept their distance from him.

He nervously straightened his tie as the clock slowly ticked down the last few minutes before five. Phillip came through the door, followed by Paul, but neither one looked his way.

Grace came up to him and smiled. "I just wanted to wish you luck," she said quietly.

"Thank you."

Phillip sat down on Ethan's left side and cleared his throat, bringing the low murmurs to a halt. "Thank you all for coming," he said, looking around the table. "Before we get started, I want to emphasize that this is a hearing regarding the conduct of Dr. Ethan Harrington on the morning of May seventh. We are not here to discuss the events that happened afterwards."

Silence and the lowering of eyes followed his statement.

He slipped on his glasses and began to read from the file in front of him. "On the morning of May seventh, I suspended Dr. Harrington for drinking while on duty. His suspension is now up, but we need to discuss the disciplinary measures, if any, that might be taken before he is reinstated."

"Dr. Harrington, do you wish to dispute the accusation that you were drinking in your office that day?" Dr. Pearson asked.

Ethan glanced down the table at him. "No."

"Well, what assurances can you give us that it won't happen again?"

He leaned forward. "I'm not sure how to answer that."

Meredith spoke up. "Have you sought any outside help for your problem?"

"No, I haven't. Because I don't have a problem."

She arched her pencil-drawn eyebrows. "I think it's abundantly clear to everyone at this table that you have a problem, Dr. Harrington. If you didn't you wouldn't have wound up in the psychiatric ward."

"I thought I made it clear that we would not be discussing that," Phillip said, giving her a harsh look.

"Well frankly, Phillip, I think we need to. I cannot tell you the number of phone calls I have received from concerned citizens." She continued on in her arrogant tone talking about Ethan as if he weren't even in the room.

Jessica sat silently, not wishing to participate in what was quickly shaping up to be her ex-husband's execution. Stealing a sideways glimpse, she saw that he was gripping the arm of the chair with his left hand as he leaned back. It was then that she noticed the tan line where his wedding ring used to be.

"I have not gotten any such calls, Meredith," Sarah interjected. "Dr. Harrington's patients have all told me that they miss him and want him back."

"We can't overlook the fact that we may be facing several lawsuits. Isn't that right, Paul?" Meredith countered.

Paul cleared his throat before answering. "It *is* highly possible."

Meredith continued on. "I think it would be a grave mistake for us, as a hospital, to let Dr. Harrington continue to practice here. The publicity we have received from all of this has been damaging enough."

"I'm sorry you feel that way, but I am not going to discuss this matter any further," Phillip said flatly.

"Phillip, I believe I speak for nearly everyone here when I say that no one coming into this hospital is going to want to be treated by a…a crazy drunk," Meredith said.

The room suddenly erupted into bickering voices.

Ethan pushed his chair back and stood up. "Excuse me, Phillip."

Every head turned to look at him.

"I think I can clear this whole matter up," he said evenly.

Phillip nodded. "All right, Ethan."

He let the tips of his fingers touch the table as he drew a deep breath. "I have made some mistakes in my life. And I'll be the first to admit that I was downright stupid at times." He glanced over at Meredith. "But I refuse to stand here and be degraded by a pompous *ass* such as yourself."

Meredith's mouth dropped open.

"The only reason you are *on* this board is because of your money," he continued. "You don't have a *clue* what it's like to be a doctor. You've never had to tell a mother of two that she's not going to be around for her child's next birthday because she has ovarian cancer. You've never had to face a set of parents and tell them that their son or daughter died in a car accident tonight, and there was *nothing* you could do to save them." Ethan looked around the room. "Just about everyone else here knows what I'm talking about. They know of the enormous pressure and stress. Everyone has their own way of dealing with it." He clenched his jaw. "I chose a different way of dealing with it, but that does *not* make me crazy." He glanced at Grace. "Am I crazy, Grace?"

She shook her head and smiled. "No, Ethan."

"Thank you. Grace has been treating me for my *problem*." He stopped and swallowed hard. "Still, I realize that I have brought an undue amount of embarrassment upon this hospital. And I would like to apologize to each member of the board for any humiliation that I may have caused them." He reached into his left breast pocket and pulled out an envelope. "So, in order to prevent any further embarrassment, I hereby tender my resignation, effective immediately." He handed the envelope to Phillip and headed for the door.

Sarah pushed her chair back and caught him by his arm. "Ethan, you can't do this," she whispered.

He leaned in close to her. "I'm sorry." He slipped out of her grasp and went out the door.

Sarah still had her back to the others when she heard Phillip clear his throat.

"Let's take a vote," he said quietly.

~

Ding-dong!

Ding-dong!

Ethan leaned his head against the back of his sofa and sighed, wishing whoever it was that was ringing his doorbell would go away. When it sounded for the third time, he stood up angrily and stalked into the foyer, jerking it open. "What?"

Sarah seemed startled by his reception. "Do you mind if I come in?"

He turned away without answering, leaving her standing on the porch.

She remained there for a moment, before following him into the living room. "I tried calling you, but the line was busy."

"I took it off the hook," he said, sounding irritated with her. He swayed just a bit before sitting on the sofa.

The meeting had taken place less than two hours ago, and she found the fact that he was already drunk, a little disconcerting. "You certainly surprised everyone today," she said, sitting down beside him, "including me."

He leaned forward and picked his glass up from off the table.

Sarah watched as he downed its contents in one swallow.

When he was finished, he looked over at her. "Did the board accept my resignation?"

"Yes."

He gestured with his hand. "Well then, there you go."

"You *did* call Meredith a pompous ass," she said, trying to get him to smile.

He reached for the bottle. "She deserved worse."

"How much have you had?" she asked, laying her hand upon his forearm.

Something that sounded like a laugh came from his throat as he shook his head. "Not enough."

"Ethan...don't do this."

His response was to drink straight from the bottle. Afterwards, he flicked his eyes, which were covered in a glassy haze, in her direction. "Why did you come here?"

"I wanted to talk with you, to make sure you were all right."

He set the bottle down and got to his feet. "Tell me the *real* reason."

A small shiver went down her spine upon hearing the anger in his voice. "That's the truth."

He shook his head. "No, the truth is that you were afraid I might try to kill myself again and you wanted to be here to *save* me!" He leaned over her. "Well, don't do me any more favors."

Realizing that it had been a mistake coming here, she stood up and started across the floor.

"Sarah, wait. I'm sorry," he called to her. "Please don't go."

She stopped in the entranceway of the living room, but didn't turn around.

"I didn't mean that." He walked over to where she stood. "I'm sorry."

She stared at the floor, refusing to look at him.

He placed his finger underneath her chin and lifted it until she met his eyes. "Please don't cry. I didn't mean what I said," he whispered, brushing her tears away with his thumb.

"It's okay," she said with a sniff. Her tears were now gone, but he continued caressing her cheek. She began to grow uncomfortable.

He suddenly leaned in to kiss her.

"I think I should go," she said, backing away.

He let out an exasperated sigh. "Oh, come on, Sarah. Gavin isn't the only man in this town who can satisfy you."

Her face turned crimson as she raised her hand to slap him. He caught her by the wrist before she could make contact, and jerked her towards him. "Let me go," she said.

He grabbed her other wrist, making her drop her purse. He then bent down and pressed his mouth hard against hers.

Sarah turned her head. "Ethan, please stop it," she begged, trying to break free of his grasp. His mouth and tongue moved along her neck and throat, causing the panic in her to rise. "Please stop!"

Ignoring her pleas, he backed her over to the sofa and forced her down.

"Ethan, no!" She tried to knee him in the groin, but couldn't move.

He held her wrists over her head with one hand as he jerked her blouse open with the other.

She took in her breath as he began to touch her. "Ethan, stop!" She managed to wriggle her right hand free and used it to pound against his shoulder. "Stop it!"

Unfazed, he fumbled with the button on her pants and yanked roughly on her zipper.

She began to feel along the table for any object she could reach. Her fingers closed around something, and without hesitation, she hit him hard on the head with it. Scotch and glass ran over both of them as the bottle broke across his face.

Ethan fell backwards, allowing her to sit up. He leaned heavily against the cushion, slightly disoriented from the blow. Blood seeped into his left eye. He looked at Sarah, the darkness in his eyes fading.

"Stay the *hell* away from me!" she sobbed as she ran to get her purse from off the floor.

He staggered after her. "Sarah, wait! I'm sorry!"

She ran out the door clutching her blouse together.

Ethan leaned against the doorway, trying to get his balance. "I'm sorry!" he called to her.

Chapter Fifty-one

The next morning, all eyes were upon Ethan as he made his way down the fifth-floor corridor towards the clinic.

"Ethan?"

He stopped and turned around.

Grace was coming towards him. "I didn't think you would show up today," she said as she drew near.

He glanced nervously around the hallway. "What are you talking about?"

She tilted her head. "Well, it's Tuesday, and it's nine o'clock."

He looked down at her and sighed. He had completely forgotten about his session with her. He had come here hoping to apologize to Sarah.

"Are you ready to go?"

He started to shake his head but stopped when he heard a man's voice approaching from around the corner. Deciding that Phillip was the last person he wanted to see right now, he gratefully followed her up the stairs to her office.

Before she could get the door closed, however, she was paged to the emergency room. "I'm sorry, Ethan," she said, sounding disgruntled. "Just make yourself comfortable, and I'll be back as soon as I can."

He flung himself down on the couch in the corner of the room. As long as he didn't move his head, it didn't throb.

~

Sarah sat at her desk staring at a patient's chart. After a moment, her eyes wandered to her wrists, which were bruised and sore. Feeling the tears forming, she placed her head in her hands.

"Sarah?"

She wiped at her eyes quickly, and nodded at Phillip. "I'm sorry, I didn't hear you come in."

He softly closed the door and sat down across from her. "I know this has been hard on you. And I know you're upset about Ethan's resigning, but I think we need to set aside some time to talk...about the clinic."

"You mean talk about getting an intern to help me."

"Yes."

"All right, Phillip. I'll look over the resumes you gave me and get back to you."

He sat there a little stunned. "You didn't even give me a chance to use my charm to persuade you."

She forced a smile. It wasn't often that he used humor. "Well, Ethan's resigned, and I certainly can't run the clinic alone. I'll let you know something soon, all right?"

~

Ethan's eyes were closed when he heard footsteps outside, followed by the sound of the door opening.

"I'm sorry about that," Grace said.

"That's okay," he mumbled.

She walked closer to him and leaned over. "What happened?" He had three butterfly bandages just above his left eye. She could see a deep cut that ran partly into his eyelid.

"I ran into a door last night," he said, slowly bringing himself to a sitting position.

Grace sat on the edge of her desk and crossed her arms. She looked at him for a moment with that disbelieving glance she had sometimes. "You certainly know how to shake up a board meeting," she said, deciding to let it go. "Why did you resign?"

He let out a long sigh. "Did you really think they were going to let me come back to my job and pretend as if nothing had happened? It was my only option."

"Do you really believe that? Or is it just an excuse to avoid the problem?"

"What problem is that?"

She shrugged. "Why don't you tell me?"

"Grace," he said with another sigh. "Please don't pick apart my words and analyze them. I'm not in the mood."

"Well, everyone is very sorry to see you go."

"Somehow, I doubt that."

"What are your plans now?"

"I don't know," he answered, rubbing his eye tenderly.

"Did you have anything to drink last night?"

He looked up, wondering why she had changed the subject. "No."

She leaned forward from her perch. "Don't play me for a fool, Ethan. I recognize a hangover when I see one."

He dropped his gaze to the floor.

"Why did you lie to me just now?"

He didn't say anything for a long time. When he did speak, there was a finality in his tone. "You know Grace, I think our sessions are over. I don't work here anymore, and I legally don't have to be here."

It was her turn to be silent.

"Don't take it the wrong way…it's just…I think we're done. I have nothing left to say. But I do appreciate everything. I mean that, Grace. You are one of the most sincere people I have ever met."

"Thank you," she said absently. "But I really wish you'd change your mind. I think there's a lot more ground to cover."

He slowly got to his feet and walked towards the door.

"Ethan, since this is now our last session, I'd like a little bit of closure. There's something I need to ask you."

"What?" he asked in a tired voice.

"Well, after everything that's happened in your sessions with me, everything we've discussed...and now with your resigning, I'd like to know where you stand."

"What do you mean?"

She hesitated for a moment. "Are you glad...that you're alive?"

"Grace," he said, sighing as he opened the door, "you picked the wrong day to ask me that."

~

That evening, Sarah walked across the parking lot looking forward to a warm bed and a cup of tea, but she suddenly stopped dead in her tracks when she saw Ethan leaning against her car in the darkness.

"Can I talk to you for a second?"

"I don't want to hear anything you have to say," she said, reaching for the door handle.

He pushed himself away from the car. "Please…just hear me out."

She looked up at him and put her hand on her hip. "What?"

He blinked, surprised that she was going to listen. "I'm sorry."

Sarah put the entire force of her body into her hand as it struck him hard across the face. "You're *sorry?* Is that all you can say?"

The skin on his cheek stung as he looked at her solemnly.

"You were going to *rape* me!" she said, keeping her voice just above a whisper.

He took her by the arms. "Can you please just listen to me?"

"*Don't* touch me," she said, jerking away from him.

He reached for her again, but dropped his hands when he heard footsteps.

They both turned to look.

Phillip was coming towards them.

Ethan put his hands on his waist and turned the other way.

Sarah folded her arms across her chest and stared at her shoes.

Phillip stopped a few feet away and nodded at her. "Sarah."

She nodded back but didn't say anything.

He started to come closer.

"I'm fine, Phillip."

He shifted his gaze from her to Ethan, who was still standing with his back to him.

"Really, everything's okay," she said, seeing the concern in his face.

"All right, I'll see you in the morning," he finally said.

After he had gotten in his car and driven away, Ethan turned back around.

"You were going to rape me, Ethan," she said again. "There is no forgiveness for that."

"I was very drunk last night. I didn't know what I was doing."

"You knew *damn* well what you were doing! I begged you to stop." Tears welled up in her eyes. "I begged you."

"I swear to you that I haven't had a drop since then."

"Well, good for you," she said sarcastically.

"Listen to me. I would understand if you were to go on hating me for the rest of your life. I would. But I don't want to lose you. You're my best friend."

She pointed a finger at his chest. "Well, maybe you should have thought about that before you did what you did."

A car drove slowly by them.

Sarah waited for it to pass before continuing. "If I ever do forgive you, it's going to be a long time coming," she said, opening her door. "So until then, don't call me and don't come looking for me. I don't even want to see you." She slammed the door and started the engine.

Ethan stepped back as she drove away.

Chapter Fifty-two

Ethan's plane touched down in Manchester, England on a wet and foggy morning. Grabbing his bag from the overhead, he followed the other passengers off the plane. A sense of misplaced belonging came over him as he walked through the gate.

David stood waiting for him at the end of the terminal, his arms open wide.

Ethan fell into them, wanting and needing the comfort of his oldest and dearest friend right now.

"I'm so glad you called," David said.

He pulled back from his embrace. "I'm very happy to be here."

"You're looking great." The smile David wore wavered slightly. "Uh, well except for that."

Ethan tenderly touched the bandage above his eye. "One of the hazards of working in the ER."

"My car's this way," he said, taking his bag from him. "Are you hungry?"

"Starving."

As they drove to the restaurant, Ethan couldn't help but look out the window. The sights and sounds of the city he had grown up in were no longer here. Skyscrapers now stood where tall buildings used to be, and highways had replaced some of the roads.

He smiled to himself remembering when he'd first moved to the U.S. how very strange it seemed to drive on the right side. Now, it seemed odd to be doing it the other way.

Over dinner that evening, the two of them sat catching up on old times. Ethan had forgotten how much he missed him. It was nice being with him again. "You know, David. I can't thank you enough for this opportunity," he said, hoping he heard the sincerity in his words.

He nodded. "I have been dreaming about this for years you know…us working together." His eyes grew moist as he adjusted his glasses. "I'm so glad you're coming home."

The hours passed as they chatted, and although Ethan was enjoying himself, he began to crave a drink. He tried to concentrate on what David was telling him, but it was becoming harder and harder to focus.

"Ethan, did you hear what I said?"

"I'm sorry," he replied, tapping his bad ear.

"I said that Joanne's friend is a real estate agent. She can meet with you in the morning to help you find a house. But until you do, you know that you are more than welcome to stay with us."

"Thank you, David. That's very kind of you."

The waitress came and poured them both more coffee.

As the night went on, Ethan found himself growing a little edgy and was ready to cut the evening short.

David watched him as he drank his coffee. "You all right?"

"Yes, why?"

"Your hand's trembling."

Ethan made a fist and then relaxed it.

David eyed him closely. "Are you still drinking?"

"No."

"Really?"

"I've got it under control."

"And by under control, you mean what, exactly?"

He leaned back in his chair. "Why are you doing this, David?"

"Ethan, I've known you for a very long time. And I know you well enough to know when you're lying."

He swallowed hard and looked down at his hand. "My drinking is no longer a problem. I've stopped."

David looked away for a moment and cleared his throat. When he looked back, his expression was serious. "You can't drink here, Ethan. Do you understand what I'm saying?"

"Yes," he said quietly.

A few more agonizing minutes went by before they walked out of the restaurant.

~

Ethan's hands were shaking so badly, he could barely get the key card into the slot of his hotel room door.

Once inside, he knelt on the floor and reached for his bag, grappling with its zipper. It had been about seventy-two hours since his last drink—the night he had hurt Sarah.

His whole body began to ache as he searched through the bag. He finally closed his fingers around the bottle and pulled it out. Unscrewing the cap, he promised himself that he would have just one drink. He brought it to his lips and let it pour down his throat.

One drink turned into many.

Chapter Fifty-three

The following Monday, Ethan stood outside his office to the clinic. He hesitated a moment and then tried the knob; it was unlocked, which meant that Sarah had not gone home yet. Cautiously, he opened the door and looked inside.

A small sense of relief swarmed him when he saw that she was not here. He set the box that he'd brought with him on top of his desk and let his eyes wander slowly around the room. It had been over two months since he'd been up here, and he couldn't help feeling like it was no longer a part of him. Solemnly, he opened up the top drawer of his desk and began putting his things in the box.

Out of the corner of his eye, he saw the door swing open. Expecting it to be Sarah, he braced himself.

A young man wearing scrubs and a lab coat walked in.

Ethan thought he was an orderly at first, but noticed the stethoscope he wore around his neck.

The man looked startled. "May I help you?"

"Uh, no. I'm Dr. Harrington. I'm just cleaning out my desk."

The man's eyes widened and then took on a sheepish look. "Oh, Dr. Harrington, I should have known. I'm sorry," he said, stepping forward to shake his hand. "It's a real honor to meet you, sir."

Ethan smiled faintly as he accepted his handshake. "Thank you. And you are?"

He pushed a lock of his sandy blond hair out of his eyes. "I'm Joshua Embry Jr. I'm working here with Dr. Williams."

Ethan tried to maintain his smile, although it was fading quickly.

"It's part of my internship," he explained.

"Well, Dr. Williams is a great doctor. I'm sure you'll learn a lot from her."

"I already am."

As Ethan began going through the next drawer, he noticed he was still standing there. "I'll be out of your way in a minute."

"Take your time," he said, but he made no motion to leave. "Um, Dr. Harrington?"

He looked up.

"I just wanted to tell you that I think this hospital is suffering a great loss by losing you. I think what you and Dr. Williams have accomplished with this clinic is tremendous. And I would have liked to have had the privilege to work under you."

Ethan's smile returned. "Well, thank you very much. It's nice to know you feel that way."

The intern nodded and opened the door. "It was nice meeting you."

"Same here." Ethan returned his attention to the task at hand, and as he closed the last drawer, he couldn't help noticing that his box wasn't nearly as full as the trashcan was.

Next, he crossed over to the coat rack to retrieve his stethoscope and collection of ties. When he turned around, Sarah was standing in the doorway, her face expressionless. "I'm just cleaning out my desk. I'll be done in a minute."

She walked past him and poured herself a cup of coffee.

He tossed his things in the box and took a last look around before letting his eyes settle upon Sarah's back. "Well," he said, "I guess that's everything." He began to dig in his pocket. "Um, here are the keys to the office."

"What are your plans now?"

He pulled the keys out and began to slide them off their ring. "I'm going home to Manchester. I'll be working at a hospital there."

There was a long silence.

"When are you leaving?"

"In about three weeks. Just as soon as I can get things taken care of here."

"Well, I guess congratulations are in order," she said sarcastically.

He placed the keys down on her desk and walked towards her. "Sarah...I can't leave with this between us. I'm sorry for what happened. You have to believe me when I tell you that I didn't mean it. Can you please find it in your heart to forgive me?"

She spun around to face him. "Do you think my forgiving you is going to make everything all right? Well, it's not, Ethan! But *hey,* if that's all that's keeping you here, then I forgive you, okay? Now, you can go."

"Look, I don't know what else to say," he said, holding out his hands in frustration. "What do you want from me?"

"I want you to admit that you're an alcoholic."

He felt his jaw tighten.

She looked at him, waiting.

He grabbed the box and turned to open the door.

"That's right. Go ahead and leave. But you just remember that changing your address and your job isn't going to change the fact that you're an alcoholic."

"You're wrong."

"Am I?"

"Yes."

"For the better part of a year, I have stood by and watched you slowly destroy your life. When Jessica left you, I tried to be there for you—to comfort you, the way you did me when *my* marriage fell apart." She shook her head. "But you wouldn't let me. Instead, I watched you drown your sorrows in a bottle. Each day I have watched you sink a little lower, grow more depressed, become more—"

"Do you have a point to all this?" he asked, not really enjoying her hateful dissection of him.

She stopped and pointed at the ceiling. "You laid up in that hospital bed unconscious for *seven* days, Ethan. *Seven days!* We didn't know if you were going to live or die. You had the D.T.'s so bad they had to tie you down. So, don't you *dare* stand there and tell me that you don't have a problem. And do you want to know what the worst part is?"

"No, but I'm sure you're going to tell me," he said flatly.

"For *months*, I lied to Phillip for you when you were late because you had a hangover. I covered for you when you left early, knowing that you were going to go get drunk. But you were my friend and I did what I thought a friend should do. And all those times...I was just enabling you to do it."

Silence, as awkward as it was damning, followed her words.

Ethan looked at her for the longest time before grasping the knob. "I'm sorry for hurting you the way I did, Sarah."

"The way you *did?* You can't even say the word, can you?" Her voice raised an octave as it shook with anger. "I want you to answer me one question before you go."

He let go of the knob and sighed, wishing that he had just stayed home.

"How can you go on drinking, knowing what you've done? How can you live with yourself?"

Ethan leaned against the door and cast his eyes downward, feeling as if his insides were being ripped apart.

She folded her arms against her and shrugged. "How? I just want to know."

His entire body began to tremble. "Because I can't stop," he whispered.

The room became so quiet, he could hear the beating of his own heart.

"There's an AA meeting in twenty minutes at the high school," Sarah finally said.

He shook his head. "I can't."

She grabbed her purse out from under her desk and opened the door for him.

"I can't," he repeated.

"I'm going over there, and I'm going to wait for you," she said, looking into his eyes. "But this is the last time I will ever offer to help you."

~

Sarah stood quietly to the side of the room keeping an eye on the door. There appeared to be about thirty or so men and women milling about in the small classroom.

"Hello," said a voice beside her.

She turned to find an older gentleman smiling at her.

"My name is Gerald." He offered her his hand.

"Sarah," she replied.

"The meeting's about to start." He gestured towards the table. "Have you signed in yet?"

"Me? Oh..." she said, shaking her head, "I'm just waiting for my friend. He hasn't arrived yet."

"Why don't you find a seat? Perhaps he'll come."

The chairs were arranged in rows of eight facing the front. Sarah chose to sit near the back so she could watch the door.

The room grew quiet as the man who had introduced himself to her walked up to the small podium. "Hello, everyone. My name is Gerald and I'm an alcoholic," he said. "I've been sober for six years, three months and eleven days."

The sound of applause echoed throughout the room.

"I want to thank you all for coming tonight," he said, looking around. "I'd like to tell you a little bit about myself. I'm a retired engineer from an automotive company. I don't really remember how old I was when I began drinking, but I do remember how old I was when I stopped." He pursed his lips. "One night I was driving home from a bar, as drunk as any man could be. I hit another car head on, seriously injuring a woman and her two-year-old daughter."

He paused, the pain from that night evident upon his face. "By the grace of God, they survived and are all right today. But while I was sitting in a jail cell waiting to hear if I was going to be charged with manslaughter...I began to realize that I had a problem. That night, I made a promise to God and to myself that if he let them be okay, I would never drink again." He held his hands out. "That was the last night I ever took a drink. I'm standing before you now to show you that it can be done."

Another round of applause broke out.

"Thank you. We have a few people here tonight who also want to share their story with you."

Sarah listened to the men and women, each one telling their stories of despair. A movement in the corner suddenly caught her eye and she turned to look.

Ethan stood uneasily in the doorway. Upon seeing her, he made his way over and sat down in the seat she had saved for him.

She offered him a small smile as she reached for his hand.

Chapter Fifty-four

The late afternoon sun spilled through the windows as Ethan stood in front of the oak bookshelf in his den. He pulled several books off at a time and placed them in the box beside him. He then took the pen that was clipped to his shirt pocket and wrote down the contents of the box on the itemized sheet that the freight forwarder had given him. When he had first started packing this morning, he had been very descriptive in writing down what each thing was. Now, he just generalized what was in the boxes.

He figured the fastest way for him to do this was to take one room at a time. He had already done the kitchen, leaving out only the essentials, but he frowned as he looked around the den. There was still a lot more here, not to mention what was upstairs.

The freight forwarding company was coming to pick up his things early next week. They would take all the boxes and furniture, load it onto their truck, and send it by rail to the harbor in Portland. From there, it would be loaded into a container and placed on a vessel bound for Manchester. The ship would take about two weeks by ocean to reach its destination.

He hadn't thought it possible to find a house that he liked in the four days he'd visited with David, but had managed to. It was situated in a suburb just outside Manchester. The house was not very big, but what it lacked in size, it made up for in character.

He glanced at his watch. The real estate agent would be stopping by shortly with the contract for him to put his house up for sale. He found himself hoping it would sell quickly, although it would not be without stipulations. According to the terms of his divorce, Jessica was entitled to half of the proceeds; it was something he was less than thrilled about, but at the moment, he would just be grateful to get out from underneath two mortgages.

He'd had to use almost all of what was left in his bank account for the down payment on the house in Manchester. He and Sarah both drew their paychecks from the hospital because they worked in the clinic, and considering that he had not been paid since early May, he was honestly beginning to hurt for the money.

A desire to have a drink suddenly crept into his mind. It was a subtle craving, but a persistent one. The doorbell rang, and he hurried to open it, shoving the thought aside.

~

By that evening, Ethan had managed to finish packing most of the downstairs. In the morning, he would do the basement, when there was plenty of daylight. He tiredly sat down on the floor in his bedroom and began to get the things out from under the bed. Stifling a yawn, he knew he was going to dream about cardboard boxes tonight.

He got on his knees and peered underneath to make sure he had gotten everything. Noticing there was still a blanket, he turned his head and reached for it, pressing his shoulder up against the rail. His fingers locked onto it and pulled it out, dragging a bottle of scotch with it.

Ethan picked it up as it rolled across the carpet. As he stared at it, that persistent little plea for a drink began to get a bit more obnoxious in his mind. Getting to his feet, he went and emptied its contents into the bathroom sink. He managed to smile at himself as he watched the amber colored liquid swirling down the drain. That hadn't been too hard.

~

At three o'clock the next morning, Ethan heaved into the toilet bowl. His fingers gripped the rim of the porcelain as his body jerked, then retched.

When he was done, he sat back in the corner, and wiped his mouth with a towel. His heart was pounding so fast it was making his head hurt.

He stumbled back into the bedroom and grasped his cell phone, but his eyes refused to focus making it impossible for him to use it. He reached for the cordless on the nightstand, and began pushing the buttons. Three tries later, he finally got the number right.

~

Ethan lay in bed as still as he could while Sarah administered an injection of Diazepam. "Thank you for coming." The words jerked out of his mouth.

She withdrew the needle and folded his arm back at the elbow. "I'm glad you called," she said softly.

He turned over on his side trying to make the nausea go away, but only succeeded in bringing it up. He leaned over and vomited into the trashcan below him.

Sarah wiped his face with a cool rag. "Try and sleep, okay?" she said, pulling the covers over him to stop his shaking.

"I can't," he whispered. Every time he closed his eyes, the nightmares would come. As a doctor, he knew that they were only hallucinations, but the large, hairy spiders that kept crawling up his bed made it hard for him to remember that.

She reached over for his hand. She had to pry his fingers off the blanket. "I'll stay here with you. Just close your eyes."

~

The birds chirped happily outside Ethan's window as the sun came up over the trees. Sarah had lost all feeling in her hand hours ago as Ethan still held it tight. It took a little doing, but she eventually managed to slip out of his grasp and stand up. She put her arms over her head and stretched, trying to make the ache in her back go away.

Stepping out into the hall so she wouldn't wake him, she called the hospital to check in and then went downstairs to make some tea. She scoured the pantry and cabinets, but could only find instant coffee. Deciding it was better than nothing she made a cup of it, and then headed back upstairs.

She quietly picked her way around the stacks of boxes and sat down in the chair across from the bed.

He began to stir. "Sarah?"

She set her cup on the nightstand and leaned over him. "I'm right here."

The panic in his eyes faded and he closed them again. "I'm glad you're not mad at me anymore..."

She smiled down at him. "Well, it's pretty hard to stay mad at you."

Chapter Fifty-five

Three days later, Ethan sat in the receptionist's office waiting to see Paul, who had called yesterday and said that he had some final papers for him to sign regarding his father's company. Finding it extremely warm in here, he reached up and unbuttoned his collar.

"Dr. Harrington, can I get you anything? Coffee? Some water?"

"No, thank you. I'm fine." He leaned back in his chair as he waited, not having the strength to sit up. He noticed that every once in a while, Paul's secretary would casually glance at him. He knew it was probably because he looked like death warmed over.

He had made it through the physical part of the withdrawal but the urge to drink was still strong, and he would've liked nothing more at this moment than to have a glass of scotch spilling down his throat.

Paul opened his door and stuck his head out. "Ethan?"

He stood up rigidly and walked into his office. "How have you been, Paul?" They had not spoken since that last day in court.

"Fine. How about you?"

"Good."

Paul narrowed his eyes at him. "Are you feeling all right?"

"I've been a little under the weather."

"Well, thank you for coming down here."

Ethan sat down across from his desk.

"These papers I need for you to sign are from the beginning of the second quarter," he said, handing him a pen.

Ethan crossed his legs, using his thigh as a table, and began putting his signature on the stack of papers.

Paul watched silently, noting that he looked to be about as broken as any man could be.

When he was finished, he handed him back his pen. "Is that it?"

"That's it. Now that Renee has your proxy, you should be receiving the papers from her attorney for you to sign—like you did with me."

Ethan looked away for a moment. He still held a lot of resentment towards Paul over losing custody of Ryan. But he also found that he missed their friendship. "Paul, when I gave my proxy to my sister…I really had no choice. I hope you can understand."

Paul nodded. He had pretty much figured that Renee had blackmailed him into signing it over to her. "That's all right."

"Have you been playing any golf lately?" Ethan asked, glancing out the window.

The corners of Paul's mouth turned up slightly. "A little here and there. How about you?"

"It's been a while," he said quietly. "Paul, I wanted to say that I'm sorry. I'm sorry for my behavior towards you these past few months."

Paul smiled. "I'll accept your apology, only if you'll accept mine," he said, offering him his hand. "I'm sorry, too."

~

The drive home seemed long to Ethan as he was stopped by yet another red light. He couldn't help but notice the bar across the street. Its neon sign flashed brightly in his eyes, beckoning for him to come inside. He tapped the steering wheel impatiently with his fingers.

Finally, the light changed and he was on his way again, but he never noticed before today just how many bars there were. He felt the burning in his stomach as he turned the corner. Just keep driving, he told himself. He swallowed hard, trying to occupy his mind with other things, but it was useless. His head began to throb as the need for a drink became the sole driving force in his body.

He quickly pulled over on the side of the road and jammed the gear into park. Resting his head against the steering wheel, he closed his eyes. There was no way on this earth he was going to get through this, he told himself. This silent revelation only made his desire for a drink worse. Feelings of despair and utter desolation came upon him.

He slowly raised his head and looked at his surroundings. This wasn't the street he thought he was on. Somehow, he had managed upon Meridian.

~

Jessica hurried to her front door as she dried her hands off with a towel. "Ethan."

"Can I please come in?"

She stepped back allowing him to come through the doorway. "Are you all right?" she asked, noticing how pale he looked.

"I know I should have called first, but I was wondering if I could see Ryan."

Silence followed his request.

He stuck his hands in his pockets to hide their trembling.

She slung the towel over her shoulder. "Well, I was just about to give him a bath—"

"Can I give it to him?" His voice was uneven.

She eyed him for a moment.

"I swear, I'm not drunk...I haven't been drinking."

She gave him another long look before turning away. "Follow me."

~

Jessica stood over the kitchen sink rinsing out her glass. She felt uneasy with Ethan being in the house, as she really didn't believe him about not being drunk. She whirled around when she heard his footsteps behind her. "Did you get him to sleep?"

He shook his head and smiled. "Hardly." He turned and looked behind him.

Ryan came tottering into the kitchen.

She bent down and picked him up. His hair was damp, and smelled of baby shampoo, and Ethan's aftershave.

Ethan remained in the doorway, sensing her uneasiness. "Thanks for letting me see him."

"You're welcome," she answered, noticing the color had returned to his cheeks.

"Well, I'll get out of your hair now," he said, turning towards the living room.

She walked him to the front door. "I drove by the house the other day and saw that it was for sale."

"Yeah," he said, stepping onto the porch.

Jessica shrugged, confused. "Are you moving to a smaller place?"

He set his jaw to mask his emotions. "I've gotten a job offer in Manchester."

"England?"

He nodded.

"Why?" she whispered, feeling an inexplicable panic rising in her throat.

"Well, I can't stay here," he said, surprised by her ignorance.

She shook her head as if doing so would dissuade him. "You can always set up a private practice."

A sad smile formed on his face. "I don't think it would thrive."

~

The smell of freshly cut grass lingered in the air as Sarah sat on Ethan's front steps, waiting. She knew he had a meeting with Paul this afternoon, but thought he would have been home by now.

He had been on her mind most of the day, and she was anxious to see how he was doing. It also had been a miserable day at work, and she really didn't feel like going home to an empty house.

Headlights flashed in her eyes as his car pulled into the driveway.

"I must be hallucinating again," he said, getting out of his car. "There's a pretty woman waiting for me on my porch steps."

She stood up and dusted the back of her pants off. "Hi."

He smiled down at her. "Hi." She had been a tremendous source of comfort to him these past few days, and he knew that he wouldn't have made it through the withdrawal without her.

"I hope you don't mind my being here. I just wanted to see how you were doing today."

"Well, I think my day was better than yours," he said, unlocking the front door.

She sighed. "It shows, huh?"

"Do you want to tell me about it?"

"No," she said, as he held it open for her. "I just want to forget about it."

"Okay," he said, eyeing her curiously.

She cleared her throat. "So, how are *you?*"

He shrugged. "Actually, I'm pretty hungry."

"That's a good sign."

He tossed his keys on the table. "Why don't I order a pizza for us?"

"That sounds great."

Half an hour later, they sat at his kitchen table devouring a double-pepperoni with extra cheese.

Sarah hadn't realized how hungry she was as she bit into her fourth piece.

"Are you going to tell me what's bothering you?"

She took a moment to swallow. "Today, I was ambushed by all sides at the board meeting."

"Over what?"

"Being over budget, what else?" She propped her elbows on the table. "No one defended the clinic. It's just hard not to take it personally."

"I'm sorry. I wish I'd been there."

"You couldn't have done anything."

Ethan looked away. He knew he had hurt her by resigning; he had taken the easy way out, leaving her behind in the wake. "I'm sorry," he said again.

She took a sip of her ice water. "Let's change the subject, okay?"

They talked about other things as the evening passed. But neither one of them discussed his leaving for England.

Chapter Fifty-six

Ethan walked around the outside of the guesthouse checking the doors and windows to make sure they were secure. Night had already fallen as he made his way along the stone path to his house. The air around him was thick and muggy, and smelled like rain. He stuck his hands in his pockets as he took one last look around.

His eyes rested on the swing set a few feet away as the moonlight reflected off its frame. Reaching out, he slid his hands up and down it; the metal was rough and damp with dew. Its condition had been unusable when he and Jessica had moved here, but last summer he had sanded it down and painted it a bright red.

A long sigh fell from his lips as he sat in one of its swings. Ryan had never even gotten a chance to play on it. He sat there slowly rocking himself as the crickets sang him a chorus of their songs. This past year had been tumultuous, at best. He had lost his entire family due to death, divorce, or anger.

Heading back inside, his footsteps echoed off the walls as he walked through each one of the empty rooms. The house seemed sad and lonely. Ethan shook his head. Maybe it was he who was sad.

The street lamp out front shone through the stained glass window above the French doors, making the prisms of light dance on his shirt. That window had pretty much been the reason why they had bought the house in the first place; set in a rainbow of colors, it was truly exquisite. He smiled, remembering the time Ryan had first noticed the colors reflecting on the floor. He had spent all day trying to pick them up.

He leaned against the now barren wall and sighed as he thought about Ryan and how much he was going to miss him. Throughout these past two weeks, Jessica had allowed him to see him while she was at work. It was nice to see him on a daily basis - and it helped get him through the day without taking a drink. Ryan was his lifeline.

Ethan closed his eyes, feeling his heart sink. It was killing him inside to leave him. He knew how important it was for a son to have a father.

Ethan's thoughts immediately turned to his own father. Yesterday, he had been going through the items from the boxes he had brought home from his father's condo. He was trying to decide what to keep and what to throw away when he came across a small wooden box that he hadn't remembered packing.

Sifting through it, he'd found several pieces of jewelry. There was a set of cuff links, which didn't seem all that nice, and a matching tie clip. He gathered that they must have had some sentimental value for his father. His fingers also touched lightly upon a woman's wedding band. He held it for a moment before placing it back inside the box.

His eyes then focused on something unusual. He picked up the small gold medallion and turned it over in the palm of his hand. It had the number five printed on it along with the words, sobriety and anniversary. Ethan was dumbstruck. He never knew his father had stopped.

He opened his eyes and ran his fingers through his hair. Had his father gone through what he had just been through? His mind went back to that day in the hospital when he'd grabbed his hand. Over the past year, he had often wondered what it was that he had been trying to say. A small part of him always hoped that it was to tell him he was sorry.

Ethan pushed himself away from the wall, forcing himself to let go of the thought. It was easier to go on hating him.

Chapter Fifty-seven

Ethan walked down the corridors of the hospital for what would be the last time. Saying goodbye to the people here had been much harder than he had anticipated, Grace in particular.

The two of them walked together, making nervous chit-chat until they came to the end of the hall.

He looked down for a moment trying to gather his thoughts. It was difficult because he could already see Grace wiping her eyes. "I don't think I can ever thank you enough..." He stopped, not knowing how to finish the sentence.

"Just remember that I'm only a phone call away," she said, giving him a trembling smile.

"I will."

She reached up to hug him. "I'm going to miss you."

He held his breath until he felt he could speak. "I'm going to miss you, too."

She quickly pulled back. "Take care of yourself."

Ethan slipped his hands in his pockets as he watched her hurrying away. After a moment, he turned and began heading towards the exit. Unfortunately, he wasn't going to be able to see Sarah. She was tied up with a patient and he had to get to the airport soon.

"Ethan?"

He grimaced when he saw Phillip coming his way.

"I was hoping I'd get a chance to speak with you before you left."

"I was just on my way out," he said, checking his watch. He wanted to have plenty of time to say goodbye to Ryan.

"I'll make it brief." Phillip walked over to a private area away from the nurses' station.

Ethan followed, his body tense.

"I'm sorry that things turned out the way they did," he said, keeping his voice low. "I hope you understand that I was just doing my job. And I was also trying to look out for a friend."

Ethan took a deep breath and looked away. "At the time…I had lost everything," he said softly. "The only thing I had left was my pride, and I didn't want to lose that as well. But I know that you were right in what you did."

Phillip extended his hand. "No hard feelings?"

"No hard feelings," he answered, realizing it was time to let it go.

~

Ethan cradled Ryan in his arms as he held him on the sofa.

Jessica stood several feet behind him looking out the window.

"Ryan, I've got something to tell you," he said, turning him around so he could see his face. "Daddy's going away for a while." He stopped and cleared his throat, trying to stop the lump from coming up. "I know you don't understand, but I promise I'll be back to see you. I promise."

Jessica closed her eyes as she listened to him talk. His voice was soft and gentle, but laden with sadness.

"I hope you don't get angry with me for leaving as you grow older," he whispered. "But just remember that Daddy loves you."

Ryan patted Ethan's face. "Daddy," he said, smiling.

His lips began to quiver. "Yes, Daddy will *always* love you."

Jessica wiped at her eyes as he got to his feet and came around the sofa.

Ethan stood in front of her, not knowing how to tell her goodbye. She was the woman of his dreams; everything he ever wanted, and yet, in the blink of an eye, he had fallen in love with her—and lost her. He took a deep breath and let it go, spilling the words. They were the only words left to say; the only words that could make amends for what had happened between them. "Jess...I've been going to AA. I've been sober for eighteen days." He tilted his head and sighed. "Eighteen *very* long days."

She opened her mouth to speak, but her voice was replaced by a sob.

Biting his tongue to keep his tears hidden, he reached out to embrace her. He breathed her in, committing her scent to his memory, knowing this would be the last time he would ever touch her. With his vision growing blurry, he pulled away and headed for the door.

"Ethan?"

He stopped and looked over his shoulder.

Jessica remained by the window, her face streaked with tears. "I wish things could have been different," she whispered.

His chin trembled. "So do I."

~

Ethan sat in the waiting area of the tiny airport. As he listened for the announcement to board the plane, he mentally ran through the checklist in his mind, hoping that he hadn't forgotten to do anything. He had turned his rental car in a few moments ago, and had given the freight forwarding company his deposit. He cringed slightly as he found himself hoping that his car made it on the vessel and across the ocean without any scrapes or dings.

Sarah rushed through the terminal as fast as her high heels would allow her, praying that he hadn't boarded yet. She rounded the corner and stopped. "I'm so glad you're still here," she said, nearly out of breath.

He stood up and met her halfway. "You didn't have to come all the way down here."

"I wanted to tell you goodbye."

A voice sounded over the P.A. system. "May I have your attention, please? All passengers may now board flight 518 to Boston."

He looked down at her. "That's me."

Sarah tried to gather her thoughts. She had planned exactly what she was going to say to him on the drive over, but now she was grasping for the words. "I'm going to miss you," she finally said, reaching up to hug him.

He felt his neck becoming wet. "Please don't cry," he said softly. "You'll make *me* do it."

"I can't help it," she said, shaking her head.

He took both of her hands in his and squeezed. "Sarah, thank you for everything. I couldn't have gotten through this...*any* of this without you. You've been a good friend to me."

She sniffed. "Well, I don't stick pencils in my nose for just anybody."

He began to laugh. That was an image he would never forget.

"May I have your attention, please? Final boarding call for flight 518."

"I better go." He bent down and kissed her on the cheek before disappearing through the gate.

She walked up to the giant window and looked out at the plane. A few minutes later, she heard the roar of its engines as it began to roll away from the terminal. She wiped at her eyes as it taxied towards the runway.

The plane traveled down the tarmac and was airborne in a matter of seconds. She watched the lights on it get farther and farther away until it disappeared into the rain-filled sky.

Chapter Fifty-eight

Six months later, Ethan was working late in his office going over some figures. It seemed that he had so much to do, yet not enough time in which to do it.

There was a short knock upon his door.

"You heading home soon?"

"I need to finish this first."

"You've been working on that proposal for two months now," David said, sitting down in the chair across from him. "When are you going to turn it in?"

Ethan looked back down at the numbers. "It has to be perfect."

"Joanne told me to bring you over tonight for dinner." He arched his eyebrows. "And she'll be very mad at *me* if you don't come."

"I think your wife is just taking pity on me," he said, pushing his chair away from the desk.

"Are you still here?" called a voice from the doorway.

Ethan glanced over. "Just on our way out, Seth."

"Hey, a bunch of us are headed over to the pub to watch the game. You chaps want to join us? First round's on me."

"Thanks for the offer, Seth, but I've made other plans. Another time, maybe."

Seth wagged his finger at him. "All right, but one of these days I'm going to hold you to it."

David watched Seth disappear down the hall before turning to Ethan. "He doesn't know, does he?"

He remained silent as he reached for his coat.

"It might be easier if you told someone."

He shook his head. "Some days it's all I can do to deal with it myself, David."

~

Thursday evening, Ethan arrived home more tired than usual. He had just come from an AA meeting, which sometimes lifted his spirits, but almost always drained his energy. He had chosen a group that met near the outskirts of Manchester. It was a little bit longer of a drive, but no one there knew who he was, and he preferred to keep it that way.

He sat down on the sofa and mentally went over the contents in his refrigerator. Deciding there was nothing inside it worth getting up for, he took out his phone and began checking his emails. He saw that there was one from Sarah and eagerly clicked on it. A smile immediately formed on his lips. She was going to be attending a convention in London and was hoping that she could see him.

Switching screens, he pulled up her number and pressed the button. After several rings, he heard her pick up.

"Hi. Did you get my email?"

"I did," he replied. "That's why I'm calling."

"So, do you think you can come to London and see me for a day?" she asked hopefully.

"Well, I can make arrangements to come and see you that Friday. But I was kind of hoping you could extend your trip for maybe another week, and spend some time with me in Manchester."

There was a slight pause.

"Well, I *do* have some vacation time coming."

He began to laugh. "*Some?* Sarah, I know you've probably got like, what? Fourteen weeks of vacation?"

"*Six.*"

"I was close. So how about it? Will you stay?"

"Why not?" she said.

He smiled inwardly. "What hotel are you staying at in London?"

"Mmm, I think it's called the Grosner House or the Grover House...something like that."

"The Grosvenor House?"

"Yeah, that's it."

"Wow."

"What?"

"Nothing, I just can't believe the hospital is paying for you to stay there. It's a five-star hotel; very posh."

"Really?"

He sensed her smile through the phone and returned it, wishing that she could see it. "Really."

Chapter Fifty-nine

Sarah sat in the lobby of the Grosvenor House on a very chilly and windy February morning. Every time the front doors opened, a cold draft filtered in. She folded her arms across her as she waited patiently for Ethan to arrive.

He'd been right when he had said that this was a very posh hotel. Her surroundings could only be described as gorgeous. Marble floors, cathedral ceilings, and crystal chandeliers decorated the lobby; while her room had been filled with very nice, very expensive amenities. The building itself was huge, taking up nearly half a city block.

She gathered that Phillip must have felt sorry for her by allowing her to come here. The nightly rate alone was over three hundred dollars.

Her last meeting had been at nine this morning, and although she had loved staying here, she was anxious to start her vacation. She kept an eye on the front doors as she settled back into her chair. It had been just over six months since she had seen Ethan, and there were times that she thought their friendship was long forgotten, but then he would call or send her an email and she would wonder why she'd been so concerned.

Just then, she saw a tall, slender man with dark hair come through the door. She sat forward as a smile broke out over her face.

Ethan glanced around the room, his eyes searching. They stopped when he saw Sarah hurrying towards him. "Hi!" he said, wrapping his arms around her. After a moment, he stepped back, and took both of her hands in his own. "It is *so* good to see you."

She shook her head and laughed. "I can't believe you're here."

He squeezed her hands and gave her a wink. "I've missed you," he said with a smile. "So, are you ready to go?"

"My bags are up in my room."

He helped her on with her coat. "I was thinking that maybe I'd show you a little bit of London, if you haven't already seen it."

"Actually, I haven't gotten to see much at all. The schedule of this convention was early morning to late at night."

He checked his watch. "Well, why don't you leave your things in your room, and we'll spend the rest of the day in London. If we head out now, I can take you to Buckingham Palace to see the Changing of the Guard."

Her eyes lit up. "Let me go get my camera. I want to take lots of pictures."

Ethan waited in the lobby as she went back to her room. In a few minutes, they were in a cab on their way to the Palace.

~

The sun peeked through the clouds as she and Ethan maneuvered their way around the crowd that was gathering.

"Here we go," he said, helping her up a slight slope. "You should be able to see it best from here."

Sarah looked out among the throngs of onlookers and took in her breath. Buckingham Palace was bigger than it looked in all those brochures. The castle seemed to go on forever.

Ethan smiled as her camera clicked away.

The crowd began to talk and point as the beating of drums sounded.

"Here they come," he said.

The guards were marching down the street in their red uniforms and big, black fuzzy hats. It was a spectacular display to watch. They marched from Wellington Barracks on St. James Park all the way to the palace. And at precisely eleven-thirty, the ceremony took place.

Afterwards, Ethan took her to the Banqueting House. This, apparently, was where Charles I was beheaded in 1649. From there, they went to a restaurant for lunch, and then he took her to a place called the New Caledonian Market on Tower Bridge Road. It was a huge street fair, filled with knick-knacks and crafts. They stayed there for most of the afternoon browsing about.

It was nearly five o'clock when they got back to the Grosvenor House, and a little while later they were on a train bound for Manchester. Sarah noticed that the trains here seemed to be about as common as a taxi was at home. It was nearly a two and a half hour ride, but she and Ethan never stopped talking the whole way. It was odd how they fell back into their conversation; it was as if they had never been apart.

Night was beginning to fall as the train pulled into the station. Walking to the parking lot, or car park, as it was commonly referred to here, Sarah immediately recognized Ethan's car. It seemed rather funny to her to see it in such an unfamiliar place.

They drove along the street that led out of Manchester, still talking. The moon lit up the rolling countryside that hugged both edges of the road, making for a beautiful night. Eventually, they came upon a small sign that read, 'Welcome to Cheadle'.

"Are we here?"

"This is it," he said nodding.

They drove another mile or two and then turned down a side street.

"Here we are," he said, pulling into his driveway. He unlocked the front door and held it open for her.

Sarah's eyes wandered around the room. "Oh, it's beautiful!" she said, noticing the sunken area in front of the fireplace.

He set her suitcases down and smiled. "Thanks. Let me give you the fifty-cent tour."

She followed him out of the living room and through a swinging door.

"This is the kitchen."

It was a good-sized room adorned with black granite countertops and cabinets that were painted a bright white.

He led her back out to the living room and down a short hall. "This is my den." He opened the door for her and flipped on the light.

She peered inside. There was a desk with mounds of paper piled on top of it, and rows upon rows of printer paper stacked neatly against one wall.

He shrugged. "It's a little messy. Come on, I'll show you the upstairs."

She followed him up the steps and down a narrow hallway. "This is the guest room and the bathroom's right in there," he said, gesturing with his arm. "I put lots of towels in there for you."

There was another room across the hall. "Is this your bedroom?" she asked, looking through the doorway.

On one side of the room was a tiny bed with airplanes and trains printed on the comforter. A small bookcase stood on the opposite wall; it was filled with stuffed animals, fire trucks, and lots of other toys. A shiny new rocking horse sat in the corner.

"This is Ryan's room," he said softly.

She glanced over her shoulder at him. "He's going to love it."

"Do you think so?"

"I can't think of any little boy who wouldn't," she said smiling.

He folded his arms as he leaned against the doorjamb. "I'm hoping that one day she'll let him come for a visit."

"Maybe she will," she replied. But knowing Jessica, she knew it was an unlikely possibility.

He pushed himself away from the jamb and turned out the light. "This is my room," he said, walking across the hall.

After the tour, they went back downstairs where Ethan got a fire going for them.

"Your house is very beautiful," she said, crossing over to the sofa.

"Thanks," he said, sitting down beside her. "Are you tired?"

"A little, but I'm too wired to sleep right now."

He leaned back against the cushion so he could see her better. "So, did you find anything interesting at the convention?"

She propped her head against her hand as her arm rested on top of the sofa. "I found lots of things that we could certainly use in the clinic. I'll put in a request for them, but I'm sure I'll be turned down."

"Some things never change," he said, picking up on her tone.

She sighed. "I'm getting so tired of fighting for every single cent while every other department gets handed a big fat check. I think if Meredith and some of the others had their way, the clinic would be shut down."

"I'm sorry," he said softly.

She shrugged as she ran her finger along the piping of the sofa. "I guess that's why I jumped at the chance to visit you. I promised myself that while I'm here I'm not going to dwell on it at all. I just want to relax and enjoy myself."

Chapter Sixty

The next morning, Sarah awoke to a wonderful smell coming from the kitchen. She hurriedly dressed and went downstairs to find Ethan standing at the stove. "Good morning."

He looked over his shoulder. "Morning."

"Something smells good. Are you making pancakes?"

"Not just *any* pancakes," he said, cocking his eyebrow. "These are blueberry pancakes." With precision, he flipped it up in the air and caught it on the plate. "Have a seat. Coffee's on the table."

She stared at the plate of pancakes he placed in front of her. "I'm impressed."

"Don't be. They came in a box."

Sunlight illuminated the table and she looked up to see where it was coming from. There were two huge skylights in the ceiling.

"Did you sleep okay?" he asked, wiping his hands on his pants before sitting down.

"I slept wonderfully," she answered, pouring a liberal amount of syrup over her pancakes.

Ethan took a sip of his coffee. "I need to go check on a few patients, and if you'd like to come along, I'll give you a tour of the hospital."

She finished chewing the big bite she had just stuffed in her mouth and swallowed. "I would love that."

"Afterwards, I'll take you to St. Ann's Square."

"What's that?"

"It's kind of like a flea market."

"Ooh, that sounds like fun," she said with a smile.

~

Sarah walked beside Ethan as they made their way along the interior corridors of Manchester City Hospital. She tried to take everything in as they went, but its size was enormous.

An older man wearing a white lab coat nodded as he passed them in the hall. "Ethan."

"Hello, Brian."

"Good morning, Dr. Harrington," a nurse said as they rounded a corner.

"Morning."

Sarah noticed that Ethan seemed to have a great deal of respect from his colleagues here. Her heart soared for him. Maybe he had truly found his home.

They stopped at the end of the hall as he fished in his pocket for the key. "See?" he said, pointing to the nameplate on the door. "It's got my name on it and everything."

Her feet sank into the plush carpeting as she stepped inside. "I'm very jealous."

He laughed. "I was practically speechless when *I* saw it."

They were on their way out when Seth popped his head in. "Word has it that you've got a beautiful woman in here." He smiled when he saw Sarah. "I stand corrected. You've got a *gorgeous* woman in here."

Ethan shook his head. "Sarah, this is Dr. Seth Young. He's the head of geriatrics, and my somewhat, irritating friend."

She extended her hand. "It's very nice to meet you."

Seth took her hand in his and kissed it. "The pleasure is all mine."

"I think I've heard Ethan mention your name a time or two," she said, feeling the heat settling in her cheeks.

"Well, only the part about me being very handsome is true."

Ethan rolled his eyes. "See what I mean?"

Seth glanced at his watch. "Have you two had lunch yet?"

"Not yet."

"How about if I take you both out for a bite to eat?" He nudged Ethan's arm. "I'll even pay for *yours*."

"Well, that would be a first," Ethan said, smiling at Sarah. "He's only doing this to make a good impression on you."

"How about if we go to the *Hole in t'Wall?*"

"Excuse me?" Sarah asked. Seth's accent was a little thicker than most.

"It's a pub, darling," he said with a wink.

She looked to Ethan, hesitating on her answer.

"They serve lunch there," he explained, seeming to pick up on her concern.

"Oh. Well, that sounds good."

~

Sarah stared out the window as they drove through the streets of Cheadle. Small patches of grass poked through the snow-covered fields that lay on either side. She leaned back in her seat, finding the town to be as beautiful as it was tranquil.

"Are you having a nice time?"

She shifted her gaze towards him. "I'm having a wonderful time." After lunch with Seth yesterday, Ethan had taken her to the flea market as promised. Thinking about it now, she wondered if she was going to be able to get all of her packages on the plane.

Up ahead, she could see the city limits of Manchester. "Where are we going?"

"Mmm, you'll see," he said, turning down a side street.

The storefronts and shops they passed looked rundown, with each one looking more dilapidated than the last.

Ethan turned down another street and pulled over, parking on the side of it. He opened the door for her and gestured for her to follow him. "This way."

They walked about half a block or so, before stopping outside a large brick building.

"What is this place?"

"Patience," he said, unlocking the door for her.

The smell of fresh cut lumber hung thick in the air as she walked across the concrete floor. A stack of lumber sat over in one corner, while sheets of drywall sat in another.

"This is going to be the Chadwick Street Free Clinic." A broad grin spread over his face. "And it's mine."

Her eyes widened. "This is *yours*?"

He shrugged. "Actually, it's half the city's, but I own it. It's for anyone who can't afford medical help. And it's going to be run *my* way."

"Why didn't you tell me about this before?"

"I was going to, but then you emailed me you were coming, so I thought I'd surprise you."

She reached up and hugged him. "I'm so happy for you!"

Ethan smiled down at her, delighted in the fact that she liked it. "Let me show you where everything's going to be."

~

Later that evening, they were still discussing his plans for the clinic. Through the course of their conversation he had told her that his friend, Dr. Straithan, used to run it, but it had closed over a decade ago. Ethan had managed to convince the city that there was a real need for this type of service again.

He explained that, along with himself and Dr. Straithan working there, he would receive an intern for three months at a time from the hospital. Besides funding from the city, the clinic was also eligible to receive several grants from the government, but she had learned that a great deal of the money had come out of Ethan's own pocket. He had bought the building, and was paying for most of the renovations himself.

"Ethan, I think this is so wonderful."

"Thanks."

"I can't believe you kept this a secret from me all these months, though."

He scratched his head. "It was very hard, believe me."

A moment of silence followed.

Ethan searched for something else to say, figuring she may be tired of talking shop. "I guess Ashley's due date is getting pretty close, hmm."

"Two more weeks."

"Are you hoping for a girl or boy?"

She shook her head and laughed. "It doesn't matter. I'm going to spoil it either way."

He cocked his eyebrow. "I have no doubt."

For the next half hour or so, they discussed the pros of being a grandmother, and all the privileges that went along with it.

Chapter Sixty-one

The wind was a little nippy as Sarah stepped out of Ethan's car and began following him down a dirt path. This afternoon he had persuaded her to go horseback riding with him. The ground was cold and hard underneath her feet as they made their way towards the stables.

Up ahead, she saw a man leading a horse out of the barn. "Hi, Doc."

"Nick." Ethan nodded. He shook the man's hand when he got there. "Thanks for getting him ready."

"No problem." He tipped his hat at Sarah before leaving.

Ethan rubbed the horse on his neck and patted him. "Sarah, this is Comet," he said. "Comet, this is Sarah."

The horse snorted at her, sending white puffs of air out of its nostrils.

Ethan had bought him a couple of months ago from one of his patients.

Sarah looked at the creature in awe. He stood a good foot or two above Ethan with a coat so black, it shimmered. "He's beautiful."

Comet affectionately nudged Ethan's arm.

He reached into the pocket of his coat and pulled out a handful of sugar cubes. "Here," he said, handing her a couple. "Feed him one. Just put it in the palm of your hand like this." He demonstrated how.

Sarah had never been on a horse before, let alone be near one; and quite frankly, she was a little terrified. She placed the sugar cubes in her palm and extended her arm. "Here, Comet."

The horse sniffed at her palm.

Upon feeling his tongue, she screamed and threw the cubes on the ground. A shudder went through her as she danced backwards.

Comet took a step forward still thinking she had the cube.

"He's going to eat me!" she said, grabbing Ethan's arm and hiding behind him.

Ethan was laughing so hard he could barely stand up.

She swatted him on the back of his shoulder. "It's not funny!"

"I wish I'd had a camera right then," he said, still laughing as he walked around the side of the horse. He put his foot in the stirrup, and in one swift motion hoisted himself into the saddle. "Give me your hand."

Sarah hesitantly took his hand, putting her foot in the stirrup the way he had done.

Comet turned his head and stared curiously at her.

"He's looking at me, Ethan."

"That just means he likes you," he said, still grinning. "Come on."

She swung her leg up and settled herself into the saddle behind him.

He looked over his shoulder at her. "How's that?"

"Okay, I guess."

"Just hold on to me."

She wrapped her arms around his waist.

"Not that tight. I can't breathe."

"Sorry," she said, loosening her grip.

"Are you ready?"

"Yes, but please don't make him go fast."

"I promise." He made a clicking sound with his tongue and Comet began to move.

Sarah felt as if she were on a Ferris wheel for the very first time.

Ethan guided the horse across the field and into a patch of woods.

After a little while, she got used to the movement under her and relaxed. The forest was absolutely breathtaking; a blanket of snow covered the ground beneath them while small icicles hung from the trees above like decorations.

The sound of a small brook was close by, and Sarah could see the sunlight glistening off the water as it ran through a bed of pebbles. She rested her chin on Ethan's shoulder and sighed contentedly. "This is very nice."

They rode for most of the afternoon.

~

Sarah got out of bed and slipped on her robe. Her posterior was rather sore from riding yesterday causing her to have to walk in a stiff and unnatural looking manner. As she stepped out into the hall, she noticed a small tray sitting on the carpet beside the door; on it sat two wrapped presents and a card.

Her legs screamed for mercy as she bent down to pick up the card. In the note, Ethan wished her a happy birthday and wrote that he hoped these gifts would give her an enjoyable day while he was at the hospital.

She smiled to herself, both happy and surprised that he'd remembered. She eagerly tore at the wrapping of the first present and lifted out a bottle of bubble bath. She laughed out loud when she opened the second present—it was a horror novel.

She turned and limped straight to the bathroom where she began pouring a liberal amount of bubble bath into the tub. It was her birthday, and she was not about to feel guilty for loafing today.

~

Sarah stood in front of the mirror, fussing with her hair. After a moment, she stepped back to get a glimpse of herself. She hoped it wasn't too much. Ethan had told her to dress up, but wouldn't tell her where he was taking her.

Downstairs, Ethan sat in the chair waiting. He checked his watch as he stifled a sigh. Why did it take women so long to get ready? It was probably the Eighth Wonder of the World. He stood up and turned around when he finally heard her coming down the steps.

Sarah met his eyes.

He immediately smiled when he saw her. She was wearing a form fitting black dress that was cut low in the front. Her hair was pinned up with a few curls hanging down. "You look very pretty," he said, meaning every word.

"Thank you," she answered, blushing. "Will you tell me now where we're going?"

"Dinner first, and then I'll tell you."

~

The restaurant was dimly-lit and quiet as she and Ethan finished their dinner. Soft music flowed from a small dance floor, and you could hear low murmurs of intimate conversation.

The waiter, who appeared to be close to retirement age, poured them both more coffee.

"Are you having a nice birthday?" asked Ethan.

Sarah nodded. "I am."

"Would you like to dance?"

"I'd love to."

He took her by the hand and led her out onto the floor.

It had been a very long time since she'd been dancing, and it was a strange, yet nice, sensation to feel his hands on her lower back. Her fingers rested lightly on his shoulders as they moved to the music.

He looked down at her and smiled.

It was at that moment, that *absolute* moment, in which her feelings for him changed. The song ended and another one began, yet he seemed in no hurry to get back to the table. She found herself wondering if he was feeling the same way.

"What are you thinking?"

She shook her head, embarrassed by her thoughts. "I was just thinking what type of birthday I would be having if I were back home."

"What would you be doing?"

"Well, for starters, I'm sure that most of the nurses would have thrown me a party—complete with dead flowers and a stripper. Not to mention the presents that would probably consist of bottles of vitamins and geriatric items. That's what they did to Kate in obstetrics when *she* turned forty." The corners of her mouth suddenly turned down. "Oh, Ethan," she said, somewhat dejectedly. "I'm forty years old. I'm *old*."

He stooped down to catch her gaze. "You're not old."

"Yes, I am," she said, starting to feel miserable.

"Sarah," he said with a sigh, "apparently, you haven't noticed how many men have been staring at you this evening. They're very envious of me."

"You're just saying that."

"I'm serious. Every man in this room would love to be the one dancing with you right now. *But,*" he added, shaking his head, "I'm not about to let them."

She felt herself smile in spite of herself.

After dancing to a few more songs, they went back to their table and sat down where she saw him glance at his watch. "Are we late for something?"

"No."

"So, where are you taking me?"

"This is it," he said innocently.

"No, no, no…" she said, waving a finger at him. "You said dinner first, and then you would tell me."

"I did say that, didn't I? Okay," he replied, reaching inside the breast pocket of his suit. He pulled out two tickets and handed them to her. "Happy Birthday."

A schoolgirl grin broke out over her face. "You're taking me to the opera? Oh, Ethan, thank you!"

The waiter approached the table. "Can I get you any dessert?"

"None for me thanks," Ethan replied.

"Very good, sir. And would you, madam, care for any dessert?"

"Oh, no thank you. I'm stuffed."

The waiter's eyes widened just a bit. A second or two passed by, and then he turned to Ethan and smiled. "Congratulations, sir."

"Thank you," he said, after clearing his throat.

The man turned and shuffled off.

"Why did he say that?"

Ethan kept his eyes on the table and shook his head. "I'll tell you later," he answered, seeming too embarrassed to look at her.

~

The sweet sounds of the opera still filled Sarah's head as she slipped out of her dress and pulled on her robe. This evening could only be described as magical.

Ethan was kneeling in front of the fireplace when she returned downstairs.

"Thank you again for tonight," she said, sitting on the floor beside him. "I had a wonderful time."

He stoked the fire, causing a burst of flames to roll out from underneath the log. "You deserved it."

"Hey! That reminds me," she said, shoving him slightly. "You said that you would tell me later why the waiter said that."

He grinned and shook his head.

"What?"

"In England," he said, putting the poker away, "when you tell someone that you're *stuffed*...that's another word for pregnant."

Sarah's face turned several shades of red, including a couple of colors that he had never seen before.

"Oh, God!" she said, covering her face with her hands, "I'm so embarrassed."

He began to laugh, but it sounded more like a snicker.

"I can never go back there."

"Don't worry," he said, still grinning. "You'll look back on this one day and think it's funny."

"Yeah. Maybe in about ten years."

He reached behind him for his coat as it lay draped across the chair. "I have one more present for you," he said, feeling in the front pocket.

"Ethan, you have given me *more* than enough presents."

He held out a small box covered in black velvet. "It's not a birthday present. It's more of a thank you present."

Seeing the serious expression on his face, she took the box from him and opened it. A heart-shaped diamond pendant winked at her. She looked up at him, completely speechless.

He drew his right knee up and rested his elbow on it. "Do you like it?"

She placed her hand over her chest. "I love it. But I can't accept this."

"It's the very least I could do...to thank you."

"Thank me for what?"

"For saving my life." He shifted his gaze to the fire. "I wouldn't have blamed you if you never forgave me," he said quietly. "I took advantage of our friendship. Lots of people had given up on me. But you didn't." He turned back to her. "If it wasn't for you, I literally would not be here tonight. So...I just wanted to say thanks, for being *my* hero."

Sarah's eyes glistened with tears as she looked at the pendant. "It's beautiful."

"No," he said. "*You're* beautiful."

She looked up, surprised by his last words.

Ethan leaned forward and kissed her softly upon the lips. It lasted only a moment and then he pulled away.

The fire roared in a whispered hush as if it did not want to disturb them.

Sarah reached out and brushed his dark locks from his forehead. Her hand then slid around his neck, drawing him closer.

He bent down and kissed her again.

This time, she felt the warmth and passion escaping from her own lips as he cradled her in his arms.

Chapter Sixty-two

In the early hours of the morning, Sarah lay quietly beside Ethan, her head resting upon his chest. She had been awake for some time now, and she knew he had been too, but neither of them had spoken.

"Sarah?" His voice broke the silence.

"Hmm?"

The awkwardness seemed to take hold of him as he searched for something to say.

She propped herself up on her elbow and smiled.

He dropped his gaze as he brushed her hair from her bare shoulders.

Several more moments of silence passed by.

Noticing his embarrassment, she took the initiative to say it. "Are you sorry that this happened?"

"Not at all," he said without hesitation. "I'm *surprised* that it happened, though."

She tilted her head back and giggled feeling the tension leave her. "I know. I never thought that one morning I would be waking up next to you."

He laughed quietly, forcing the corners of his mouth to turn up.

"Is there something wrong?" she asked, observing the rigidness in his face.

"No. I just don't want our friendship to change because of this."

She laid her hand upon his chest. "I know. I feel the same way. But it *is* going to change. We've gone somewhat beyond the boundaries of just being friends."

He nodded, not wanting to think about it anymore.

"What's going on behind those dark eyes of yours, Ethan?"

He turned his lips towards hers. "I'm thinking how very much I'd like to kiss you again."

Sarah leaned over and placed her mouth on his.

Ethan took in his breath as her bare breasts brushed against his skin.

~

That evening, Sarah and Ethan were having dinner at David and Joanne's—except, *dinner* had ended nearly four hours ago. The conversation, however, had never ceased.

David was an American so it was nice that Sarah didn't have to listen so hard when he spoke. At the moment, he and Ethan were on the other side of the living room having a serious discussion about the clinic.

"Here you are." Joanne handed her a cup of coffee.

David's wife was a very pretty woman with grayish-blonde hair. She was tall with a slender frame, and had just a few crinkles around her eyes.

Sarah had been telling her a little while ago about Ashley and the excitement of becoming a grandmother. Joanne nodded and listened enthusiastically, but didn't mention if she and David had any grandchildren. She casually glanced around the room and noticed that there were no pictures of any children hanging on the walls.

Joanne sat down on the sofa beside her and crossed her legs.

"How long have the two of you been married?" asked Sarah.

She paused a moment as if to think. "It will be thirty-one years this June." She took a drink of her coffee and looked at Sarah expectantly. "How long have you and Ethan been together?"

Sarah smiled not really knowing how to answer. This evening, Ethan's body language with her had been subtle. She wasn't sure that he wanted anyone to know what was going on between them.

"I'm sorry, dear. I didn't mean to put you on the spot."

"That's all right," she replied, as her mind still frantically searched for something to tell her.

Joanne shifted her gaze to Ethan. "It seems like it was just the other day when he was helping my Davy in his clinic. He was just a boy, really." She shook her head. "Oh, how these years have gone by."

Sarah smiled, trying to picture Ethan when he was younger.

"Davy was absolutely devastated when his clinic closed. He had put most of his life into that place," she spoke with a touch of sadness in her voice.

"Why did it close?"

The older woman sighed. "It all came down to bloody politics. Nothing more."

Sarah nodded, thinking about her own battles. "I can certainly understand that."

"I must tell you," Joanne said, leaning in close, "that I've never seen my Davy happier. He is so excited about this clinic and getting to work with Ethan. I think it's a dream come true for him."

~

Ethan slid his tie from his collar and peered through the blinds. "I think we're going to get a thunderstorm tonight."

Sarah sat in his bed watching him get undressed.

"Did you have a nice time this evening?" he asked, sitting on the edge of the mattress.

"I did. Joanne and David are very nice." She covered her mouth in an attempt to hide a yawn.

"I'm sorry I kept you out so late," he said, pulling his shirt off.

"That's all right. We don't have to get up early for anything."

"That's true."

"You know," she said, running her fingertips along his shoulders, "I could get used to this vacation thing."

Ethan closed his eyes and breathed deeply as she rubbed the area between his shoulders. He tensed up, however, when he felt her touching the scars on his back.

"How did you get these?"

He quickly turned around and forced a smile. "You tell me about that itty-bitty, teeny-tiny tattoo on your left shoulder blade, first."

She grinned and shook her head. "I got that during one rebellious semester in college."

He cocked an eyebrow as he leaned in to kiss her. "Rebellious, hmm? Tell me more."

"No, it's your turn."

He kissed her long and hard on the lips as he pulled her towards him. "Later," he whispered.

She lay back against the pillow as his lips fell upon her breasts. His hand moved up her thighs and pulled her panties down. His fingers began caressing her, slightly probing. She breathed in, moaning softly.

He undid his pants and straddled her.

Sarah felt his breath quiver as he pushed inside. His thrusts were slow and gentle, his lips soft. She closed her eyes and took in her breath, wishing this moment could last forever.

~

Ethan fought his way through the darkness, feeling the familiar sense of dread that always surrounded him. He could smell the dampness of the concrete as he crouched on the steps, desperately banging on the door. "Please, let me out!"

Something brushed against his feet making his entire body tremble. He banged harder on the door. "I'm sorry!" A shrill squeak sounded behind him making him turn around. A pair of red eyes was ascending the steps in front of him. "No!"

"Ethan, wake up!"

He opened his eyes and sat up, fighting to catch his breath.

"It's all right," Sarah said, stroking the back of his head. "You were just having a bad dream."

He swung his legs over the side of the bed and gripped the edge of the mattress.

Sarah pressed her lips to the back of his shoulder. "It's all right."

He wiped the sweat from his face and nodded, but refused to look at her. "I'm going to go downstairs for a little while."

She pushed the covers back to go with him, but stopped, sensing that he wanted to be alone.

Ethan made his way down to the kitchen and flipped on the light. After his eyes had adjusted, he opened the cabinet above the stove and reached in the very back, grasping the neck of the bottle. Pulling it out, he cradled it in his hands as if it were a priceless artifact.

Bought during a moment of weakness one night a few months ago, he had managed not to drink it; but he couldn't seem to throw it out either. It gave him a sense of security.

His fingers trembled as they tore at the seal and unscrewed the cap. The bottle clunked against the glass as his unsteady hand poured the liquid into it. Its aroma was strong, making his jaws ache for it as he brought it to his lips. He suddenly lowered his hand and set the glass down. He closed his eyes and gripped the edge of the counter.

"Ethan?"

He opened his eyes and looked over his shoulder.

Sarah stood in the doorway.

Something between a sigh and a sob fell from his lips. "I really need a drink," he whispered.

Thunder shook through the house, rattling the floor beneath his feet.

She walked up to him and looked at the bottle on the counter. "That must have been some dream," she said, reaching out to touch his arm.

He turned away and sat down at the table.

"What was it about?" she asked softly.

He shook his head.

She knelt beside him. "You can tell me."

"It won't help," he said in a broken voice as he bowed his head in his hands. There was only one thing that would make it better, and it was calling to him from its perch on the counter.

"I'm a very good listener," she said.

Ethan pressed his fingers against the sides of his temples, turning the tips of his knuckles white. "When I was nine, my father took me out to the storm cellar for punishment. He left me down there all night." Tears began to fall down his face. They followed the contour of his chin and dropped onto the table one by one. His body jerked and shivered as the images of the rats replayed before him. "I begged for him to let me out."

Sarah got to her feet and wrapped her arms around him. "It's all right," she said, kissing his tears. "It's all right."

Chapter Sixty-three

Sarah leaned against the headboard watching Ethan sleep. The sun had risen hours ago, but she couldn't bring herself to wake him. Her fingers lightly touched the scar over his heart; the skin was raised and slightly wrinkled from where the bullet had gone in.

Ethan's hand suddenly moved to hers.

She pursed her lips in an effort to hold back her tears.

He moved his arm, inviting her to lie down beside him.

"I'm sorry," she whispered.

"There's nothing for you to be sorry about."

She stroked his chest with her fingertips. "How did you get those scars on your back?"

He took a deep breath and let it out slowly. "For lying."

She wiped at her tears. The polite man that had walked her to her car that night was a far cry from the father Ethan had known.

~

Sarah's breath came out in clouds of white as she sat on the back porch. The day had passed by without her and Ethan saying much of anything to one another.

"Aren't you cold?"

She looked over at him and shook her head.

Ethan sighed. He hated the fact that she was leaving in the morning. He put his arm around her and kissed the side of her face. "I wish you didn't have to go."

"Me too."

The front doorbell rang.

When he made no motion to answer it, she realized that he hadn't heard it. "Ethan, someone's at your door."

Getting to his feet, he hurried inside.

She remained on the porch for a bit, trying to sort out her feelings for him, but couldn't. The only thing she knew for certain was that she didn't want to leave him.

"Who was it?" she asked, walking into the living room.

"A courier," he answered, tearing open the thick envelope. After a moment, he looked up at the ceiling and swore.

"What's wrong?"

"Renee has contested my father's will. She is forcing me to take a DNA test to establish the paternity of Ryan!" He flung the papers across the room as he uttered a few more obscenities directed at his sister.

Sarah bent down and picked up the pages from off the floor. "She's placing a hold on the company? Can she do that?"

He nodded. "Every stockholder in the company is going to be issued a letter on the first of May when the hold goes into effect. Whether I take the test or not won't matter after that. The question of doubt will have already spread. It won't take people very long to figure out who the father is." He clenched his fists. He should have known better than to think that this was going to slide. Renee had been true to her word; the two years were almost up.

Sarah looked back down at the letter. It stated that a copy had also been sent to Jessica and Gavin. She covered her hand with her mouth and closed her eyes. The personal ramifications of this were overwhelming. It would set off a chain of events that could never be undone.

~

Early the next morning, Ethan fumbled on the nightstand for the phone. "Hello?" He sat up and swung his legs over the edge of the bed. "That's all right."

Sarah turned over in bed and listened.

"Mmm-hmm. I got it yesterday."

She soon realized that he was talking to Jessica. An inexplicable feeling of guilt came over her as she lay there next to him.

"I don't know what I'm going to do," he said with a sigh. "I need to get in touch with Paul first of all."

She slipped out of bed and went across the hall to give him some privacy. Glancing at the clock on the wall, she decided that she had better take a shower. Her plane would be leaving in a few hours.

She turned on the water and waited patiently until she saw a cloud of steam rising above the curtain. She then let her nightgown fall from her shoulders and stepped inside. Closing her eyes, she let the spray run over her wishing that a blizzard would come along and cancel her flight.

A few moments later, she heard the rings on the curtain scrape across the rod and then felt Ethan's hands upon her.

"Mind if I join you?" he asked, letting his lips roam along her neck.

Sarah kissed the side of his face, feeling his stubble as the water ran over her tongue.

He kissed her full on the mouth, and then turned her away from him.

She leaned forward, placing her hands against the stall as he rubbed himself between her buttocks. Her whole body tingled with anticipation. She felt so alive.

Ethan placed a hand on her shoulder, gently bending her over. He glided slowly in as he held her tightly around the waist. He began to thrust softly, each time going a little deeper.

She felt her body become rigid with excitement. Her breath shook as she released it. "Oh, Ethan," she whispered.

~

After checking her luggage in at the gate, Sarah joined Ethan in a corner by the terminal.

He put his arms around her and drew her close. The airport was bustling with activity, but Sarah was the only one he saw. He bent down and kissed her, wishing she could stay.

"How are we going to work this?" she asked, smiling through her tears.

"Well, I'll call you every day. And I'll be down in a few weeks to handle this thing with Renee."

"Promise?"

"I promise."

An announcement was made calling all passengers to the gate.

Ethan's lips were full of warmth and tenderness as he kissed her once more. "I'll miss you."

Unable to speak, she turned and began walking away.

As he watched her disappear through the gate, he found himself missing her already.

Chapter Sixty-four

On a windy night in early March, Sarah stared anxiously at her cell phone, willing it to ring. Ted had called her at work this morning to let her know that Ashley had gone into labor.

After making him promise to call the minute the baby was born, she had immediately told Gavin, who in turn, had invited himself over to wait with her after work. Hearing the doorknob jiggle, she looked over her shoulder.

He came in carrying a pizza. "Has he called?"

"Not yet," she answered, irritated that he hadn't bothered to ring the bell.

Every sound they made while eating seemed to be magnified in the quietness. She was still carrying a grudge from last summer when he'd implied that Ashley's pregnancy was all her fault.

He wiped his mouth with a napkin. "So, how was your trip?"

She shrugged. "It was nice."

"Did you see Ethan?"

"Yes."

"How's he getting along?" he asked, in what sounded like to her, a rather petty tone of voice.

"Great. He's starting his own clinic. It's getting ready to open in a month or so." As she spoke, she saw him pull out his cell phone and check his email.

"Did he happen to mention to you what he was going to do about the paternity suit?"

"He told me he would be coming down in a few weeks to handle it, but I don't really think he knows what he's going to do about it."

Gavin shook his head as he pressed the phone to his ear. "This whole thing makes me nervous."

Sarah felt herself shiver at the thought of the truth coming out. Everyone would then know why she and Gavin had divorced, along with Jessica and Ethan; not to mention, the shame and humiliation the four of them would have to face.

~

Ethan leaned back in his chair reading over the information in front of him. It was nearly midnight and his body told him it was time for bed, but he needed to get this report finished. The only problem was that every other minute he found himself thinking about Sarah, and then Renee. He rubbed his eyes and tried to concentrate. The projected figures for the first month of the clinic looked good. The overhead was low. Not extremely low, but he felt confident about it.

He stood up and stretched, decidedly giving up for the night. His cell phone rang as he was turning off the lights. He smiled when he saw who it was. "I was just thinking about you."

"Really?"

"Mmm-hmm."

"I've got some good news," Sarah said, her voice laced with excitement.

"What?"

Ethan sat down on the arm of the sofa as he listened to the details, important or not, surrounding the birth of her granddaughter.

Sarah stopped and took a deep breath, feeling as if she were rambling.

"And how's the grandmother doing?"

Her eyes immediately moistened upon hearing that word. "I'm fine. I'm just so happy."

"I miss you," he said softly.

She paused to wipe her eyes. "I miss you, too."

"Are you doing anything this weekend?"

A smile formed on her lips. "No, why?"

"I have an appointment with Renee and Paul. But it's also an excuse to see you."

Chapter Sixty-five

The following Saturday, Ethan drove his rental car down Orchard Lane and pulled into the parking lot of Serenity Harbor City Hospital. He turned off the engine and swallowed nervously.

After a few more minutes, he opened the door and got out, deciding he couldn't wait any longer to see Sarah.

The first person he bumped into when he stepped off the elevator was Trish. "Dr. Harrington!" She ran around the nurses' station to hug him. "Dr. Williams told us that you were coming in this weekend. How are you?"

Before he could answer Kellie and two other nurses came up to him. Ethan felt himself relax a little as he chatted with them.

Sarah rounded the corner. When she saw him standing there, she started to run but caught herself, making the hesitation in her gait look like a retarded skip.

He held his arms out to her. "Hi."

"Hi," she answered, giving him a brief hug.

"It's good to see you again," he said formally, his eyes saying much more.

"How long are you going to be in town?" Trish asked.

"I'll be heading back Monday." He pretended to notice that Sarah had her coat on. "Are you heading home?"

"Yes, I'm finished for the weekend, thank goodness."

"I'll walk with you," he said, turning to say goodbye to the nurses.

On their way out, they ran into several more colleagues. Ethan talked politely with each of them, acting as if he had all the time in the world, but his anxiousness made his accent thick.

Finally, they made it to the parking lot and got into their respective cars where he followed her home, parking his car on the side of the street in front of her house.

Once inside, Ethan closed the door and turned the lock. She immediately fell into his arms, allowing him to kiss her in a fiery embrace. "I have missed you so much," he said, pulling back to look at her.

Sarah hurriedly undid his coat. "I haven't been able to think about anything else all day."

They made their way across the living room, with articles of clothing being dispensed along the way.

~

Night had fallen as the two of them walked hand in hand along the beach. The moon reflected off the ocean illuminating the tide as it rolled softly in.

Seeing that they were completely alone, Ethan let go of her hand and wrapped his arm around her, enjoying the opportunity to hold her.

She laid her head upon his shoulder, letting her shoes dangle precariously from her fingertips as the waves lapped at her toes.

They walked on in blissful peace, just happy to be with each other.

He kissed her gently on top of her head and then took a deep breath. "There's something I've been wanting to tell you for a long time."

"What's that?"

"That I love you."

She stopped walking and looked up at him. His eyes were full of tenderness. She touched the side of his face. "I love you too, Ethan."

Taking her by the hand, he led her away from the water. He sat down in the sand and drew his knees up to his chest.

"What's the matter?" she asked, sitting down beside him.

He shook his head. "Absolutely nothing." He rested his elbows on his knees and looked out over the ocean. "I like the way I feel when I'm with you, Sarah."

His words brought a smile to her face.

"There's something about you. You seem to have a calming effect on me. There are things that I've told you about my father...that I've never told anyone before." He placed his hand over his heart. "I had a huge void inside me...like a black hole. And no amount of alcohol, or displaced happiness could ever satisfy it. I was so certain that I could go the rest of my life without loving someone again. But now, there are days that I don't think I'll survive if I don't call you."

Sarah swallowed the lump that had risen in her throat as he leaned in to kiss her. She breathed in, enjoying the feeling of his lips against hers.

He drew back and smiled. "Marry me."

Before she could say anything, he reached into his pocket and pulled out a ring. The diamond twinkled like a star in the moonlight.

Her mouth started to tremble. "Ethan."

Chapter Sixty-six

Sarah stood in front of her bedroom window watching a squirrel trying to fit its large head through the birdfeeder that she had hung from the branch of her oak tree last fall. Every now and then, she would glance down at the ring on her left hand, and Ethan's words would come flowing back to her. She brought the ring to her lips and closed her eyes. His proposal had taken her by surprise.

Ethan raised his head up and squinted open one eye. "Sarah?"

She turned away and sat down on the edge of the bed.

"What time is it?" he asked, searching for her clock.

"It's a little after nine."

He pushed himself up to a sitting position and gently touched her cheek. "Have you been up long?"

"A little while. What time do you have to meet Renee?"

"Ten-thirty," he answered, taking a moment to rub the sleep from his eyes. When he opened them, he noticed her looking at her ring.

She saw him watching and smiled awkwardly. "Do you like it?"

"I love it. It's beautiful." She reached out and brushed his hair with her fingertips. "And I love *you*. I don't want you to think I'm hesitating on giving you an answer because of that."

"I know. It's a big decision, and I want you to take as much time as you need." He tilted his head upon seeing the distance in her eyes. "Is there something else?"

Her lips folded tightly together as she looked down.

"What is it?"

She began picking at the pattern on her comforter. "You know that I can't have any more children."

He sat up and put his arm around her. "I'm not marrying you for children. I want to marry you because I love you."

"You say that now," she said, shaking her head, "but you're still young, Ethan. It wouldn't be fair to you."

"Please don't let that be the driving force of your decision. I've got Ryan and that's enough for me." He touched the side of her face with the back of his knuckles. "I mean that. I want to spend the rest of my life with you." He kissed her tenderly on the lips. "Okay?"

Not wanting to discuss it any further, she returned his kiss full on.

Ethan lay back against the pillow as she straddled him with her knees. Grasping the hem of her nightgown, he pulled it up and over her head. She leaned forward, letting her breasts graze across his chest, as her legs slowly intertwined with his.

Placing a hand on her lower back, he rolled over, switching places with her. Her hips rose and fell, moving in rhythm with his as he thrust inside her. A soft moan escaped her lips as his kisses became fervent upon her neck and breasts.

Ding-dong! Ding-dong!

They both stopped in mid-stride.

Ding-dong!

"I'm sorry," she said, pushing against him. "I'll get rid of whoever it is."

"Hurry back."

She put on her robe and ran downstairs. "Gavin."

"Did I wake you?" he asked, sounding somewhat apologetic.

She gathered her robe tighter against her as he walked right in. "Um, no. I was getting ready to take a shower."

"I'm sorry to bother you, but I just came by to get my baseball glove."

"Your glove," she repeated, still holding onto the doorknob.

"Yeah, I'm going to teach Ryan how to play catch today. I can't find it at my place. I think it's still upstairs under the bed." He started across the living room. "Do you mind if I go look?"

She quickly closed the door. "Gavin...Gavin, wait!" she said, hurrying after him.

He stopped and turned around.

"Um...I have company."

He looked at her for a moment. Then his face turned red. "Oh, I'm sorry. I didn't know."

"It's all right. You wait here, and I'll go get it," she said, heading towards the steps.

Gavin glanced around the room, trying to rid himself of his embarrassment. He caught sight of a briefcase lying open on the coffee table and took a step closer. His discomfort was immediately replaced by anger when he recognized the initials engraved on its side. He turned around, his eyes locking with Sarah's.

Ethan was getting dressed when she returned to the bedroom. "It's Gavin," she stated.

"I heard," he said, leaning over to tie his shoes. "Does he know I'm here?"

"He figured it out." She tossed her robe on the bed and reached for her blouse.

"I'm sorry."

"There's no need," she said, slipping into her blue jeans. "I was going to tell him anyway." She just hadn't wanted it to be *this* way.

Gavin stood up when he heard them coming.

Ethan glanced sideways at him as he walked into the living room. "Gavin."

"Ethan."

"Here's your glove," Sarah said quietly, holding it out to him. "Do you have a minute? I'd like to talk to you."

"I don't have much time," he answered, keeping his eyes on Ethan. "I'm going to go play ball in the park with *my son*."

Sarah dropped her gaze to the floor, unable to look at the hurt that was now visible upon Ethan's face.

Clenching his jaw, he brushed past Gavin and snapped his briefcase shut.

"Good luck," she said, walking him to the door.

"After I get through there, I'm probably going to go see Jessica and tell her," he said in a low voice. He put a hand on her waist and bent down to kiss her, but stopped, glancing at Gavin.

Sarah looked over her shoulder and found him still glowering at Ethan.

When he noticed her staring at him, he turned away and put his hands on his hips.

Satisfied she'd gotten her point across, she stood on her tiptoes and gave Ethan a kiss. "I'll see you later."

"'Bye."

She watched him walk down the drive to his car before pushing the door shut. She bit her tongue for a moment, and then turned around. "What you just said to him was *very* cruel."

Gavin tossed the glove on the chair and shrugged. "He's a big boy. I think he can take it."

"Look," she said, crossing the floor to stand in front of him. "I'm sorry you had to find out this way. I was going to tell you."

"How long has this been going on?"

She tilted her head. "Well, *not* that it's any of your business, but we've been seeing each other since I went to visit him."

"Are you in love with him?" he asked pointedly.

"Yes."

The redness in Gavin's cheeks turned dark.

"He's also asked me to marry him," she said, figuring it would be best just to get it over with.

Silence hung in the room for a long time.

"What did you tell him?" he finally asked.

"I haven't given him my answer, yet."

"I can't believe this, Sarah," he said, shaking his head. "I can't believe that you are actually considering marrying him."

Any regard she had for Gavin's feelings suddenly left her. "Would you care to explain that?" she asked, although she was certain she knew what was coming.

"Oh, come on, Sarah. Are you going to make me say it? The man has *issues*. Everybody in this town knows that he's a drunk."

"He has not had a drink in over seven months."

"And I suppose you're just going to take his word for that."

Her anger began to rise. Besides his obnoxious behavior, he'd also managed to ruin a perfectly good morning for her. "Look, Gavin, I am only telling you all this, because I felt that you deserved to know before everyone else. I don't particularly give a *damn* what you think. And just in case you've forgotten, we're not *married* anymore."

He folded his arms and sighed. "I know that I hurt you with Jessica, and I'm deeply sorry for that. But don't you think you might be doing this just to get even with me?"

She threw her arms up in disgust. "My God, Gavin, I cannot believe the size of your ego! You are so damn shallow, it's pathetic!"

He spread his hands out to her. "Well, what else am I supposed to think?"

"I don't care what you think!"

"I'm just trying to make you understand what a big mistake you'd be making by marrying him."

She spun around and marched towards the door. "I want you to leave." She jerked it open and looked expectantly at him.

He grabbed his glove from off the chair. "I hope to *hell* you know what you're doing."

~

"I really appreciate you coming down here on a Sunday to do this for me, Paul," said Ethan as he waited with him in his office.

"It's no trouble. But I must confess, I'm a little surprised." He peered at Ethan over his glasses. "Are you positive you want to do this?"

He rubbed the back of his neck and sighed. "This is really my only option."

They heard the unmistakable clicking of Renee's high heels in the lobby outside. The two of them stood up as she entered the room.

"Hello, Renee." Paul walked around his desk to shake her hand. "How are you?"

"Fine, thank you." She turned to her brother. "Hello, Ethan. You're looking well."

He directed his gaze to Paul. "Shall we get started?"

Paul gestured towards the small table in the room. "Renee, will your attorney be joining us?"

"No," she said, sitting down in the chair opposite of Ethan. "I don't think there's any need."

Paul took a seat at the end of the table and handed a document to her. "This is the proposal we've come up with to counter your placing a hold on the company."

She laid it in front of her and leaned forward to read it.

He continued on. "Ethan is willing to sell Harrington Enterprises to you—"

"You *can't* be serious," she said, looking over at Ethan. "This is bloody nonsense!"

Ethan's jaw twitched. "Paul, would you mind leaving us alone for a few minutes?"

"Of course."

He waited until the door was closed before turning his eyes upon his sister. She was leaning back in her chair, arms crossed, mouth sneering. It was hard to believe this was the same little girl who used to wear pigtails. "I strongly suggest you take this offer," he said in a low voice.

"Let me get this straight. I am suing you with a paternity suit and your only solution is to sell me the company?"

Ethan's face was expressionless.

"Not to mention..." she said, grabbing the document, "you want eleven million for it."

"I think that's fair. The company is worth more than three times that."

"Why should I buy the company from you, when I can have it for free with this lawsuit?"

"Because this would be the easiest way for you to get it. I will fight you all the way on this one, Renee."

"You don't have the money to fight me."

"I have enough to keep this tied up in court for the next two years." He stood up and placed his hands on the edge of the table. "And during that time, this company will take a nose dive with your freeze on it." He shook his head slowly. "When this is all over, you'll be lucky to get two million out of it."

"Why are you doing this, Ethan? Is it your idea of revenge, or just a desperate attempt to cover up the truth?"

"You listen to me, Renee," he said in a threatening tone. "Don't you think for a minute that I've forgotten what you did to me. But I'll be *damned* if I'm going to just stand by and watch you drag my little boy through the mud."

"*Your* little boy." Her tone was laced with sarcasm.

"That's right. He is *my* son. Now, do we have a deal or not?"

She looked away angrily. "Will you forfeit all the earnings being held in Ryan's trust fund?"

"Once you buy the company, the trust will be dissolved and the money turned over to you. So what's it going to be?"

"I don't guess I have much of a choice, do I?"

Ethan's knuckles turned white as he pressed them into the table. "Then sign the *goddamn* papers and we won't have to see each other ever again!"

Something flickered in her eyes. "Fine."

He stepped around her and opened the door. "Paul?"

"What did you decide?" he asked, returning to the room.

"I'm accepting your offer," Renee said dejectedly.

Ethan stood behind her, watching as Paul showed her where to put her name. She may as well have been signing it in blood the way she looked. The smallest sense of satisfaction began to creep into him.

"I'll have the necessary papers drawn up for the transfer and you can have your attorney look it over. And then, come May first," said Paul, "Harrington Enterprises is all yours."

Renee stood up and left the room without saying another word.

A smile of relief broke out over Ethan's face as he turned to Paul. "Thank you," he said, shaking his hand.

~

Ethan squinted against the sun as he walked across the parking lot to his car. His lips were still curled into a smile as he reached into his pocket for his keys. It was if a huge weight had been lifted from his shoulders.

As he went to unlock the door, he noticed Renee making her way towards him. "Did you forget something?" he asked, tossing his briefcase in the front seat. "One last snide comment before you go, maybe?"

She stared at him for a long time before speaking. "Did you really mean what you said in Paul's office? About not seeing me ever again?"

He nodded. "Yes, I think I did."

A look of hurt came across her face. He couldn't tell if it was real or pretend.

"I don't want you to hate me, Ethan. You're all I've got."

"That's not true. You've got the company now. You can do whatever you *damn* well please."

She looked down at the pavement for a moment. "When I saw you the last time in the hospital, I told you that I was angry at you for leaving me. That's not entirely the truth." She let out a long sigh and shook her head. "I was angry at our father. He wasn't there, and I took it all out on you. I guess I just needed someone to blame."

"Blame for what?"

She shrugged. "For my miserable life."

He laughed. "You just took the company from me for less than one-third of its worth. What the hell do you have to be miserable about?"

"Never mind." She turned and began walking away.

He ran after her and caught her by the arm. His smile faded when he saw her face. "What do you have to be miserable about?"

"Nothing," she said, prying his fingers off of her.

His voice softened. "What?"

Her eyes suddenly filled with tears. "My life is miserable, Ethan, okay? I mean, look at me. Do you honestly think I'm happy?"

"You've never been happy, Renee. It's nothing new."

"What about you, Ethan? Can you honestly say you're happy?"

He looked at her solemnly for a moment. "I try to be."

"Really? Why did you try to kill yourself then?"

"We're not talking about me," he said in a curt tone.

"No, we're talking about you *and* me, and what happened to us when we were kids."

He narrowed his eyes at her.

"My *God,* Ethan, I'm not an *idiot!* I had eyes and ears when we were growing up. I knew what was going to happen when he took you into his study. I could hear the strap hitting your skin."

Ethan set his jaw to mask his emotions.

"Have you ever wondered why I don't drink? Or why I keep marrying these losers? Or why I don't have children?" The tears that had been pooling in the bottoms of her eyelids spilled over onto her face. "I don't *drink* because I don't want to be like him. I marry those *men,* because I'm looking for someone to take his place. I don't have *kids,* because I'm afraid I'll inflict some sort of emotional damage upon them and they'll wind up exactly like us." She looked at him through her tears and began to shake her head. "Our father was a *bastard,* Ethan. A *goddamned bastard.*"

He put his arms around her and hugged her tightly. She kept her hands clenched as she sobbed into his chest. "You're right," he whispered, holding the back of her head. "He was a *goddamned bastard.*"

Chapter Sixty-seven

Ethan stood on Jessica's front porch for a moment before ringing the bell. His mind was still on his conversation with Renee. He was trying to collect his thoughts, when the door suddenly opened.

"Hi," Jessica said, "I saw you pull in." She stepped back allowing him to come inside.

They stood there for a moment, neither one of them knowing what to do.

He finally leaned forward and kissed her lightly on the cheek. "It's good to see you again."

She walked rigidly over to the sofa. "Please, have a seat."

He followed and sat down beside her, leaving one cushion between them.

"Can I get you anything?"

"No, thank you."

"I'm sorry that Ryan isn't here, but Gavin has him today."

"Yes, I know," he said, settling against the back of the cushion. "I ran into him earlier."

"Well, I feel bad that you didn't get to see him. I didn't know you were coming down until the other day, and he had already made plans," she said apologetically.

"That's all right," he replied, hiding his irritation that she once again put Gavin's feelings ahead of his. "I'd like to see him in the morning before I go, if that's okay."

She nodded. "That's fine."

A few moments of silence went by.

"How did your meeting with Renee go?"

"Well," he said, switching gears, "I think I have managed a deal to keep Renee out of our lives forever."

She laughed. "What did you do? Put a contract out on her?"

He laughed with her. "No, but that's not a bad idea."

"What kind of deal did you make?"

"I sold the company to her." He shrugged when he saw her expression. "It truthfully belonged to her anyway."

"I'm sorry you had to do that."

"Well, I wasn't about to let an innocent boy get caught in the middle of all this," he said, shaking his head.

"So she agreed to drop the paternity suit?"

He nodded. "That was the deal. "*That*, and she had to pay me eleven million for it." A wry smile broke out over his face.

"Well, you're quite the businessman. Your father would have been proud."

He scratched his head, still grinning. "I think I made a nice little profit. It should go a long way on my clinic."

"Oh, yes, your clinic. Sarah was telling us about that. I think it's great!"

"Thanks."

Jessica noticed that there was something different about him, but she couldn't quite put her finger on it.

"Part of the reason I came over here today was to tell you about the situation with Renee, but I have some other news as well."

"What is it?"

"I wanted to tell you this before you heard it from anyone else." He cast his eyes upon the floor as he spoke. "Sarah and I…are seeing each other."

Jessica sat there seemingly in a stupor. She couldn't have heard that right. "Um...what—" She stopped, fumbling for the words. "When did this happen?"

"When she came to visit me." He gave her a moment to absorb what he'd just said before continuing. "There's something else. I'm in love with her, and I've asked her to marry me."

Jessica looked at him, her expression unreadable. Then a small smile formed as she began to shake her head. "My, my. You're just full of surprises today." She stood up quickly and turned away. "I hope you can forgive me for not saying congratulations."

"I didn't expect you to, Jess," he said, picking up on her tone. "I just wanted you to know what was going on before finding out from someone at the hospital."

"Has she given you an answer yet?"

"No."

She turned around. "She was only there for what—two weeks? How can you be ready to marry her?"

"I don't think I need to explain myself to you," he said, getting to his feet.

"Well, I'm sorry! But this is just a little hard to take!" she shouted. "Of all the women in the world, why does it have to be Sarah?"

"Why do you care if it's Sarah?"

"Because."

"Because why?" he pushed. "Is it because she used to be married to Gavin?"

"That is *not* it and you *know* it!"

"Well, tell me what it is, then!"

"I don't want to have her as Ryan's stepmother for starters."

His face grew dark. "Well, I didn't particularly want Gavin to be his *father!* It was supposed to be *me!*"

~

The sun was just beginning to go down as Gavin played with Ryan in the side lot of his apartment complex. He admitted to himself that he had not been very good company to him today. The baseball glove remained in his car. The only thing he had on his mind was Sarah and what she had told him.

"Daddy!" Ryan ran past him.

Gavin turned in time to see Ethan sweep him up into his arms. Anger began to churn inside of him as he walked towards them.

Ethan swallowed the lump in his throat as he lifted Ryan high above his head. "When did you get so big?" he said, being ever so grateful that he still recognized him. Out of the corner of his eye, he saw Gavin approaching. "Listen, Daddy just came to give you a big hug and kiss. And I promise I'm going to come play with you tomorrow."

"You know," Gavin said, putting his hands on his hips, "seeing you twice in one day is about all I can stand."

Ethan set Ryan on the ground and watched him head back to his toy trucks. "The feeling is mutual, I assure you."

"Tell me something. Just what is it that you hope to accomplish by doing this?"

"Doing what?"

"I don't want her getting hurt by you."

"You mean the way you hurt her?"

He took a step closer. "I don't know what it is that she could possibly see in you."

Ethan folded his arms and looked down at him. "Why should *you* care?"

"Because I still care a great deal for Sarah, and I don't want to see anything bad happen to her."

"No, that's not it. You see I know you better than you *think* I do, Gavin." He tapped him on the chest with his finger. "You're nothing but an arrogant *son-of-a-bitch* who can't get past the fact that your ex-wife is sleeping with someone else."

Gavin's eyes smoldered as he pushed his hand away.

"How does it *feel*, Gavin? It hurts, doesn't it?"

He grabbed him by his shirt and drew his right fist back.

"Go ahead. Take your best shot," Ethan said. "But I promise you it will be the last one you ever take."

He gave him a slight shove and dropped his hand. "You haven't changed at all."

"No, that's where you're wrong," Ethan said in a low voice. "If I hadn't, you'd already be lying on the ground. But *you*, on the other hand, will never change. You're always going to be a little *prick*."

~

Sarah sat on her back porch, nursing a glass of wine as she replayed her conversation with Gavin over and over in her mind. At first, she deeply regretted him finding out the way he did, but as the day wore on, she found herself feeling glad that he had. There was the smallest part of her that hoped he was hurting. She ran her fingers along the rim of the glass, wondering when it was that she had become so vindictive.

She had phoned Ashley a little while ago and had given her the news. She had been stunned, of course, but before they hung up her daughter told her that she was happy for her; however, Sarah doubted her sincerity.

"Hi," Ethan said, opening the screen door.

She moved over so he could join her on the step. "How did it go today?" she asked, emptying the contents of her glass on the lawn.

"Well, Renee accepted my offer. She's dropped the paternity suit in exchange for the company."

She breathed a sigh of relief. "Thank God."

"So how did it go with you?" he asked, sitting down beside her.

"Not good. Gavin was very hateful about the whole thing."

"I gathered that when I saw him a little while ago."

"What do you mean...*when you saw him?"*

"I stopped by to see Ryan on my way back," he explained.

"What happened?"

"We…had some words. Don't worry, I didn't hit him," he said, smiling slightly when he saw the worried look on her face. "Not that I didn't *want* to."

"I'm sorry," she said in a tired voice. "Did you tell Jessica?"

"It didn't go very well, either." Ethan rested his head on top of hers as he slipped his arm around her waist. "If it makes any difference to you...*I'm* very happy. And I don't give a *damn* about anyone else," he whispered.

Chapter Sixty-eight

A bitter sigh fell from Ethan as he watched Ryan playing with the fire truck he had bought for him this morning. Seven months was far too long to go without seeing him.

His attorney had told him that he could appeal the custody decision after a year, but Ethan knew his attempted suicide would ultimately cause him to lose again. The likelihood that Ryan would grow up without being close to him began to weigh heavily upon his heart.

"That's quite a present," Jessica said, interrupting his thoughts.

He looked over his shoulder, and saw her coming down the stairs. "Do you think it's too much?"

"Would it matter if I said yes?"

Sensing they were about to argue, he grabbed his coat and knelt in front of Ryan. "Daddy's got to go."

"Ethan, wait..." Jessica shook her head in dismay. "I don't want to leave things like this. Can we talk for a minute?"

He tousled Ryan's hair and went to sit beside her on the sofa.

"You were right yesterday," she said quietly. "You don't have to explain yourself to me."

"Jess, I don't expect you to understand this, or to even be happy for me. I just wanted you to know before everyone else did, that's all."

"Well, you're right on the first part. I *don't* understand." She paused a moment. "But I *am* happy for you."

He looked over at her. "Thanks…I think."

"I must say, Ethan," she said, smiling in spite of herself, "I've never seen you like this."

"Like what?"

She shrugged. "So content."

"It shows, hmm?"

"Sarah must be doing something right, because I've never seen you happier."

~

Sarah was deep in thought when Ethan came through her office. She glanced down at her watch and frowned. "Is it that time already?"

"I'm afraid so. But I do have time for a quick lunch if you care to join me."

"I'd love to." She wrapped her arms around his neck and looked into his eyes. "I'd *love* to have lunch with you...and I'd *love* to marry you."

He looked at her blankly for a moment. "Really?"

"Really."

He suddenly picked her up and twirled her around in his arms, making her throw her head back and laugh. He set her feet back on the floor and bent down to kiss her. "Where's *Junior?*" he asked, pausing to come up for air.

A smile formed on her lips. "I sent him down to radiology. They're really backed up. He could be there for a while."

"That's too bad," he said, embracing her in another kiss.

Sarah closed her eyes as their bodies pressed against one another.

Neither of them was aware that the door had opened.

The sound of a small gasp made Sarah break away.

Trish stood there, mouth gaping. "I'm so sorry," she stammered. "I'll...I'll just uh...come back." She groped behind her for the door handle.

"It's all right," Sarah said, taking a step towards her. "What do you need?"

"I need you to sign off on Mrs. Blandford."

Sarah took the chart from her and began flipping through the pages, trying her best to pretend that nothing had happened.

Trish glanced at Ethan as she waited.

He wiped his mouth and smiled nervously.

"Here you go." Sarah handed the chart back to her.

"Thanks," she mumbled, unable to find the door fast enough.

Ethan looked down at her and smirked. "Now, where were we?" he said, drawing her to him.

"You know..." she said smiling, "she's going to tell."

~

Denise turned around when she saw Trish returning to the station. "What's wrong?"

"Nothing."

"You're all flushed."

She kept her eyes on the chart in front of her.

"What is it?"

"You wouldn't believe me if I told you," she whispered.

"Told me what?"

She looked around for a moment to make sure no one else was within earshot. "If I tell you, you have to promise me that you won't tell another soul."

"I promise. Now, what's the secret?"

"What secret?" Kellie asked, coming up behind them.

Trish groaned. "Nothing."

Denise and Kellie exchanged glances.

About two seconds passed by before Trish caved. "I can't keep this to myself!"

"Tell us!"

She held her hands up. "Okay, but *first*," she said, giving Kellie a warning look, "promise me on your very life that you won't tell anybody."

Kellie crossed her heart. "I promise."

Trish looked around once more. "When I went into Dr. Williams' office just now, I walked in on her and Dr. Harrington kissing!"

Denise tilted her head. "Kissing how?"

"I'm talking serious lip-lock."

Sarah and Ethan rounded the corner to find the three of them huddled together, giggling and whispering. When they saw them approaching, they scattered like mice.

Trish ducked behind the counter, seemingly interested in a particular chart tucked away in the bottom cubbyhole.

Sarah placed her hands on the counter and peered over it. "Trish?"

She stood up, clutching the prized chart against her chest. "Yes?"

"Did you tell anyone what you saw a few minutes ago?"

She shook her head emphatically. "No, of course not."

Sarah glanced at the other two nurses for confirmation.

They both dropped their eyes to the floor.

"I think she told them," she said, looking back at Ethan.

Denise was having a very hard time keeping a straight face, which had now spread over to Kellie.

Trish had been able to keep it together up to this point, but a sideways glance between her and Denise ended it.

The three of them began to snicker uncontrollably.

Sarah sighed and shook her head. "Well, I guess the cat's out of the bag now," she said, placing her hand on Ethan's chest.

He slipped his arm around her waist. "We should have locked the door."

"Oh, come on, we're dying here! What's going on with you two?" Denise asked.

"Okay," Sarah said. "Ethan and I have been seeing one another, and…we're getting married."

The squeals could be heard all over the fifth floor.

Chapter Sixty-nine

Three weeks later, Sarah was leaning against the back of the elevator taking a quick moment, in between patients, to go over her list.

Tomorrow was to be her last day at work. She had given Phillip two weeks' notice, and he had agreed to oversee the clinic until they could find a replacement. She feared, or rather knew, however, that after her departure there would be no one left to fight for it, and guessed it would be closed within a year.

Her pen solemnly moved on down the list.

Packing: She put a check mark beside the word. Most of her things were on their way to Ethan's house and should be arriving within a few weeks. A secondhand dealer had agreed to come on Friday and take the pieces of furniture that she had chosen to leave behind.

House: Her house had gone under contract and was now in escrow. The closing date was set for the end of the month, which would allow her enough time to finish moving.

Church: It was hard finding a church to get married in, as most of them were booked in advance. Not to mention the fact that most pastors would not marry you in a church at all if you had been divorced. After a lot of searching, Sarah finally decided that the small chapel in the hospital would be the perfect place. She had known the chaplain, Tom Stephenson, for years, as had Ethan. He had told her that he would be more than happy to marry the two of them. It really was for the best, because this way nearly everyone could attend the ceremony, and then go back to work.

The elevator stopped and opened its doors.

Sarah felt her body tense when Jessica stepped on. She folded her checklist into several squares before cramming it into the pocket of her lab coat. She had purposely been avoiding her and had hoped to escape the hospital all together without having to speak to her.

Jessica kept her eyes on the light above the door. "So, I guess Saturday's the big day."

"Yes."

The elevator hummed along, taking its time. After what felt like an eternity, it finally came to rest on the seventh floor and chimed; the pleasant tone of its bell a stark contrast against the tension that filled the air around them.

Jessica slipped through the doors and stopped to look over her shoulder. "Take good care of him," she said softly.

Chapter Seventy

Friday evening, Ethan stood solemnly over his father's grave, his emotions wound tight. The scars he bore, inside and out, made it easy to justify his hatred for him. These last few months, however, he had grown weary of carrying around all this anger. Unforgiveness was far more damaging than the alternative, and he did not want to be consumed by it the way his sister had.

The power of forgiveness was healing, as he had learned from Sarah. He looked down at the gold medallion he held in his hand. He had been carrying it with him in hopes that one day he would be able to say it was his.

He slipped it back into his pocket and turned his eyes upon the marble headstone. "I'm getting married tomorrow," he whispered.

~

Sarah sat in the middle of Denise's living room, opening up her gifts. So far, she had received two pairs of lace underwear, a see-through bra, and a book about different sexual positions.

She stuffed the black panties back in the bag and shook her head. "You guys have really outdone yourselves tonight."

"Open the one in the pink paper," Trish said grinning.

Sarah reached for the present. The entire room grew silent as she began to tear at the paper.

"It's from all of us," Denise chimed in.

"Well, I can only imagine what it might be, then." As she sifted through the mound of tissue paper, there were hushed whispers and giggles. She picked up the garment and held it up.

The room erupted into laughter.

It was a silk teddy, with detachable pieces and holes where certain parts of her anatomy went. She shook her head and laughed. "My...I think I may have to take a look at that book before I wear this."

Another round of laughter sounded, along with several speculations about what Ethan's reaction would be when he saw her in it.

Chapter Seventy-one

Ethan turned over in bed and opened one eye. For just a brief moment, he didn't know where he was, but then a small body cuddled up next to him and he immediately remembered. He was at the Clearwater Hotel...and this was his wedding day.

He quietly slipped out from underneath the covers and stole into the bathroom to take a quick shower. Last night when he had picked Ryan up, Jessica had told him that she would consider letting him come visit for a couple of weeks over the summer. His heart surged at the thought of being able to spend such precious time with him, and he couldn't help smiling as he shut off the water and drew the curtain back.

"Hi, Daddy!" Ryan was sitting on the toilet seat waiting for him.

"Hi," he said, wrapping a towel around his waist. "Daddy's going to shave, okay?"

Ryan watched intensely as he rubbed the white foam on his face and then drew the razor across it.

"Daddy?"

"Hmm?"

"Me shave," Ryan said, patting his face.

Ethan smiled. "I'll be right back. Don't move." He grabbed a chair by the door and placed it in front of the sink for him to stand on. "Hold out your hands," he said, picking up the can.

Ryan did as he instructed. Ethan helped him spread the foam on his face, and then snapped the cap on the razor before handing it to him. "Now, you start up here..." he said, standing behind him as he guided his tiny hand downwards.

After he had scraped the shaving cream from his cheeks, Ethan rinsed him off and dried him with a towel. "The last thing you do is put on some aftershave." He poured a small amount into Ryan's hand and then some into his own. "Mmm," he said, patting his face and neck.

Ryan rubbed his hands together and slapped his face and forehead, somewhat missing the intended target. "Mmm."

"Okay, let me see." Ethan turned him around and stroked the side of his face. "Smooth."

Ryan reached up and touched the side of Ethan's face, imitating him. "Smoove."

Ethan carried him out of the bathroom and turned on the television for him. He then got himself dressed and sat down on the bed to slip on his shoes. When he was finished, he slid open the top drawer of the nightstand. Sarah's ring was inside it, as well as two plane tickets to Sydney. He was going to surprise her with them after they were married.

Considering the fact that she had not gotten to visit her daughter last summer because of him, a honeymoon in Sydney seemed appropriate. It would give her a chance to reconnect with Ashley, as well as the opportunity to bond with her granddaughter.

Knock-knock.

Ryan turned his attention away from the television and ran to answer the door.

"Well, hello." David knelt down in front of him. "Don't you look handsome?"

Ryan hid behind Ethan's leg and smiled bashfully.

"Ryan, can you say 'hi' to David?"

"Hi," he whispered, burying his face in Ethan's pants.

David smiled as he laid his jacket on the bed. "He's *tall* for two. He's going to be just like you."

"Yeah," Ethan said, wishing that were the case.

"Well, I'm here. Ready to do whatever a best man does."

"Can you tie this for me?"

David's mouth twitched as he looked at the jumbled knot underneath Ethan's collar. "You seem to be just a tad bit nervous."

"Just a tad," he replied, raising his chin up so David could work.

"You know, Ethan, I haven't gotten a chance to tell you yet how very proud I am of you. You've overcome a lot of things to get to this point..." He stopped for a moment and cleared his throat. "I'm really happy for you."

"Thanks," he said, trying to hold his own emotions at bay. "It means a lot that you could be here."

David finished the task of fixing his tie and took a small step back. "Well," he said, in a quivering voice, "it's not every day that a man's son gets married now is it?"

Ethan swallowed hard as his feelings for his father and his love for David suddenly converged. His eyes grew wet as he reached out to hug him.

~

Sarah stood in front of the mirror in the women's restroom, making some last minute adjustments to her hair and makeup.

Trish came through the door. "Are you almost ready?"

She turned around and held her arms out. "What do you think?"

"Oh, Sarah," she said, clasping her hands together, "you look gorgeous!"

"Thank you," she replied, looking down at herself. She had chosen a creamy off-white dress. It was cut low around the neck with satin-covered buttons lining the back.

"Here's your bouquet," Denise said, bursting in behind her.

Trish and Denise had graciously agreed to be Sarah's bridesmaids, and between the two of them, had done a terrific job of getting everything ready for today. Her chin wavered as she thought about how much she was going to miss them.

Denise took her by the hands. "Are you ready?"

She took in her breath. "Is it time?"

"Almost. I'll come back and get you when it is." She headed out, taking Trish with her.

Sarah looked at herself in the mirror once more. A soft smile shone back at her. Everything inside her told her that she and Ethan were going to have a nice life together.

She reflected a moment on the last two years. Through it all, she had learned one very important thing; after all is said and done, the only thing that matters is what's in your heart.

The door swung open again.

"Ethan's here," Trish said smiling. "He's waiting in the chapel, and he looks so handsome!"

~

Ethan stood off to the side of the chapel with David. "Do you have the ring?"

"For the third time, yes."

He glanced nervously around the room, letting his eyes settle upon Grace. She was sitting in the front row holding Ryan in her lap.

The chaplain came up to them. "I think we're ready."

Ethan walked behind him and took his place in front of the altar.

The organist began to play as Trish made her way down the aisle, followed by Denise. There was a moment of silence, and then the wedding march sounded, bringing the guests to their feet.

David patted him on the shoulder and smiled.

Ethan turned around and felt his breath leaving him. Sarah was coming down the aisle looking more beautiful and radiant than he had ever seen her, or could ever imagine seeing.

~

Jessica stood in her office staring out the window. She guessed that Ethan and Sarah were probably married by now. When he had told her that day about the two of them, she had felt something burning inside of her. Perhaps it had been the tiniest bit of jealousy, or hurt. She crossed her arms and sighed.

"Jessica?"

She glanced over her shoulder. Gavin stood in the doorway.

"Mind if I join you?"

"I guess we're probably the only ones not at the wedding."

He slid his hands in his pockets as he walked in. "The two of them getting married is kind of ironic, don't you think?"

"It's kind of like a kick in the teeth, isn't it?" she said bitterly.

He looked at her for a moment and then nodded, his face blank.

~

The reception was being held two doors down from the chapel. Everyone milled about nibbling on cake and sipping punch. Every now and then, a nurse or other member of the staff would come in to wish the bride and groom their best before scurrying back to their duties.

Sarah and Ethan stood in the middle of it all, talking with Phillip.

Ryan, who had fallen asleep a little while ago, slept soundly in his daddy's arms.

"Well, I sure hate to lose one of my best doctors," Phillip said. "But I wish you both nothing but happiness." He leaned over and gave Sarah a kiss on the cheek.

"Thank you, Phillip."

He extended his hand to Ethan. "Now you take good care of her."

"I will."

"Sarah, over here!" Trish motioned for her to come over as Phillip left.

"I'll be right back," she said, turning to Ethan.

He was watching her go when he felt someone tap his arm.

"Poor thing's tuckered out." Grace patted Ryan softly on his back.

Ryan's head rested upon Ethan's shoulder as his breath, warm and soft, fell against his neck. "He's had a big day," he said quietly.

"I wanted to tell you congratulations, and that I wish you all the best."

"Thank you, Grace." He hadn't really gotten a chance to say much of anything to her today. "You know, I think I finally have an answer to that question you asked me so long ago," he said in a low voice.

She gave him a curious look and then nodded, remembering what it was she had asked him. *"Are you glad that you're alive?"*

Ethan glanced across the room at Sarah as she stood talking to Trish and Denise.

She saw him looking at her and smiled.

A feeling of peace suddenly washed over him and began to fill his heart. It was a peace like he had never known. He smiled back at her. "Yes," he answered.

~~~
~~~

Thank you for taking the time to read After All Is Said And Done. If you enjoyed it, please consider telling your friends or posting a short review. Word of mouth is an author's best friend and very much appreciated.
~ Thank you, Belinda G. Buchanan

SEASONS OF DARKNESS

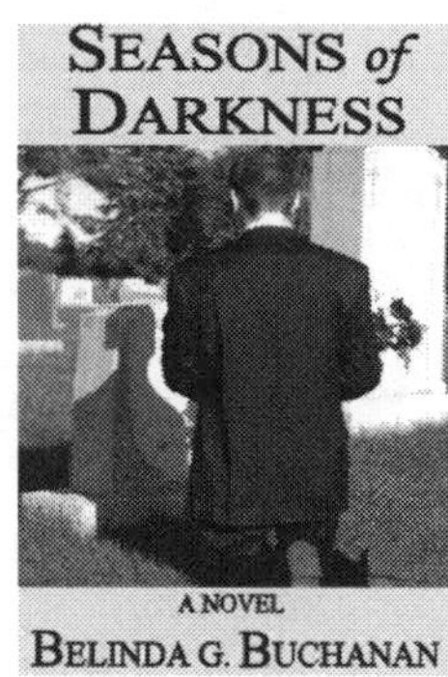

Long before his turbulent marriage to Jessica, Ethan Harrington was just a lonely young man trying to cope with his mother's suicide. Left alone with his controlling father in an isolated farmhouse, he struggles to live among the shattered remains of a family that was never functional to begin with.

A kindhearted doctor, a beautiful girl, and a caring nanny all love him in different ways, but Ethan—now sixteen, and still ravaged by his mother's death, turns to what he has seen his father take comfort in time and time again—thus giving rise to an inner demon that will not turn him loose.

THE MONSTER OF SILVER CREEK

Terror has come to Prairie County, Montana…

A sinister killer is on the loose. A serial killer who feeds off of young women's fear...and leaves a most unusual calling card. Police Chief Nathan Sommers is on the hunt, but every road leads to a dead end.

Nathan is battling his own personal demons as he tries to cope with the death of his wife. He feels her dying was a direct result of his actions and is consumed with guilt.

As he draws nearer to the killer, everything in his life suddenly comes undone. He is forced to deal with his feelings for Katie, the pretty new owner of the bakery that he is struggling to build a relationship with, as well as his love for his dead wife.

About the author

Belinda Buchanan is an author of edgy Women's Fiction and Mystery novels. A native of the bluegrass state, she currently resides there along with her husband, two sons, and a menagerie of animals that includes two persnickety cats, a hamster, and one dog that thinks he's a person.

Please visit Belinda's website for the latest updates about her upcoming novels, read the first few chapters of all her books, play games, and take a peek inside her character gallery:

belindagbuchanan.com

27162596R00380

Printed in Poland
by Amazon Fulfillment
Poland Sp. z o.o., Wrocław